REI
ME

RELEASE ME

The Wolf Hotel Mermaid Beach
Book One

K.A. TUCKER

ISBN 978-1-990105-54-8 (paperback)

ISBN 978-1-990105-53-1 (ebook)

Edited by Jennifer Sommersby

Cover design by Shanoff Designs

Published by K.A. Tucker Books Ltd.

Manufactured in the United States of America

Author's Note

This is a book where Ronan is with more than one woman, at least until he figures out his shit. And Connor is, well, Connor. If you haven't read the other books in the series, you don't know these two, and they may take some getting used to.

Release Me is divided into two parts, and these parts straddle the Wolf Hotel series featuring Abbi Mitchell (Books One through Five.) Part One is referred to as Before Abbi, and it is the prequel novella, Ronan, originally published in 2016. It was published as ebook-only, and many of you have asked me to make it available in paperback and audiobook. Here you go! I've revised the story, adding in new scenes, and I had it re-edited. I think it's *definitely* worth a reread.

Part Two is After Abbi, and takes place after Own Me. The storyline picks up one year after Part One. Do you need to read Wolf Hotel Books One through Five to understand what's happening? It's not required, though there will be spoilers from those books woven into this part. I tried my best to keep them to a minimum, but it's impossible to avoid them all.

This story ends in a cliffhanger. For content warnings, please visit my website.

PART ONE
BEFORE ABBI

1. Ronan

"What'd I tell you?" My new roommate, Connor, stretches his beefy arms out to either side, grinning at the crowded boardwalk. There must be thousands of people. Tens of thousands, even. Everyone says nights in Miami are crazy. The street festival only ups the mayhem.

His bright blue gaze rakes over three girls who stroll past, their matching black shorts like second skins hugging their perfectly round ass cheeks. They smile, they wink, their made-up eyes flash from Connor to me—to my sleeve of ink, to my face where they linger, not even pretending to play coy.

"All right. Time to move," Connor announces.

"Give me a sec to finish this." I puff on my Marlboro while appreciating the balmy evening temperature and soaring palm trees. It was forty degrees Fahrenheit when I left home this morning.

He frowns. "I need a solid wingman, so ease up on the chain-smoking. That may have worked for you in Indianapolis, but chicks don't dig it down here."

"Don't worry about chicks digging me." The problem is that *I'm* having a hard time being interested in any of *them*. I'd rather just lean against this stucco wall and smoke my brains

1

out than go to the effort of searching for a girl, striking up a tedious conversation, and pretending I care what she has to say, all while waiting for her to inhale enough drinks to embolden her hands.

Why can't they make cigarettes to replace a good fuck? I mean, sure, a smoke is a nice way to cap it off when you've blown your load and you're sprawled on your back, sweaty and panting. But when you're alone—because your girlfriend of four years decided you needed "time apart" and is riding someone else's dick already—and you're not in the mood for the energy it takes to pick up, it sure would be nice to pull a smoke out of your pocket and get your release that way.

It would be effortless.

Peaceful.

Uncomplicated.

I can't say any of this to Connor, though. I only met him two hours ago, fresh off the plane. He gave me just enough time to drop my luggage in my new bedroom and take a piss, and then he announced we were going out to "pop my Miami cherry." I can't help but feel like this is some sort of vetting process, a test to see if he and I can be friends. And I can tell he's the type to tell everyone I'm a pussy if I don't go along with it.

I snuff out my cigarette. "Lead the way, Casanova."

―――――

"BETTER LUCK TOMORROW NIGHT." I light up a smoke the moment my sneakers touch the sidewalk.

"I fucking hope so," Connor grumbles, slamming the taxi door and earning a curse from the driver. "I was so sure I had that redhead."

"And I was so sure you were gonna get your skull crushed in by her boyfriend." An angry beast who could pass for a professional wrestler, bulging arms, veiny trunk of a neck and all. Not that Connor isn't equally threatening. He looks like a juiced-up Ken doll.

"You weren't exactly a big help." He punches my shoulder playfully.

"Sorry, man. I haven't slept much. The guys at work had a little going-away party for me last night." At Racey's, a low-class downtown strip club, where the drinks are overpriced and the girls are extra sleazy.

We stumble past a guy taking a piss against a wall, the stench of booze and fresh urine assaulting my nostrils.

"Don't worry. It's a good area. Mostly a young crowd." Connor waves it off and climbs the steps to the front door of our condo building. It's not high-end, but it's definitely not the slums. There are six identical structures in a row—all white stucco with red tile roofs, clean pathways lined by shrubs that get bare-bones landscaping attention. Lots of palm trees. The best part, though, is that we're a five-minute drive to the beach and our jobs at the Wolf Miami Hotel. That was a selling point for me when I was searching for a place to live, seeing as I have no plans to buy a car.

"So, what do you think about Miami so far?" Connor keys in the passcode to get into the main entrance.

"Helluva lot warmer than back home." It was gray and miserable when I kissed my mom's worried cheek goodbye and walked out the front door, nothing but a duffel bag slung over my shoulder.

"Enjoy it now. You'll be sweating your balls off come summer. Still, it's worth it. I've been here for six years. Can't get enough of the ocean and the nights." He leads my travel-weary body toward the elevator. "And our team at Wolf is kick-ass. Good bunch."

"Great, because I left a good team back home." For two years, I've worked in outdoor maintenance at the Wolf in Indianapolis, doing landscaping and other grounds work for the luxury hotel chain. Not a glamorous job, but it's stress-free, pays decent, and there are certain perks, like discounts to book rooms at any of the Wolf locations around the world. Not that I could afford to.

"Why'd you leave Indy, anyway?"

I hesitate. "Needed a change, is all."

He grins. "A chick."

Connor's more perceptive than he lets on. "Something like that." More like the girl of my dreams. The one I'm still madly in love with, even though she pulverized my heart.

He leans back and closes his eyes, his gelled blond hair leaving smudges against the mirrored elevator wall. "Don't worry. You'll get enough Miami pussy to forget that one. You're gonna fit in great with the guys here."

And I meet them in ... five hours, based on my watch. I groan. The plan was to fly in tonight—Thursday—and get settled so I was ready for a Monday morning start. But HR called me yesterday, asking me to start tomorrow. I agreed.

I probably shouldn't have drank so much tonight. Connor's a bad influence—not that I need much help. But at least we get along well. Thank God, seeing as I have to live *and* work with him.

I had very few requirements when I answered the housing ad on the online Wolf employee bulletin board while planning this job transfer.

Four walls and a bed? Check.

Bathroom? Check.

Cheap rent? Check.

Connor asked me where I'd be working. I said outdoor maintenance, and he told me the room was mine. Just like that, thirty seconds into the conversation. No reference checks, no "I'll call you back." That probably would have raised some red flags with other people, but I didn't give a shit. I needed to get as far away from everything as I could. Beach and sunshine seemed like a no-brainer.

I follow Connor along the bright hallway of the fourth floor to our condo on the end.

"Shit." Connor drops his keys twice before managing to get the door unlocked, only to drop them again once inside. They land on the doormat, on a pair of women's gold sandals. "Why is she home?" he mutters, more to himself.

"*Who*?"

"Ryan."

I can't tell if Connor is a bit dense or hammered. "Who's Ryan?"

Connor tosses his keys on the counter, causing a loud clatter. "My sister."

I stop dead. "Your *sister* lives here?"

"Yeah. Didn't I tell you?"

"No." And the ad neglected mention of a second roommate.

"Oh. Yeah, my sister lives with us. She has the room next to yours." Connor stumbles over to the fridge to pull out two Gatorades, tossing one to me. "She said she was staying at her boyfriend's tonight. Don't know what happened." He chugs half the bottle and wipes his mouth with the back of his hand. "Why? You got a problem with my sister?"

"Nah, man. It just would have been nice to know that I was living with two people instead of one."

He waves me off. "Whatever. She's easy to live with. She's always at work, or in class, or at the library. She's tidy and super nice. Cute. You know, in that smart-girl way. You guys share the bathroom, but you'll be heading to work before her, so it's not a big deal. Make sure you put the toilet seat down and you'll be fine."

I shake my head and ask sarcastically, "Is that all?"

"Uh ... yeah?" He smirks at me like *I'm* the idiot.

I crack open my Gatorade and take a big swig while I digest this latest surprise. Connor has a sister. A college-aged sister, from the sounds of it. And "cute," whatever that means.

He peers at me oddly. "What's that look for?"

"Nothing." I shrug. "Aren't you supposed to warn me not to get into her pants?"

Connor bursts out with hearty laughter. "Yeah, good luck with that. I doubt her boyfriend can get into her pants half the time."

I frown at his back as he staggers down the hall toward his room on the opposite side of the condo.

2. Ronan

They may as well make alarms to buzz like a hundred jackhammers drilling into concrete, because that's basically what it feels like against my skull right now.

I groan, wishing I'd been smarter about the beer intake last night. But stupid is as stupid does, and I must have been hitting the snooze button because now I have ten minutes to get ready before we have to leave for work.

I kick off the blanket I snagged from the living room—I didn't think to bring sheets and there was literally nothing in this room except a naked mattress on a frame, a nightstand, alarm clock, and a dresser—and haul my weary body out of bed. Making for the door with my toiletry kit tucked under my arm and my eyes half closed, I narrowly avoid doing a face-plant as I trip over the heap of clothes from last night. "Fuck," I grumble, stumbling out my door and toward the bathroom.

A small form plows right into me.

The girl bounces back into the wall, her headphones and water bottle dropping from her grasp to hit the floor. She looks like she just came back from a run, her fair skin glowing, her T-shirt drenched in sweat, her brown hair pulled back into a damp, matted ponytail.

"Sorry," I apologize as she reaches down to collect her things, well aware that my briefs can't possibly hide my morning wood. At least I'm wearing briefs. I normally sleep naked.

"Ronan! Hurry up or I'll leave you here!" Connor hollers from the kitchen. He's already dressed in Wolf Hotel's maintenance crew garb—beige cargo work pants, a forest-green collared golf shirt, and steel-toe boots.

When I turn back, the girl has ducked past me and disappeared into her room without giving me so much as a glimpse of her face.

"That was Ryan," Connor says.

"Yeah, figured as much." I head for the bathroom. "I'll be ready in five."

————

WHEN I USED the bathroom last night, there were no hints of a female. But now that I'm in the shower, there's no missing the evidence—colorful bottles and razors line the shelves, a shower cap hangs on a nearby hook, a giant pink puffy thing dangles from the shower handle.

Stepping under the water stream, I wrestle with the showerhead to raise it to normal height, accidentally knocking several shampoo bottles to the tub floor. The puff ball ends up there too, along with one of her razors.

I don't have time to be picking up all this shit right now. I don't even have time to shave the stubble from my jaw, and the Wolf employee code requires a stubble-free face. Hopefully, my supervisor won't be strict about it. It's not like we interact with the guests, anyway.

Standing under the steady stream of hot water, I attempt to scrub my brain awake. My hair is buzzed so short, I don't really need to shampoo, but the minty scent usually wakes me up. A minute of soaping down with my basic Irish Spring bar and then I'm slapping the tap and climbing out.

Shit. I forgot to pack a bath towel too.

Sheets ... a pillow ... I better make a list for tonight.

I open the narrow closet behind the door and find it fully stocked with everything one could possibly need plus more. There's an entire shelf of various creams and bottles and boxes for monthly female issues, all lined up and facing out. Organized to the point of obsessiveness.

So, Ryan likes things neat. I should probably remember that, if we're sharing a bathroom. Something else to think about ... later.

I grab a fluffy pink towel and wipe down quickly. Then, cinching it around my hips with one hand, I leave the bathroom.

And plow into Ryan again, this time on her way out of her room toward the kitchen.

"I'm sorry." She takes a step back, giving me an opportunity to get a good look at her face, still sweaty, flushed, and disheveled from her run. She looks nothing like Connor. Her eyes are large and round and hazel-colored, her cheekbones are high, her nose small and buttonish. Overall, kind of average, to be honest. Probably not a girl I'd take a second glance at, but by no means unattractive. She's short, five foot two, if I had to guess, the top of her head meeting my collarbone. She's compact. One of those little body types that's curvy but proportionate to her height.

"Dude! Hurry up!" Connor hollers.

Right. "Hey, I'm Ronan."

She stares up at my face for five long seconds, her expression unreadable, before her gaze drops. "That's my towel."

I open my mouth to explain—and apologize—when she cuts me off, outrage twisting her face. "Are you kidding me? You can't just move in here and take whatever you want. That's not how this works!"

Whoa. "I'll wash it tonight."

She throws a glare toward the kitchen. "Did you even vet this Neanderthal before you let him move in here?"

Huh?

"Relax, Ry," Connor says around a sip of his coffee, seemingly unbothered by his sister's explosive reaction.

"*Relax?* How can I when you're making me share a bathroom with one of the Screw Crew! I'm probably going to contract gonorrhea from the shower!"

What the ... I give Connor a bewildered look.

He merely shrugs in response, the small smile telling me he finds this amusing.

I don't. And I have exactly two minutes to get dressed before I am left behind—because I believe Connor's the type to do that. I don't have time to stand here and be yelled at by my new pint-sized roommate. And if she's going to be hurling insults at me ...

I release my grip and let the towel drop to the floor. "You want it? There you go. Thanks for letting me borrow it until I can get to the store."

Whatever Ryan was going to say gets lost on the tip of her tongue, her eyes widening as she takes in my naked body.

Behind me, Connor bellows with laughter.

Her cheeks flaming, Ryan spins and darts back into her bedroom, slamming the door shut behind her.

"*Screw* Crew?" I echo.

"She doesn't have the best opinion of our work colleagues. And you didn't prove otherwise with that little stunt right there."

Fair enough. If the Miami guys are anything like the ones back home, they've got well-earned reputations for their conquests of the housekeeping staff. At least Connor doesn't seem to be pissed at me for flashing my junk. "I thought you said she was nice."

"You didn't think that was nice?"

Jackass. "When did you tell her I'd be moving in?"

"When she left for her morning jog."

I level him with a glare.

Still grinning, he nods toward my bedroom. "Come on. We gotta go."

3. Ryan

I crack open my bedroom door and pause to listen before venturing into the hall.

They're gone.

Thank God they're gone.

The wood floor creaks beneath my feet as I step over the towel.

My towel, that's been rubbed all over some guy's ass crack. Now I'll have to burn it. Or, at the very least, soak it in a vat of bleach.

"You *really* suck sometimes, Connor!" I growl into the empty living room. How could he spring this on me? A thirty-minute warning is all I get after living here for three years?

To be fair, the big oaf knew I'd complain, that I'd demand a say, and never in a million years would I have agreed to one of Wolf's grounds guys moving in. I work in the hotel's administration. I see—and hear—enough to know what they're like.

Case in point—the guy has already exposed himself within five minutes of an introduction! And now I have to share a bathroom and a wall with this ... this ... obscenely attractive flasher.

My cheeks burn anew with the image of his body scorched

onto my brain. Why couldn't he have a pot belly and a coat of fur, instead of that eight-pack and pristine V-cut pelvis? I know why. Because my scamp of a brother had to find a partner in crime for his scandalous lifestyle.

"Ugh!" With a heavy groan, I barge into the bathroom, the remnants of steam from Ronan's shower lingering in the air and fogging up the mirror. A gob of toothpaste smears the porcelain sink, and the counter looks like it was half submerged in water. What did he do, bathe in the basin?

"It's okay, Ryan. It's all going to be fine. Just breathe." I coach myself through several long deep inhales and exhales, as tears of anger and frustration prick my eyes. Today was already lining up to be horrible, given last night's unexpected breakup with David.

I still can't believe it's over.

Is it because I told him I loved him last week?

That painful lump in my throat flares. I considered calling in sick to work while on my jog but talked myself out of it. Distraction is key.

Peeling off my sweat-soaked running clothes, I throw open the shower curtain.

And make a strangled sound.

4. Ronan

"Of course we're gonna work together!" Connor exclaims, as if any idea otherwise would be crazy.

Charlie, my new supervisor, no doubt strong but with a thick layer of cushion to disguise muscle, frowns up at me from behind his desk in the maintenance office. "You sure you want to put up with him all day? It's already bad enough that you have to live with him."

I chuckle. "I'll survive."

"All right. You two are stuck with each other, then. You're on trash today." His slate-blue eyes roll over my stubbled jaw. "Is this the beginning of a new look, or were you two out too late last night to shave?"

Fuck. Not fifteen minutes in and I'm already getting grilled. "Which answer do you want?"

He smirks. "The one that means I don't have to cite you for breaking the conduct code. I'll give you a pass today because you just came in from the Midwest and they're lax up there. But make sure you come in clean-shaven next week. Besides, the hipster thing wouldn't suit you."

"Yes, sir."

We're almost out the door when Charlie hollers, "And trash duty on the beach does not take four hours, fellas."

Connor offers an innocent look that's as fake as a three-dollar bill. "Never, boss. Two hours, tops."

"Uh-huh." Charlie buries his nose in his paperwork again, not buying the act for a second, but not reprimanding us further. I get the impression Connor is one of those guys who gets away with a lot of things he shouldn't get away with.

I'm not one of those guys. "Okay. So, where do we start? Parking lot? Kitchen?" If this place is anything like the Wolf back in Indianapolis, management is extra vigilant about keeping those areas clear of rodent-attracting debris.

Connor checks his watch. "If we hurry, we'll catch the last half of the women's volleyball practice on the beach." He sighs. "And let me tell you, it's a beautiful sight."

———

"This isn't gonna take long, is it?" Connor grumbles. Our heavy footfalls echo along the corridor in the employee-only area. The Wolf hotel chain may be ritzy, but they've saved their building budget for the parts that guests see. It's beige walls and dim lights here.

"I don't know. She said she needs a signature. Shouldn't be more than a minute." I got a message from an admin this morning, asking me to come in and sign some payroll papers that got messed up in my transfer. I'm not shocked. The guy who handled my move isn't playing with a full deck.

"A minute, my ass. Do you know how slow they work in here?"

"You really are a whiny bitch when you're hungry."

"Warned you, didn't I?" Connor pushes through the glass door marked Employee Administration and into an office as plain as a hospital waiting room—windowless and beige, the kind of place that makes me only too happy to be picking up trash out under the hot Florida sun. I'd hang myself if I had to sit in here all day.

"Look, if I don't do this, I don't get paid, and if I don't get paid, you're not gettin' rent money. So shut the fuck up." It hasn't taken long for Connor and me to get into a groove. We already sound like we've known each other for years instead of less than twenty-four hours.

Connor walks up to the counter that runs the full length of the room, keeping Wolf's various "white collar" office admin staff (payroll, finance, customer service) and the "blue collars" (housekeeping, kitchen scullery, maintenance crew) separated. He slaps the little bell.

And we wait, listening to the medley of fingertips tapping on keys, phones ringing, a low buzz of voices, an occasional cough.

Not one head pops up from a cubicle.

"Told you. An hour." He hits the bell again, this time twice and harder. "And fix your laces while you're at it. Doesn't that drive you nuts?"

I glance down to see that one of my laces is indeed undone and dragging. "Actually, I didn't notice." As I'm crouching to retie it, Connor bellows, loud enough to carry through the entire office, "Yo, Tatum! Can you help us out so we can go eat? You know how I get when I'm hungry!"

Fucking guy is going to get us both in shit, hollering like that.

"Would you be quiet? People are taking reservations in here!" a female whisper-hisses.

I stand to find a brunette on the other side of the counter. She's wearing the standard-issue Wolf admin staff uniform, and my attention can't help but veer downward to where the white blouse stretches across her tits.

When I lift my eyes again, I find her scowling at me.

It takes me a good five seconds before I realize that I recognize that scowl. "Oh, shit."

"I told you Ryan works here, didn't I?" Connor's grin says he damn well knows he didn't mention that and he's enjoying every second of this. "She's the coordinator for the house-keeping division."

Ryan is no longer sweaty and disheveled. Her hair is piled on top of her head, and her rich hazel eyes are hiding behind a pair of dark-rimmed glasses. No makeup touches her creamy skin, from what I can tell.

"What do you want?" she snaps, but I don't miss the blush crawling up her cheeks.

"Someone left a message about signing a payroll form so I could—"

"Jean! Crew guy is here for you." Ryan stalks away before I can finish, leaving me with my mouth open midsentence, staring at the way her hips swing in that tight purple skirt, her tiny waist making her ass seem bigger than it is. Not that I mind an ass that I can fill my hands with.

"Dick," I hiss. "You could have warned me."

"Hell no. Not after this morning. That was priceless, by the way."

"I'll bet. Anything else important you want to share with me?"

"Yeah. I'm fucking *starving*."

A cute Asian girl appears. "Ronan Lyle?"

"That's me. I got a call about paperwork?"

She sets a form in front of me. "I need you to fill this out."

"Hey, Jean." Connor rests his elbows on the counter and flashes her the same stupid smile he was using at the beach all morning. The one that got him four different phone numbers. "Big plans for the weekend?"

She dips her head to hide behind heavy black fringe as she lists her itinerary, hour by hour, it seems. I tune her out right after "sewing club" comes up and set to quickly filling out the form.

"What's our address again?"

Connor recites and I fill it out, all the while feeling Jean's black eyes appraising me.

"So, *this* is your new roommate?"

"Yeah. Why?" Connor grins. "What did Ryan say?"

"Nothing." The expression on Jean's face says Ryan had things to say and they weren't at all pleasant. She drops her voice. "She's in a bad mood today."

"I noticed. Something going on with the douchebag?" Obviously, Connor doesn't like Ryan's boyfriend and doesn't care who knows it.

She glances over her shoulder and then whispers, "I heard they broke up last night, but I'm not asking."

Connor's face fills with understanding. "No wonder she's being such a bitch." A little louder, "Hey, Ry!" When she doesn't answer, he raises his voice. "Ryan Tatum! I know you can hear me! Come over here!"

The sound of sandals slapping along the tile floor announces her approach before she appears. And the look on her face ...

Connor really doesn't want to keep his skin today.

"Would you stop being an idiot!" she hisses.

He ignores her tone. "What happened with David?"

I keep my head down, pretending not to listen as I fill out the rest of my form.

"Nothing." But by the tone of her voice, it's definitely something.

"You two broke up?" Connor pushes.

"So what?"

"So ... you should tell me these things."

"Why? You don't give a damn. And it's none of your business." She's trying to play it cool, but the slight waver in her voice betrays her.

"Come on. Don't be like that." The ever-present humor in his voice fades a touch.

"You want to talk about something? Fine!" Her voice raises

an octave. "Let's talk about our new roommate and his nudist tendencies."

Heads pop up over the cubicle walls now. Jean stares at me, her mouth hanging open.

"You had to be there," I explain with a shrug.

"I'll bet." Her gaze skims over the ink on my forearm. If it were cooler outside, I'd have to cover that up with a long-sleeved shirt. Employee conduct manual, page four.

"Oh, come on, that was funny. And besides"—Connor reaches up to seize my chin between his thumb and index finger—"how could you be so mean to this poor guy? He just had his heart ripped out. All he wants is to be loved. Can't you show him some love?"

I slap his hand away.

Ryan's hazel eyes shift to my face. She has pretty irises. I'll bet her smile would be pretty too. If she's capable of one. To Connor, she says, "Go eat. You're more annoying than usual."

"Yeah! That's the point!" He taps on the counter as he strolls away, a wordless gesture to hurry up.

Jean breaks out in a fit of giggles, like he's said the funniest thing. I want to offer her a bib to keep the drool from her blouse. I slide the completed form over instead. "Anything else?"

"No, you're all set. Thanks for coming quickly."

"That's Ronan. He 'comes quick.' Tell all your friends," Connor quips from behind.

I wait until the door is shut behind us before I punch him in the shoulder. "There's something wrong with you."

He rubs his washboard abs. "Yeah, my impending starvation."

"You and Ryan have a strange relationship."

"What are you talking about? It's totally normal."

"She hates your guts." And yet she still lives with him.

Connor grins. "Yeah, maybe a little."

I shake my head. "How old is she?"

"Twenty-five."

So is Connor, and I remember this because he's one year older than me. "So, you're twins?" I wouldn't put it past him not to mention that.

"Nah. Half sister. Our dad was a little busy cheating on my mom that year."

This is all starting to make sense. "No wonder you guys don't look anything alike."

"I only met her a few years ago. She was moving to Miami from Orlando, and she needed a place while she figured things out. My dad asked if she could crash with me." He shrugs. "I said sure, I didn't care. And she hasn't left yet. She stays out of my life, I stay out of hers. It works, for the most part."

"That explains a lot."

"Like?"

"Why you haven't threatened to pound the shit out of me if I bang her." Like I did to all my friends back home when they so much as glanced at my baby sister Brittany.

"You kidding? I *want* you to try something with her. Just let me be there to see it. It'll be fun watching her kick you in the nuts."

I sigh. "Something is *seriously* wrong with you."

He's distracted from a retort by another crew guy coming around the corner. "Yo, Baker! What's up? This is Ronan. He's new."

The blond nods once my way. "Not much. Did you read that email about Alaska?"

Connor's eyebrows rise in question.

"They want us there a week earlier."

"Seriously? But that's like ... two weeks away, then!"

Baker shrugs. "I know. They said they'll reimburse flight changes, though."

"I haven't booked my ticket yet."

"What? You're crazy!" Baker shakes his head. "I booked

mine months ago. I'll let you know what I move it to. We should fly up together."

"Definitely. Hey, we're heading for Chipotle. Want anything?"

"Nah, I'm good. But thanks. See you guys around." He keeps going down the hall.

And I'm left with yet another surprise courtesy of my new roommate. "You're going to Alaska?"

"Yeah. That resort is opening."

I remember the intercompany memo that went out last fall, encouraging Wolf employees to apply for jobs at the new seasonal hotel near Homer. I didn't even open it. I mean, it's Alaska. Who the fuck wants to go there?

Apparently Connor. And in two weeks, based on what these guys were just talking about. "How long are you gone for?"

"Five months."

"Jesus. You *are* crazy."

"What? Didn't you ever go to camp?"

I burst out laughing.

"They're putting the whole staff up in a village of cabins. And paying us better than what they're paying here."

"Yeah, it's called danger pay, because you're gonna get mauled by bears and cougars and shit."

"Nah, this is a Wolf luxury resort, not some Ramada Inn. They'll have all that sorted."

"You're gonna be bored."

"You're kidding me, right?" He grins. "How long were you pussy-whipped by your ex?"

"Four years," I admit reluctantly. "Why does that matter?"

"Because have you not noticed the housekeeping staff that Wolf hires?"

"Of course I have." Our employer is notorious for hiring young, attractive employees. I don't know how they get away with it without any labor discrimination charges tossed their way.

"Well, all those housekeeping girls are gonna be in cabins a stone's throw away from me, all summer long. Stuck at a resort with nothing to do but fuck crew guys. The *last* thing I'm gonna be is bored."

"Fair enough." I should have opened that email. Had I known Tasha was going to dump me, I'd probably be going to Alaska too. "Well ... shit. You could have told me." Here I am, making a fast friend of Connor, and he's leaving.

He shrugs. "You should see if they're still hiring."

"What?" I chuckle. "I just started here. They won't let me take off."

"Won't know if you don't ask."

"I don't know."

"Suit yourself." He squeezes the back of my neck. "You and Ryan will have a *great* summer together."

I groan.

5. Ronan

Connor lingers at the door, watching me empty two grocery bags' worth of food onto the counter. "You sure you don't want to come? Someone will be selling a ticket outside."

"Scalper prices to sit by myself at a concert? Nah, I'm good." As much as I'd kill to see the X Ambassadors, the cost will be way too steep.

"'Kay. I'll swing by to change and grab you when it's done. That blond from the beach today texted me. She's gonna meet us at the club and she's bringing a hot friend for you."

"Hot by whose standards?" I ask around a sip of beer. Usually when girls have to sell their friends like that, the results are underwhelming.

"Does it matter? Sherrie said she likes to suck dick. You gonna say no to that?"

Tasha loved to suck my dick.

My cock twitches with the memory, even if that memory is now laced with bitterness. Maybe a good blow job from another woman is what I need to get over her.

Connor nods toward the fridge. "Bottom shelf is yours."

The lowest shelf, when I'm over six feet tall. "Shouldn't Ryan take the bottom shelf?"

"If you wanna move Ryan's food, be my guest. I'll be home in about three hours. You might not have fully bled out by then after she stabs you for touching her things." With a slap against the wall and a "See you in a few," he's gone.

I study the fridge, shaking my head at the middle shelf, which is clearly hers. Everything is neatly lined up and packed in glass containers. Fruit, vegetables, yogurt. Food groups that are sorely lacking from Connor's shelf, which is basically beer, hot dogs, and ketchup.

The bottom shelf is on the lowest rung, leaving little room. I don't need a lot, but this is ridiculous. Ryan's a good foot shorter than me. The shorter people get the lower shelves. Those are the rules of life. She's going to have to learn to deal. And if she wants to yell at me about it?

Fine. So be it.

I take a big swig of my beer.

And then set to shifting things around.

———

"Is that all you got?" I watch highlights of the Panthers getting their asses handed to them by the Leafs. I guess I can't say much—Indiana doesn't even have an NHL team. Still, I can't get behind this.

I check my watch for the hundredth time. It's after eleven. I'm showered and dressed and finishing off my fifth beer. This big, fluffy brown sectional may be the most comfortable thing I've ever sat in. If Connor doesn't get back soon to drag me out, I'm not going anywhere tonight, no matter how hot this friend of Sherrie's is. And based on the picture he texted me, she's a solid nine, though I'm reserving final judgment until I see her in person. The catfish stories are real.

Keys jangle in the hallway outside our door. A few seconds

later, the door flies open and Ryan strolls in, arms laden with textbooks and a grocery bag. Her eyes skate over me as she kicks the door shut behind her, but she doesn't say anything.

"Hey. You need help?" I offer, a blip of regret stirring in the pit of my stomach as she heads for the kitchen. I shouldn't have taken the liberty to change things around without talking to her. Not until I smoothed over this morning's debacle.

I don't feel like getting yelled at again.

"No thanks," she says curtly, dumping everything onto the countertop.

I watch her as she opens the fridge.

And stops dead.

"Hey, I hope you don't mind, but I swapped our things around, seeing as you're shorter than me. I lifted the shelf though, so you have as much space as before." After a lingering pause, I add, "Connor said you'd be okay with it." I owe him one for not telling me about Ryan in the first place.

After another long moment of silence, she sets to sliding her groceries onto her shelf, not saying a word, but also not threatening bodily harm. I watch, because I can't help myself. She's wearing black leggings, and her firm ass looks fantastic bent over in the fridge. My dick starts to harden.

I sure as hell can't let *that* happen.

And I can't let this tension go on either. We just got off on the wrong foot is all. Collecting my empty beer cans, I climb off the couch and make my way over to the kitchen to stack them in the case. "I'm sorry about this morning."

I get only a small grunt in response as she rips the cardboard sleeves off her yogurt and snaps the little containers apart to line them up neatly in two rows.

"I picked up towels at Walmart after work. They're gray, so they won't get mixed up."

"I doubt that would happen, anyway. I don't buy my towels from *Walmart*."

I fight the urge to roll my eyes at her snotty tone and

25

instead turn my attention to the textbook on the counter. "You in school?"

"Yup."

I flip open the cover. "For what?"

"My MBA."

"That's—exciting." I pull my fingers away just in time as she slaps the cover shut and collects the textbook along with the others. Hugging them to her chest, she grabs her purse and stalks toward her bedroom.

"Hey, hold up." I tack on, "Please?"

She slows with reluctance.

"This is dumb. Can we start over?"

"Why?"

"Because we have to live together?"

She peers over her shoulder at me, her eyes flickering down. I'm ready for the club, in black pants and a baby-blue button-down that hugs my torso. I don't often dress in anything but jeans and a T-shirt, but when I do, I like to think I clean up well. "Did you really just break up with your girlfriend or was my brother talking out of his ass again?"

I falter at the unexpected question. "Yeah. A few months ago."

"How long were you together?"

"Four years." And the last thing I want to talk about in my new life is Tasha.

She snorts. "Wow. And here I was, crying over eighteen months wasted."

"That's a good chunk of time too." This is good. We've found something in common—our broken hearts. I lean against the wall. "Why'd you guys end things?"

Her jaw tightens. At first I think she's not going to answer. "He said he loves me too much and he's not ready for that kind of commitment yet." She pauses to chew her bottom lip in thought. "Do you think that's some 'It's not you, it's me' bullshit?"

Yes. "Hard to say. You'll probably find out soon enough." With a line like that, my gut says the guy is already dick-deep in another girl. But I can't tell Ryan that. "Tasha told me she needed some space to make sure she loved me." I smile bitterly. "She hooked up with one of my best friends two weeks later."

"Ouch." Ryan slides off her glasses, cleaning the lenses with the hem of her T-shirt. When she glances up at me, I see hints of sympathy. "So, you moved down to Miami to what? Get over her?"

Get over her. Forget about her. Keep myself occupied until she decides she loves me again. That last one sounds about right. I couldn't stand being in the same city as her, knowing she would be out with other guys. "I needed a change, and I've heard this city is the place to be."

"If you're like my brother, then it is."

"I'm not like your brother."

"I guess we'll see." Again, that shrewd gaze drifts over my body. She's already seen me naked; I wonder if she's picturing me naked right now.

Blood starts flowing south and I have to shift my stance, ever aware of how fitted these pants are and that they don't hide raging erections well.

Her eyes widen, as if she caught herself checking me out. Standing taller, she says, "Don't touch my stuff anymore. I'm weird about my space. I like things a certain way." With that, she disappears into her room.

I heave a sigh, glancing at my watch again. I'm no longer tired; the five-minute exposure to her, first to her sharp side, followed by something softer, has my pulse buzzing. I need to get out of here.

Thank God, Connor plows through the door. "Two minutes! The ladies are waiting."

6. Ronan

"And then she said 'No way! You first!' and I said 'No way, you first!' and none of us went at all!" Sherrie and Georgia throw their heads back and cackle with boisterous laughter.

I gulp my drink, long since needing to move on to the hard stuff.

"Another round?" Connor's eyes twinkle. Sherrie's hands have been glued to his chest since we walked through the club doors. It's only a matter of time before they make their way south to his lap. He knows he's getting laid tonight and he's as happy as an alley cat in a tuna factory.

Georgia hasn't been as forward, but I'm guessing that's more on account of me being ... me. I'm not outgoing and flirtatious like Connor. That's not to say I don't know the right words or that I even need to say anything to attract women. But I've had plenty of them tell me that I'm intimidating—my green eyes are broody, my hard jaw is unyielding to easy smiles, my tattoos and buzz cut give me a dangerous edge. Whether they find all that attractive or they're attracted to the idea of taming me, I can't be sure. Either way, women throw themselves at me without me having to lift a finger.

It drove Tasha crazy. She'd get so jealous, accuse me of cheating on her. No one seems to believe that I never touched another woman while I was with her, but I didn't.

I have since she dumped me. Twice, back in Indy. Both were girls I picked up at a club. I ended up at their places. Neither were anything to think twice about. Pretty, but without personalities. Decent lays, but nothing mind-bending. I was relieved to be walking out their doors, tossing their phone numbers as soon as I rounded the corner.

Maybe that's why I'm not making too much of an effort tonight. I'd be just as happy to go home alone and sleep. Banging strangers from bars isn't for me. I like to know the woman I'm sliding my dick into.

"I think I want to switch to something less sugary. What are you drinking, Ronan?" Georgia sidles closer to me. That's what it's been all night—her nudging my thigh here and there, grazing her fingers over my biceps occasionally. She's batted her lashes plenty. Subtle moves to let me know she's interested but unsure how aggressive to be. But with each drink, the leash that holds her self-control back slackens.

"Jack and Coke."

"Is it any good?" She smiles sweetly at me. She really is as stunning as that picture I saw, though a lot of it is makeup.

I hold out the drink to her.

She leans over, parting her lips for the tip of the straw. She makes a point of looking up at me through those soulful milk-chocolate eyes as she sucks. "Mmm ... Yes. I definitely want this." She finishes it off with a swipe of her tongue along her bottom lip.

Yeah, I'm definitely getting laid tonight, if I want it.

"All right, this waitress of ours is never coming back. We'll go to the bar and grab a round." Connor tilts his head, signaling for me to follow. "Don't let anyone take our spots."

"Never." Georgia giggles as I climb out of my seat in the shadowy alcove at the back of Sin. We're in the nightclub's

VIP section, and apparently, it's impossible to get a table back here, but Sherrie is best friends with one of the managers.

I'm not gonna lie: I'll take a VIP booth in the dark over the crowds of sweaty bodies.

But that's where we're heading now, as I follow Connor toward the closest bar, hordes of people surrounding it, the music pulsing louder with each step.

I've never seen so many scantily clad, beautiful women in my life. The per capita of hot bodies in Miami is off the charts. I guess there's something about beach life—when you live in a place where you own almost as many bikinis as you do other outfits, you tend to go the extra mile to look good in them. And damn, these women look good.

I spot our cocktail waitress approaching. Full gold, orange, and black paint from head to toe, and she's wearing nothing but heels, a G-string, and pasties to cover her nipples. It's one helluva uniform for a nightclub. All the servers are dressed and painted like various animals. Ours is a lion. Or a lioness, to be exact.

"I was coming over to you guys," she purrs, not an ounce of shyness over her revealing outfit or my appraisal of it as she steps closer to me. There's maybe an inch between my chest and her double-D tits. They're obviously fake but beautiful, nonetheless. "I'm so sorry. We're short-staffed tonight."

It could be the Jack, but damn, this costume is sexy. So is her confidence. If I had her in the VIP area instead of Georgia, I'd be more eager. "It's okay. We needed to stretch our legs."

"What's your name?" Her lips graze my earlobe.

"Ronan."

"Hi, Ronan. So, is the brunette at your table your girlfriend?"

"Just for tonight."

She grins. "My name's Becca."

"Hey, Becca. Does that paint rub off on hands?" My gaze

drops to her breasts, my palms itching to feel the weight of them.

"It will if they're wet. And my boss wouldn't be too happy about smudges this early in the night."

"That's too bad."

Her lips part. "But how about later?"

I jump at the feel of a palm smoothing over my groin; I don't have to check to know it's hers. I can't get away, even if I want to. I'm surrounded by people in every direction, all of them clueless as the lioness server rubs my dick.

"I think you are incredibly sexy. Why don't you give me your number and we can ..."

From the corner of my eye, I notice Connor's large frame about ten feet away, standing too close and menacingly to some lanky guy for it to end well.

Shit. "I'm sorry, I've gotta help my friend. Come by the table." I skirt past her and push through, trying to will my erection down as I close the distance. I grab hold of Connor's shoulders and squeeze. "Hey, what's up, bro?"

"Look who I ran into!" Connor exclaims with mock cheeriness.

"I don't know this guy." He's skinny and has a vibe to him —his pants are tapered, his shirt fitted and untucked. I can't see his shoes, but I'd bet they're polished and slightly wing-tipped. He's nervous, that much is obvious by the way he keeps glancing around him, running his fingers through his shaggy brown hair, pushing it off his face.

For Connor to lose his charming edge, he must be pissed. And he's a big guy. Whoever this hipster-fucker is, he better be afraid.

"*This* is Ryan's ex, David," Connor explains through gritted teeth.

Oh.

"He works at Wolf, in accounting. And that girl over there

works in reception." He nods toward a pretty, tall blond standing about five feet away.

Ohhh.

"I was telling David how sweet it is, the way he had his arm wrapped around her. You know, since he broke up with my *sister* last night."

Fuck. The dick isn't just with another girl. He's with a hotel coworker.

Poor Ryan. She's gonna hear about this by Monday morning. The fact that she has to work in the same place as her ex is bad enough, and now he's dating someone else there. What is it with hotels and staffers banging each other like rabbits, thinking no one will find out about it? The outdoor crew guys have a bad rep, but these office people aren't much better.

A quick glance around shows me that five different bouncers are watching, ready to move in. I don't want to get kicked out. Not before I see Becca again. "Come on. You've gotta let Ryan deal with this in her own way. You'll only make it worse. Let's go."

At first, I don't think Connor's going to listen. But finally, he moves away, carving a path straight to the bar.

"How the fuck does *he* land a chick like that?" Connor yells over the music. "He's got to be a hundred pounds soaking wet. Does he have a giant curved dick or something?"

"I don't get it either," I agree.

"I mean, my sister and him were one thing, but ..."

"Ryan's not exactly hard to look at." She has a sweet, wholesome face and a killer ass.

"You know what I mean. She's all scholarly, doing her master's and shit."

"Yeah, I guess."

Connor eyes me. "Why? Have you been checking her out?"

"*No way.*" It's an automatic response. A lie, but a necessary one. Sisters are off-limits.

Connor leans over the bar, sizing up the choices. "Good. Because I don't think I'd be okay with that."

I snort. "Dude, then why do you keep trying to push her on me?"

"Because I like to bug the shit out of her. But if I ever thought she'd actually bite, I wouldn't."

"Oh, I'm sure she'll bite. My dick. No thanks. I like it whole and attached. But you know what?" I pat Connor's back. "I'm glad to see you actually do know how to be a good brother and give a damn about something besides getting laid."

The bartender comes by. Connor orders and pays for the round, his gaze roving over the women around the bar. "Ah, well. She'll find someone new soon enough. And speaking of getting laid ..." He grabs two of the drinks and carves a path through the crowd, back to our table.

What I could really use is a cigarette.

It's so dark in the VIP section that we have a hard time finding our corner, stumbling up a step or two to where Sherrie and Georgia are on their feet, their scantily clad bodies gyrating against each other to the heavy beat.

"I don't know which one I like more," Connor muses, watching.

They're all the same, I want to say, but I hold my tongue.

"What do you say we swap halfway through?"

"What do *I* say?" I chuckle through a sip. "What do *they* say about it?" Tasha's rage would go nuclear if my gaze so much as inadvertently skimmed one of her girlfriends. I made an offhanded swinging joke once, and she didn't talk to me for almost a week.

"Oh, they're down. Sherrie already said as much."

"Damn." This city really is something, or maybe this is what single life is like. I'm not against it, but neither of them is doing it for me. "Why don't you take both, and I'll take our server instead."

His brow arches knowingly. "The paint, right? You wanna leave fingerprints."

"*All* over her."

Sherrie notices that we've returned and waves at the row of shot glasses on the table. "Look what our waitress brought over to apologize for taking so long!"

They're all empty.

I lift one to sniff it.

"Tequila!" They both shout, lifting their arms over their heads.

Connor and I share a glance—one that says neither of us is getting laid tonight, unless it happens soon.

"I was just thinking the same thing." He nods to my glass. "Drink up."

Georgia's hips sway as she rounds the table. Still dancing, she runs her hands from my stomach all the way to my chest, her fingertips curling around the collar of my shirt. "You took too long."

Not more than ten minutes, but in drunk-girl time, I guess that's forever. "You should have water."

"Hmm ..." She's so close, all I can smell is her lotus flower perfume. "I don't want water. Do you know what I do want?"

I chuckle. "I think I can guess."

She steps in close enough to grind against me. Her eyes sparkle. "It looks like someone's excited to see me."

Or just excited, thanks to Becca.

My hands are occupied so I can't do much when Georgia's fingers slide over the hard ridge in my pants, rubbing back and forth.

"You're a big boy," she purrs into my ear, and my dick jumps, like a lap dog responding to praise. With a giggle, she draws my zipper down and slips her hand inside to grip me, the warmth of her palm through the cotton of my briefs bringing a soft groan to my lips. I glance over to see Sherrie push Connor back into the lounge chair and climb onto his lap, her short skirt riding up to show the black lace of her G-string. All around us, people are in their own worlds, laughing, dancing, semicovertly sniffing lines of coke off side tables. I wonder if it's this place or Miami in general, but no one seems to care who's watching.

And truthfully, I don't care much either. I suck back half my drink, knowing I'm going to have to finish Georgia's too. And then we're gonna have to get out of here because I need those red lips around my cock.

She must be able to read my mind because I feel the sharp tug of my belt buckle being unfastened. Fuck ... is she actually going to—

Cool fingers graze against my skin as she peels my briefs down and pulls my dick right out into the open.

Jesus. At least my back is to the crowd.

I'm too stunned to speak as she seats herself on the chair in front of me. Giving me a lascivious smile, she leans forward and runs her tongue along my full length, nearly buckling my knees.

I glance over to see if Connor knows what's going on. But he's otherwise occupied, his hands gripping Sherrie's ass as she straddles his lap, riding him so hard there's no way he's not going to come in his pants.

Just like there's no way I'm going to stop Georgia now.

I chug the rest of my drink and gently toss the glass toward the couch. Bits of ice scatter onto the smooth surface. It's a bar —they must be used to spilled drinks around here. With my free hand, I weave my fingers through the back of Georgia's hair and guide myself into her warm mouth. She accepts me without hesitation and fully, until I feel my tip hitting the back of her throat. A groan slips from my mouth.

Sherrie wasn't kidding—her friend loves to suck dick and she's damn good at it, her deceptive doe eyes locked on mine as her head bobs up and down, her long fingernails digging into my hips. She has literally no gag reflex.

35

I feel myself swelling and tightening. I may actually blow my load in her mouth, right here in the back of this club. Something I can't say I've done before. While Tasha was wild between the sheets, it was always behind the safety of a door, and with just the two of us in the room.

But Tasha isn't in my life anymore, so what the hell do I care?

A light hand settles on my shoulder. I turn to find Becca standing next to me.

"I'm sorry, I can't let you do that in here," she purrs in my ear.

"Why not? Because you want to be the one doing it?" I'm turning into an obnoxious ass, thanks to the Jack. But seriously, people are practically fucking on the dance floor, and I'll be done in a few minutes.

"Because it's considered public indecency. It's frowned upon."

Something about the way she says that makes my dick swell more.

Her eyes drop from my face to where Georgia sucks. When her gaze lifts again, I see the heat in them. "You better finish up before the bouncers come."

I smirk. "Define finish up?" Does she mean stop or …

Becca adjusts her grip on her empty drink tray, tucking it under her arm to block the view of passersby as she settles a hand over mine.

"Holy fuck," I hiss, as she guides Georgia's head, urging her on faster, deeper, her painted breast rubbing against my biceps. Even the pasty can't hide her hardened nipples.

This lioness is something else.

Over her shoulder, I see that Sherrie has reversed on Connor's lap and is grinding her ass into him now. Connor's head has fallen back against the couch, his lips parted, a euphoric look on his face as he stares up at the ceiling.

I can't believe this is happening. "Fuck me ..." I'm in heaven.

"I was hoping to," Becca murmurs.

I chug Georgia's drink and toss the glass aside, my gaze locked on Becca's stunning body. It's probably wrong to be drooling over her while Georgia is blowing me, but I can't help it, and neither Georgia nor Becca seem to mind.

"I *really* need to touch you." I'm ready to explode.

A small smile curls Becca's lips as she adjusts her stance. "Nowhere that I'm painted."

That leaves me only one place.

I graze my finger along the front of her G-string, waiting for her to stop me.

She goads me on with a jut of her chin.

Carefully, I slip my index finger down the front of her smooth mound and through her slick center. She parts her legs, inviting me inside her.

I take the invitation, sliding two fingers into her wet heat.

The simple move is my undoing. My head falls back as all the muscles in my stomach, my groin, my legs constrict and my balls tighten. Pulling Georgia's head flush against me with my other hand, I spill into her mouth with a strangled curse.

Becca abruptly steps away from me, my fingers gliding out from her.

And I find myself flanked by two truck-sized bouncers.

———

"It's almost impossible to get kicked out of Sin. Well done, buddy." Connor chuckles as we stumble through our front door and into the dark living room, Georgia and Sherrie giggling as they cling to each other's arms.

Despite the sudden end to things at the club—my pants barely done up as I was escorted out—I would have been satisfied to call it a night. But Sherrie's mouth found its way around my cock the second we climbed into the cab and now I need another release.

"I'm this way." Connor leads Georgia toward his bedroom, giving me a thumbs-up. I'm not even sure when it was decided that we'd swap and who made that decision, but it seems everyone's game.

"You've got paint on your shirt." Sherrie's hand slides over my sleeve where I'm smeared in orange from Becca.

"Shit. I hope that comes out." It's one of my favorite shirts.

"We should throw it into the wash now." She begins fumbling with the buttons, her lips moving for my mouth.

I step out of her reach, not interested in that level of intimacy. "Let me do that. My room's down there, on the right. I'll be there in a sec."

She takes three staggering steps toward the hallway, using the couch's back to guide her.

"You sure you're up for this tonight?" I ask. "'Cause we've both been drinking and we don't have to ..."

My words trail as she pushes down the top of her dress, showing off a set of perky tits before she saunters away.

I guess this is happening. I head for the closet off the main room, peeling off my shirt on the way to chuck it in the washer. It's too dark and I'm too drunk to read all the controls, so I hope I'm doing this right.

"What the hell!" a female shrieks.

Shit.

I rush toward the voices, tripping over the heels, dress, and panties strewn along the floor, to find Ryan's door wide open and a naked Sherrie scampering out.

Granted, the condo is an odd design, with Ryan's bedroom at the end of the hall and mine kitty-corner to it. Still, it's not hard to figure out. "Your *other* right."

Sherrie darts across to my room. I dare hazard a glance to find the bedside lamp on and Ryan sitting upright in her bed, her scowl full of venom.

"Sorry." I close her door before I feel the sharp edge of her tongue.

"Who was that?" Sherrie's lying on my bed, her legs spread wide, her fake, plump breasts sitting on display, watching me strip off my pants. She's got a nice body, as nice as Georgia's, I'd guess. I doubt this will take long. And then what? How am I going to get rid of her? I don't want to wake up next to this girl. Why did we bring them back here?

"Roommate." I tear open the fresh box of condoms and fish one out, ripping the foil packaging with my teeth.

"I don't think she liked me climbing into her bed."

"I can't imagine why. Turn around."

"Aren't you going to get me off first?" Sherrie gives me an exaggerated pout and runs her fingers along her core as if to taunt me.

I seize her by the hips and flip her over. Pulling her up onto her knees, I climb onto the bed behind her. "Don't worry. You'll get off." I made it a personal challenge, figuring out exactly how to get Tasha to orgasm every time. Sherrie can't be that much different. Plus, I don't stick my tongue between just anyone's legs. Definitely not a woman who rode my friend's lap in a bar, and who I won't be seeing after tonight.

With one hard thrust, I'm inside her.

She cries out.

I give her a moment to adjust to my size. "How does that feel?"

"So good," she moans, turning her face to the side. This angle—ass up—is one of my favorites. Though, asses in general are my kryptonite.

I close my eyes and move my hips, pushing in and out of her with ease as I dare let myself imagine Tasha's hips between my grip for a moment. It doesn't feel the same, though. Nothing about this woman feels the same.

My ex is tall and athletic, with small tits and washboard abs. She smells like the almond cream she uses every day—a subtle but intoxicating scent. Her hair is silky soft, free of hairspray. It always slipped through my fist like a feather when I tried to grip it.

The headboard bangs against the wall. I'll need to pull my bed out tomorrow so that doesn't happen again. There's not much I can do about the frame, creaking noisily with each thrust.

Sherrie doesn't seem to notice or care, her moans coming more frequently and loudly each time I plunge into her. It takes me a minute to find that spot deep inside, but now that I have, I angle so I slam into it mercilessly.

"Oh my God! I'm coming! I'm coming! I'm ..." Coherent words fail her and soon she's crying out with her orgasm. The muscles in my stomach tighten with anticipation at my own release, which is taking its sweet time, thanks to the booze.

An angry fist pounds against the wall on the other side, slowing me down.

Ryan's voice is muffled but loud enough to understand. "You are so full of shit! No one's *that* good!"

Sherrie giggles through her pants. "I guess you haven't fucked her yet, then. She wouldn't be saying that otherwise."

No, I haven't. And I can't see that changing. Her pussy probably has teeth.

Still, I can't help but smile at what my dick registers as a challenge. Setting one foot on the floor, I hook my arms around Sherrie's thighs and lift her lower half right off the mattress.

"Oh my God," she pants. "You're *so deep*."

"You ready to prove my roommate wrong?"

———

THE CLOCK SHOWS twenty minutes have passed by the time I unload into my condom, my body coated in a sheen of sweat, my chest heaving, my muscles exhausted.

Sherrie came two more times and is now a floppy doll on

her back, legs limp within my grip. "I don't think I'm going to be able to walk." Her voice has turned raspy from all the screaming.

No sooner does the last squeak of the mattress sound than my door opens and Connor appears in his boxers.

"Come on, man ..." I'm still inside her, for fuck's sake.

Connor doesn't even pretend to apologize. "We've gotta get up in a few hours for work, remember?"

I frown. Tomorrow is Saturday. We're not scheduled to work.

He sets the clothes Sherrie scattered down the hall onto the dresser. "Your cab will be here in five. Georgia's waiting for you."

I struggle to hide my smile.

I think Connor may be my soul mate.

––––––

"You'll call us?" Both Sherrie and Georgia clumsily paw at my bare chest.

"Sure." I turn my head as Sherrie leans in, and I end up with a sloppy kiss on my cheek. At least Georgia doesn't bother.

"I'll walk 'em down. Make sure they get in their car safely." Connor trails them out in his boxers, throwing me a thumbs-up on his way past.

I stagger back toward my bedroom, fully intending to stick my head out the window to grab a smoke before I face-plant into my pillows.

Ryan is standing in her doorway, her hair a wild mess and hate in her eyes, even as they dance over the briefs I threw on. "You're *nothing* like my brother, right?"

I groan and pinch the bridge of my nose. "Can we do this tomorrow, please?"

"Do what?"

"This thing where I accidentally offend you and then you yell at me and storm off."

"You call what happened tonight 'accidental'?" Her nostrils flare. And here I thought she couldn't look angrier. "Your *whore* climbed into my bed."

"That's not a kind word."

"*Naked whore.*"

"Sherrie got confused." So confused that she swapped guys halfway through, I want to add, but humor won't help my cause.

"That doesn't mean it's okay!"

I hold up my hands in surrender. "You're right, it's not. I'm sorry. It won't happen again."

"Until tomorrow night, with the next *whore* who can't tell the different between right and left."

"I'm not gonna be doing this every night." I don't think I can handle it. The familiar tingle of regret is settling in. I feel like I've cheated on Tasha, even though she's with other guys.

"Bullshit." Ryan shakes her head. "I work all day, and I have class four nights a week, plus a shit ton of schoolwork to do on weekends. Some of us don't get to coast through life drinking and partying. We have to use our brains."

These verbal lashings are getting tiresome. "I said I was sorry. What else do you want me to say?"

"That you won't bring home whores!"

"She wasn't a whore."

Ryan crosses her arms over her chest, the stance screaming doubt.

"Hey, I might need to get laid every once in a while. Don't tell me Connor doesn't bring home girls."

"He's at the opposite end of the condo. I have to share a wall with you!"

"Fair enough. I'll be quieter next time."

"It's 2:00 a.m. and I had to listen to some drunk woman scream—practically in my *ear*—for the past half hour. Now I'm going to be exhausted. And don't tell me this isn't going to happen again. Neither of us are dumb enough to believe that."

I sigh, my patience wearing thin. This is exactly why I don't want female roommates. "I've barely looked at another girl since Tasha dumped me, and I wasn't planning on bringing anyone home tonight. It just ... happened. I'll do my best to keep it to a minimum, but I won't commit to living like a monk."

I could be mistaken, but I think I see sympathy flicker in Ryan's eyes. She pauses for a long moment. "I could give you my schedule for when I'm extra busy and you can work around that?"

I burst out in laughter. "Are you serious? I'm not fucking on your schedule, Ryan." My focus drops to scan her bare legs. They're short but shapely beneath that oversized, unflattering sleep shirt with the picture of a crab and the words *I'm crabby in the morning* scrawled across it. "Not unless you're the one in my bed."

"As if," she stammers. But her body betrays her, her gaze flickering over my chest, her lips parting with a sharp inhale. She gives her head a shake. "I'm not into your kind."

"*My* kind?" I smirk.

She sets her jaw. "No ambition and low standards."

I don't like her tone or her words. They're laced with disdain, like she's too good to be with me. I don't bother bringing up the fact that I have a business degree. I'm guessing she'd use it to prove her point, how a guy with a degree is doing manual labor at a hotel because he lacks ambition. I've heard it more than once from Tasha. "That's right. You like accountants. They're all so honorable, right?"

Pain flashes in her eyes.

Bringing him up was a jerk move. I open my mouth to apologize—

"You need a shower. You reek." Her nose wrinkles with disgust.

I can't help myself. "That's because I just finished fucking a woman into three orgasms." I take a step closer to her. "Have you ever been fucked like that?" *Is Ryan quiet or does she scream when she comes?*

Her mouth gapes with shock for a split second before her small hand flies out to slap my cheek. With a huff, she storms back to her room.

"Yeah, I didn't think so." I chuckle all the way to my bed, ignoring the sting.

I definitely deserved it.

7. Ryan

I 'll bet the prick is sleeping soundly on the other side of this wall.

I stare listlessly at my clock, willing my brain to shut off, but all I can do is replay the events of the night—from waking up to a woman wearing nothing but overpowering perfume sliding *into my bed*, to the sound of her lust-filled moans and the repetitive thump of Ronan's headboard that seemed to go on *forever*.

That couldn't have been real. I've watched porn before. That's what she sounded like—like she was being paid to perform. Granted, she was drunk, but still ...

If she enjoyed it half as much as she faked it, she had a *great* night.

Worse, I heard Ronan when he came—a deep, guttural sound that spiked my pulse.

That spiteful bastard *clearly* dialed it up ten notches after I banged on the wall, slamming into her so hard that I thought his headboard might break through the plaster. He got what he was probably aiming for—my rage—but the longer it went on, my anger began to compete with illicit thoughts I *do not want* of my dirty roommate. Especially not while the memory of him in our hallway, freshly showered, buck naked, and arrogant is still fresh in my mind.

It's the last bit of our heated conversation that I can't shake.

"I'm not fucking on your schedule, Ryan."

"Not unless you're the one in my bed."

An unwanted flutter stirs in my lower belly as those words replay through his deep, raspy voice. Ronan is gorgeous, even if he knows it. Those sharp green eyes and angular jaw are enough to stop anyone in their tracks. There, I admitted it.

And I'm not the only one who has noticed. There were plenty of whispers about "the new guy." The moment he strolled out of the office last Friday, I saw the stares and mouthed *oh my God*s. The furtive questions followed quickly. *What did you mean when you said he was a nudist? What does he look like naked?*

How big is his you-know-what?

But even with all his arrogance, there's something acutely sad about him. It makes me hate him a little less ...

Just a little.

8. Ronan

"Ready?" Connor hollers from the living room.

I grab my wallet, cigarettes, and keys from my dresser, and on second thought, abandon the keys. They'll only annoy me on the volleyball court and besides, what's the point? I'm always with Connor. We've become attached at the hip.

Ryan's door opens as I'm stepping out of my bedroom. It's the first I've seen of her since our 2:00 a.m. confrontation on Friday night. It's now Sunday. "Hey, what time do you need the shower in the morning?" she asks, not a hint of the usual venom in her voice.

I falter, not familiar with this docile version. "My alarm goes off at 6:20."

"Great. Have a good night." She ducks into her room and closes the door without another word.

I exchange a confused look with Connor, who only shrugs. All right, then ...

Maybe she's realized what a shrew she's been and is coming to terms with this new arrangement.

That'd be nice.

——————

I pound on the bathroom door. It's 6:30 a.m. Ryan knew I needed to hop in the shower ten minutes ago to get to work on time. So why the hell did I hear the water start at 6:15?

This is intentional.

And she's not answering.

My irritation flares. "Come on, Ryan!"

Connor staggers into the kitchen, a little rough around the eyes after our late night at the bar down the street. But he's clean and in uniform, coffee in hand, ready to go. "What's goin' on?"

"Your sister is being as sweet as ever, that's what's goin' on." She's gonna make me late.

He nods toward his side of the condo. "Use mine."

I'm about to concede, but ... "No! Fuck this!" I like *my* razor and *my* shampoo and *my* soap. She's doing this to piss me off. I bang on the door. "If you don't answer me in five seconds, I'm gonna assume you've slipped and fallen, and I'm gonna kick this door down! Consider this fair warning. One! Two! Three—"

The water shuts off.

Seconds later, the door opens, and Ryan emerges in a cloud of steam, still in her pajamas, her hair dry, a book tucked under her arm.

What the ... "You didn't even take a shower."

She lets out an exaggerated yawn. "Oops! Silly me, I can't believe I forgot to actually get in!"

My face screws up. *"You forgot to get in?"*

She shrugs innocently.

"And let me guess—you forgot my schedule too?"

"Whoops! Totally slipped my mind. I guess I was just *so* tired after losing all that sleep this weekend. You know, with all the *whores*."

"For fuck's sake. That was Friday night and stop calling

women whores!" I don't often let my anger get the better of me, but now I'm struggling.

Ryan strolls past me and into her room, kicking the door shut behind her.

I turn to Connor, who's devouring a banana and grinning. "Is she for real? Did that just happen?"

"You two kids better figure out how to get along. And hurry up. We've gotta go soon."

Fuck. I duck into the bathroom and turn on the tap, waiting impatiently for the water to turn hot.

There's none left.

9. Ryan

My hands tremble as I lean back against my door and listen to Ronan's brief exchange with my brother and his even briefer shower. I've complained to Connor at least a dozen times about how small our hot water tank is. For once, I'm glad his cheap ass refused to upgrade.

I hatched this plan on Friday night while the asshole slept soundly after his sexcapades and have been fine-tuning it all weekend instead of giving my school assignments the attention they deserve. The good news is it was a suitable distraction from my heartbreak.

I'm not a spiteful person by nature. I thought I was going to pee my pants when he started counting to five, and when those smoldering eyes landed on me, I almost abandoned my nerve.

All in all, though, I think it went off rather well.

This will teach Ronan to be a little more considerate toward his roommate.

With my plan successfully executed, I get dressed for work.

10. Ronan

"You're lying. It's *impossible* to get kicked out of Sin!" Dean, a leggy guy with a protruding Adam's apple and glaring tan lines, exclaims around a mouthful of his sub sandwich, thin strands of lettuce spilling out of his mouth as he talks.

"And yet superstar here managed it, all by himself." Connor's heavy hand falls on my shoulder. "I can't decide if it was the blow job or you fingering the cocktail waitress that pissed off the bouncers more."

A raucous chorus of applause and laughter erupts in the staff area behind the Wolf Hotel—a plain fenced-off area of picnic tables and a few planters—as the guys react to Connor's dramatic retelling of Friday night.

"And then what happened?" Lopez, a guy from customer service whose first name evades me, asks. He seems decent. The kind who lives at home and does everything his mother asks of him, including marry the good Catholic girl from down the street. She wouldn't approve of him sitting with our degenerate lot.

"We left." I ball up the wrapper of my own sandwich and chuck it into the trash can, then lean back on the park bench and revel in the warm sun. Unlike Connor, I'm not one to fuck around and talk about it.

"Yeah, but—"

"Come on, now." I nod toward a group of female employees sitting at the table next to us, pretending not to listen. They don't need to hear a bunch of pigheaded crew guys talking about blow jobs and fingering.

"And then we swapped," Connor goes on to say. "And damn, did that girl know how to suck a cock."

"So, you basically had three chicks that night?" Lopez gazes at me with awe.

"In one form or another," Connor answers for me, earning my warning look.

A group of women emerges through the back door, and the guys shift their focus off the topic of me and my dick to ogle them.

"How did David manage to land her?" Franco, another crew guy, asks, as we watch the blond who was at Sin with Ryan's ex stroll out, a flowery lunch bag dangling from her fingers, sharing a secretive laugh with her friends as they take a nearby table.

And so it begins, the gossip, the speculation. These guys all know about it, which means Ryan would have heard about her ex by now. I wonder how she's taking it.

After this morning's shower stunt, I shouldn't care, but I actually find myself replaying the exchange and chuckling. Good for her. Nothing wrong with a little spite fuel.

"I'd tap that." Connor tips his head back to finish his can of Coke. He lets out a loud belch, earning frowns from their table. Of course, most of them melt away when they see who it's coming from.

"How do you get away with that?" Franco gapes at Connor.

"Same way I get away with asking a girl if her friend can

join." Connor's face splits into a wide grin, showing off his dimples. "I'm so damn irresistible."

Another round of laughter erupts.

I'm reaching into my pocket for my Marlboros when the exterior door swings open and Ryan steps out, her brown paper bag in hand. Heads automatically turn. Her cheeks flush as she quickly seeks us out and begins walking over.

"She eats lunch with you?" I ask.

"Never, which means something must be seriously wrong." Connor grabs the trash from the space between us, making room for her. "Baby sis! What a rare pleasure!"

"Shut up. I'm only three months younger than you." She wipes the bench with a readied napkin before sitting down gingerly.

I shake my head.

"What? I just picked up my clothes from the dry cleaners." Her gaze skims my dusty pants, telling me without words that she thinks I'm dirty. At least she doesn't sneer.

The other guys have drifted off into their own conversations—which, thankfully, are too low for us to overhear because I'm sure they'd only prove Ryan's theory that the crew is a bunch of STD-riddled cavemen.

Connor nudges her shoulder with his and asks softly, "What's goin' on?"

"Nothing. I ... needed to get out of there." She quickly unpacks her lunch onto her lap. Yogurt, apple, grapes, and a cheese sandwich on thin dark bread that is probably healthy but is cosplaying as cardboard. I'll bet her meals are as predictable as the sun setting each night.

Connor must be thinking the same thing. "Don't you ever get sick of eating the same thing *every single day*?"

"No."

His baffled expression is comical. "But don't you ever want to order a big, greasy burger?"

"No." She glances at the messy remnants of his pizza sub.

"Do you understand how bad it is for you? It's full of fat and salt and preservatives."

Connor lifts his shirt up and smooths his hand over his belly, as hard and sculpted as mine. "Does it look like it matters to me?"

She snorts. "You need to start eating better."

"Fine." He offers a one-shouldered shrug. "You cook and I'll eat better."

"*As if*. It's bad enough I have to clean the bathroom after *him*." She jerks her chin toward me.

"Well, you won't have much to clean today, what with my two-minute cold shower and all," I remind her dryly.

"You deserved that."

I smirk. "Yeah. I did. You win."

She falters. "Wow, conceding already."

"What can I say?" I tap my chest. "I have no ambition, remember?"

Her gaze follows my gesture, and the hint of a smile curls her lips. It's wiped off quickly as the door creaks open and her ex steps out.

David's eyes skim over the area. They pause on the bench where the three of us sit, widening slightly—I can almost hear the curse in his head—and then he quickly averts his gaze to where his new girl sits.

"Hey, David!" Connor hollers, waving at him. Ryan lets out a noise of mortification. "How was the rest of your night on Friday?"

David's shoulders sink a little as he heads for the other table, claiming the spot next to Ryan's replacement.

Connor watches them, perfecting a menacing stare I didn't think he could pull off. "I should nail her just to piss him off. What do you think, Ry?"

Her face is pale as she takes in the scene, and I can almost see the pieces click in her mind.

Fuck.

She didn't know.

"I think I'm going to finish my lunch inside." She begins collecting her food, her hands shaking.

"No. Stay." I settle my hand on her leg, just above her knee, before she has a chance to stand. "Make him think you don't care."

Her body tenses in response. To my touch or my words, I can't say. Probably both. "You don't get it."

"Don't I?" I study her profile in the noon sunlight. She has smooth skin, not a scar or pimple in sight. And her face is actually *a lot* prettier than I first appreciated, in a wholesome way.

I know *exactly* what she feels like. Two weeks after Tasha and I broke up, I was sitting in a bar when she walked in with Anthony—a guy I'd known since I was seven. I had three choices: leave, pick up a chick, or start a fight.

My knuckles took a while to heal.

"If you get up and go, you're the heartbroken girl who's running into the bathroom to cry. Is that what you want?" Because it's not the person who's been causing me stress at home.

She shakes off my hand from her knee. "No."

"I didn't think so. You want to look like the woman who doesn't give a shit and has moved on already. Fake it till you make it and all that. Let him be uncomfortable." That's what this sourness is, I'm guessing—a shield. Unfortunately, she doesn't know how to wield it properly. Everyone gets the brunt.

"He's right. Just sit here between the two of us and eat your weird bread and pretend you don't care." Connor stretches his legs and, leaning back into the bench, closes his eyes.

With a deep breath, Ryan shifts her focus to her yogurt, peeling off the foil lid. "You saw him on Friday night?" she asks quietly.

"Yeah," I admit without hesitation.

"So, you knew about *her*?"

I can see Ryan replaying our conversation that night, when I brought up her honorable accountant. "Yup."

Her jaw clenches. "Why didn't you tell me?"

"When was I supposed to do that?" I give her a pointed look. "You were too busy yelling at me and plotting revenge. I figured you'd hear about it soon, anyway."

"Still, I would have liked more warning."

"We should get off on another foot, then. A friendlier one."

Her gaze cuts to me before refocusing on her lunch. "Do you think ..." Her voice drifts.

"That he was with her before you broke up?" I finish off the question that would be on my mind if I were in her shoes. Hell, I did ask it. To this day, I'm not convinced Tasha and Anthony weren't fucking around behind my back.

She peers up at me, blinking repeatedly. I don't need to say it aloud; she's figured it out.

"This is humiliating," she whispers under her breath.

"Forget about that loser." I collect her apple and toss it in the air once before setting it back gently in her lap. "He doesn't deserve you."

Her brow flinches as if she wasn't expecting that answer. After a long pause, she says, "I'm trying, but it's not easy."

"Find a fuck buddy," Connor drawls lazily. "Works like a charm."

She scowls. "Great brotherly advice."

"What?" Connor shrugs. "You know, everyone thinks you're banging Ronan. You may as well start."

"No, they don't."

"Am I lying, Ronan?"

I can't tell if he's being serious or being ... Connor, but I'll play along. I stretch my arm along the back of the bench and start twirling the ends of Ryan's brunette hair through my fingertips. It's silkier than I expected. "I wouldn't say *everyone* thinks that. Not yet, anyway."

"Bullshit." She shifts her head away, making me lose my grip.

I reach for another strand and continue toying. "What did you expect? We live together. You've seen me naked—"

"Because *you* flashed me."

"Great foreplay, by the way," Connor offers. "Good job, man."

"And everyone knows what those dirty crew guys are like," I mock. "And yet here you are, eating lunch with us. *You* came out to *us*."

"To *Ronan*," Connor interrupts, egging her on. "A lot of flags, if you ask me. Everyone's gonna be talking."

Ryan's cheeks begin to flame. "This is payback for the shower this morning, isn't it?"

"Yup." I steal her apple right off her lap and take a big bite. And I'm going to enjoy every second of it.

11. Ronan

"What is that smell?" Connor steps through the front door.

"You." We just finished playing Frisbee tag with his league and we're drenched with sweat.

"No, man. That's food." He inhales deeply. "And it smells delicious!"

He's right. Someone's been baking. A rack of muffins sits in the middle of the island, still warm from the oven. A note next to it reads, "Eat better."

"Has hell frozen over?" Connor asks, confusion on his face.

"They must be laced with arsenic." I glance down the hall. Ryan's door is closed but the light peeks through the crack. She would have had to come home from class and baked them right away.

"That or Ex-Lax."

"She has to share a bathroom with me, though, remember."

"Fair point. Definitely arsenic, then." We stare at the muffins for another five seconds.

"Fuck it. I've led a good life." Connor takes one and shoves it into his mouth. A deep frown furrows his brow as he moans and gives the thumbs-up.

We each polish off three before we part ways. I head straight for the bathroom, intent on taking that long, hot shower I didn't get this morning.

Through the crack at the bottom of Ryan's door, I spot toes.

———

I'VE JUST STEPPED out of the Wolf employee restroom, my pants barely done up, when Connor grabs my arm and tugs me down the hall. "Come on."

"Fuck. I get it! You're hungry! Relax already." I jerk my arm from his grip. He can be so annoying sometimes.

"Baker just found out that his mother has cancer."

"That sucks. And?" Not to be insensitive, but I don't know the guy.

"He's bailing on Alaska. So you're taking his spot."

"*What?*"

"Just keep paying rent on your room here and it's yours when we come home in the fall."

"But—"

"Dude, trust me. This is gonna be a summer you'll never forget. I heard this is a big gamble that Wolf is taking, opening a seasonal hotel up there. No one thinks he can pull it off. Do you know what that means?"

"No?"

Connor pauses his mad dash down the hall to meet my gaze. "It means he's going to bring up the hottest fucking chicks you've ever seen in your life to work there. He's all about image. Hottest chicks in cabins, all summer long. *And us.*"

I chuckle. Every decision Connor makes seems to be driven by one thing and one thing only—his dick. "Okay, you're beginning to sell this idea to me. But I doubt they're going to let me and Baker swap. I just got here. Life doesn't work like that."

Connor grins. "Wanna bet?"

———

RYAN IS at the counter when we step through the door, helping one of the housekeeping staff, a polite smile painted on. It's not exactly genuine, but it's nice to see all the same. I was beginning to think her lips couldn't curve upward.

Her attention flickers to us, and rests on me for a long moment before shifting back to the girl in front of her.

"Jean! Hey, Jean! Where are you?" Connor whisper-hisses, leaning over the counter as if she might be hiding behind it.

Ryan shoots her brother a dirty look but doesn't say anything as her coworker appears from around the cubicle partition.

"Oh, thank God you're here. We need your help, *stat*." He's borderline frantic.

Jean tucks her hair behind her ear and bats her eyelashes. "With what?"

"Baker's not going to Alaska. Ronan's going to take his place."

"Oh? Okay?" Her onyx eyes flicker between the two of us.

"So ... we need you to make that happen."

Surprise lifts her brows. "I don't have anything to do with Alaska recruitment. I don't even know who—"

"You *must* know someone. Come on! You're the outdoor staff coordinator! You're our one contact in here, and Alaska is taking two of us from you. You *must* know who to talk to."

"I don't, really ...?" Her small, round face scrunches up with apology.

"Belinda Cartwright," Ryan cuts in, pulled into the conversation despite the housekeeper in front of her. "She's the general manager for Alaska and she's in Miami right now, down in one of the conference rooms. Try the Pacific."

Connor slaps the counter. "Beautiful. Thanks, sis."

"Of course. Anything for Ronan." She smiles sweetly at me. It's fake, but it's pretty, all the same.

"Wow, you *really* want me out, don't you?" She'd get an entire condo to herself for the summer.

"So, you're not *completely* clueless after all." She adjusts her glasses and continues to stare at me. Her expression is unreadable.

"Come on." Connor tugs my arm. "Let's get you locked in."

———

"WHY DIDN'T you apply during the recruitment process?"

It's a struggle not to gape at the soft mounds peeking out of Belinda Cartwright's silky white blouse. The general manager of Wolf Alaska—a gorgeous blond who made my blood race just watching her stroll toward us in her red stilettos—has managed to make her suit look both professional and slutty at the same time. "I was in a different place in my life."

She folds her arms over her chest, a knowing smirk touching her lips. "And now?"

"Now I'd really like the opportunity to go to Alaska." Am I even saying these words? What the hell do I know about Alaska? Nothing except that it's far away and cold.

"It's an easy swap," Connor adds.

Her sharp eyes size him up behind a pair of designer black-rimmed glasses. "Yes, that's already been established. And you started in Miami when?"

"Last Friday," I admit reluctantly.

"Last Friday," she echoes. "You'd be leaving your team short-staffed."

"They would have been short-staffed, anyway, if Baker had left."

Her painted lips twist in thought, and I find myself staring at them, wondering what they'd feel like wrapped around my—

"What's your name again?"

"Ronan Lyle."

She unlocks her phone and begins typing out an e-mail. "Well, Ronan Lyle, assuming you have a positive work record—"

"I do." At least in Indianapolis, I did. I have a feeling being friends with Connor might earn me some strikes on my good name.

"Well then, I don't see there being a problem with this."

"Seriously?" Connor's face lights up as if she announced that he's won a million-dollar cash prize.

"I don't normally get involved at this level of hiring. But since you two hunted me down ..."

I can't help but note the absence of a wedding ring or the way she keeps sizing us up. "So, will HR give me the okay or—"

"*I'm* giving you the okay. The job is yours. I'll handle HR. You'll get an information package by the end of the day and then you can book your flight. You know it won't be cheap, this close to travel dates, right?"

"I'll make it work." For what they're paying up there and the money I'll be saving not going to clubs, it will all even out.

"You are *amazing*, Belinda." Connor gives her his thousand-watt smile.

All he gets back is another long, intimidating gaze. "Shouldn't you two be working right now?"

"Lunch break."

"Hmm. Well, I doubt you're supposed to be roaming the conference area in your soiled boots. Okay, then. I'm sure I'll see you in Alaska at some point."

Connor and I watch her stalk away, her heels clicking loudly and hips swaying suggestively with each step, like she knows we're standing here, gawking at her.

"Did she just make your dick hard?" Connor whispers.

"Like a flag pole. How the hell is she a general manager?"

"You kidding?" Connor snorts. "Henry Wolf handpicked her."

"Of course." Rich bastard. I've never met the guy, but I've heard enough. The one time he came to the Wolf in Indianapolis, the staff wouldn't shut up about how attractive he was. I'm sure Belinda will be taking care of more than his hotel for him. Still, she must be good at what she does.

"So, we're golden. See?" He slaps my arm. "Told you I'd make this happen."

"Yeah." I guess I'm going to Alaska. Like, next weekend. "What the fuck, man." How is this my life now?

"It'll be worth it, I promise." Connor pats his stomach. "Now I need food before I pass out."

12. Ryan

Heels click past, drawing my attention upward in time to see *her* pass by.

Eliza, her name tag reads. She has the longest legs I've ever seen on a human and she started working at the front desk six weeks ago. That's all I know about her.

But there's no way she didn't know about me.

My insides clench with anger and hurt as I watch her blond hair sway with her steps. She's tall and willowy, with tan skin and big, bright white teeth. Pretty, in a sorority sister sort of way. And she's heading toward accounting as if I'm not *right here*.

"*Hey*." Jean slides into my cube, strategically blocking my view of David's desk hidden behind a tall gray divider. "How's it going?" She's always been soft-spoken but now she sounds like she's consoling a grieving widow.

When I started working at Wolf, I didn't think much of my counterpart. All she talked about was her sewing club, knitting scarves, and her four cats. Fast-forward two years, I consider her a friend. She's certainly one of the few people around here who I truly trust. Her only flaw? Her colossal crush on Connor.

"I've been better." I sink back into my chair. "So, I guess *everyone* knows?" Because I've felt the prying glances all morning.

The sympathetic smile I get in return is answer enough.

Bitterness and hurt flares. "He's such a jerk." How do you do this to someone?

"*Big* jerk," Jean agrees, her arched eyebrows disappearing behind a heavy, dark bang.

"Do you know when they started talking?" Because Eliza and I haven't crossed paths once. She's not part of our circle.

Jean hesitates. "I heard something this morning." If there's been any talk, Jean would have caught it. She's quiet, unobtrusive. She's a human fly. Even if people notice she's there, they assume she's not listening.

"Like?" I push.

With a covert scan over her shoulder for eavesdroppers, she leans in and whispers, "Remember that Thursday night when a bunch of people went out to the pub after work and ended up at that club?"

"Yes," I say warily. I have economics on Thursdays so I missed out, not that I would have followed the crowd to their debauchery. "Everyone came in late and reeking of alcohol." Except for David. He called in sick. Claimed he ate bad sushi.

"Rumor has it David and Eliza left in a cab together. They were pretty close."

"Define 'pretty close.'" Did my coworkers watch him cheat and say *nothing* to me?

She winces. "It didn't sound like they were only sharing a ride."

Her words are a punch to my stomach. But this is all beginning to click. Aside from a text to tell me he was lying low on account of his food poisoning, I didn't hear from David all weekend, and when I offered to go over to take care of him, he was quick to hide behind explosive diarrhea.

Was it all a lie?

And come to think of it, he's been acting strangely since. Distant. That's what inspired me to declare my feelings.

Jean stares at me like a scientist with a bug under her microscope on which she's conducting an experiment.

How will this organism react to the truth?

"Whatever." My eyes sting with threatened tears. Does it matter *when* they hooked up? I told David I loved him and a week later, he dumped me. We're over and he's already moved on, with no qualms about flaunting it in front of my injured heart. "I wish it wasn't with another staffer. I wish I didn't have to see it at work."

Jean's lips purse. "Well ... what about Ronan?"

I frown. "What do you mean? What about him?"

"I don't know. You sat with the crew guys at lunch, and you, like, *never* sit with your brother—"

"It had nothing to do with Ronan. I needed to get away from David!" I whisper-hiss. Not that it helped because in the end, he came out there to see *her*. I veered for Connor and Ronan out of desperation because they were the only faces I recognized and I didn't want to be that awkward girl standing in the middle of the high school cafeteria, clutching her lunch tray with nowhere to sit. "Why, are people saying I'm hooking up with Ronan?" Damn it, those two may have been trying to get a rise out of me, but they weren't wrong.

"Most of them are talking about how *they* want to hook up with him." She snorts and then quickly covers her nose with her hand, embarrassed. "He's hot, Ryan. Like, *really* hot."

"I hadn't noticed," I lie. That angular jaw? Nope. His intense green irises? Nada. The way his full lips kick up at the corner in the slightest, most hidden smile? Does nothing for me.

But I'm not even fooling myself. The truth is, Ronan keeps sliding into my thoughts even though I don't want him there. I've secretly admired that body from the first moment I saw it, even when I was yelling at him about my towel and calling him an STD-laced Neanderthal. It didn't help that he was so kind to me the other day when he had every right to be a dick after my shower stunt. My first impression of him was way off. He's not actually *that bad*.

Jean snorts again.

"If he wasn't leaving for Alaska, I'm sure everyone drooling over him would get a ride." Connor always wins, which means this latest scheme to swap Baker for Ronan will work and I'll have the condo to myself this summer. No complaints there.

"That's right. You're running out of time." She waggles her eyebrows.

"No way." I emphasize that with a head shake.

"Then why are you blushing?"

"Okay, go knit something." I wave her off, my cheeks on fire.

"You don't always have to be *so* sensible." Jean slides off my desk. "It wouldn't be the worst thing, you know, especially since he's leaving. Easy break, no commitment ..."

"I wouldn't even know what to do with a guy like that," I scoff. "It's *not* happening."

13. Ronan

It's after ten when Ryan walks through the door, throwing her backpack onto the floor with a thud. She looks exhausted.

And miserable, like she's fighting the urge to cry.

"You're gonna have this place all to yourself for five months!" Connor bellows, oblivious to her mood. Or he's trying to cheer her up. He's not as obtuse as he plays at.

Ryan's gaze drifts over the laptop on the coffee table, to the cans of beer in our hands, and finally to me. "I take it you got the job?"

"I did." The welcome package arrived two hours ago. For whatever else Belinda might be, she's definitely on top of things.

"We booked our flights. We leave next Saturday." Connor throws up his arms in celebration.

"You two gonna share a bed up there too?" Ryan wanders over to the fridge. I expected more excitement from her than she's showing. She hasn't hidden the fact that she doesn't want me here.

"Depends how many girls are in it with us," Connor chimes in, earning my chuckle.

Her face contorts with a grimace. "Gross."

He climbs off the couch and carries the empties over to the waiting case. Living with this guy is going to turn me into an alcoholic. "No, it's not. You need to get back to your Greek roots."

She flashes an incredulous look his way. "I have no Greek roots. Neither do you."

"So?" He shrugs. "Live a little."

"That's your solution to every problem, isn't it? Get laid?"

"Hasn't failed me yet." He belches. "I'm crashing. See you guys tomorrow." With that, he vanishes into his bedroom.

I watch quietly as she rifles through her food, pulling out glass containers. Moving her things to the bottom shelf was brilliant on my part. It makes her bend over further, giving me a better view of that round ass, especially when she's wearing leggings, and she wears those a lot. She's got solid, muscular thighs. Not skinny but proportionate to the rest of her. The only part of her that isn't proportionate is her waist, which is tiny. It works well on her, though, making her breasts—I'd put them at a C—stand out and her hips all the more provocative.

Abruptly, she turns and catches me ogling her.

I'm slow in averting my gaze, not really caring if she knows I'm checking her out. "So, how are you doing?"

"How do you think?" She tosses a bag of carrots onto the counter. "He sits two rows over and she comes in to visit him all the time. Walks right past my desk too. Doesn't even bother to go another way. And then *everyone* notices. I can feel them watching me to see how I'm going to react. And I'm pretty sure he hooked up with her before we broke up."

"That sucks. I'm sorry." If I had to see Tasha and her new conquest every day, I think I'd have been arrested by now. As it is, I left my entire city to get away.

Her eyes glisten. "It really does."

"I guess they have those office dating rules for a reason."

"Those are for managers and subordinates. I don't report

to David." She bites down hard on a raw carrot and the sound of her crunching is the only noise for a long moment.

"Still ... it'd be a lot easier if he didn't work in your office."

"I'm never dating anyone from work again, *ever*," she declares through a nervous laugh. "It's like high school—people gossiping about how David cheated on me and wondering if I had a clue. Don't they grow out of that?"

I ease off the couch. "No, a lot of them don't. And they get worse as their lives get more boring. Sitting in those cubicles all day? Pretty fucking boring. They can't keep their mouths shut."

"Please. This coming from the guy who told everyone he messed around with *three* women last Friday night? Yeah, that's right. I heard about it." There's no missing the disgust on her face.

"I didn't tell anyone about anything. Thank your brother for that."

"So, your big ego doesn't need stroking like Connor's?"

"My big *ego* is not what needs stroking." Her jaw drops, and I smirk. She walked right into that. "But I never talked about it. It's none of anyone's business who I'm with or what I do with them."

"Unless they're unfortunate enough to share a wall with you," she says dryly.

"Hey, you questioned my skill. I had to prove you wrong."

She rolls her eyes.

"Fine. I was drunk. It wasn't one of my finer moments," I concede.

"That was all an act for me? How sweet," she croons in a mocking tone.

I'm not going to be able to convince her that I'm actually a decent guy. And I'm tired. "Don't worry, your ex and front desk girl won't last long. I give them a month."

I say it to give her hope—that it won't be thrown in her face every day for too much longer—but her crestfallen expression tells me I haven't helped much.

"Glad he threw away a year and a half with me for something meaningless."

"I didn't mean it like that." *Shit.*

Her lips purse. "It's okay." There's a long pause. "So, what do I do now? How do I keep going to work every day and stop caring?" She peers up at me, a rare vulnerable expression on her face, her eyes begging for an answer.

Her mouth isn't very wide, but her lips are plump. Lipstick free. Soft. What would they feel like wrapped around my dick? What would they look like, parted as she moans? What would she do if I leaned down and kissed them right now? I haven't kissed anyone besides Tasha in over four years. I haven't felt any urge to.

Until now.

Too bad Ryan can only barely tolerate me. But she's vulnerable, which is why I need to leave, stat. I don't want to be *that guy.*

I finish off my beer and dump the empty into the case. "Your brother was right. Find someone to fuck until the pain dulls or you get back together with that loser who you're too good for."

She hesitates. "Is that what you're doing?"

"Trying. But I need someone who can tell their right from their left." I should hit up that lioness server at Sin. If they'll let me back in.

She chuckles, and her focus drifts to my mouth before averting quickly. "Good luck with your search. Maybe you'll find her in Alaska."

"Maybe." Just a stone's throw away in a nearby cabin, as Connor promises. Easy. Not as easy as it would be to have Ryan, on the other side of my wall. "Too bad my roommate is such a shrew. I wouldn't have to go so far."

Her cheeks flush. "I don't like you."

Damn it, I can't help myself. I lean over the island. "Then why can't you stop watching me?"

"I can .... I mean, I don't ..." She stumbles over her words, completely disarmed.

I grin. The exact reaction I was going for. "You don't have to like me to enjoy what I can do for you. In fact, it's better if you don't." That way she won't fall for me because I can't give her anything more than a quick fix. "'Night."

Her gaze bores into my back all the way down the hall.

———

It's still dark when I wake. Checking the clock—2:00 a.m.—I roll onto my back with a groan, my eyes adjusting to the dim light of the room. It's too bright for my liking, thanks to the shitty curtains that don't block the street lights beyond.

A figure stands beside my bed.

"Jesus." I jolt. It takes me a moment to calm my racing heart. "Ryan?"

She doesn't answer, simply stands over me, her arms at her sides, her long hair down, framing a tortured face. Her over-sized white T-shirt hides her curves, reaching down to mid thigh. Without her glasses, I can easily make out the almond shape of her eyes.

"You're here to kill me, aren't you," I say, half joking, although a part of me wonders. I shouldn't have taunted her. "What's wrong?"

She swallows. "Did you mean what you said?"

"About?"

Her gaze drifts over my bare chest and downward, to where my sheet covers my naked lower half.

Holy shit.

Am I dreaming?

I covertly pinch myself. Nope, awake. *Wide* awake.

The way she's standing there, staring at my body ... my

blood starts pumping. I'm going to be hard in about twenty seconds. "Okay, the shower was one thing. But this is hitting below the belt."

"It's not a prank." Her gaze lifts to meet my face, letting me see a lustful heat in her eyes for the first time. She isn't kidding.

Seriously, is this happening? Is this a test? Because I'll fail miserably. "You can't come in here like this and expect me to be a decent guy." If I weren't groggy, I'd already have her on her back.

She reaches down to tug at my cover. It slides to my thighs, leaving me exposed. Her lips part with the softest sigh as my dick hardens in front of her. "You promise you won't tell anyone?"

"I won't tell anyone."

"Not even Connor?"

Fuck me ... Connor has quickly landed a spot at the top of my friend list, and Ryan is *his sister*. What will he do if he finds out?

I can't do this. I just ...

Ryan seizes the hem of her T-shirt and lifts it up, over her head, letting it fall to the floor.

14. Ryan

*Y*ou *don't have to like me to enjoy what I can do for you. In fact, it's better that you don't.*

After lying in bed for two hours, replaying those words while a countdown clock to next Saturday's flight ticked inside my head, I must have snapped because *this is insane.*

I'm trying not to shake and probably failing miserably. I don't want Ronan to know how nervous I am. Heck, I'm always nervous around him. He's one of those intimidating guys—tall, dark, and ominous, with his piercing eyes and his wicked smile and that swagger.

But right now, standing naked in front of him, his burning gaze searing my body, his face full of shock, I feel like my legs are ready to give out. I work hard to keep my figure lean and hard and healthy but I will never win when pitted against the long legs and trim torsos and slender hips of women like Eliza's.

The kind of bodies Ronan likes, if the naked girl who fell into my bed last Friday is any indication.

Ronan groans, his hands settling on his forehead. "Ryan, I can't ..."

My stomach drops. I can't believe this. I'm standing naked

in front of Ronan—a guy who fucked around with *three* different women in one night last weekend—and he's turning me down. Have I totally misread him?

With my face on fire, I dive for my T-shirt and make to run from his room.

He can move awfully fast, though, for a guy half-awake and sprawled out in bed.

I make it all the way to the door before his giant, calloused hand slams against it, stopping me from escape. "I didn't say that I didn't want to."

"It sure seems like it." I despise the sound of my voice, brimming with rejection.

He steps in close behind me, pinning my chest to the cool door, his body heat searing my skin. "Does it *feel* like it?" He presses his hard length into my back.

I can't help the gasp. I got a good look at his dick as it swelled under my gaze. I've only been with three other guys and none of them compared to Ronan's size.

It's not just his lower extremity either. It's *all* of him—his solid muscles and ridges, his height, the way his forearms naturally tense as he moves. He's a ten on anyone's scale.

I steel my nerve. "Well then, what's the problem? I thought you said you wanted this." I may come off as confident, but I've never been forward when it comes to sex. I've *never* propositioned a guy. The fact I even came in here tonight is pure recklessness.

Pushing my hair to the side, he leans over and settles his lips on my nape, his tongue grazing me ever so gently, sending shivers all the way down to my core.

I make to turn, to face him, wanting to see his chiseled muscles, feel how hard his chest and stomach are beneath my fingertips. But strong arms seize my hips, keeping me in place as his bare foot slides in between mine, gently prodding my legs farther apart.

"I'm leaving for Alaska next weekend," he whispers.

"I know. It's perfect." It was probably the biggest factor in my wild decision to come here tonight.

Ronan chuckles. The depth of his voice against my spine makes me shudder. I hold my breath as his hands slide from my hips, one traveling upward to cup my breast, the other moving lower to rest along the inside of my thigh, his thumb smoothing over my skin. "Okay, just this once. But I can't give you more than that. This won't turn into anything. I mean, it can't. I'm ..." His voice drifts.

He's still in love with his ex-girlfriend.

It takes me a moment to find my voice. "You honestly think I'm looking for a commitment? I don't even like you, remember?" That's not entirely true. Sure, I was angry with Connor. And when I first saw Ronan—all dark and gorgeous six-foot-something of him, towering over me—I immediately wrote him off.

But Ronan also tried to make me feel better about being dumped and apologized to me when I was being a bitch to him, overreacting over a towel because it was either that or burst into tears.

Most important, though, he's right: I don't have to like him to enjoy sex with him. At least this way, my heart won't get tangled with emotion.

And maybe sleeping with Ronan will erase the overwhelming rejection I'm drowning in, the feelings of inadequacy that I've woken up to and fallen asleep with since I found out David dumped me for a tall, willowy blond. I'd do *anything* to stop feeling this pain, even if for just a night.

As it turns out, *anything* includes sleeping with my hot pig of a roommate.

I inhale sharply as Ronan's hand shifts to cup between my legs, his thumb sliding over my clit. I'm already wet for him and, with each pass, growing more so. But any embarrassment I feel quickly evaporates under his touch.

"For someone who's disgusted by me, you have a funny way of showing it." He leans forward until his face fits into the crook of my neck, just far enough that his hot breath skates over my skin. And then he pushes one finger deep inside.

A sigh escapes my lips.

"I wondered what you would feel like."

He did? I close my eyes as my senses go into overdrive. "And?"

He slips a second finger in, stretching me as his thumb draws circles. "You're even softer and tighter than I expected." His mouth closes over my earlobe and he bites down gently. "Definitely no teeth in here."

I'm struggling to stay on my feet as the heat between my legs intensifies. If he's this skilled with his hands and his mouth …

I want to turn around, to touch him. To kiss him. Badly.

Suddenly, I'm off my feet and cradled in his arms, being carried to his bed. With ease and speed I don't expect, he has me on my back. I watch in a mute state of shock as he pulls a condom from his bedside drawer, tears the foil package with his teeth, and rolls the condom on, all with smooth precision.

Seizing me by the thighs, he pulls my body to meet his.

And then he's pushing in.

I gasp at the intrusion as I stretch around him, my heart hammering in my chest. From the moment I entertained this crazy decision to now couldn't have been more than five minutes and yet here we are. It's like some weird out-of-body experience. There is no way Responsible Ryan would stroll into her new roommate's room in the middle of the night and demand—beg for?—sex. This is a different version of me, a careless version.

And I must admit, she's enjoying this.

Ronan's muscles strain beautifully with each hip roll, until he's filling me completely.

He pauses, grins devilishly at me, sprawled out and exposed before him. "You good?"

"Yes," I manage. Am I? Or have I gone completely insane? Am I going to regret this?

"Get out of your head for a bit, Ryan," he warns softly, as if he can read my mind.

"Okay," I squeak.

Adjusting his grip on my thighs, he thrusts in and out, the bed creaking with each move, the headboard banging against the wall. It's as noisy as the night he was with that woman he picked up at the club. I try not to think about that right now. I'm nothing like her. Almost as an act of defiance, I press my lips together, intent to not let myself *sound* like her.

"Fuck," he groans, cords of muscles tensing.

He's so deep, and he keeps hitting one spot each time he goes in. It's not entirely comfortable.

"Don't worry, I know what I'm doing," he promises, his heated gaze trailing from my face to my breasts, down to where we're joined.

And he must, because with each stroke against that spot, my body opens to him, the dull ache turning into something entirely pleasurable.

"You're so wet," he murmurs through ragged breaths.

I am. And offering no resistance to him anymore. It's almost embarrassing. I'll never be able to deny my attraction again.

Ronan shifts one arm to splay a hand across my pelvis, pressing down slightly as his thumb starts rubbing my clit.

I can't help the low moan that escapes.

"That's it, Ryan. I know you're not shy." He suddenly changes his tactics, rolling his hips rather than thrusting.

It brings out a second, lower moan from me, unbidden. This view of him—naked and confident and between my legs —might be the sexiest thing I've ever seen.

I can feel the beginnings of an orgasm deep in the pit of my stomach, the blood flowing fast to my core.

Ronan grips both my thighs again, lifting my hips a little higher, squeezing a little harder as he changes his rhythm, plunging into me hard and fast. I've only ever come during sex once—during a rare night of no inhibitions when my then boyfriend and I smoked a joint and *everything* was a major turn-on.

I'm dead sober now, but the sight of Ronan's body, straining and glistening, his dark, lustful gaze locked on me, pumping in and out—the very idea that a guy like this, who could have any woman he wanted, is going to come because of me ...

I don't care if I sound like that drunk idiot from the other night as the rush of blood hits my nerve endings and my muscles tighten around him. I cry out, bucking against him where we're joined.

Ronan's head falls back, his sharp Adam's apple jutting out from his strong neck, and he groans as the muscles in his stomach tense. I feel him pulse inside me, his thrusts slowing until they've stopped altogether.

Our panting breaths fill the silence in the room.

Now what?

If he were my boyfriend, this is where he would lie down beside me. We'd kiss, I'd nuzzle my nose in his neck, I'd draw patterns along his chest, I'd ask him if he enjoyed that.

But this is Ronan.

My new roommate, my brother's friend, an outdoor crew guy, a man whore. A guy I had sex with for the soul purpose of forgetting my ex. A guy who's still in love with *his* ex.

I can't believe I just had sex with him.

He slides out of me and checks the condom—I assume for holes. Seemingly satisfied, he pulls it off and reaches for a tissue.

I use that opportunity to bolt, grabbing my T-shirt on the

way to the door. "Good night." I duck out without a backward glance, not breathing until I'm behind my closed bedroom door.

My forehead hits my wall as a wave of shame washes over me.

Oh my God.

What have I done?

15. Ryan

I press my ear against the door, listening for the soft pad of Ronan's bare feet. His alarm went off a few minutes ago. It's an awful, blaring sound. I'm usually out for my daily jog when he wakes up, so I haven't had the displeasure of hearing it until now.

But I skipped my jog this morning because I was afraid to risk facing him.

He didn't even kiss me before he dove in.

Was that by choice or by omission, because I woke him up at 2:00 a.m. for surprise sex? I've heard of guys who don't kiss. Guys who sleep around a lot and make it a habit of *not* kissing women on the mouth. I'm not going to fool myself into believing I've had Ronan all wrong and he isn't a guy who fits that description.

"Dude! Hurry up, we've gotta leave soon."

I roll my eyes at my brother even as my heart races. He says the same thing to Ronan *every* day.

"Yeah, yeah," Ronan mumbles, his gravelly voice so coarse this morning, I can feel it skittering across my skin. That's perfect, seeing as I can still feel where he was inside me too.

"You look rough, man. Didn't you sleep?" Connor asks.

"I guess not." A pause. "Where's Ryan?"

"Probably out for a jog, burning off her anger issues. Why?"

My jaw clenches. *Don't you dare say a word about last night, you son of a bitch.*

Maybe I'm imagining it, but I sense Ronan glancing over his shoulder at my closed door. I skitter back, afraid he'll know I'm hiding back here, listening.

"No reason. I'll be ready in fifteen." A moment later, the bathroom door shuts.

I bury my face in my hands. I can't believe I slept with him! I can't believe I barged into his room, woke him up, and practically begged him to give it to me. I'm not that girl. I just lost my mind temporarily. I was blinded by my heartache, by his sexual innuendo, and that gorgeous face and intoxicating smirk.

Worse, I'm still waiting for the regret to kick in. Shame, yes, I have oodles of that, soaking into my bones. But if I was going to declare temporary insanity with anyone, something about Ronan feels right. For some bizarre, inexplicable reason, I trust the guy.

Just not enough to face him again.

———

"You'll get that staff report to me by noon?" Geraldine peers down at me from behind her glasses.

"Sure thing."

With a nod, she moves on to the next line on her to-do list.

As far as bosses go, she's tolerable. A bit of a micromanager, but I guess that comes with the territory of working with things like payroll, where missing details—a check box, an input cell—can mean someone doesn't get paid.

"Hey." Jean peeks around the corner of my cube. She's in the one next to me. "So, Ronan is for sure going to Alaska."

My stomach spasms, hearing that name. "Yeah, they booked their flights last night." That's not the only thing Ronan did last night. Am I stupid to believe he'll keep quiet? It seemed like a no-brainer at the time, that Ronan wouldn't be in a hurry to tell Connor. It's not like Connor has ever given any indication that he'd care if I slept with our new roommate, but I can't see how *Hey, I screwed your sister last night* would slide smoothly out of Ronan's mouth.

And if Connor ever learns about it, everyone at Wolf—right up to the big boss Henry Wolf himself—will know.

Jean sighs heavily. "It's going to be so boring here this summer."

My nose wrinkles. She's been in love with my brother since the first day the idiot strolled in. And she's not the only one. There are at least three others in the office who perk up every time he comes in here to annoy me.

I guess I can't blame them. We were complete strangers when we met, and I noticed his bright blue eyes and dimpled smile right away. No one can honestly claim he isn't handsome. But the fact that we're blood related instantly diminished his appeal.

As does the fact that he's a pig. He'd nail every last girl in housekeeping if he could. Everyone knows it, and it still doesn't seem to sway them from their adoration. I don't understand.

The fawning over Ronan hasn't been much better. You'd think he were some sort of god who walked on water to get here. Though, after last night, I might agree with that.

David was never able to get me to orgasm during sex, and he tried. Eventually, he insisted it had to be my issue, and I agreed.

I swallow the rising bubble of nerves as a memory hits, of

Ronan kneeling in front of me, gripping my thighs tight. I can still feel him with each step I take. Just the thought of him now stirs a throb between my legs.

Giving my head a shake, I push all thoughts of Ronan aside.

16. Ronan

"Six people to a cabin?" Connor's jaw drops.

"Yeah. And bunk beds." Dean shakes his head. "Didn't you read the email? It was all spelled out in there."

"I top-lined it." Connor shrugs. "Caught the important things."

Apparently not. "I sure as shit don't remember you telling me I'd be going back to *camp*," I glare at my idiot roommate. "Seriously, is it too late to back out?"

"Fuck that, you are not backing out. Trust me, this summer is gonna be life-altering." Connor slaps my shoulder. "I'll even take the top 'cause I'm such a good friend."

"And you get to bottom, Ronan," Dean gibes.

"Whoa there." Connor waggles his finger. "We're not at the crossing-swords stage of our friendship yet."

"*Yet?*" I throw my hands out in a *what the fuck* gesture. "I like you, man, but not like *that*."

His eyebrows arch. "What if we're tag-teaming and we accidentally—"

"No." I shake my head. I'm willing to embrace my single life wholeheartedly, but dicks don't make mine hard.

Meanwhile, Dean doubles over with laughter.

The sound of approaching heels stalls our highly inappropriate conversation. Three front desk clerks stroll along the hallway, dressed in matching fitted skirts and blouses, Starbucks cups in their manicured hands.

"Hey, Eliza." Dean waves at the leggy blond, the one boning Ryan's ex.

"Hey." Her fingers wiggle with her returning wave, giving him a brief glance before her attention shifts first to Connor, then to me, where it lingers until she's forced to break her gaze.

Connor tracks her ass as they head down the hall. "Damn, those are some legs."

"Yup." She's about as opposite to Ryan as one can get.

He shakes his head. "Seriously, she's one of the hottest girls at this location. What does she see in David? The guy's as exciting as a colon cleanse."

"Probably the same thing Ryan saw in him," I counter.

"Yeah, but that's *Ryan*," he scoffs, as if it's self-explanatory.

"Legs has nothing on your sister." I may not have seen it when I first met Ryan, but now that I have, I can't unsee it. Especially not after last night, with her compact naked body splayed out before me, as she bit her bottom lip to keep from making noise. I can say with one hundred percent certainty that no woman has shocked me like she did, showing up in my room like that. "Seriously, she's a catch." Who is currently freaking out about hooking up with me last night if skipping her jog to hide behind her bedroom door is any clue.

I expected as much, though.

"Dude, your sister's hot," Dean jumps in to echo. "Like, in that nerdy school librarian way. But she's got that ass—"

Connor cuts off his words with a warning index finger shoved to Dean's face.

My phone chirps then and I use that excuse to avert my guilty gaze and read the email that just came in from Jean in HR.

I smile. "I need to sign more paperwork for the transfer."

17. Ryan

"Hey, Tatum!"

My back stiffens at the sound of my brother's booming voice. I'd like more than anything to pretend I'm not here, but he'll holler until people glare at me.

With a reluctant groan, I stand.

And inhale sharply at the tall form standing next to him. *Of course* they're together. They're inseparable.

Except at night, when I'm propositioning Ronan in his bed.

He watches me approach, the tiniest smile curving his full lips. Lips I have yet to kiss. Yet? *No! It's not happening!*

I lock my focus on Connor. Does he know? Has Ronan told him?

If he has, and Connor announces it in here, which I wouldn't put past him, I will stab him with the pencil in my grip.

"What do you want?" It comes out harsher than I intend. That's the way my anxiety reveals itself—I turn into a bitch. And boy, am I anxious.

Connor leans over the desk, his massive body dusty and

sweaty from being outside in the heat. "You didn't meet us out back today."

"I *never* do." I've intentionally kept myself busy over the lunch hour, eating at my desk or running errands, not wanting to risk an awkward situation where my teammates get together and David is there. With *her*.

"You did on Monday."

"Yeah, well ... that was once." My voice cracks over those words. Ronan basically said that to me last night. *Just this once.*

Connor shrugs. "We missed you."

I search for some hint that he knows. I see nothing, and he's not good at keeping secrets. Especially not one like that.

Ronan hasn't told him.

A small sigh of relief escapes me, even as the other side of the coin shows itself. Does Ronan regret last night? Did he wake up this morning, dreading seeing me? Did he enjoy it? Oh my God. What if it was terrible for him?

I clear my throat to calm my nerves. "Why are you *really* here?"

"Jean asked Ronan to come down and sign some things for Alaska."

"And here they are." Jean sidles up next to me, laying out a few forms on the counter in front of her, giggling nervously. "I feel like we just did this."

"Because we did."

I watch him take the pen in those strong, calloused fingers —the same fingers that were inside me last night—and begin filling in the boxes. His penmanship is surprisingly neat.

Connor's phone rings in his pocket. "I gotta take this. I'll wait for you in the hall."

"All right. I'll be done in a minute."

Connor ducks out.

I can't help myself. "Can you survive without my brother next to you for that long?"

"I guess we'll find out. Hey, Jean, I heard there might be an extra copy of the Wolf Alaska brochure here somewhere. Would you mind checking?" Ronan smoothly asks.

"Could be one in the mail room? Give me a sec." She trots off, leaving me alone with him.

I turn to go back to my desk.

"Stop."

The single word stalls my legs. "What?"

He makes me wait for an answer, leisurely signing and dating the bottom of the form. I use that time to study his sleeve of tattoos. I've caught nothing more than glimpses so far —of an angel, a woman's face, an old-fashioned scale, a skull. The designs are both beautiful and raw. And so masculine.

I've never found tattoos appealing until now. It's more likely the canvas that I'm becoming infatuated with. Ronan could model, as handsome as he is. I could see him on some edgy, black-and-white magazine cover, with motorcycles and leather and cigarettes.

Finally, I can't stand the silence. "You know you don't need the pamphlet. You can get all the Alaska info on the website."

"My mom asked me to send it. She likes things in print."

Ugh. Why does him saying that make him even hotter? Bastard.

A secretive smile curls his lips. "No jog this morning?"

So, he knows I was hiding in my room. "I wasn't up to it."

"Avoiding someone."

"Just didn't feel like it," I lie. A run would have been a fantastic way to burn anxiety.

"Hmm ..." He sets the pen down and slides the paperwork forward, the side of his thumb grazing mine as his piercing eyes lift to settle on me. "Didn't take you for a chickenshit."

"I'm not." I fight the urge to pull away. Not because I don't want to touch him, because I so badly do. I glance around to make sure no one's watching. "You didn't tell him, did you?" I whisper.

He leans in, dropping his voice to match mine. "Did you honestly think I'd tell Connor that I fucked his sister last night?"

A shiver skates down my spine with his crass words. "It's not like he'd care."

Ronan chuckles. "I think you're wrong about that."

"Well ... remember your promise."

"What's it worth to you for me to keep it?" A rare and wicked smile curves his lips, his focus dropping to my mouth. "Because I'd love to watch you give me a—"

"The last one!" Jean speeds toward us, waving the colorful pamphlet in her hand.

I step back, breaking contact.

He settles that devastating smile to Jean. "Thank you. I appreciate it."

"No problem." She fumbles with her hair. "Do you need anything else?"

"Nope. Thanks." His gaze shifts back to me. "School tonight, Ryan?"

"As usual." When I enrolled in the master's program last fall, I had this crazy idea that it would be manageable. Work full time, go to class four evenings a week, use my weekends for assignments ... easy enough. Clearly, I was delusional. Thank God it's Thursday and my last lecture for the week.

"I guess I'll see you at home, then."

"Maybe." I try for casual indifference. It comes out strangled.

Ronan swaggers out the door, chuckling.

———

I HIT the button for four and let my backpack fall to the elevator floor. It lands with a thud and then topples. My textbooks spill out.

"Shit." I stoop to pick them up just as someone stops the sliding doors from closing.

"I hate it when people jump into a closing elevator," a guy says, out of breath, reaching to help me.

I look up to find a man smiling at me. He obviously came from the gym or a jog because his shorts and T-shirt are drenched with sweat and his blond hair hangs limp around his forehead.

I stand. "I wasn't cursing you. I was cursing these."

Blue eyes take in the textbook in his grip. "Economic policy. My favorite."

"You're lying, right?"

"If I say that I'm not, will you think less of me?" He flashes a boyish grin. "I majored in economics at Cornell."

"Impressive." Only one of the top schools in the country. This guy must be smart. And I've never seen him before. "Did you just move in?"

"About a month ago." He pauses for a second, then thrusts out his hand. "I'm Kyle."

I fumble to free myself and take it. "Ryan."

The elevator opens to the fourth floor. Kyle holds the door and waits for me to step out.

"It was nice to meet you," I offer.

"Yeah, you too." He hesitates. "I'll see you around the building?" It comes out sounding like a question—or an invitation?

But I'm too focused on my next run-in with my new roommate to give it much thought. "Yeah, sure." I sling my backpack over my shoulder and head for the end of the hall, equal parts excited and panicked.

It's Thursday. Connor always goes out on Thursdays, and since the two of them have been attached at the hip, I have to assume Ronan's gone too. They're likely at the bar. Will Ronan pick up someone tonight?

Is he going to bring home a woman?

An unexpected wave of dread hits me, even as I remind myself that he was up front with me last night about it being a onetime thing. He's going to do whatever he wants with whomever he wants tonight.

I'm so dumb.

Why did I think sleeping with him was a good idea?

By the time I walk into our empty condo, I've worked my stomach into knots.

Now I get to sit here, my guts twisted with all kinds of terrible ideas. Seriously, this is why I can't have casual sex.

With a groan, I throw my bag to the floor and head for the fridge, even though my appetite is dead.

"What the ..." I frown as I take in my shelf. Everything is shifted around, out of order. The large containers are sitting on top of small ones. And my yogurts are flipped upside down. It's utter chaos.

Connor wouldn't do this. He knows how much I hate people touching my things. This had to be Ronan's work. Is it payback for something or is he trying to get under my skin? Is this the equivalent of pulling pigtails in twenty-something-year-old Man Whore Land? I actually don't know how old he is. Or anything about him.

Shaking my head, I spend a few minutes reorganizing everything before I grab an apple and head to my room.

Things are out of place there too. It's all subtle, and for someone who isn't particular probably wouldn't be noticeable. A picture that's not quite straight, a book that's flipped upside down in a stack of right-side-up books, a necklace dangling oddly on its hook.

My stomach erupts in butterflies even as my jaw tenses, knowing Ronan was in my bedroom. He's testing me.

But to what end? To tell me he's thinking about me?

Or simply to piss me off.

No. It's to get a reaction out of me and force a confrontation.

Two can play at this game.

I hesitate with my hand on his doorknob, listening intently. No sound. The door creaks as I push it open. My pulse skips a beat at the sight of his bed—unmade, the sheets tangled in a ball. His work clothes are strewn over the dresser, along with a fistful of change and scraps of papers. Receipts, though I see phone numbers scrawled on the backs. God, he's as bad as my brother. Did he get those numbers today while trolling the hotel beach, pretending to work?

Another wave of dismay washes over me. If he brings someone home and I have to listen to them have sex ... I don't think I'll be capable of shrugging it off so easily.

There's not much I can do in here to irritate him. It's already a mess. I could clean his room, toss out all those phone numbers. Would he care?

I know one thing he *will* care about.

I dart over to his nightstand. Inside the top drawer is a box of condoms—economy size. "Pig," I mutter. Let's see how far he gets without these.

There's not much else in the drawer. A tube of lubricant, unopened. My cheeks flush. We definitely didn't need that. There's also a framed picture. I pull it out and study it. It's of Ronan in a graduation gown, his arm around a stunning brunette. She's smiling broadly, her arms wrapped around his waist. They look like they're in love. I'm guessing this is his ex.

He's holding a certificate in his hands. It's difficult to read, but I manage to make out the University of Indianapolis label.

Ronan went to college?

Why the hell is he working in the outdoor crew at Wolf, then?

Shaking my head—I really don't know anything about the guy I slept with last night—I set the picture back into the drawer and slide it shut.

The sound of keys jangling in the front door has my heart racing. I bolt, intent on getting out of Ronan's room before he catches me. But my baby toe catches the corner of the bed frame, and I go down like a sack of rocks, my vision blurring as pain shoots through my foot.

I'm fighting the tears as I hear Connor's booming voice from the living room and footfalls approaching in the hallway. I have just enough time to shove the box of condoms under the bed before Ronan appears in nothing but shorts, his T-shirt thrown over his shoulder, his bare chest glistening with sweat.

Surprise hits his face. "Ryan?"

"What?" I snap. The pain is beginning to subside. I force myself to stand and face him.

He leans against the door frame, a knowing smirk growing on his face.

Connor appears behind him. "Ry? What the hell are you doing in here?"

"Looking for something."

His face screws up. "In Ronan's room?"

"Yes, in Ronan's room. Because Ronan likes to touch my things without asking."

Ronan settles a heated gaze on me. "I can't help myself. I like it when you scream. At me."

Struggling to keep my cool—even as my cheeks grow hot— I hobble toward the door, noting the volleyball under Connor's arm. "Trying to pick up women at the beach again?"

Connor grins. "Not trying. Succeeding. They're meeting us later."

The change of topic worked. Unfortunately, the answer isn't what I wanted to hear. My stomach flips. "Great. Let me by, please?"

Ronan watches me intently as I squeeze past, making every effort not to touch him.

I don't come out of my room again until they've left.

18. Ronan

Ryan certainly didn't tidy while she was here.

"What were you up to?" I muse, scanning my room for evidence. I knew messing around with her carefully organized belongings would get a reaction out of her.

My nightstand drawer is cracked open. With curiosity, I pull it all the way.

Tasha smiles up at me.

Collecting the framed picture, I study the two faces within for a long moment. That was a good day. We'd only been together for a year or so, but I distinctly remember thinking she was the one. We'd even talked about marriage once but agreed we weren't in a rush—she's a few years younger than I am— and things were perfect the way they were.

A mix of hurt, disappointment, and anger swells inside me. We were perfect, and she threw it all away for random dick.

This picture is the only tangible thing of her I brought with me. It's time I toss it and be done with mourning. I'm not ready yet, though.

Gently setting the picture back, face down, I slide the drawer shut. At least she's out of sight.

And out of mind for today. I've barely thought of Tasha,

too preoccupied with my late-night visitor and how much I enjoyed it. Ryan and I may not be friends, but we've become a hell of a lot more than strangers.

Truthfully, I'd rather stay home tonight and see if I might get another visit, but Connor's already tapped me as his wingman and resisting might make him suspicious.

Peeling off my socks, I head for the shower.

19. Ryan

I didn't think I was going to fall asleep, but I must have drifted off, because I'm awakened after 1:00 a.m. by the sound of female laughter in the living room.

The sharp edge of jealousy pricks me. Ronan brought someone home. *Of course* he did. But this is my fault, I remind myself. *I* went to *him*. He was open and honest. He doesn't owe me anything.

I close the book I fell asleep to and set it on my nightstand, shut off my lamp, and then curl up into a ball and fight the painful disappointment I didn't expect to feel.

I guess the plus side is that I'm not thinking about David right now.

Someone uses the bathroom and then footfalls trail into Ronan's room. The door closes, and a moment later, the bed creaks. The whole process is much quieter and less dramatic than last Friday.

I stare up at the white ceiling with knots in my stomach, waiting for the moaning to start, reminding myself that Ronan is an ass and a pig, and that I don't want him, I don't like him, and I brought this on myself.

K.A. Tucker

It's an hour before I drift off.
Right around the time it dawns on me that Ronan is alone.

20. Ryan

I squeeze through the elevator doors as they're closing, forcing them to open again.

Kyle is standing to the left, dressed in a dove-gray suit. "We're taking turns."

"Huh?" I'm breathing raggedly and drenched in sweat. So stupid of me to go out. I don't enjoy jogging in the heat of the day. That's why I always go in the mornings, when it's cooler and quiet. Peaceful.

But then I had to go and sleep with Ronan.

Yesterday, I skipped my run altogether, avoiding him. Today, I bolted at 6:00 a.m. and didn't come home until I knew they would've left for work. But that hour-long run wasn't enough, apparently, because after a full day of struggling to focus, I came home, changed, and took off, pushing myself to add another five miles to my day's count.

"I was coming home from the gym yesterday. You're coming home from the gym today," Kyle explains with a dimpled smile. Now that he's freshly showered and dressed, I can see just how handsome he is, in a clean-cut, mama's boy way.

"Oh. Yeah." My thighs are on fire.

"Fourth floor, right?" He pushes the button without waiting for my answer. I notice that the second floor is already selected. He got off on my floor yesterday. Maybe he's going to a friend's or a girlfriend's place. "So, Ryan ... are you studying for exams?"

"I've started. Can't wait until it's over."

The doors open on the second floor, and he steps out, but pauses. "I'm in 255, if you're ever need help. I'm an economics analyst, so it's kinda my thing."

"Oh, thanks. Yeah, I'll let you know."

He steps back, watching with a friendly smile as the elevator closes.

Sweat is still dripping down my cheeks as I plow through our front door. I'm praying that Ronan's not home.

No such luck. They're both loitering in the kitchen.

I duck my head, heading for the bathroom, intent on avoiding them until after I've showered and my face isn't so red.

"Two runs in one day, sis?" Connor calls out. "You have some pent-up frustration you're trying to burn?" There's no missing the amusement in his voice.

I stumble a step. "What is *that* supposed to mean?" Oh my God. Did Ronan tell him?

"Nothing! Relax. Jeez. You need anything at the store?"

"Nope. Thanks." I lock the bathroom door behind me and let my head fall back against it with a thud. Just one more week until Ronan's gone to Alaska and I won't have to see those piercing eyes, or watch those muscles move with that sexy swagger, or wonder who he might bring home next.

I inhale deeply. It smells like Ronan in here—like his minty shampoo and his soap. He must have had a shower while I was running.

One more week and I won't have to smell him.

Unexpected disappointment twinges deep inside me with that thought, and it doesn't take a genius to figure out why. It's the same reason I felt immense relief last night when I realized Ronan was alone. All he has to do is glance my way to make my pulse race.

The truth is ... I want him again. That's the real problem here. I let him screw me and now I want it again. He said only one night, and I want another night, and there's no way in hell I'm going to him again.

Worse, he knows I want it, too, the bastard.

One more week.

Just one more week.

Starting the shower, I peel off my clothes and climb in, reveling in the hot water until it turns tepid, trying to not think about a naked Ronan in here.

All is quiet when I emerge, towel wrapped tightly around my body, my sweat-drenched clothes in my fist. The boys have left for the store.

Good.

The tension eases from my shoulders as I head for my room. I'll get dressed, grab a bite to eat, then go to the library to study. By the time I come home, they'll have gone out for the night.

I find Ronan stretched out on my bed.

It takes me a moment to gain my composure, to smooth my expression to one of disregard before I give him the reaction he's fishing for. I toss my dirty clothes into my hamper. "I thought you were going to the store?"

His gaze crawls over me. "I never said I was going anywhere."

My towel doesn't feel secure enough, as if merely a look from him could pull it down. I resist the urge to fumble with it. "What do you want?"

He swings his legs off the edge of the bed and pulls himself up to sit. "Seems I'm missing something important from my room."

I turn my back to him and begin shuffling through my

dresser for clothes. I'm assuming he's talking about his condoms. "Oh yeah? When did you notice it missing?"

My bed creaks as he stands. "Last night." Suddenly, Ronan's directly behind me, his strong frame looming. "When I was going to come in here to see you."

My fumbling hands freeze. He was going to come in here last night? That means he would have been going for a condom.

That means he wanted sex again.

From me.

I struggle to keep my voice indifferent. I don't want him to know how he affects me. "You should keep better track of your important things."

His deep chuckle vibrates along my spine. I watch with shock as, reaching around me, Ronan collects the framed picture of my mom and me, the three books, and the jewelry box that decorate the top of my chest of drawers, and tosses them to my desk.

"Hey! What are you—*ah!*" My words drop with a yelp as he grabs my hips, spins me around, and hoists me up to sit atop it. It's a five-drawer chest, and he's so damn strong.

Without any preamble, he tugs at my towel until it falls open, laying me bare. Pushing my thighs apart, he leans forward.

I watch, my jaw hanging open in shock, as Ronan's mouth settles between my legs.

"Have you ever heard of foreplay?" I finally manage in a hoarse whisper.

"This *is* foreplay."

Whatever resistance I might have put up dissolves in a puddle as his tongue slides over my center.

"Why'd you take my condoms?" he asks, his hot breath against my sensitive flesh.

Because I didn't want you sleeping with anyone else while you're here?

I don't answer, instead reaching down to grab the back of his head, his short, near-black hair unexpectedly soft against my fingertips.

He smiles, his hands gripping my thighs tighter, pulling me forward until I'm afraid I might fall right off the dresser. Ronan would never allow that, though. I don't know him, but I know that.

His tongue takes another long, leisurely swipe. "You *are* sweet. Who knew?"

"I thought this was a onetime thing."

"Do you want it to be a onetime thing?"

I hesitate on the lie. "This doesn't mean I like you."

He chuckles, the grating sound and his mouth so close to me pooling heat in my core. "Wouldn't expect otherwise."

I gasp as he pushes his tongue inside me and then takes off, a relentless barrage of licks and swirls that demonstrates his expertise. Not like David, who only occasionally did this for me, and only for long enough to mark off an invisible check-mark in the decent boyfriend column.

"Do you like doing that?" I dare ask.

He pauses long enough to show me a lust-filled gaze, his fringe of eyelashes thick and long. "Do I like doing what?"

"*That.*"

"Eating you out?"

Oh my God. My stomach tenses. "Yeah."

"I love it." Releasing one of my thighs, he slides two fingers inside me, drawing my gasp and pooling heat into my lower belly. His mouth seals over me again, and my inhibitions quickly fade as his tongue explores and his fingers slowly thrust, building an intense pressure deep inside. I relax and open to him, stroking the back of his head while I coax him with garbled, half words.

When I finally come, it's with Ronan's tongue deep inside me, bucking against his face, crying out with complete abandon.

He stands. His lips graze over my nipple, teasing it with his breath. "How was that for foreplay?"

"Fine," I manage through ragged breaths. He could teach a class on the art of going down on a woman.

"Where is my box of condoms, Ryan?"

"Under your bed," I answer, my eyes closed.

He pulls me down off the dresser with ease, setting me on the bed, where I sprawl out, boneless. I'm vaguely aware of him leaving the room, only to return thirty seconds later, his shirt missing and a foil packet in his hand, his track pants hanging low on his hips, the V of his pelvis leading down to the hard ridge of his erection.

His body truly is a work of art.

Ronan pushes his waistband down to his thighs and takes his length in his palm. With languid strokes, he rubs himself in front of me. "You thought I was going to bring someone home last night, didn't you? That's why you hid these?"

"Yes," I admit. "Why didn't you?"

He opens his mouth, but falters. "I didn't feel like it." I get the impression he was going to say something different.

He tears the foil wrapper with his teeth and rolls the condom onto himself with one hand, his gaze never leaving mine.

For the briefest of seconds, I consider closing my legs, denying him. But I quickly dismiss that crazy thought, because the truth is I'm aching to feel Ronan inside me again. I enjoy the idea of him wanting me.

He flips me over and pulls me to my knees with no warning, smoothing his palms over my backside. "Damn, this ass." The mattress sinks under his weight as he kneels behind me.

"What about it?" I fail to keep the apprehension from my voice. I've always been self-conscious about my round hips, emphasized by my slender waist. In fact, this is my least favorite position because of it. I never let David take me like this.

"It's beautiful."

"Really?"

He drags his thumb along my crack, making me tense. "I could stare at it all day." He grips each side tight, and I feel his tip prod my opening, still swollen and sensitive.

And so wet.

I close my eyes as he pushes into me, overwhelmed by his size from this angle. I take him in quickly enough, though.

His phone chirps. "Shit ... you took too long in the shower." He pushes my chest against the mattress and hikes my ass up higher in the air.

"What do you mean? Is Connor on his way—" My words are cut off with a cry as he thrusts into me at that same relentless pace as the other night, just before he came.

I don't fight the sounds that slip from my mouth this time, fisting the covers, his skin slapping against mine, a repetitive and tawdry sound. It's almost unbearable, my mind torn between the odd pleasurable pain he's delivering and worry that my brother's going to walk in. It's distracting enough that my orgasm catches me by surprise, just as Ronan's pulsing deep inside me with his own.

My muscles barely have time to stop constricting around him when he abruptly pulls out. He leaves, clicking my bedroom door shut behind him.

Disappointment doesn't even have time to settle in before I hear Connor hollering at the door for Ronan to give him a hand unloading the car.

My heart is still racing. That was so close.

I press my lips together to keep from laughing.

What the hell are we doing?

And why am I enjoying this so much?

21. Ronan

I hold my ground at the bar as I savor my last drink. It's almost one. Connor no longer requires my services of wingman based on how far down that woman's throat his tongue is, and I'm doing my best to avoid her friends, one of whom can't keep her hands off me. She's beautiful, I'll give her that. But she's drunk and obnoxious.

And she's not Ryan.

I chuckle at myself as I think of that smash-and-dash earlier. World record, I think. At least for me. I haven't come that fast inside a woman since my first time in one. But it was fun, all the same. Even more fun was hoisting Ryan onto the top of her dresser. A thousand bucks says she's never had a guy do that before. It only took ten seconds for her to let go of her apprehension and enjoy it. I can still feel her fingertips against my scalp.

"You work at Wolf, don't you?"

The feminine purr in my ear catches me off guard mid sip. More unexpected is the face I find next to me.

It's the girl David cheated with. I can't remember her name. Don't care to. "I do." A quick scan around us turns up empty for her new boyfriend. "You here alone?"

"Oh, no. My friends are over there ... somewhere." She gestures behind her into the sea of faces, casually flipping her hair. "I'm Eliza. You're Ronan, right?"

"Right." I hide my smile through a sip. Eliza isn't at all subtle—not that I didn't pick up on her interest in the hallway. Is this how she swooped in on David and convinced him to abandon a year-and-a-half relationship?

"So ... what are you doing here?" she asks, prodding the conversation along.

I rattle the ice in my glass in answer.

"Well, yeah, obviously." She giggles. "I mean, why are you alone?"

"I'm not. My friend is ..." She follows my pointed finger to the corner where Connor has his arm around his conquest to not-so-discreetly hide the fact that his other hand is under her skirt. "Preoccupied."

Eliza's mouth gapes. "Wow, I guess what they say about you crew guys isn't far off."

"Connor's a special breed."

She peels her focus away from them, her blue eyes sparkling when they return to me. "Is it true he's leaving for the Alaska Wolf?"

"Yup. So am I." It still doesn't feel real.

"You *are*?" She pouts. "But you just started in Miami, like, yesterday!"

A bit of an exaggeration, but it does feel like it. "You know quite a bit about me." I'm no idiot. She's as good as mine if I want her. But the last thing I'd want to do is hurt Ryan. In fact, I wish I'd left an hour ago, so I could get home and tug off that crab-faced T-shirt she loves to sleep in and pick up where we left off.

Her cheeks pink. "Not enough. Like, why did you transfer down here only to turn around and go to Alaska?"

"What can I say but my roommate's persuasive?" One of my roommates. The other one is probably lying in bed, over-thinking her life decisions in part because of this woman who is angling to hook up with me. "Aren't you dating David from accounting?"

"Oh! That's new. I mean ..." She's flustered. "It's not serious."

"It's not?" Does he know that?

"No." Her headshake emphasizes her answer and then a playful smile curls her lips. She adjusts her stance closer to me, her chest subtly nudging my biceps. "So, you *do* know who I am."

Maybe I'm extra sensitive because of Tasha, or because I consider Ryan a friend, but I don't want to play this game anymore. Tipping back my drink to down the rest of my whiskey in one gulp, I set the empty glass on the counter. "Yeah, you're the girl who my other roommate's boyfriend cheated with. Have a good night." I leave her gape-mouthed, carving my way through the crowd to Connor and the glaze-eyed brunette he's finger-banging while they sway to the pulsing music. "Heading out now. It's late."

Connor pulls his hand away from the girl to check his watch, earning her frown.

"Damn, it is." Leaning down, he whispers something in her ear.

She nods and, holding up a wait-a-second finger, scuttles over to her friends.

"Which one do you want?" Connor calls out over the music, and I feel the girls' excited eyes survey me.

What is this, an auction? "Neither."

"Dude," he chastises with a *what's wrong with you* look.

"I have a headache," I lie.

"You know what fixes that? *Both* of them."

I shake my head, hoping the girls get the message. "Ryan's got her exams coming up. She'll kill me if she loses sleep."

Connor shrugs. "My room's big enough for all of us."

I chuckle. He is, by definition, the opposite of a cock-blocker. "Nah, I'm good. I'll see you at home." We're only a fifteen-minute walk away.

I hightail it out of there before he can convince me to reconsider.

22. Ryan

"She lives!" Connor exclaims as I emerge from my room around eight on Saturday night, my stomach growling with hunger. He and Ronan are lazing on the couch, watching a basketball game. "What have you been doing all day?"

"The same thing I do every Saturday. My assignments. Studying." I stroll toward the fridge, stealing a lightning-fast glance at Ronan. A wave of excitement courses through me.

"How many more years do you have, anyway?" Connor caps off the question with a belch.

"Just one." If I can concentrate enough to pass my exams. It's been a struggle, staring at my books and notes all day while my ears remain open, listening for any sound that might indicate Ronan's going to pay me another visit. They were out late last night, and Ronan came home alone again. He went straight to bed, while I lay in mine for a good hour, listening, thinking that maybe he was waiting for me, that I should go over there. Finally, I drifted off.

"Hey, would you be a sweet, kind sister and bring over another round for us?"

"It's not fair." I pull two beers off the top shelf. If I ate and drank like they did, I'd balloon. Keeping my expression smooth, I wander over to the couch, handing Connor's can to him first, then one to Ronan.

Ronan's fingers graze mine in the exchange.

Connor frowns up at me. "You look different."

"That's because you're drunk."

Ronan snorts.

"No ... are you wearing makeup?"

"So what?" I turn my back to him, wanting to hide the flush in my cheeks. I went to Ulta this morning to pick up my face moisturizer, and I was waylaid by a saleswoman who asked if she could try out a new mascara on my lashes. Normally I pass, but she was beautiful and claimed she was wearing that very brand. I wanted to see what it could do for me.

I bought the mascara, along with the gold eye shadow she swiped across my lids.

"So, you never wear makeup," Connor says slowly.

"Not *never*." Just hardly ever.

"Not when you're sitting in your room all day, studying."

"Whatever. It's no big deal. Drop it."

But he's not relenting. "I think she's trying to look good for you." He elbows Ronan in the ribs.

"*What*? Why would I want to do that?" I force scorn into my voice while my face burns. This is humiliating.

"Leave her alone," Ronan warns. "You're going to make her angry, and she'll take it out on me."

"Fine." Connor belches again, earning my grimace. "By the way, we're having a goodbye party here next Friday."

I groan loudly. I knew it was coming, but I can't stop it. This is Connor's condo, and I pay very little in rent.

"It'll be tame," he promises.

"The cops showed up last time," I remind him.

"We'll keep it under control."

"I had to buy new sheets!"

"Ed's not invited back. I promise."

Ronan's stony expression softens with his chuckle.

My pulse skips a beat, even as I try to argue against this. "And who's going to clean up if you two are gone the next morning?"

"Maria from the first floor. We'll get rid of all the trash and empties and leave cash for her."

"Don't you just have *all* the answers." I sigh heavily. "I want a lock on my door."

"For what?" Ronan blurts, and then his jaw tenses. "I mean, no one's going in your room. We'll make sure people know the rules."

"People break rules when they're horny." I stare at him pointedly. Like the one where he wasn't going to fuck his friend's sister.

The corners of Ronan's mouth curve through a sip. "Fair enough."

Connor's phone chirps with a text. He dismisses my request with a "Fine" as he reads his message, then elbows Ronan. "Sherrie and Georgia are going to Sin tonight. You in?"

His words feel like a gut punch. Sherrie. She's the one who doesn't know her left from her right.

"No thanks," Ronan says without missing a beat.

"Are you kidding? Dude! They were smoking hot."

"Been there, done that." His eyes glimmer across mine before he takes a long sip of his beer.

Connor is not accepting his answer. "What's wrong with you, man? You turned those girls down last night. Now you're saying no to these two. Is your dick not working or are you getting something somewhere that I don't know about?"

Please be too dense to figure it out, dear idiot brother.

I stick my head in the fridge, afraid Connor will see the answer in my face. Or that he'll see my stupid grin of satisfaction, hearing that Ronan isn't picking up other women.

Thankfully, Connor's phone rings, distracting him before he forces an answer from Ronan. "Shit, I gotta take this. Hey,

Mom ... Yeah, I know. I'm sorry. I've been busy ... You know, same old. Next Saturday ... Yeah, it should be a blast."

I take the opportunity to glance over and catch Ronan's focus on my ass. He lifts his gaze to meet mine, to see my quirked brow, the one that says I've caught him.

He subtly nods toward our rooms and then, easing off the couch, saunters down the hall, disappearing into the bathroom.

"Five months ... Sorry, I don't think I can make it." Connor's mom is no doubt asking him to visit her in Orlando. "Yeah, she's here. Studying. Always studying. Finally broke up with the douchebag."

I roll my eyes but throw a wave Connor's way. Danielle has always been kind to me, even though I'm a byproduct of her ex-husband's affair.

"She says hi."

With nervous flutters in the pit of my stomach, I collect my container of veggies and hummus and my water and head toward my room. I get as far as the bathroom when Ronan reaches out and, grabbing hold of my wrist, pulls me in.

"What are you doing?" I hiss.

He takes my dishes and sets them on the vanity. "How long do you think he'll be occupied?"

"At least twenty minutes." Danielle loves to talk and now that she's pinned down her son, she won't let him go so easily.

"That should be enough time."

"We can't! Connor's *right there*." Even as I deny him, my hands smooth over Ronan's chest, the soft cotton of his T-shirt hugging his curves. It's the first chance I've had to touch him so freely like this and he is all hard muscle.

His fist curls around my ponytail and he pulls, tilting my head back until I meet molten eyes. "Then you shouldn't have stuck your ass in the air like that, wearing these." His gaze settles on my mouth as he pinches at my leggings, stretching them.

A giggle slips from my lips as my confidence soars, earning a crooked smile from him.

This is surprisingly fun.

And I so badly want him to kiss me.

Ronan leans forward, and I think he's read my mind, he's going to grant my wish. But he veers at the last second, the heat of his breath skating over my cheek. His lips settle on my neck. "I need to come, Ryan," he whispers, his tongue dancing over my skin, sending shivers all the way down to my nipples. "I need you to make me come right now."

"Okay" slips from my mouth, unbidden.

He leads me back three steps until the backs of my legs hit the toilet and I'm forced to sit. His calloused fingers are gentle, grazing the underside of my chin, smoothing over my bottom lip. "I've been waiting for this since last night." His thumb slides into my mouth and I suck it involuntarily.

With his free hand, he tugs his track pants down, and his hard length springs free.

It's another first for me, the chance to grip him in my hand, to revel in the feel of his smooth, soft skin against my palm.

I shake my head.

"What's wrong?"

"Nothing. It's just ... we seem to be running around the bases in the wrong direction."

He groans, his head tipping back as I run the pad of my thumb over his tip. "I don't care which direction we're running in, as long as it ends with me coming in your mouth."

No one's ever talked to me like this before. I never thought it would be a turn-on, but coming from Ronan, with that deep, raspy voice, it makes my pulse skitter every time.

My mind snags on his words. He's been waiting since last night? I hesitate. "Why didn't you bring a girl home from the bar?"

He frowns. "Did you want me to?"

"No." Is that wrong to admit?

"Well then ..."

"Well then, what?"

"Suck my dick, Ryan." His hand slips from my jaw around to the back of my head and he pulls me forward.

I resist, even though desire burns hot between my legs. "Say please."

His brow arches. "Please take my dick in that vicious mouth of yours."

I oblige, running my tongue along the underside of him. When I glance up, he's staring down at me with a hard look.

I part my lips. An invitation.

He accepts it, sliding in. I close over him, molding around his shape.

Connor's voice carries from somewhere in the living room and it must be bothering Ronan, because he flips the switch for the fan, drowning it out.

I've never really liked giving head, but it's different with Ronan. Maybe because our relationship is purely physical, and he turns me on like no other guy I've ever been with. I want him to enjoy this as much as I enjoyed him going down on me yesterday. So, I do my best, pushing myself to take him in as deep as I can, until I'm forced to relent or gag. He seems to appreciate it, smoothing loose strands of hair off my forehead gently, sweetly whispering words of encouragement, his hand controlling the tempo. When it starts to speed up, when his breathing starts growing ragged, I know he's close.

"That's it." His hips start thrusting into my mouth and he suddenly swells even more. "Almost there ..." His hand closes tight over my hair until it almost hurts.

A stream of warm salty liquid hits the back of my tongue as he orgasms, but aside from one low grunt, he manages to stay quiet.

Ronan spends a moment simply standing there, his breathing heavy, his hooded eyes settled on my face, his fingers stroking my hair. "Thank you." He takes a step back, tucking himself into his pants. Hitting the fan switch, he pauses to listen.

All I hear is the buzz of the voices on the TV. It sounds like Connor's off the phone.

"See you later." Ronan winks and steals a carrot before ducking out.

Did that just happen?

Yes. It did. And I enjoyed it.

I take a moment to study myself in the mirror—my puffy lips, my mussed hair, the smears of black mascara around my eyes—and then I brush my teeth, grab my containers of food, and sneak out to my room.

———

IT'S ALMOST two in the morning when commotion stirs in the living room and female laughter carries. I sit up to listen intently.

Plural female laughter. Ronan's courtesy must have run out. He's brought someone home the same day I gave him a blow job in our bathroom.

I flop back into bed, disappointment overwhelming me. It's followed closely by anger, at Ronan, but mostly at myself for allowing our little charade to continue. I'm not programmed for casual sex. I can't do it, even with a guy I have no interest in hanging out with outside of what we do in bed.

My pulse hammers in my ears as I lie in the dark, listening to the floor creak in the hallway, his door opening.

Waiting for the inevitable bed-frame thumping to begin.

I stiffen when my bedroom door swings open instead. For a split second, I think it's another directionally challenged naked drunk girl, but the brief stream of light allows me a glimpse of a naked Ronan instead.

He shuts the door behind him. A moment later, the sheets shift and pull, and then he's lying down beside me, heat radiating off his body. "I know you're awake," he whispers, the sound of his voice stirring my blood. His breath—a mixture of toothpaste and a sweet liquor and tobacco—skates over my face.

"How?"

His hand slides between my legs, his fingers slipping under my panties. "Because you've been lying in bed for hours, wondering what I'm doing at the bar, waiting for me to come home." His finger draws along my slit. "Thinking about me."

I *have* been doing that.

But now I shove his hand away. "Don't you have someone waiting for you?"

"What?" I can hear the frown in his voice even if I can't see it.

"I heard more than one woman come in."

"You're right. There are two, and they're with your brother."

"*Both* of them?"

I sense his smile. "Both of them."

"Oh." Relief overwhelms me even as I try to block out that visual.

Ronan's hand slips back, this time peeling my panties down past my knees.

I lift my legs until they fall to my ankles and I can shake them off.

"You thought I'd bring someone else home while we're doing this?" he asks, the soft pad of his thumb finding my clit to draw teasing circles.

"Well ... yeah. You said only the one night."

He chuckles. "Obviously we're not following that rule."

"What changed?"

There's a long pause as if he's considering his words. "I don't enjoy picking up girls at the bar."

I can't help but laugh. "I heard how much you enjoyed Sherrie, remember?"

"The part where I came, sure," he corrects with a dark chuckle. "But it's all pointless, impersonal. And it didn't make me feel better about Tasha leaving me." His breath skates over my cheek. "You don't feel pointless or impersonal. And even though this is just for now, I feel better when I'm with you." He pauses. "Is that wrong?"

My God, how did I not realize before that I'm not the only one needing a confidence boost? "No, I get it. You're still in love with someone else." My heart pangs in my chest with a rare glimpse at Ronan's pain. He seems so lost. "And here I thought you were just another cocky asshole taking advantage of a vulnerable girl."

"I *am* a cocky asshole. But I'm not a dick, and I don't fuck over friends."

"Is that what we are? Friends?"

"Aren't we?"

I consider that. "I guess you could call us that."

He nuzzles my cheek with the tip of his nose. "While we're messing around, I won't be with anyone else. That's the only commitment I can make. If that's good enough for you."

"Yeah. And same. I mean, not that I have a line of guys waiting—" A soft gasp slips from my lips as his fingers slide inside me with ease, proving my readiness for him.

"You don't need me in your bed to feel good about yourself, Ryan. You're incredible and David is an idiot, but that's his loss, not yours. You'll find someone else who makes you ten times happier, and you'll wonder how the hell you ever thought he was the one."

A warm feeling erupts in my chest with his encouraging words. I hesitate. "Actually, there is one other thing I want from you."

"Yeah? What's that?" he asks, never breaking his tempo.

I reach up to touch his stubbled cheek and run my thumb over his bottom lip. I'm torn between wanting to see his face and enjoying the liberty that comes with darkness. But there's one thing I know I want. "Kiss me."

"Ryan..." I sense him searching for a way to deny me.

"Please?" I thought I was done begging this man for things.

A long moment passes and then he leans forward and presses his mouth against mine. His lips are softer than I imagined, moving in a sweet, sensual way that I hadn't expected from him. "Like that?"

"Yes. Exactly like that." A sigh escapes my lips, and he slides his tongue along the seam. I open wider, my tongue reaching for his, needing it against mine, needing to taste his mouth. He obliges, pressing in deeper, his hand down below stalled, as if his undivided attention is now above. I could do this with him all night long.

"Finally. First base," I murmur.

His lips stretch against mine in a smile, and then they're shifting south, along my jawline, my throat, leaving a trail of wet heat. He toys with the spaghetti strap of my nightie. "This is different."

"Easier to remove." And a lot sexier than the oversized T-shirts I've grown accustomed to sleeping in.

He tugs at the top, uncovering my breast. I moan as he pulls my nipple into his mouth and sucks. How is he so good at *everything* he does?

Experience, I guess, but I don't want to think about that. This Tasha girl's loss is my gain. "What you said earlier to me, about me finding someone else who makes me ten times happier? The same will happen for you. I promise."

He pauses a moment, and I think he's going to respond, but then he occupies his mouth once again.

My legs stretch apart without thought, opening for him, a deep ache growing between them that he works to satisfy, stretching me with first two, then three fingers as I roll my hips against his hand, all while I grip the back of his head, holding him against my breast.

I'm writhing under Ronan's touch, moments away from coming, when heavy footfalls pound in the hallway.

There's a knock and then, a moment later, Ronan's bedroom door creaks open. "Hey, bro. I need your help with these two. I'm way too drunk to handle them both." A pause. "Ronan?" Connor slaps the wall. He's turning the light on, no doubt.

"Shit," Ronan hisses against me, pulling away.

Shit is right. Connor may be dense, but even he will put two and two together now. If he does, will that be the end of this?

I don't want that.

Scrambling out of my bed, I adjust my nightgown and then open the door a crack. And quickly avert my gaze. "What the fuck, Connor!" He's naked.

"Sorry! I didn't think you'd be awake."

He didn't think, period. I keep my eyes on his face, shielding any risk of a downward view with my hand. "Of course, I'm awake, when you're yelling outside my door."

He points to Ronan's room. "Where is he?"

"How the hell should I know? I heard his door open a few minutes ago, so I guess he went somewhere. I can't keep up with all the whoring going on around here. Yours included."

Connor furrows his brow in thought. "I'll bet he hooked up with Vera. She was all over him in the elevator the other day, using that 'broken light in her bedroom' trick."

Vera—a fifty-year-old divorcée with enormous breasts who wears skintight gym clothes and bright pink lipstick. Connor slept with her about a year ago and still talks about it to this day. "Good for him. Now go back to your room and let me sleep." I slam the door for effect.

And hold my breath.

A moment later, Connor's footfalls pad against the hardwood as he leaves.

Ronan groans. "That was close."

I push the straps of my nightshirt down, letting the thin cotton fall to the floor before I climb into bed. "Do you think he'd actually be mad at you for this?" I fumble in the dark until I feel his smooth, warm skin beneath my fingertips again.

"It's hard to tell. I know I'd kill him if he got into my sister."

I ignore his crude choice of words. "You have a sister?"

"Yeah. Younger one. Brittany. Or Britt."

I didn't know that. Of course I didn't. I know nothing about this guy I'm living next to and sleeping with. *And that's how I want it*, I remind myself.

I reach out, tracing his stomach muscles. "Well, I don't think he'd have a right to be. He practically forced you on me by letting you move in. What did he think would happen?"

Ronan rolls on top of me, positioning his hips between my legs. "That you wouldn't be able to keep your hands off me, obviously."

With crisis averted, my thoughts turn to something else. "So, do I want to know what he meant by 'helping' him?"

His lips trail over my jawline. "Probably not."

"Do I want to know the kinds of things you've done?"

"Definitely not."

He's right. Because I've heard a couple stories at work—including one about my brother and another crew guy named Jake sharing a girl—that have dropped my jaw.

And I'm not with Ronan for anything but the very thing he's giving me, and knowing that is liberating. There's no pull on my heartstrings, no desire to stay up until the morning learning everything there is to know about him, no wondering if this will last. I know exactly how long it'll last—for one more week. And then he'll go to Alaska and try to fill the void in his heart by screwing who knows how many women, and I'll get back to my life, hopefully feeling a little better about David.

That's what this is all about—me, helping myself move on after a horrible breakup.

The foil wrapper tears and latex crinkles as Ronan sheaths himself.

"You're always careful though, right?" I ask.

Collecting my hands in his, he pins my arms above my head, pressing his whole body against mine. I revel in the feel of his weight. "Always." He traces my jawline with kisses, all the way to my lips, whispering, "I'm completely yours for the week, Ryan. Use me."

I angle my hips upward. "Gladly."

With our fingers entwined, he lines himself up and pushes into me.

I close my eyes as the first moan slips out.

23. Ryan

All is quiet in the condo on Sunday when I wake up, two hours later than I should have. Ronan went back to his room after a slow and sensual round of sex, very different from the last two times but no less pleasurable. He still made me orgasm. That's something I'm going to sorely miss when he's gone.

I heard nothing from the women Connor brought home. Either he quietly packed them off last night, or they're all still in bed together. I cringe at the thought of all those limbs and other body parts. It's not for me.

But maybe it *is* for Ronan. Had Ronan and I not been doing whatever this is, would he have gone to Connor's room? What would have gone on in there? I can't even imagine. It's a good thing this little fuck-buddy arrangement expires soon, because I doubt I could keep him interested for much longer.

I'm brewing myself a coffee when a door creaks open.

It's Ronan, staggering from his bedroom, eyes still half closed, buck naked, his dick long and hard with morning need.

I don't avert my gaze.

With a lazy wave, he disappears into the bathroom, and I go back to fixing myself a coffee, struggling to hide my grin.

A few moments later, he pokes his head out. I can hear the shower running. "Hey." I love how gravelly his voice is in the morning.

"Hey."

He crooks a finger, calling me to come. To take a shower with him, I gather.

My stomach tightens in anticipation. But I set my jaw and plaster my face with a mock frown instead.

His brow arches. "Really?"

"I'm busy." Leaning against the counter with my coffee in hand, I sip away.

A slow, wicked smile curls his lips. He steps out and stalks toward me.

I stand up straight, my eyes flashing to the short hall leading to Connor's room before turning back to Ronan in all his beautiful nakedness. "What are you doing?" I hiss.

He takes my cup from my grip. "I can't wait until tonight. We're either fucking in the shower, or right here in the kitchen. You have until I'm finished this coffee to decide where you want me to take you." His free hand leisurely strokes over his length as he takes long gulps from my mug, his heated gaze on me.

I swallow. His words, the sight of him ... Damn it. There's no way I'm getting an ounce of schoolwork done with this on my mind. I want to be naked with him. I want him pressed against me, inside me. Right now.

With a shuddering sigh, I stroll toward the bathroom.

24. Ronan

"Wonder if there'll be enough staffers to get some games going in Alaska," Connor muses as I trail him through our condo building's front door.

"In the forest?" I mock, wiping the sweat off my brow with my palm. I never would have guessed Frisbee tag took that much effort, but the way Connor's league plays, I thought I was going to collapse on the field. It could be the nicotine tar in my lungs, though. "You can build a team with the human-sized mosquitos."

The elevator doors open with a ding, and out steps Vera's surgically enhanced breasts, followed by the rest of her. The first time I met the single, older lady, I'll admit, I had a hard time focusing on her face, as pretty as it is.

"Boys!" She appraises our bare chests and soaked shorts. "What have you two been up to?"

Connor grins as he reaches out to hold the elevator door, showing off his ripped biceps. "You know us. Always looking for a good workout."

Her eyes light up with heated interest. "You can find one of those at my place. Come by anytime. And *you*." She sizes me up like, well, a cougar deciding where to start on its fresh kill. "I still need that light in my bedroom fixed."

"Didn't he *fix that* last weekend?" Connor muses.

Her brow pinches with confusion. "Last weekend ..."

The elevator alarm screams at us.

I slip past them and jab the button for our floor. "I'll come by next week to help you with that, ma'am."

Connor releases his hold, blowing a kiss at her as the doors are closing. And then he turns to me. "Did you just *ma'am* Vera?"

"Yeah, why wouldn't I? My mother raised me to have manners."

He chuckles. "Anyway, we're not here next week."

"Exactly. And the light in her bedroom is not broken." That's code for *I'm going to break your dick sex* if I've ever heard one.

"It's not," Connor agrees. "I fell for it and, bro ..." He shakes his head. "That was a night. She pulled out a strap-on and—"

I hold up my hand. "'Nough said."

The elevator doors open on our floor and we step out.

"Hey, if you weren't with her last weekend after the club, where were you? I came to your room."

Shit. "Went out for a smoke."

"At two in the morning?"

I shrug. "I needed one, and you said I couldn't smoke inside."

His eyes narrow suspiciously while he digs for his keys. "You really need to quit that shit. It's not good for you. And you missed out because of it."

"Yeah, too bad." With a smirk, I trail him in.

25. Ryan

Kyle is emptying his mailbox when I walk into our building on Wednesday night, struggling with my overloaded backpack. "Fancy meeting you here."

"Hey, stranger." He reaches for the strap. "Let me help you."

Normally I'd decline the offer, but I'm too tired and it's too heavy.

He grunts under the weight. "God, I don't miss these days."

"Trust me, I can't wait until it's over." Do I *really* need my MBA?

He presses the button for the elevator. "It's been four years since I graduated and I still sometimes wake up in a panic, thinking I'm late for an exam."

"Is that what I have to look forward to?" Four years. That would make him around twenty-seven or twenty-eight, if I had to guess. Not that much older than me, but older. I like that.

The door opens and he hangs back, gesturing for me to go first. An older gentleman. I like that too.

"So, when do you write?" he asks.

"First one's next Wednesday."

Kyle hits the button for the fourth floor. But not the one for the second floor, *his* floor, I notice. "Are you ready?"

"Honestly, I don't know. I work full time, I just broke up with my boyfriend, I've been ..." *Fucking my roommate every single night.* "The last couple weeks have been distracting."

The elevator opens. Kyle holds the door for me and then steps out behind.

I reach for my backpack but he's already moving around me and down the hall. "If you're free on Friday night, you could come over and I'll help you study. We could order in Thai or something."

He says it so casually. Is he being a nice, helpful fellow building dweller or did Kyle just ask me out on a date?

"Actually, my roommates are leaving for Alaska and they're having a goodbye party that night."

"Alaska. Wow." His eyebrows pop with genuine amazement.

"Yeah, for the summer."

"Oh." He nods. "Well, you probably don't want to miss that."

"Actually, I probably do. It's liable to get out of hand, knowing my brother." I peer up into kind, blue eyes. Kyle really is handsome. "Can I let you know?"

He grins, revealing deep dimples. "Sure. I'll be home, reading about statistical probabilities or something equally *wild*."

I giggle as I collect my bag from him. "Thanks for carrying this."

"No problem. Maybe I'll see you Friday?"

I watch him stroll to the elevator, stealing a glance back at me ... twice.

Okay, Kyle's definitely into me.

I'm smiling as I walk into our condo. Ronan's in the kitchen, hovering in front of the open fridge, shirtless, the view of his muscular back mesmerizing.

He turns to me. "Good night in class?"

"Kind of." I drop my bag, exhausted. "Where's Connor?"

"Concert."

"I swear, he spends half his salary on tickets." I frown. "Are you eating my yogurt?"

Ronan licks the spoon. "Yup. It's my second one."

My jaw hangs. "Why?"

He shrugs. "I was hungry. And bored."

"You shithead!"

"Yeah. What are you gonna do about it?" he taunts, his eyes roving over me, the simple act raising my pulse.

Oh my God, this guy is a machine. I've never had so much sex in my life. Every single night, sometimes twice. There's no denying him either, not that I'd want to. But still, I pretend that I have the willpower to say no. It usually lasts all of ten seconds. As soon as his lips are on me, I'm a goner.

"Nothing. I'm going to sleep." I bolt for my room with a shriek, making it all the way to my door before his arms rope around my waist and I'm laughing hysterically. "Put me down!"

He tosses me onto my bed and yanks off my shoes and socks, followed by my pants, then my panties. I help him by tugging my own shirt off and unfastening my bra. In seconds, I'm lying naked in front of him. Waiting.

He pauses, his gaze softening for a moment. "I'm gonna miss you."

"I'm gonna miss you too." But I don't think I'd be so cavalier if he wasn't leaving.

Still, next week will be quiet, lonely.

Ronan drops his pants—he's not wearing briefs tonight, and he's already fully erect. "How do you want it?" The deep rasp in his voice is intoxicating.

"Well, seeing as you ate my snack, it's only fair." I stretch my legs wide.

With a grin, he drops to his knees.

———

"Did you hear?" Jean hisses, startling me in my cube.

My stomach clenches. What will today's gossip be? Hopefully nothing David related. "I doubt it."

"Henry Wolf is in Miami." Her onyx eyes dance with excitement.

That piques my interest. The CEO of Wolf Hotels, who will one day officially take over the luxury hotel chain from his father, is a celebrity to most Wolf employees and the source of a lot of racy gossip. I've only seen pictures of him, but the man could easily grace a "most beautiful people" magazine cover. No wonder I've sensed a strange buzz around the office today.

Everyone's in heat.

And the rumor is, that's exactly the way he likes it.

Regardless, I've always wanted to see him in person, to understand what all the hype is.

"They're in the Pacific, having some big meeting, but Dana said they called her to arrange for a car to take them to lunch, off-site, for noon."

I glance at my watch. That's in five minutes.

Jean grins. "Feel like a walk to the lobby?"

"My legs could use a stretch." I lock my computer and grab my lunch bag.

———

"They're saying it's going to be one of the nicest Wolf locations in the world," Dana gushes. The towering, lithe brunette is a popular concierge. There's usually a circle of businessmen hovering around her desk when she's on shift.

"That's what I keep hearing too," Jean says. "Plane rides and tours to see grizzly bears. And the scenery alone, with all the mountains and lakes and wilderness!"

I've seen the brochure. It's going to be an incredible place.

Had I not been in school, I would have considered applying. Then again, I don't know if I could handle the living conditions. "The staff are all in cabins. Like six people to each or something like that."

Dana and Jean both look at me with blank expressions.

"Absolutely *no* privacy?"

"Oh, yeah," Jean agrees. "I don't know how Connor and Ronan are going to handle that."

"Something tells me they won't care one way or another," I answer dryly. Ronan might be keeping his pants on while he's messing around with me, but he leaves for Alaska on Saturday morning, and tomorrow's the party. My fun time is coming to an end.

A prickle of jealousy sparks in my chest. I quickly chase it away. I don't want to date Ronan. It's just ... I guess I don't want to think about him with someone else either. Not yet. I've selfishly enjoyed him too much. I've barely thought of David.

That Connor hasn't caught us yet is mind-boggling. I'm beginning to question how he functions at the basics in life.

"You know, you're going to miss them when they're gone," Jean says.

"I know," I admit with reluctance. I'll even miss my big, dumb brother. But it's also for the best, because I can't concentrate on anything when Ronan's around. I'm going to fail my exams if I can't clear my head.

"Oh, speaking of those two, guess what happened!" Dana's chocolate eyes twinkle with juicy gossip. "The front desk girls went out last weekend, and the guys were there. Apparently, Eliza hit on Ronan."

My stomach clenches with dread.

"And?" Jean pushes, asking the question I can't.

"And he turned her down. Basically called her out for messing around with David behind Ryan's back."

A mixture of relief and adoration for the guy swells inside me. Despite our sordid relationship, he is actually a real friend.

"See?" Jean elbows me. "You should have hooked up with him!"

I did, at least twenty times, in every position you could imagine—many I never imagined. I bite my tongue against the urge to say it, especially now that I know Eliza had her sights set on him. My vindictive side wants it to get back to her.

"Anyway, from what I heard, Eliza and David are over." Dana looks at me when she says this, as if gauging my reaction to the news.

"*I* don't want him back," I blurt, and the moment the words are out there, I know them to be true. There's not an inkling of "what if" stirring. An invisible weight lifts with that comprehension.

"There he is!" Dana suddenly hisses, derailing all talk of David and Ronan.

The three of us—and pretty much every other female in the lobby—zone in on the five-man conglomerate that strides out of the elevator, heading for us.

Speaking of not being able to concentrate ...

I'm not one to openly fawn, and yet there's no ignoring Henry Wolf. Not his piercing blue gaze, or his sharp, angular features, or his dark, thick hair, styled in sexy waves. I watch the way his fit body moves smoothly, how his tailored suit falls perfectly with each step as he approaches, preoccupied with conversation.

I'm mesmerized.

"What's with the beard?" Jean whispers. "Is he going lumberjack for Alaska?"

Dana giggles. "I heard he's going to be up there a lot. The hotel is his pet project."

Henry Wolf's eyes slide over Jean and me before moving on to Dana. My face instantly flushes.

"I believe there's a car for us?" he says smoothly. Beneath

that scruff, I can make out a set of plump lips. If rumor is correct, those are reserved for Victoria's Secret models and other gorgeous celebrities, not lowly Wolf staff.

Dana glances over her shoulder to check the carport. A doorman waves at her. "Yes, Mr. Wolf. It's already waiting." She beams at him.

He responds with a cool, polite smile. "Lead the way then, please." He and the other men follow Dana out.

Jean sighs. "What I would do for a night with that."

"Are you cheating on Connor?" I tease as we head toward the doors to the staff area.

"Connor doesn't even know I exist, and you won't help me," she mutters sullenly.

"I am *helping* you by not letting you subject yourself to an STD cocktail. My brother doesn't do relationships, and I'm not going to be his pimp."

"But I want to come to the goodbye party!"

"How do you know about that?"

"*Everyone* knows about that."

Great. "Trust me, you don't belong there. *I* don't belong there. I'm probably going to leave so I can study." Will it be to Kyle's or the library? I've been too distracted by Ronan to give my cute neighbor's invitation any real thought, but I actually could use the help.

"Why? What's going to happen?" Jean asks warily.

"Let's see ... the last time Connor threw a get-together, there was a naked girl stretched out across the kitchen island and people doing body shots off her. Off *every* part of her." I give her a knowing stare.

Jean's face pales. "On second thought, I think I have a sewing club engagement."

"Good call."

26. Ryan

I come home from work to a living room littered with shopping bags.

"Did you know how cold it is in Alaska?" Connor exclaims, holding up a fleece sweater. "Even in summer?"

"Compared to Miami? I had an idea, yes. I guess you're packing?"

"Won't have time tomorrow." He stuffs it into his duffel bag. "So, I've written down a bunch of things that you need to do. Bills to pay, that sort of thing."

"Connor, I do that stuff ninety-five percent of the time now."

He shrugs. "Figured it can't hurt to have a list."

"You're right. Thanks." At least he's making an effort rather than taking off and assuming everything will magically take care of itself.

"I'm sorry, excuse me, what was that? Did I hear you say, 'Connor, you're such a smart and handsome big brother and I'm going to miss you'—"

"Enough." I hold up a hand but cap it off with a chuckle.

He grins. "You know, you've been in a way better mood lately. Who's been getting into your pants?"

I screw up my face to try to hide my panic. *Our roommate and your partner in crime. That's who.* "Not everyone's life revolves around getting laid."

"Yes, it does. They just don't have the guts to admit it."

"Whatever."

His lips purse. "I'm glad you and Ronan are getting along better."

Mention of Ronan's name stirs a flutter in my stomach. "Like I had a choice. But only two more days." I duck into the fridge so he can't read the lies in my expression.

"Either way, I was worried for a bit."

"*You*, worried?" My fake laugh comes out extra forced.

"Yeah, fine, I wasn't, really."

Grabbing a water, I head for my room, itching to change out of my staff uniform before class.

"Oh yeah. Some guy came by. Kent, I think he said?"

"Kyle?"

"Yeah, that's it."

"Really?" I frown. "Did he say what he wanted?"

"Something about tomorrow night. Where'd you meet him?"

"In the elevator. He lives on the second floor."

"That's it. *Get it*, baby sis."

"I'm not—" There's no point. "You're ridiculous."

Connor drops a heap of socks into his bag. "Glad to see you're moving on from Dickface."

I roll my eyes at his crassness. "Kyle's helping me study for my exams."

"Uh-huh. Call it what you want. Smart move to be out of here tomorrow, though, because it is gonna be lit."

I hold a finger up in warning. "If *anyone* goes into my room—"

"Relax, Ronan put a lock on it when he got home."

I peer down the hall to my door. Sure enough, there's a

shiny new handle with a key sitting inside. "Oh, thanks." I guess Connor paid for that. A rarity.

"Uh-huh." Connor salutes. "New guy seems decent. You have my seal of approval."

"You barely met him." He couldn't remember his name!

"Don't forget to rubber up."

"Great brotherly advice." I hesitate. "Is your sidekick in his room?"

"He had a few last-minute things to pick up at the store. Everything's so expensive in Homer, we're better off flying up with it."

"Okay. Have fun packing." I wander down the hall, stealing a glimpse to see Ronan's black duffel bag packed and sitting on the floor beside his bed. Unexpected sadness fills my heart. He's only been here two weeks, I was a bitch to him for half that time, and yet I'm going to miss him terribly.

With an unexpected heaviness in my chest, I head into my room.

A scrap of paper sits on my nightstand. I recognize Ronan's neat scrawl.

On it is Kyle's phone number along with a message:
Go get him, Tiger.

———

A NAKED RONAN slips into my bed at midnight, bringing with him a pleasant scent of mint tinged with a touch of tobacco.

"Hey." My voice cracks over the word as I study the hard lines of his face in the dim light of my lamp.

His warm hand slides around my waist to my back. He pulls me closer until we're both lying on our sides, our chests pressed against each other. It's unexpectedly intimate, and we stay like that, quiet, for a long moment. "Hey."

"You ready for Alaska?"

"Fuck ..." He rolls onto his back. "I still don't know why I'm going."

"Because my brother lured you there with tales of beautiful, loose women?"

He fits an arm under my head and then pulls me in to rest on his hard chest. "How did you know?"

"Wild guess."

"Does that bother you?"

"A little?" I'm not ready to say goodbye. "But we knew what this was when we started, right?"

"Right." He skates a finger across my cheek. "I met Kyle today."

I swallow, trying to read his thoughts in those four words. "Yeah."

"Could there be something there?"

"Nah."

He sighs. "Ryan."

"What?"

"I've spent the last week fucking you in every position I know. I can read your body language. And your bullshit."

I smile sheepishly. "I've run into him a few times in the elevator. He offered to help me study. That's all."

"Is that what the kids are calling it these days," Ronan says dryly, staring up at my ceiling.

"He was an economics major. I think he actually means to help." Partly, anyway.

"I'm only teasing. I think it's great."

I rest my chin on his pec and study his face for anything that says otherwise. "You do?"

He smiles softly. "Yeah."

"Does it bother you?" I echo his earlier question.

"A little," Ronan admits, sending a thrill through my body. Whatever I'm feeling for him seems to be mutual. "But he seems like a good guy, and I like the idea that you'll know someone in the building. That you won't be alone." His fingertips skate over my bare shoulder.

I shiver beneath his touch. "He invited me to his place tomorrow night."

"I know. You should go."

"What if he tries to kiss me?"

"Do you *want* him to kiss you?"

"I don't know." A beat later, I confess, "He's hot."

Ronan chuckles. "Then he's one lucky motherfucker."

"But I can't start something with him and then come back here and do this with you."

"No, you can't. That's not your style."

I sense that he's given this thought already. "That would mean tonight's our last night."

"You're right. It would have to be." He slides one of my nightgown straps down. "What a good run it was."

I inhale the scent of Ronan. It's odd, how addicted I've become to him. "I'm going to miss you."

"You and Kyle will hook up and you won't miss me at all."

"And you'll hook up with half the women in Alaska and forget about me too," I tease.

"Connor will take the other half."

"And then you'll swap."

"Probably." Ronan flinches as I smack him, but then he chuckles, the deep melody of it comforting to my heart.

"I can't believe I'm saying this, but I'm happy you moved in here, even if it was only for a couple of weeks." I'm not sure I loved David. How could I have gotten over him so quickly if I did?

Ronan hesitates. "I still love Tash and miss her like crazy, but you've made it easier for me." Pain glints in his eyes but only for a second and then it's gone.

I stretch up to kiss his jaw, a hint of stubble tickling my lips. "You know, you're a decent guy. In your own twisted way."

"Thank you." He presses a kiss against my forehead. "I hope you still feel that way after tomorrow night. I don't know what your brother has planned, but he's up to something."

I groan. While I know Ronan will be with other women at some point, and soon, I don't want to bear witness to it. "I should crash at Jean's."

He hums. "Probably a smart idea. So ... friends?"

"Yeah." I smile. "Yeah, friends."

He reaches over to rummage in my nightstand drawer where he tucked several condoms. Holding one up, he says, "Once more for shits and giggles, *friend?*"

"Fine, *friend*, but make it good."

"Don't I always?" He readies himself.

I straddle his hips and close my eyes, reveling in the feel of Ronan as he sinks deep inside me one last time.

27. Ronan

"I'm gonna miss you, man," Lopez slurs as he leans into me, struggling to reach my shoulder with his arm.

I hide my smirk behind a sip of beer. I don't fucking know him. I don't know any of these people who have packed into our place. I only came to Miami two weeks ago and I'm leaving for Alaska tomorrow.

This party is really for Connor, and he is having a great time, over in a corner, pretending to listen to some chick talk while he stares at her chest, a stupid drunk grin on his face. If I know Connor at all—which, oddly, I do—he's planning on motorboating those soon.

I wander to the kitchen to dump my empty and collect a few others while I'm there. Half an hour and a few trash bags and we'll have this place ready for the cleaner. If I could crash now, I would. Tomorrow's going to be a long-ass day of airports and uncomfortable seats.

Strong hands land on my shoulders. "My man! You havin' a good time?"

I chuckle. "You're gonna be a wreck on the plane."

"No shit. But did you see the tits on Mary?" Connor

glances over his shoulder at the girl, now huddled with her friends. "I think they're real."

"You'll find out soon enough." They're real. I pride myself on being able to tell the difference. That, and she already pressed them against me earlier tonight.

"Hey, has Ryan been home?"

"Came and left." She put on a cute little dress that made me want to drag her into her room and bend her over her bed. A pang of disappointment stirs in my stomach that I won't feel the inside of her again. She turned out to mean a lot more than I expected. Without Tasha's shadow hanging over me, I might have developed feelings for Ryan beyond friendship.

"She coming back tonight?"

I shrug. "She's going to hang out with that guy she met in the elevator. You tell me if your sister is gonna bang him or come home early." If this Kyle guy turns out to be a dick, I'll fly home from Alaska to kill him myself.

He checks his watch. "I warned her not to come home before three, if she does at all."

I frown. "Why?"

"Because I made plans for you." Connor nods toward the door, where an orange-and-gold lioness stands, painted from head to toe, naked except for a pair of heels, a thong, and pasties.

Becca spots me and her face breaks out in a wide smile.

My dick instantly swells. "You're kidding me." How did he manage this?

"Good surprise, right?"

"Yes," I agree.

"All right, then." Connor's hand tightens around the back of my neck. "Maybe now you'll stop fucking my sister."

My mouth drops open as I turn to meet his glare.

"You two *actually* thought I wouldn't figure it out? Dude, I can sniff out fuckery from a mile away."

Shit. "Sorry, man. I ... it just ..." I'm at a loss for words.

"Your dick just fell into her?"

Fuck. I set my beer down and take a step back, forcing my arms to my sides. "Just not the nose. I can't be on a plane for that many hours with a broken nose."

Connor's scowl fades with a chuckle. "Come on. I'm not gonna hit you."

"Oh, thank God." He may be easygoing, but those fists would do some real damage. "Why didn't you say something?"

"Because Ryan's been happier than I've seen her in a *long* time." A rare, serious look passes over his face. "And I knew you'd treat her well."

"Yeah, of course I would. I mean, I *did*."

"I know you did. Just do me one favor and don't tell her that I know."

I frown curiously. "Okay?"

"It's a fun game we have, where she thinks I'm a clueless idiot and I play into it." Connor slaps my back. "Okay, your lioness awaits. Merry Christmas. See you in the morning. Make sure you leave yourself enough time to wash off all that paint."

28. Ronan

"Cab's waiting downstairs," Connor hollers from the kitchen.

Stuffing my ruined sheets into a trash bag—there's no way that paint is coming out and I don't give a shit—I sling my duffel bag over my shoulder and walk out of my room.

Ryan is standing in her doorway in her crab shirt, half asleep, her hair mussed. "I just wanted to say bye." Her voice has that early-morning scratchiness I love.

"Hey, I was gonna text you." My unease stirs. "I didn't think you'd come home last night."

"It was late. Around four."

My shoulders sink with relief. Becca left before three, so Ryan wouldn't have seen or heard anything. Even though we ended things, I don't ever want to hurt her. "So ... last night with Kyle was good?"

Ryan dips her head and smiles shyly. "Yeah. He's a nice guy."

"A real prospect?"

"We'll see." She reaches up to smooth the wrinkles in my T-shirt. "You've gotta go."

"I do." Still can't believe I'm going along with Connor's

harebrained plan. "Keep in touch, and good luck with your exams."

"You kidding? I have my own condo now. I'm gonna ace them."

I hesitate and then, dropping my duffel bag, rope an arm around her shoulders and pull her to my chest. "Take care of yourself, and text me *anytime* you need to talk, or for whatever reason. I'm serious." I press my lips to the top of her head. Her hair smells like her strawberry shampoo.

"You too." Her arms tighten around my waist for a moment before she pulls away. "September, Connor?"

"Yup. No parties or boys while I'm away."

She rolls her eyes.

"We took out the trash. Maria will be here around ten to clean."

"Oh, by the way, I'm hiring someone to steam-clean the jizz out of the couch, and I'm sending you the bill."

"There's no jizz on the couch," Connor argues.

"You didn't see what I saw when I came home. *Believe me*, there's jizz on that couch," she counters with a shudder.

"Fine." Shoving the rest of a banana into his mouth, Connor strolls out the door, hollering, "See you in a few, baby sis."

I collect my bag. "Stay out of trouble."

Ryan folds her arms. "I'd say the same to you, but ..."

With a wink at her, I trail out the door after Connor.

He slings an arm around my shoulders. "Ready for the adventure of a lifetime?"

I cringe and shove him away. He's way too loud for this early in the morning. "Don't make me regret this."

PART TWO
AFTER ABBI

29. Ronan

One year later, Wolf Cove, Alaska

THE O-SHAPED SMOKE ring floats upward from my lips and dissipates in the frigid spring night, polluting the otherwise pristine northern air. Another bad habit to add to the lengthy list of stupid decisions I've accumulated over the years. I may as well set fire to my wallet for all the money I've handed over to good ol' Marlboro, and that says nothing about the health risks.

How many of these did I smoke last summer, sitting in this very spot by the water—with Connor, with Abbi, by myself—savoring all that this resort in the middle of nowhere has brought to my life?

Too many.

But it ends tonight.

I mash the last of the cigarette into a stone and tuck the extinguished butt into an empty beer bottle. If this weekend has proven anything to me, it's that I need to grow the fuck up. Make serious changes. I'm turning twenty-six in the fall and what have I accomplished in the last year besides getting over Tasha?

I snort.

Yeah, I got over my ex-girlfriend by falling for someone else. I knew from the day I laid eyes on her that Abbi Mitchell and I would never be anything more than what we are, but that didn't stop me. What was it, though, that hooked me so thoroughly? Her fiery red hair? Her innocent yet curious golden hazel eyes? The way she blushes as she tells you the dirty things she wants you to do?

All of it, probably.

She's perfect in every way. Any man would be lucky to have her heart.

And I just watched her—hell, stood beside her as her bridesman or man of honor or whatever my official title is—as she married fucking Henry Wolf. As much as I like to hate on the billionaire asshole, he's not all bad. Except for that nagging little reality—*he*'s the one Abbi loves. *He*'s the one who gets to wake up beside her every morning.

I stretch out on the shoreline, the cold from the sand seeping into my custom suit. I shouldn't be lying in dirt, given it's the most expensive thing I'll ever put on. It's not even a rental. Wolf paid for it. A gift to wear while I watched him claim the woman of my dreams.

Damn.

How long will it take to shake Abbi from my system?

How long before I'm not pining over one woman or another? Who knew I was such a romantic. Not me.

I need another smoke.

Digging into my pocket, I pull out my Marlboros. And groan into the empty carton. I guess that decides that. I'm turning over a new leaf in three ... two ...

No more cancer sticks.

Lay off the booze.

And stop thinking with my dick, which has brought me as much heartache as it has pleasure.

In fact, no more women, period.

"You dead, man?" Connor's booming voice echoes over the silent lake.

The guy can't handle being away from me for more than an hour. "No, but you will be once Wolf sees that picture with Violet, you dumb fuck." The wedding photographer is going to have a lot of explaining to do with those after-party pics in the staff mess hall.

"As if. We were goofing around. She didn't touch a drop of alcohol. Where is the little Wolf, anyway?"

"In her room with her grandparents, where any *fifteen-year-old* belongs." I walked Wolf's daughter back and then headed here for some peace and quiet while questioning my sad existence.

"It's *so cold*!" a female whines.

It's then that I turn to regard Connor and note the two women huddled against him, one on each arm. Staffers for this coming season, still in uniform. I recognize them. They were servers tonight, carrying out plate after plate of everything from Alaskan snow crab to filet mignon—no expense spared for this reception. Young, but not too young. Beautiful ... but they all are. Wolf Hotels has clear hiring criteria and somehow gets away with it time and time again.

"It's Alaska." I pull myself to my feet. "Shocked it's not snowing." The guys from the outdoor crew said there were still patches in the woods.

"Fresh one for ya. Cheers, mate." Connor sheds the girls to meet me halfway and hand me a beer, his blue gaze on the darkness and water beyond. "Being here brings back memories, huh?"

"Does it ever." The best summer of my life. I twist off the cap.

"Regret not coming back this year?" he asks through a sip.

When the offer came through to work another season up here, we both sat on it for weeks, undecided. In the end, staying in Miami seemed like the better choice.

"Nah. Those days are done." As much as I'd kill to go back to them. "It's time to move on."

Connor peers over his shoulders at the two girls. "Bella and Jenny are in cabin seven. Remember that one?"

I smirk. "Of course. That was Red's." A lot went down in there, but the most memorable night was the one where I held Abbi in my arms as she cried over the guy she ended up marrying.

"We're going there now," the girl on the left—a ginger, go figure—says with a shiver, her arms curled around her chest. "You guys coming?"

"Oh, I'm *definitely coming*." Connor grins, earning their giggles and my eye roll.

How he gets away with saying shit like that and still ending up balls deep by the end of the night is beyond me.

"Ronan? You gonna quit sulking out here and head back with us?" Connor pauses, lifting an eyebrow. We've never talked about what went on with Abbi or where my head's at with this whole wedding, but Connor is not nearly as dense as he pretends to be. "For old time's sake?"

I sigh heavily. "Yeah, fuck, why not. One last kick at the can."

I'll change my ways starting tomorrow.

30. Sloane

M*ermaid Beach, Florida*

"B*EGIN by taking cleansing breaths to shake off the day's
stresses and be truly present for these next ten minutes—*"

A skill saw whirrs, cutting off my online yoga instructor's
soothing voice. I grind my teeth. Will the construction ever
end? They've been building that bloody hotel for years. At
least it's not the constant hammering today. I can't sit out here
and enjoy the gulf breeze on those days.

"*Now let's roll our body up and head into our downward
facing—*"

"I'll park wherever the hell I want. I live here too!" Cody's
raised voice carries out an open window a moment before our
front door slams.

So much for shaking off the day's stresses. With a heavy
groan of defeat, I flop backward onto my yoga mat and wait for
my fiancé to march out here and complain about our tenant.
Again.

The late-afternoon sun is warm, the palm trees providing

no more than dappled shade over the white sand. The summer's unbearably humid heat is around the corner, so I'll enjoy this while I can as I study my little beach house.

I owe it all to my grandmother, Ruby Parker, affectionately known to all as Gigi. She bought this home and the land it's on forty years ago when she moved back to Florida from O'ahu, freshly divorced and with a young daughter—my mother—in tow. Back when Mermaid Beach was nothing more than a quaint fishing community.

When Gigi signed the property over to me eight months ago and moved into Palm Oaks, a home for the elderly twenty minutes away, she warned me not to skip a year of maintenance or this place would start fading away like a derelict shack and, as usual, she was right. The sun and salty sea air from the Gulf have done a number, washing out the turquoise siding and leaving the white porch floor raw in patches. At least the silver metal roof I installed last fall looks new.

"Frank's being a prick again!" The back door swings open and slaps shut as Cody plows through, Gatorade in hand, his cut arms on display in a tank top. He's fresh from the gym and still sweaty.

"What now?"

"I parked my truck like I always do, and he told me to move it."

"You mean, you backed up to his porch so he can barely squeeze out his front door?" Frank has lived in a trailer on our property for fifteen years, since Gigi hired him to help run the Sea Witch, a coffee and rentals shop on the beach. I arch a judgment-laden eyebrow at Cody. "I told you to stop doing that."

"I'm not parking near the coop. The birds shit on my hood!"

"They shit on your hood, anyway."

"Yeah, 'cause Frank trained them to do it."

I roll my eyes. "How has Frank trained a bunch of chickens, whose brains are literally the size of marbles?" Though it's hard to ignore the fact that they seem to target Cody's fire-engine-red Dodge Ram while Gigi's old Jeep Cherokee, painted the color of a clear summer sky, remains unscathed.

Cody trots down the eight steps to the sand. "I don't know, but I'm tellin' ya, I've had enough of him."

"That's too bad for you because Frank's not going anywhere." We see each other every day. We celebrate holidays together. He's family to me.

"Unless he decides to leave." Cody's voice rings with challenge.

Tension cords my muscles. I know where this is heading if I push it—a huge fight about Cody doing his damnedest to make Frank feel unwelcome. I don't have the energy for that battle today, so I steer the conversation to a safer topic. "We need to paint the house before high season. I figure between the three of us, we can have the whole place done in no time."

"That's actually what I want to talk to you about." He bends over to press a kiss against my lips before pushing his hand through chestnut-brown hair. His thick mane was the first thing I noticed about him, followed quickly by his bright crystal blue eyes and flirtatious smile.

"Painting the house?" I say doubtfully. Cody is a lot of things—charming, spirited, attention-grabbing gorgeous—but eager to do physical labor is not how I would describe him.

"No. About *selling* it."

My jaw hangs. "Did someone drop a weight on your head at the gym?" Gigi signed the beach house over to me so I could call it my own, not so I could cash in.

He crouches beside me, his face earnest as his palm smooths over my bare thigh. "Come on, babe, you've been complaining nonstop about that hotel." He gestures behind me to where it looms in the near distance. "It's not even open yet. Imagine how much worse it's gonna be? How much busier? You won't be able to sit out here anymore without being gawked at by strangers on the beach. It's not gonna be the same quiet place anymore."

My stomach knots as he voices my ongoing worries. We've been fighting the powers that be since the first notice went up on the vacant lot five years ago but have gotten nowhere, evidenced by the modern behemoth that now waits to house wealthy tourists.

Cody peers at me. "Look, I really didn't want to say anything, but you haven't been yourself lately and people are noticing."

"People?" I frown as his words prick my pride. "What people?" Who's been talking about me?

"Just ... *people*, you know. About how this whole thing has taken a toll on you, made you bitter."

I roll my eyes. "Let me guess—your mother." Who despises me and has never hidden her feelings. I'm the one who stole her precious baby away.

"Things haven't been the same for months. I'm talking about between *us*. Tell me you haven't noticed it."

"I ... guess?" We've definitely been fighting more—about work, about Frank, about money. About everything, it seems. "I don't know why."

"I chalked it up to Gigi leaving and the pressure you're under with the business, plus the hotel. But I'm not gonna lie—it's been hard on me. I don't want to start regretting giving you that ring—"

I flinch.

"Oh no, don't worry, babe, I don't!" he rushes to say. "But I don't want to see us lose what we have." He cups my cheek, adding softly, "Do you?"

"*Of course* not." I smooth my thumb over the diamond solitaire on my ring finger, remembering the night Cody proposed, a day after Gigi moved out.

"Okay. So, then ... stop being so stubborn. Let's find a new place for the two of us to start our lives together. This isn't my house. It's not even yours."

I inhale deeply. Is he right? Am I being stubborn? My gaze wanders to the little Florida cottage behind us. I was born here, when my mom went into labor during a hurricane and couldn't get to a hospital in time. Twelve years later, my mother died here. This is where I'm happiest, listening to the waves lap and inhaling the salty air. Gigi always jokes that she raised a mermaid masquerading as a human.

Indignation swells in me. No ... Cody's not right. This *is* *my* house. But I can see his point, that it's not his.

Unless I make it so.

I've been thinking about this lately. Gigi will skin me alive for it, I'm sure, seeing as she was adamant everything be signed over in my name, so I owned it outright. But Cody and I are getting married. He's going to be my husband. We're going to share our lives and everything that comes along with that.

I open my mouth, ready to suggest adding his name to the deed after we're married, when he digs a folded paper out of his back pocket and holds it out for me.

I frown. "What's this?"

"Remember that hotel lawyer who came by here a few weeks ago?"

"The one I threatened?" That slimeball also handed me a piece of paper, a bid to buy my property that I ripped up into no fewer than twenty pieces without reading.

"He came by the Sea Witch a few days later."

Unease slips down my spine. I guess it wouldn't take more than a few questions around town to figure out where else to find me. Mermaid Beach is growing, but it's still small and we've been here a long time. "You told him to fuck off, right?"

"He came to talk to me."

"*You?* Why?"

"I guess he thought I'd be less emotional, and he wanted to make sure we saw what he was offering." Cody shrugs in that one-shouldered way that says he's leaving details out.

"*And*?"

"And I figured why not see what I could get out of him. So, I named a whole bunch of demands. You know, more money, a closing date in the offseason."

Anger prickles my skin. Cody keeps saying "we" and "us" as if he has a say in what I do with *my* house.

"I even asked for lifetime passes to the hotel. And guess what? I got it all for us! Not the passes," he quickly adds, "but an annual golf membership and a week's stay in one of their penthouse suites. We could go there for our honeymoon."

I stare at Cody with incredulity, trying to process what he's saying, making sure I'm hearing correctly. This isn't the first time he's floated the idea of selling. He used to hint casually, wondering how much *we* could get for this little cottage by the sea. Then his hints grew into late-night post-coital ponderings, our naked bodies sweaty and tangled up in each other, about what we'd do if someone handed us a million dollars. In reality, I could get far more than that. My bramble of land stretches all the way back to where the road curves inland. It's prime real estate in a thirsty market.

But this behind-my-back action? This is brazen and a new side of Cody, one I don't like.

"So, you negotiated to sell *my* house with this sleazy lawyer after I've made it crystal clear *how many times* that I am not selling this property to Wolf Hotels or any other money-hungry asshole?" I say slowly, icily.

"You're being selfish! And, well ..." He falters. "What about what *I* want?"

"What exactly do *you* want?" Because my cynical side is beginning to spin dark theories.

"How about living in a house we both own!" He throws his hands in the air, sloshing Gatorade.

"We can't buy another place like *this*." These little beach-side homes are all but gone, absorbed by developers building four-story monstrosities.

"It doesn't have to be like this. There are tons of great places for half the price a few blocks inland."

"*In*land!" I spit the word with disgust. Why would I ever trade my view of the ocean every morning for watching neighbors pushing lawn mowers?

"Come on, would you read the deal before you flip out?" With one of his crooked smiles that normally wins me over no matter how angry I am, he unfolds the page and thrusts it in front of my face. "Look at how many digits there are! And we won't have to leave here until the fall so we can get married out on the beach like we planned and take our time finding another place."

"And you don't think Wolf would just tear this place down?"

"So what? We can have something ten times nicer! Plus, we can pay off all our debts."

"I don't have any debts."

But he goes on like I haven't spoken. "And buy that cabin cruiser we've always talked about getting. And we could get my mom a new trailer ..."

Cody's words fade as his intentions scream to me, and seemingly obscure details click into place—about the timing of his proposal and his behaviors since. Frank had tried to warn me. Small, subtle comments that made me lash out at him. But he was right! How did I not see this before?

"Babe? Did you hear me?"

"I am such a sucker," I whisper, a sheen of tears coating my eyes as I give my engagement ring a tug, letting it drop to the sand.

31. Ronan

O*ne year later, Miami*

TASHA

> Hey … I've been thinking about you a lot
> lately. I'm going to be in Miami this weekend.
> If you're around, I'd love to hook up. I fly in on
> Thursday night.

I READ over the text three times to make sure I'm not hallucinating. Two years ago, I prayed for these words, but I never expected to see them.

Connor pauses mid beach chair setup to study my deep frown. "Why do you look like our cat just died?"

"We don't have a cat."

"We *could* have a cat. I'd name it Ronaldo."

I ignore his dumbassery and hold up my phone. "The ex."

Abandoning the beach chair, he wanders over to read the message. "Damn. *The ex* ex?"

"Tash. Yeah." Not that Connor and I have deep heart-to-hearts, but Tasha's the only one I've ever mentioned besides Abbi, and I've only mentioned her once or twice.

He brushes a bead of sweat off his brow. It's early morning and already sweltering. "How long has it been?"

"Since I've heard from her directly? Two years." Before I transferred jobs and moved to Miami. Not a call, not a text. But my little sister ran into her at the bar last fall in Indianapolis. The way Britt tells it, Tasha interrogated her about all things *me*—what I've been up to, if I'm dating anyone, how I ended up in my billionaire boss's wedding party. She seemed especially curious about that one.

Connor shifts back to setting up the beach for hotel patrons—that I was helping with until this little bomb went off in my pocket. "Hookup, huh?" He spares me a smirk. "You know what that means, right?"

I shrug. "That she's gonna be in Miami and she knows I'm here?" Who does Tasha know in this city? No one I'm aware of and we dated for four years. I knew *all* her friends back then.

"Nah, man. That there is an 'I want to get back together' text." Connor points at my phone to emphasize his point.

"That's not it." But I scan it again. Is it? After all this time?

"Next thing you know, she'll be asking to stay with us because Miami's *too expensive*." He jams the end of the umbrella anchor into the sand and screws the top. "And you'll say, 'Sure! We have an extra bedroom now that Ryan is living with Kyle,' and then, whoops, the ex is riding your dick at dawn like the cavalry charging in for the kill."

"Shut the fuck up." I burst out laughing. But inside, my nerves churn. What would it be like to see Tasha again? Would I want something to happen? I'm in a good place in my life—*not* pining over her and reluctantly accepting that I'll never have Abbi again.

"Then again, maybe she can fix your dick, seeing as it's been broken since Red's wedding."

Before I can offer a retort, my radio crackles. "Ronan, you on the beach?" Charlie's brusque voice calls out.

"Yeah, boss. What's up?" I respond into the receiver.

"You're wanted in the conference center. Pacific Room, stat."

I frown at Connor, who matches my confusion. "What for?" That's *inside* the hotel. Not a part of our crew's jurisdiction.

"Don't question me and get the fuck over there now!" Charlie barks.

I roll my eyes. The outdoor crew supervisor is an asshole to me in front of others, but we get along well behind closed doors. I can't tell if it's because he likes me or because I'm tight with the big boss's wife, but ever since the wedding, he's been giving me extra responsibility. Six months ago, he added the label "assistant supervisor" to my job description and bumped my pay. I never asked for any of it. "On my way."

"See? That's why you don't become the supe's bitch." Connor pops open the umbrella and moves onto the next one.

"I'll send Dean over to help you finish."

"Don't bother. I got it handled." His gaze snags on a pair of blonds in string bikinis strolling the shoreline. All it takes is a half wave from him and they're veering this way, flipping hair over their shoulders.

Connor ends every work day with at least a half dozen numbers in his pocket. He can never remember which number belongs to which face. It's always fun to watch him make plans and wait patiently to see who shows up.

"As long as you get this done before the guests complain." I can see them hovering around the poolside desk, waiting for the clock to strike beach time.

"Aye-aye, boss," he mocks, saluting me. Technically, Connor reports to me now, not that it's changed our dynamic at all. But he busts my balls about it every day.

I take one last look at the unexpected message on my

screen and then tuck my phone into my pocket, leaving Tasha on *Read*. Savage, I know, but she did break my heart.

————

"You've gotta be kidding me," I call out, a rare wide grin stretching across my face as I spot the female form ahead, her back to me. I could recognize Abbi's fiery red hair from anywhere.

She spins around at the sound of my voice and her face lights up. "Surprise!"

My feet falter. I haven't seen Abbi since the wedding and definitely not since she called to tell me she was pregnant.

"Wild, huh?" With a nervous giggle, she smooths her manicured hands over her emerald-green sundress—and her swollen belly—and waits for me to close the distance.

Fuck, she's even more beautiful.

Swallowing against the unwelcome burn of jealousy, my pace speeds up, my work boots clomping along the marble floor. The cleaning team will curse me for the trail of dusty prints I'm leaving.

Scooping Abbi up in my arms, I lift her off the ground in a fierce hug, inhaling the floral scent of her hair. I don't care if this is highly inappropriate. Having her pressed against my body again feels like breathing in air after being buried alive.

"Stop! You're going to hurt yourself." But her arms tighten around my neck, returning the affection.

"Shut up. You're all baby." I wait a beat and add in a low voice so no passersby will hear. "And boobs. *Damn*, Red." They were handfuls before ... and I would know.

Wolf's a lucky fucker.

Her cheeks burn as I set her back down. "Yeah, this whole pregnancy has been ... interesting."

I grin, unable to temper this temporary high I feel every time I'm near her. "How much longer?"

Abbi's hands are on her belly again. "She comes in four months."

"*She?*" My head tips back with a deep bellow of laughter. "That'll make it *three* females under his roof. Amazing."

She giggles. "I know, right? Henry's already so overprotective with Violet. I think I saw a gray hair the other day."

"Good. I hope you have five more girls. It'll serve him right." I lean against the wall and fold my arms, drawing her hazel eyes to my sleeve of tattoos, my arms, my chest. They stall on my dark hair, the ends bleached brown from long days in the sun. She reaches up to toy with a strand. "You're growing it out."

"Yeah. I needed a change." I forgot how wavy it can get. The back tickles my neck.

A memory flashes briefly through my mind—Abbi with her hands on my buzzed head, her body writhing, while my face was buried between her legs—and I have to shove it out before my dick reacts.

She swallows hard, as if she can see my depraved thoughts. "You look good."

"I *feel* good." I was a bear for the first few weeks after quitting cigarettes and booze cold turkey, so much so that Connor bought a carton of Marlboros and pleaded with me to give up. But the gym has helped. I've added thirty pounds of muscle and can jog without feeling like I'm going to leave my lungs on the pavement.

A staffer passes, her curious gaze on us. Thankfully, it's quiet in here otherwise.

"So, what are you doing in Miami? And up so early?" I ask.

"I've got a few Farm Girl things to do." Abbi shrugs, as if it's no big deal that the little soap company she started in her Pennsylvania barn at, like, age twelve is now taking off across the country, with enough contracts that she has a full-time staff of twenty and is opening a second production location on the West Coast. "It was too late to call you when we came in last night, but I wanted to catch you before you spoke to Henry."

"Wolf's here?"

"Yeah, in there." She points to the heavy wooden doors of the Pacific, one ajar.

I frown. "I have a meeting with *him*?"

She collects my calloused hands in hers. "Yes, and he has a proposition for you. I know it's going to sound crazy at first, but Ronan? *Please* listen to him?" She pleads with her gaze.

"Is this going to be like the last proposition he had for me? Because *you know* I'll say yes." That night in Alaska will live rent-free in my mind for the rest of my life and then haunt me in the hereafter. In fact, I could die right here and be satisfied.

Abbi bites her bottom lip to hide her grin as she tightens her grip. "No, it's not *that*. But it's a great opportunity and you would be perfect for it." Her chest lifts with a deep inhale. "And you deserve it. So, please, say yes?" That last part is delivered softly.

"Well, now I'm intrigued."

A throat-clearing pulls our attention to the gaping door and the billionaire luxury hotel owner looming, an annoyed look painted across his face.

"You better go. He doesn't like to wait." Abbi pulls me in for another hug and a kiss on my cheek.

I think it's more about him not liking how close his wife and I are, but I can't help myself, holding her a few extra beats before releasing her.

"Call me later!" She blows a kiss at her husband, whose annoyance breaks instantly with a warm smile for her, his eyes shifting briefly to her belly.

Abbi strolls down the hall, her sandals slapping the floor, the material of her dress swaying with her hips.

Both of us stare at her for far too long.

"Get in here before I change my mind," Wolf barks before disappearing into the room.

Release Me

"I can barely contain my excitement." I drag my boots all the way.

32. Ronan

"This is a fucking joke, right?" I check around for hidden cameras.

Henry's smarmy smile says he's enjoying every second of my confusion. "If there's one thing I would never joke about, it's a business decision."

"And you can't think of a single other shoulder to tap besides mine? *Really*?"

The boardroom leather chair creaks as he stands, relieving it of his weight. "I can think of several." He wanders over to peer out the window, his hands tucked into his pockets. It's rare to not see him in a suit, but today he's dressed down in a golf shirt and plain black pants. Still looks like he bleeds hundred-dollar bills. "So? Are you interested?"

I stall on an answer. I'm shocked is what I am. "Why me?"

Wolf pivots, setting his hands on the back of another chair, his ice-blue eyes settled on me. I can't argue that I don't see the appeal. The guy won every lottery at birth, including the physical genes. If my proclivities leaned that way, I'm sure I'd be eager to impress him. "Because you've earned my trust, and I trust *very* few people."

"I'm ... honored?" What else do I say? "But how does that translate into running a hotel for you?"

His chuckle is dark. "Don't get ahead of yourself. Not *running* the hotel. You'd report to the general manager."

"But the grounds and facilities *and* admin managers would all report to *me*."

"Yes."

I sink my teeth into my bottom lip as I consider this. "*Why me?*"

"You have a degree in business administration and management from Indianapolis, don't you?"

"It's a piece of paper."

"Graduated near the top of your class too," he goes on as if I hadn't spoken. "And you were hired as a staff coordinator at Wolf there—"

"Before I begged them to move me outside because I hate being stuck behind a desk."

"This will be nothing like that, I can promise you." He chuckles. "I have to say, I've never had anyone try to talk their way *out* of a huge promotion."

This isn't a promotion. This is a joke. "I have no experience with this type of role," I say instead.

"True," he concedes. "But in the last year, your supervisor has been giving you more responsibility, has he not?"

"He's definitely unloaded his job responsibilities onto me, if that's what you mean."

"Because I asked him to."

My eyebrows arch. "That was coming from *you?*"

"It sure as hell wasn't coming from Charlie. He's still paranoid we're replacing him." Henry pauses. "But he's been impressed. Says you're not nearly as stupid or lazy as he assumed."

I snort.

Wolf settles into the chair he was leaning on. "If you

165

haven't figured it out yet, I make a lot of my decisions based on my gut, and it has rarely steered me wrong."

"Whatever you base it on, you seem to be winning at life," I agree begrudgingly. The guy has more money than he knows what to do with.

"My gut says you are capable of a hell of a lot more than popping umbrellas and stacking firewood. In the last two years, you have proven your loyalty—"

"To your wife, not you," I cut in.

His jaw clenches. "Don't think for one second that I'm clueless about your feelings for Abbi. Now shut the fuck up and listen."

After a beat, I purse my lips and nod.

Taking a deep breath, he continues, "You've proven your loyalty to my company and to those I would kill for. You keep your mouth shut when you could be cashing in on the things you know. You've got solid instincts. From what Abbi says, you've been trying to turn your life around, make better choices. You're not fucking every female that walks across your path."

Hey, Pot. I bite down on my tongue.

"You keep calm and pragmatic in the face of pressure." He rubs a hand across the back of his neck, as if uncomfortable. "You crawled into a collapsed mine shaft to get me out. I literally owe you my life."

My chest rises on an inhale, but I have no answer. Again, that was for Abbi.

"What do you know about Mermaid Beach?" he asks, swinging our discomfort to safer waters.

"There aren't actually mermaids there?" I flash a crooked smile before I shift into semiserious mode. "It's an up-and-coming area on the north side of the Gulf of Mexico." I've overheard more than one person talking about getaways there lately.

"It's exploding. This location is primed to become one of

our most successful." He tosses a travel magazine across the table toward me, to where a modern white Wolf Hotel graces the cover—a luxury resort on the Emerald Coast. "My father saw the potential decades ago when he bought that land. He knew the area would draw tourism one day, and here we are. They're calling it the Hamptons of the South. The sand is made of white quartz crystal from the Appalachian Mountains, carried down by rivers and bleached by the sun. It looks and feels like sugar. I've never seen anything like it anywhere else in the world." He hesitates. "This was William Wolf's baby, and I'm determined to make sure it exceeds expectations."

I don't know much about Henry's father except what I've heard from Abbi. It sounds like their relationship was complicated, but Henry obviously respected him greatly. "Which is why, again, I'm wondering how your gut says a guy from your outdoor crew is the right call. I'm a little worried. Should I call Abbi in here?"

He smirks. "I thought you'd be more excited."

"Did you, actually?" I counter dryly.

"Why does everything with you feel like a test? I'm seconds from pulling this offer."

"Okay, okay," I hold up my hands in surrender. "Say for a second I was mildly intrigued. What if I go out there and it doesn't work? What if I hate it? What if I fuck it up?"

"You have a team of experienced managers who know how to do their jobs, and you have Belinda to help you get a handle on things. I'm sure you remember her," he adds.

"Vaguely," I lie. "Is she on board with this?" With having a supremely underqualified guy run all the facilities, one she got caught on a security camera fucking two summers ago?

"Of course she is," he retorts without missing a beat, his lie delivered as smoothly as mine. "Give it six months. If you hate it or still feel like you're not the right person, you can demote yourself and go back to doing grunt work. Here is your contract, which includes compensation and perks." He slides a sheet across the table with his index finger.

I scan the page.

And struggle to keep my calm. "That's ... enticing."

"I thought it would be." He pauses. "So, is that a yes?"

"*Wait*, you want an answer right *now*?"

"Before I leave this room in ..." He glances at his gold watch. "Four minutes. We've moved up the start dates for the last wave of hires to next week. I need you in your new office by Thursday."

"Fuck, man! I knew you were impatient, but that's in, like, *three days*." Today is Monday, which means I'd be leaving Miami on *Wednesday*. "That doesn't give me any time to sort out my shit."

"And what *shit* do you need to get sorted, Ronan? Rent for the condo you share?" He leans back in his chair, a triumphant expression on his face as if he's already won. The truth is, he probably has. I don't have anything tying me down here. This new salary is more than enough to cover my rent—which is higher now with Ryan moved out—*and* wipe out my student loans, forget the perks of a company vehicle and paid accommodations.

I'd only be committing myself for six months.

Still ... that's a long time in a place where I don't know anyone, while I prove to this arrogant prick that his gut isn't always right.

A thought strikes me. "Hiring decisions are mine?"

"Theoretically, yes. A lot of the staff is already in place. We still need to fill seasonal roles, which we'll do at this Friday's job fair. Your managers will take care of that, but you'll oversee final decisions."

"So I could bring in my own people?"

"*You* have people?" he asks smugly.

I grin. "One extremely annoying person."

Henry's lips twist with his curse. "Let me guess ..."

"Hey, you're asking me to pick up my life in three days, and I don't know a soul there besides Belinda, and we both know exactly how that's going to go." After that fateful day, she avoided Connor and me like we were carrying no less than ten communicable diseases. "Besides, Con and I are a package deal." We've been attached at the hip since the day I stepped off the plane two years ago. Something tells me he will riot if I don't negotiate on his behalf.

"That'll leave Charles two bodies short," Henry says after a moment.

"You and I both know he can replace us like that." I snap my fingers.

With a heavy sigh, he concedes. "If you want to bring your man-child with you, that's your call." He leans in, suddenly serious. "But this is not Wolf Cove. I can't have my director of operations fucking every staff member there."

"It would only be the female staff." The flat look I get back has me retreating. "Those days are done, I promise you." I'm not about to admit that I haven't had sex since New Year's Eve and even that interaction left me feeling hollow.

"Yes, Abbi alluded to that." He hesitates. "You'll be senior management, and Wolf Hotels has strict policies in place about managers engaging in intimate relationships with their subordinates ..."

His words drown out with my bark of laughter.

A ghost of a smile grazes his lips. "Fair enough, but the policy is real, even if I didn't follow it."

"Can I hire my own assistant?"

"*No*. Belinda has taken care of that, and *he* is getting your office ready as we speak."

"Probably wise." When Henry replaced Abbi, it was with Miles—a gangly, nervous guy who Abbi never has to be jealous of.

"Also, the neighbor is off-limits."

I frown. "The *hotel's* neighbor?"

"The owner of the property beside us, yes. They've caused me plenty of legal issues and I'm dealing with them accordingly."

"That sounds ominous."

"They picked the fight. And they'll end up regretting it, believe me. Now, unless there's something else, sign that and get your ass to admin." Henry Wolf doesn't wait for my answer, sliding out of his chair and strolling out of the Pacific Room without another backward glance.

33. Ronan

"Come on, man. It's been ten hours. Can we switch it up?" We left Miami before sunrise with our belongings stuffed in the back seat, and I've been subjected to Connor's never-ending country music playlist the entire ride.

"You can listen to whatever you want when you're the one driving."

I throw my hands up in the air. "I said I'd drive!"

"Yeah, but no one else handles sweet Darla." He smooths his hands over the steering wheel of his fully loaded, limited edition red Bronco.

"Am I gonna find you with your dick jammed into the fuel hole one day?"

"It's too small for me," he retorts, as if the thought has already crossed his mind.

I shake my head. "If you paid half as much attention to the women you hook up with as you do this thing ..." Connor drove *Darla* off the lot four months ago and has spent every day fawning over her since, polishing rims and wiping off dust that dares to settle.

"I must be doing something right 'cause the ladies keep coming back." He winks at the elderly toll booth operator as he hands her four bucks, earning her cackle. Cranking the volume up as he passes through the gate, he shouts, "Quit bitching, boss! We're almost there!"

"Stop calling me that." My stomach flips with excitement as we head for the three-and-a-half-mile bridge that connects the peninsula to the mainland.

Henry Wolf wasn't exaggerating when he said he wanted me at Mermaid Beach in three days. Within an hour of me accepting the position, I was signing my life away in front of an HR manager and choosing my company car. The deal included a one-way plane ticket, but I decided to keep Connor company on the ride here.

A decision I'm regretting now that my eardrums are threatening to bleed.

But at least the view is spectacular. I open my window and revel in the cooler temps. I won't let it fool me, though—if the last two days of research taught me anything, it's that I'll be spending my days drenched in sweat soon enough.

Connor's eyes sparkle as we regard the deep blue water on both sides of the two-lane passage ahead, speckled with fishing boats, pontoons, and a few Jet Skis. Neither of us grew up on the coast, so the sea and palm trees haven't lost their luster for us yet. "Something tells me we're in for another adventure."

"We're in for something, all right."

A gut full of shame when Abbi appreciates just how wrong she and Henry are about my potential.

———

"Ronan. *Dude.* Where the fuck are we?" Connor hasn't stopped cursing since he turned onto the Coastal Highway—named as such, even though it's a two-lane road with a speed limit of thirty-five miles and a pedestrian crosswalk every time I blink.

Along most of the drag are luxury beach houses. They go

on forever, broken up by a restaurant here and a bar there, and on the other side of them are miles upon miles of white sand beach and water that earns its emerald-green description with nothing more than a glance.

"Turn right up ahead," I instruct, pointing at the street that leads into a twelve-foot-tall metal gate.

He punches in the code and the gate glides open without a sound.

I feed Connor directions, and he follows them while humming to the music, winding Darla through the community streets until we reach the house wearing the right number on its wall.

I double check the address. Is Wolf for fucking real? *This* is part of my compensation package?

"Well, *damn*." Connor eases his driver door shut. "This whole thing is *ours*?"

"No, it's mine. You're squatting, remember?" I'm struggling to play it cool as I check the number in the email for the third time. I did not expect beachfront and I sure as hell wasn't expecting this four-story behemoth. There must be an error. I keep telling myself this as I make my way to the ornate solid wood front door to punch in the code. It works. This is definitely our place.

I lose my cool in the entryway. "Holy shit."

"There's an elevator!" Connor echoes my inner thoughts as he jabs at the button and a door opens instantly. He files in. "All aboard!"

"I'll meet you at the top." Because I need a moment alone to digest Henry's generosity and find the trap hidden within.

I take the stairs, sizing up the suites of lavish furnishings and ocean-view balconies off the back, until I reach the kitchen and living area on the third floor. This feels like something Henry himself would stay in, with all its French doors and high-end appliances and designer décor. It's way too rich for my blue-collar blood.

"Ronan! Get up here!" Connor's voice booms from some-where above.

I take the set of stairs leading up two more flights and find him standing in the middle of a rooftop deck. "Is this for fucking real?"

"I keep asking myself that. Seems like it." I rest my elbows on the rail balcony and take in the five-million-dollar panoramic view of emerald waters and white sand as far as the eye can see in both directions. Below is our private pool.

We have a fucking private pool because having the ocean *right there* isn't enough.

Connor's penetrating gaze is on me.

This is going to be good. "Yes?"

"Do you top or bottom with him?" he blurts.

I laugh. *"What?"*

"Come on, man. You're practically a monk, turning down women left and right. And then you go into a room with Wolf and come out with this huge promotion? Might I remind you that you were a crew grunt days ago."

"Trust me, I don't need reminding."

"So then, what gives? Because I don't see him doling out special perks to me and I dragged my ass into that cave just as much as you did."

"You're here, aren't you?"

"Because of *you*, not him. He doesn't even like you. So, what is it? You got dirt on him? You blackmailing him?"

"Shut up, man. As if I'd ever." I glare at my friend for suggesting it. Connor has no idea what went on that night in Alaska between me, Abbi, and Henry, and he never will. That's no one's business.

But the wheels in my brain are churning. Is this Abbi's doing? No hotel operations director gets a perks package like this. A VP, maybe ... but a guy helping run one hotel? Abso-lutely not. I dig out my phone.

"What are you doing?" Connor's voice is laced with accusation.

"Calling Red. Either this is a mistake or her husband is playing some sort of game." He's right—Henry has never liked me. He's probably setting me up to fail so he has an excuse to fire me once and for all and not feel any guilt over it. If a guy like that is swayed by guilt.

"Are you nuts?" Connor grabs my phone out of my hand. "You're not saying a fucking thing! We are gonna live here like two Cinderellas, and you're gonna pretend like you can do that job until you screw it all up."

I snort. "Thanks for the vote of confidence."

"You're welcome. What are friends for?" He slaps my phone into my palm. "Do you think they stocked the place?"

"Who's 'they'? The royal 'they'? Doubt it," I say but he's already ambling back inside, surely heading for the fridge.

With a sigh, I check my texts. A congratulatory one from Abbi full of champagne and fireworks emojis, and one each from my mother and Britt, with ten questions apiece.

And the one from Tasha that I've read no fewer than twenty times but never answered.

I figured three days and a spontaneous move across the state later, I would have already forgotten about it, but here I am, considering what to say.

Fuck it. It's not like I'm still in love with her. Time fixed that. Time and Abbi—another woman I can't have.

> Hey, long time no hear. Enjoy your trip to Miami. I just moved to Mermaid Beach. Got a big promotion.

I send it before I can waste another second dwelling on my response. Why I felt the overwhelming urge to add that last part, I don't know. Maybe because when Tasha and I broke up, she said I wasn't going anywhere and fast.

Heavy footfalls pound up the stairs. "Nothing in there, and I need chow."

As much as I don't want to get back in a car, I'm curious to see what this town has to offer. "Yeah, fine. But I need to hit a coffee shop first." I gave up a lot of vices, but caffeine was not one of them. The pressure behind my eyes warns me I better get my fix soon.

"They'll have coffee wherever we go to eat."

"No, they'll have swamp water."

"Dang, you're whiny today. But fuck, fine."

I pause to admire the view one last time.

"Pretty sweet, huh?"

"I *do* feel like Cinderella."

Connor snorts. "Yeah, if Cinderella sucked her fairy godmother's dick."

34. Sloane

"New girl's been here two weeks and still doesn't know how to clean the machines!" Frank hollers, his gruff voice thick with annoyance.

I scroll through new bookings, the coastal radio tuned to a comforting mainstream pop station playing in the background. "Aren't you the one who trained her?"

"Yeah, and I don't have time to run a remedial program." He turns his broad frame sideways to move through the narrow doorway that connects the Sea Witch's café to the rentals side, cash bag in his meaty grip. "Business is definitely picking up."

"Yup. Ten new bookings came in this afternoon." I tap my computer screen to show him the reservations for the floating tiki bar cruises. We have three custom chartered boats available, and they're fully booked for Memorial Day weekend. "And we're already getting beach chair and umbrella bookings well into next month." For all the people who lug their own equipment in, there are still plenty who'd rather pay fifty bucks and not deal with the hassle.

Frank's hulking form leans over my shoulder to read the

screen. He nods with approval. "We're gonna be begging for the offseason by June."

"Don't I know it." The warmer weather is already luring visitors to our white sugar sands and idyllic coastal vibe. Once school lets out? Mermaid Beach will explode with families. They'll jam the roads with their cars and golf carts, create hour-long waits at restaurants, and fill the hotel and rental beach houses. Every local business will work themselves to the bone while earning enough to stay afloat for the remainder of the year.

"When are Skye and Rebel comin' in?" Frank asks.

"Tomorrow night." It's the third season working here for the two college girls from Cincinnati. They'll arrive in Mermaid Beach with their car loaded the day after they write their last exam.

"Good, 'cause I'm getting sick of making lattes."

"But you're so good at it!" I grin at his retreating back. At six five, wearing a perpetual scowl, and heavily tattooed with his Native Pacific Islander markings, Frank's appearance behind the till usually causes our customers to stumble a beat. He doesn't seem the type who should be inquiring about their dairy and froth preferences.

He answers with a grunt as he disappears into the back office. A moment later, the telltale beeps of the safe's keypad sound as he deposits the day's earnings.

Some business owners might not so freely trust their staff with the code to their safe, but Frank's more than staff. He has been a fixture at the Sea Witch for sixteen years. He's become a big brother and protector. I trust him more than I trust anyone else, and I lean on him a lot.

The door jangles and I look up to see Dave and Ted stroll in.

"Hey, strangers!" My face splits with a genuine smile. "What are you doing here?" These two travel from Louisiana every spring like migrant birds, here for the work and the fishing. Dave has managed Sea Witch's beach equipment for eleven years, ensuring every last piece goes out in the morning and returns before dark. Teddy's one of his crew—a tall, quiet guy who shows up every day and lets Dave do all the talking for him.

I round the desk to give the guys hugs.

"Hey, Sloane."

I can't help but notice Dave's returned affection is uncharacteristically subdued. He's normally lifting me off the ground.

Frank reappears. "Guys. Long time, no see." They exchange firm handshakes; Frank doesn't hug anyone except Gigi.

"Seriously. I wasn't expecting you until Sunday. It's not an issue, right?" I peer up at Frank, who's been doing all the maintenance on the trailers we rent to out-of-town staffers.

"Ready to go," he confirms.

"Yeah ... about that." Dave scratches the back of his head as his gaze darts to the HELP WANTED sign in our window. "There's no easy way to say this, but I figured I owed it to you to tell you in person." His chest puffs with a deep inhale. "We got hired at the new hotel. Full time. We won't be working for the Sea Witch anymore."

His words feel like a punch to my stomach, and it takes me a few beats to process, to make sure I heard them correctly. "But ... we just talked on Monday. You're supposed to move all the equipment out *next week*." Hundreds of chairs and umbrellas that need to be hauled from offseason storage to the compound—our nearby summer lot. It's grueling work that *has* to get done, and we're already shorthanded.

Teddy's focus hasn't left his shoes once.

Dave's face pinches with apology. "Just got the call. They moved up our start date. There's no wiggle room. Sorry."

"But ..." I'm struggling to wrap my head around this bomb. "When did they hire you?"

He falters. "A month ago."

"*A month!*"

"And you thought waiting until the last minute to tell us was what *you owed us?*" Frank erupts, his deep voice filling the small rental office.

Teddy edges toward the door.

Even Dave, who at six foot three isn't a small guy, takes a step back. "I don't know what else to say except we're sorry. We wanted to tell you as soon as we could." And, for his part, he *does* sound sorry.

I stare at their backs as the door jangles closed.

Frank's giant hand settles on my shoulder, giving it a squeeze. "It's gonna be fine."

"*How? How* is it going to be fine?" I blink against the threatening tears. "We've already lost five people to that fucking hotel!" First Jay, one of my tiki cruise captains, quickly followed by four new seasonal hires who got "the call" and promptly ditched us. Now, Dave and Teddy?

"We'll replace them."

"*This close* to the start of the season?"

"Mick can take over running the crew."

"Mick is indecisive, and he panics when he has more than one thing on his plate. He can't supervise. He does what he's told, not the other way around."

"Okay, then *I'*ll supervise until we find someone to replace Dave."

"And what about hauling everything out?" It was already going to be hell and now we're down two more capable sets of hands.

"I'll take care of it. I'll call the crew in to start earlier. Don't worry, we'll get it done."

My body sags, but it's not with relief. It's with overwhelming disappointment that Dave would do this to me. More, though, it's with a heavy sense of foreboding, that worries tucked into the back of my mind have a good reason to reemerge in a *told you so* fashion.

"Have you heard from Jeremy?" He's played captain for six seasons, shuttling groups to Starfish Island, a popular sandbar. He's funny, outgoing, and a favorite among the tourists.

"He called in after getting back to the dock." Frank drags the elastic from his hair to free his lengthy black locks from the braid he wears at work. "Why?"

"I'm getting a weird vibe from him lately. Like he might be leaving us too."

"Nah, he'd already be gone if they scooped him up." Frank's heavy brow furrows with doubt. "And he makes a killing in tips. He'd work here year-round if he could."

"Yeah, I know. That's the problem. Two weeks ago, he asked me if I'd consider hiring him on full-time." But I can't afford another salary. Frank helps me run the coffee shop year during the offseason, and the tour and rentals side shuts down at the end of October until March. "And now there's *this*." I stab the local newspaper with my index finger, drawing Frank's attention to the job fair announcement at the Wolf Hotel.

He tips his head to read it, showing off the hint of gray at his temples. At forty-four years old, Frank looks closer to my thirty-one. "This is for seasonal, not full time."

"To start, sure, but as if they wouldn't be clambering to hire Jeremy year-round once he's proven himself." He's reliable, punctual, and the hardest worker Sea Witch has ever had.

Frank pauses as if in thought. "You honestly think he'd leave us for Wolf?"

"I never thought Dave would leave us, and see what just happened!" I throw a hand toward the door. "Jeremy booked Friday off. He *never* books time off." Luckily, we don't have any cruises scheduled for that day.

"No, he doesn't," Frank agrees reluctantly.

"What if he leaves me? We'll be down to *one* captain." AJ, who worked for us last year and is reliable enough, though not the most personable. Honestly, I wasn't going to hire him again this year, but I'm desperate. "How am I going to replace someone as good as Jeremy? People ask for him *by name!*" I stab at my computer screen, to the notes section of repeat bookers. Whininess laces my voice.

"He still works here today. If he's gone next week, we'll deal with it then." Frank gives my shoulder another comforting squeeze. "This isn't the first time someone has quit on us out of the blue."

"I knew this was going to happen. I *knew* that stupid hotel was going to swoop in to take *all* the best workers, and then what are we going to be left with? The lazy, untrustworthy plugs. Wolf is ruining Mermaid Beach's entire vibe, and it's not even open yet!"

Not that the feeling hadn't already shifted for those like me who grew up here, casting fishing lines and running barefoot to the ice cream shop. Somewhere along the line, the quaint Florida cottages were replaced by looming coastal mansions and condos, and dozens of new businesses cropped up almost overnight—there are now three other tiki bar cruise companies to compete with ours. Popular travel magazines wrote articles about the area, throwing around comparisons to the Hamptons and Nantucket, and all these bougie Northeasterners who can't afford to vacation in those areas flocked here, driving up the prices of everything—houses, taxes, food. A lot of locals can't afford to live here anymore. So many of them are cashing out and leaving.

Some people argue the change has brought good things to the community, but I disagree. We were doing just fine. Change is what brought those surveyors to the land next door to my home—acres that had been sitting vacant for decades, not worth developing. Fast-forward five years and there's now an eyesore where only swaying sea oats along sand dunes and a serene grove of bramble and copper woods existed before.

"Sloane ... Don't start up on this again. It does you no good," Frank warns.

"I'm not. I swear." Poor Frank has had to listen to me rant about all things Wolf Hotel for years. I dragged him to town council meetings to try to stop the build, but all those assholes care about is how much money and prestige the Wolf name will bring to Mermaid Beach. "But tell me it doesn't bother you that it's there. *Right* beside our home."

"It is what it is. There's no point fighting it anymore. You tried, and you lost. Now, it's time to let go. Who knows, they could bring us more business."

"People who pay a thousand bucks a night for a hotel room aren't coming to the Sea Witch to stand in line for syrup-laced coffees and to rent beach equipment, Frank."

He shrugs. "You could have sold to them. They made you a good offer."

"I'm not selling!"

Frank's eyebrows arch with reproach.

"I'm *not* selling Gigi's house," I repeat, tempering my tone. She bought that property back when you could still scoop up acres for cheap. And while she claims she prefers her nursing home now that her body is giving up on her, it would kill her to see the place torn down for more sterile mansions or, worse, an expansion on that hotel. "I've lived in that house all my life. *You* live there. A lot of our staff consider it their home over the summer." In trailers Gigi collected over the years to provide cheap accommodations to the Sea Witch family, as she likes to refer to them. Hell, Dave and Teddy are supposed to stay there!

"And you don't have to," Frank says calmly. "Now, speaking lazy, untrustworthy plugs, guess who I heard is applying at Wolf?" He waits a beat before relieving me of the suspense. "Cody."

I snort, even as hearing that name makes my stomach clench with dread. "Good. They deserve that sorry sack."

"They won't hire him."

"Please. If there's one thing Cody is good at, it's fooling people into thinking he's a decent guy." He sure fooled me. He had zero experience and yet I hired him as a captain, and then I dated the bastard for a year before saying yes to his proposal.

"I always knew what he was about."

"Yeah, thanks for warning me."

The flat glare I get in return is almost comical. Frank's not one to stick his nose into other people's business, but he did grumble about Cody's work ethic. I ignored him because customers loved Cody so much. And because I loved him.

After Gigi officially signed the properties and the business over to me and left for the nursing home, things changed. Cody moved into my house and began introducing himself as an owner around here. He helped himself to cash from the safe on occasion, to cover his truck payments and other loans. He picked fights with Frank almost daily to try to force him to move.

But it was the day Cody showed up with that negotiated offer for my land that the light bulb went off and I realized we were *never* going to work. He might have truly loved me, but he loved the idea of getting his hands on all that money more.

It's been a year since I kicked Cody's ass out and I'm still angry with myself for not seeing through him from day one. When I think about that momentary lapse of judgment where I considered putting him on the deed to my house, I feel like vomiting.

"Good thing I've added vetoing my dates to your job description then, huh?" I say half jokingly as I refresh my computer screen. I no longer trust my gut where men are concerned.

Another cruise booking appears. "It's like everyone woke up from hibernation all at once. At least we're getting bookings, even if we don't have staff."

"Hibernation sounds good." Frank checks his watch. He's been here since 5:00 a.m. "Other side's locked up for the day. If you don't need me, I'm gonna head home and grab a few hours of sleep."

"Okay, I'll see you later. Hey, can you stop by Dollar General and grab me some more poster board?"

"No, Sloane." He shakes his head fervently. "This isn't healthy—" His scolding words are cut off at the ding of the doorbell, as two brawny male customers step inside.

"The bros are back in town," Frank murmurs under his breath, earning my elbow. If there's a type that annoys him, it's the loud, obnoxious twenty-somethings whose mamas have told them they're God's gift to the world enough times that they wholeheartedly believe it. Their type flocks here for guys' weekends like perverts to a wet T-shirt contest.

I can't tell if these two fit that mold. They're certainly *fit*. The blond has to be a gym rat, given the size of his chest and arms. The tattooed one is also built, but not nearly as bulky. He certainly doesn't scream frat boy or easygoing, his angular face stony, his eyes hidden behind aviators.

I splash on my customer-friendly smile, despite my sour mood. "Can I help you two with something?"

"Yeah, this whiny little bitch needs a coffee before he'll let me eat." The blond jerks his thumb at his friend, showing off perfect teeth with his grin. I'll bet that gets a lot of women giggling like fools.

The dark-haired guy's hard expression doesn't so much as crack, as if he's used to his buddy's digs. Or he's just had a really long day.

"Coffee shop is on the other side, and it's closed." Frank folds his brawny arms.

"See?" Blondie smacks the other's chest. "What'd I tell you. It's officially beer o'clock." He looks around. "You don't serve beer here, do you?"

"Nope," Frank says with forced patience.

The blond scans the white shiplap-clad space, waving a hand at the beach chair and umbrella set up in the corner. "What's all this about, then?"

I'll bet this one's a lot to handle. But I may as well promote us while they're here. Surely they have thick wallets. "We rent them out to tourists. We also rent paddleboards, and we now have Jet Skis available. *And* we do tiki bar cruises, if you and your friends want a tour around the area with a drink in your hand."

"Hence the BREWS AND CRUISES on the sign," he muses.

"Exactly. We still have slots available for this weekend. It's a great way to spend an afternoon."

Frank taps the wall next to him, plastered with bikini-clad groups toasting drinks and splashing water for the camera.

The blond edges over to investigate the customer photos with interest. "Where's this at?"

"Starfish Island. It's about a ten-minute ride out, past the ..."

While Frank describes the idyllic spot where tourists linger for hours during high season, the other guy meanders to my desk with a lazy stride. "Connor can be loud and annoying, but underneath it all, he's a mediocre friend and an exhausting roommate," he says by way of greeting, his voice deep and raspy.

I chuckle at his dry humor. "You're lucky to have him."

"That's what he keeps telling me." The guy's attention lands on the framed photo hanging on the wall next to me. "'Gigi, the original sea witch,'" he reads out loud. "Who was she?"

"She *is* my grandmother. That picture was taken in front of the shop the first day it opened, almost forty years ago." I smile at Gigi back then—her blond hair tied back in braids, a traditional lei hanging around her neck.

He slides off his aviators. "Disney or Greek?"

"Huh?" I manage, caught off guard by both his question and his piercing green eyes.

He smirks. "Which version of sea witch?"

"Oh ... I don't know. It was what my grandfather called her." I stumble over my answer. Since when are bros interested in plaques and family history? "He was Hawaiian, and he believed in mermaids."

His gaze drifts over my face, as if searching for hints of island ancestry in my ashy blond hair and olive skin. "And sea witches, apparently."

"Apparently."

"Weird pet name." This guy has a cool, calm way about him.

"Actually, it was meant to be an insult." Once, Gigi and my grandfather had a huge fight before he went out fishing. He lost his boat—and nearly his life—in a squall that day and accused her of putting a curse on him. She didn't deny it, figured she'd let him fear her a bit. After that, every time something went wrong in their lives, it had to be the work of the sea witch in her. "They divorced, and she moved to Mermaid Beach out of spite."

The corners of his mouth curl. God, he is a beautiful man. "Your grandmother sounds like a smart woman."

"She's the best." I bite my bottom lip to stop from grinning like a fool. "First time in Mermaid Beach?"

"First time."

Strange. There's something familiar about this guy. I feel like I've seen his face before. "Where are you from?"

"Miami, most recently."

"We'll hook something up. Right, Ronan?" The blond—Connor, he called him—booms, cutting into our conversation.

"Yeah, I'm in," Ronan says, but his weighty gaze never leaves me, and it feels like his answer has nothing to do with a tiki cruise or beach chairs.

A tremble runs through my body.

Frank appears at my side and announces, "You can book online. Coffee shop opens at 7:00 a.m.," in that brusque way of his that borders on rude, even if he doesn't mean it to be.

Ronan's smile grows wider. "I think that's our cue to leave."

"Good, 'cause I'm gonna pass out." Connor pats his stomach, drawing my focus to the ridges of muscle. He's annoying but hot, I'll give him that.

Sliding his glasses back on, Ronan collects a business card from the counter, pausing to read it. "See you around, *Sloane*."

I let out a shaky breath as I watch their backs disappear out the door.

"Veto," Frank says on the tail end of the door jangle.

I roll my eyes. "You honestly think I could spend more than two minutes in a room with him before I stabbed him?"

"Not *that* idiot. This one." Frank taps the counter where Ronan stood a moment ago. "He's dangerous."

"They were here for, like, two minutes!" I laugh, and it lifts a bit of the cloud that has settled on this place. "Dangerous *how*?"

His brow pulls together tightly. "Like he'll teach you things you don't need to learn."

"Ooh, that sounds like fun." I waggle my eyebrows, earning his glower. "I'm a grown-ass, thirty-one-year-old woman." Who has never woken up in bed next to a guy I met the day before or had a casual fling. I've lost the interest of more than one guy because I didn't put out by the third date. Gigi swears it's a good method for weeding out the assholes. It wasn't foolproof, though. Cody put in the time—we didn't sleep together for almost two months. Turns out he was hooking up with weekend beachgoers behind my back—something I learned after our breakup.

"You know, I should start having one-night stands. Relationships don't seem to be working out for me."

"Great idea. Let me know so I can get my BB gun ready."

A mental image of the giant guy sitting on his trailer porch steps taking aim at some poor, unsuspecting fool hits me and I start giggling.

A rare—and I mean cougar-sighting rare—smile splits Franks face in two.

So, naturally, I ruin it. "Now, about that poster board ..."

35. Ronan

Nuts! I was hoping you could show me around town. I'm there for Sandra's bridesmaid party. Remember her? Congrats on the promotion. Still with Wolf? How is Mermaid Beach? I've always wanted to go.

My thumb floats over my phone's keyboard as I consider a suitable response. The text came in last night while we were elbow-deep in wings and beer. I should ignore it, is what I *should* do. Do not engage, do not pretend that I care what my ex is doing with her life, two years later.

Why does that seem easier said than done?

"Fucking Wolf, man." Connor eases Darla into a parking spot at one minute to 9:00 a.m. "How does *one guy* control all this?"

"With the silver spoon he was born suckling on." Easing out of the car with a groan, I pause to take a good look at the new hotel. I have to hand it to the architects—Wolf Hotels may be a chain, but no one could ever label the actual hotel properties cookie-cutter. They all ooze luxury, and every single one

I've seen has character. Wolf Cove is a ritzy timber wood lodge; Miami's has a southern Florida charm with Latin flair. This one? It's an elegant boxy white exterior with rows of groomed palm trees and a giant mermaid water fountain leading up to the grand front entrance.

And it's *huge*. Bigger than I'd anticipated.

"Where to, boss?" Connor asks, sucking back a mouthful of coffee, his eyes bleary from the rounds of Fireball and tequila last night. Siren's Call, the beachside bar we chose for dinner, morphed into a party. Scantily clad women showed up and everything quickly went downhill from there. Thank God my bedroom is on the top floor and has a lock.

I check my watch. "To meet *my* boss."

"You think he's gonna be a dick?"

"Shit." I pinch the bridge of my nose to quell the hangover headache. The last few days have been such a blur. "I forgot to tell you ..."

"You're late." Belinda's nose curls with displeasure as she sizes us up and down in the lobby of the hotel. "And you smell like tequila."

"Unexpected night." For a guy who hasn't touched hard liquor in a year, I have regrets. But they're momentarily cast aside as I gape in awe at the vacuous space, the vaulted ceilings lined with windows to show off the azure sky beyond.

Connor greets her with a megawatt smile. "If I'd known you were in town, I would have called."

"I wouldn't have answered," she throws back without missing a beat.

"You look well." His gaze slides down to where the buttons of her flamingo pink silk blouse open just enough to showcase her cleavage. "Vibrant."

And not at all fitting the traditional Wolf colors of white, black, and plum. Instead, the few staffers floating around are clad in shades of orange, pink, and leafy greens.

"As will you, soon enough." Belinda's white teeth flash with her sneer. "Orientation has already started so you'll have to run to catch up. You'll also need to stop by administration. They can finish up your transfer and get you a uniform. I guessed at your size based on what I remember."

Don't do it. I glare at Connor in warning, able to read his dirty thoughts from a mile away. I had them too, but I can control myself.

This fucker can't. "You remember my size, do you?"

Belinda's gaze narrows to slits. If it were humanly possible to shoot daggers from eyeballs, Connor would be hemorrhaging all over the marble floor.

The last thing I need is the general manager having it out for me on day one. "Can you find your way there, Con?"

Before he can answer, Belinda snaps her fingers in the air. "No need. Holly will show you."

A petite brunette in a peach blazer and skirt charges forward.

With a wink at Belinda and a half salute at me, Connor focuses on his new victim.

Belinda's sigh is soft. "I was stupid enough to think I would escape Henry's punishment."

I smirk. "Missed you too."

She steps closer and, taking a cursory glance around to check for ears, she lowers her voice to say, "It was a terrible mistake that will *never* happen again."

I can't help but inhale her spicy perfume. It brings back fond memories. "If you say so." I'd call it one wild, unexpected day at work. We didn't instigate it. We never dreamed of it. Belinda is the one who was waiting for us at the old Wolf house during our routine check, who led us upstairs to help her deal with "an issue," as she called it. What the hell were we supposed to do when the blond smoke show stripped and demanded we follow?

She studies my face behind thick-rimmed glasses, and I sense a rare moment of vulnerability in the woman who can otherwise only be described as cold and calculating.

"It will never happen again, and no one's going to talk about it to anyone, I promise."

"I appreciate that," she forces out, as if the words were difficult to conjure.

I smoothly shift the topic away from our sordid history. "How about you show me to my office?"

She turns abruptly, equally eager to move on. "This way." Her heels click on the marble tile as she leads me down a long hall, past staff members who offer her polite greetings and me curious looks. Day one on the job and I'm late, hungover, and dressed in jeans and a Blink-182 concert T-shirt. A lot of people would consider that three strikes.

I admire the arched ceilings with detailed cornice in gold and giant painted tropical plant leaves. "I didn't know what to expect, but this place is something. Very retro and yet modern."

"Yes, the designer, Maude Claret, was aiming for a vintage aesthetic circa 1969 Palm Beach." She gestures at a small fountain where the path splits off down another hall. "But with mermaids instead of flamingos."

"Makes sense." Mention of mermaids makes me think of sea witches, which makes me think of that coffee shop we stopped in yesterday. Sloane, the original sea witch's attractive granddaughter. I smile as I remember her pale jade-green eyes and full lips. It's been a while since any woman has sparked my interest like that. Well, since Abbi, I guess.

And though I've sworn off entanglements with women, sheer curiosity had me planning to jog over to her coffee shop this morning. That is until I woke up.

Maybe tomorrow.

It's just coffee.

Belinda leads me past the entrance to the hotel's convention center and then pushes through a set of glass doors. The hall ahead opens and a soft buzz carries where people sit at desks with their computers, fingertips clacking away at keyboards, a murmur here and there, the odd ringtone. I remember that sound from not too many years ago when I sat in their same position, helping push the bureaucratic pen along.

I hated it.

It's not as dark and dreary as in the admin office in Miami. Here, they have windows, and the cube walls are low. Plus, there's no counter to keep the riffraff like Connor from wandering in. I'll bet they regret that design decision before too long.

"This is the pit," Belinda explains. "All the hotel's administration works here. Department managers' offices are on the far end."

I note the glass wall and the desks behind it, with people in various states of business—taking calls, answering emails. One is in a meeting. They work in fishbowls.

Several people pop up over their cubicles, their curious gazes landing on me, eyeing my attire. Maybe I should have made more of an effort to dress like a Wolf executive, rather than a hungover groundskeeper.

Belinda guides me to the left and we're moving down another narrow hall of closed frosted-glass doors. "These are our boardrooms. Lena, who is in charge of hospitality and entertainment, is here. That's my office." Belinda stabs the air with a lengthy pink fingernail, pointing out the opaque glass door at the end, before pushing through another one beside us. "This is yours."

The room isn't huge—enough for a desk and two visitor chairs, a clothing rack, and a giant leafy palm in the corner.

Not that I care. I wander over to the one window. Beyond the foliage is the golf course. "No ocean view?"

Belinda grunts. "That's valuable real estate. Besides, if you have any time to stare out the window, you're not doing your job."

I reach up to flick the sleeve of a green pinstripe suit. Behind it hangs an array of button-down and golf shirts in both white and pink, as well as dress pants in dark green and beige. Below are several pairs of dress shoes. "This better not be what I think it is." Wolf didn't say anything about a uniform.

"Henry insisted that I ensure you dress the part and, based on how you've arrived today, I see he wasn't wrong to worry. I've taken the liberty of acquiring a few key pieces. Abbi sent me the measurements they used for the wedding tuxedo as a guide, though she warned me you're a size bigger." She scrutinizes me, and I'm beginning to feel like a lamb chop on a dinner plate, its recipient deciding where to start. "I have a tailor coming this afternoon with more suits and to adjust this one as needed."

Henry is a controlling prick. "But fucking *green*?"

"It's a nice green! And it's a fifteen-hundred-dollar suit. Besides, it's only for select events."

I hold up a palm-leaf print tie. "I'm not wearing this."

"It's standard attire."

"For waiters and desk clerks, of which I am neither."

Her beautiful face cracks with a sardonic smile as she holds her arms out at her side. "You think *this* would have been my first choice?"

My gaze lingers over her curvy frame, clad in a botanical green blazer and pencil skirt that shows off shapely legs and calves that strain in hot pink, four-inch heels. "It works for you." The truth is, Belinda can make anything work. I'd put her in her early forties and one of the sexiest women I've ever met. It's not even her body, which is firm and curvy. It's her poise, the way she can walk into a room and command it. She's

195

the only person I've seen order Henry to do anything, besides Abbi. Probably the only one with the guts to try.

Belinda used to intimidate me, but now all I have to do is remember her on her knees with her mouth open, waiting, and that unease fades. In fact, if she offered a repeat, I'm not sure I'd be strong enough to deny her. I already know I'd enjoy it, even if it's meaningless.

Her nostrils flare as if she can sense my dirty thoughts. "Ronan, do not look at me like you want to—"

A knock on my door cuts off the end of what would likely have been a crass sentence.

Belinda remains silent, staring at me in challenge.

It dawns on me. This is *my* office. "Come in."

A pint-sized, ginger-haired guy with a face full of freckles peeks in, his green eyes darting between Belinda and me before he clears his throat. "Hello, sir. Ms. Cartwright told me to come and introduce myself when you arrived. I'm Archie, your assistant."

"Uh ... Hi." How old is this guy? It's hard to tell. He could be twenty-one or thirty-five. And *sir*? Fuck, that is not happening. "Call me Ronan."

He dips his head once. "I've already sent you the day's TCIP report and the weeklies will be in your inbox by eleven."

"*Right.*" I draw out the single word. *TCIP? Weeklies?* "Thanks."

"I'll get to scheduling meetings for you and the managers. What's your window?" His thick, bushy eyebrows lift as he waits for my answer.

"My window ..." For fuck's sake. This guy is a ball of energy.

"Why don't you and Ronan have a meeting after lunch today to go over his general expectations of you?" Belinda cuts in.

"Oh, right. One p.m. sound good?" he asks me.

"That will work perfectly," Belinda answers, her smile

thin-lipped. "He has a 2:00 p.m. already and I'll introduce him to the managers myself."

"Oh, okay. Thanks, sir. I mean ... uh ... Oh! Here, I almost forgot these." He hands me a thick envelope. "The dealership dropped off your company car. It's parked in one of the executive spaces."

Executive spaces?

Archie disappears out the door.

I feel Belinda's sharp gaze on me from behind those dark-rimmed glasses and I meet it head-on.

"Do you have *any clue* what your new position entails?" she blurts.

"Nope." I've been waiting for her to call a spade on this bullshit situation. "But I'll bet you're one hell of a teacher."

She grinds her teeth.

———

"Left up here," Belinda orders, pointing at where the paved path forks.

I smoothly steer the golf cart in that direction. This, I can do. "Nice course."

"It is. They've struggled to finish it in time." Her tone is crisp. "Elias Brown designed it."

"Is that name supposed to mean anything to me?" I've picked up a golf club exactly once in my life, fifteen years ago at a father-and-son tournament. I thought I'd die from boredom.

I feel her incredulous look in my peripherals. "He's the best course architect in the world."

"Of course he is." Only the best for Henry. "You expecting a lot of golfers here?"

She snorts. "This *is* Florida, isn't it?"

I purse my lips tight. Everything that comes out of my mouth proves how truly out of my depth I am. Henry's gut is going to need a steady dose of antacids when he realizes that.

With an incoherent mumble and a shift in her seat, Belinda continues, "This location is meant to be a year-round retreat. The winter months are cooler here but ideal for golfers who prefer to play their sport while not sweating through their khakis. That, along with the luxury spa and heated pools, will draw the spouses. We see this as an adult resort mainly, given the cost. Surely, we'll also attract small groups. Bridal parties and such."

Mention of bridal parties makes me think of Tasha in Miami. I was *this close* to seeing her again because knowing me, I would have been too curious to stay away.

Also knowing me, I would have even bigger regrets by the end of the weekend.

"Is *that* part of this Elias Brown's design?" I point to the puddles of water pooling on the ninth hole green. "Because I may not know much about golf, but I know that's a drainage problem." The course at the Wolf in Indianapolis had the same issue. We had to rip up the entire area to fix it. I'll never forget how sore my back was after that ordeal.

Belinda's brow wrinkles. "This construction crew has been disappointing, to say the least. Talk to Dorian."

"How did he not pick up on this?" How has nobody noticed? There are people out here cutting grass daily.

"You can scold him when *you* deal with this issue. Keep going." Belinda waves a hand forward.

We wind around the bend. Fluorescent red, orange, and pink squares catch my notice. "What is that? Up there." I point ahead, past a chain-link fence to where handmade signs dangle off tree branches. I squint to read the words. "'Mermaid Beach doesn't want this.' 'You're not welcome.' 'Take your money and go away.'" A longer one hangs nearby. "'Wolf Hotel Billionaire Owner Questioned in Brother's Death.'"

"That is the reason I wanted to bring you out here."

"Ah, yes. The neighbor." The one Henry specifically warned me about.

"Drive." She gestures toward the area.

"Okay, even I know to stay off the green—"

"Anyone who has a problem with it can speak to the general manager. Oh wait, that's me," she snipes. "I am not ruining my heels."

"Whatever you say, boss." I veer off the path. The cart bumps along, the tires leaving imprints as we move closer toward the fence. "So, what's this all about, besides old news?" Scott Wolf died a year and a half ago and deserved his untimely end. Abbi told me what happened—the grim details that they managed to keep out of the news to protect her from becoming more of a media spectacle—and if someone else hadn't killed the son of a bitch, I would have with my bare hands.

"Our neighbor isn't a fan of us."

"A giant hotel right next door? Can't imagine why. Is that one lot?" It's hard to tell beyond the thick, wild bramble.

"It is. Stretches all the way from the main road to the beach. The family purchased it decades ago."

I let out a low whistle as I slide out of my seat for a better view, feeling the itch to dig into my pocket for a smoke that's not there.

More handwritten signs come into view.

Wolf Heir and Assistant Spotted at Exclusive High Society Sex Party with Friends Margo Lauren and Hedge Fund Playboy Preston Abbott.

I remember that headline circulating. Connor still asks for an invitation every time he talks to Abbi.

Henry Wolf Breaks His Own Rules to Marry His Assistant. Was She Prey?

Wolf Hotel Billionaire's Innocent Farm Girl Not So Innocent After All

That last one spikes my anger. It's about Abbi ... and me,

and moderately fabricated nonsense from a spurned reporter who was trying to cause trouble ahead of the wedding. Connor and I were named in the article. Our full fucking names.

It caused Abbi such stress and unleashed a torrent of online bullying from brainless losers with no lives of their own, so they spend their time taking sides of strangers they'll never meet and trying to tank Farm Girl's business.

"That's gotta be worth a pretty penny." There's at least ten to fifteen acres there. I'm surprised they haven't already sold to a developer. I crouch to find a view past an especially full bush. "Are those trailers?"

"Yes. Painted every shade you can find." Belinda's disgust is plain in her voice.

"Campground?"

"I don't know what you call it. The mobile homes are occupied during the season, except for one tenant who lives there year-round. The owner lives in a dilapidated house. You can see it clearly from the beach."

I shift my position. "Yeah, I see it now." Or the back porch, anyway, of a house sitting off the ground on a pier-and-beam foundation, to help fend against a flood, though the sand dunes already form a natural barrier.

A pink hut sits on the far end. "Is that a chicken coop?"

"Yes, one that houses the noisiest rooster I have ever heard. I called bylaw but, shockingly, you're allowed to have one in this county if you have a lot that size. We've already petitioned to have the law changed."

"Over the neighbor's rooster?" I can't help the amusement in my voice.

"We can't have it disturbing our guests."

"From way over there?"

"Wait until you hear it!" she snaps. "Besides, it's the principle. These people have been a royal pain in Henry's ass for years. From the moment they found out about the hotel, they've been trying to stop it. Circulating petitions, rallying local interest groups to storm council meetings, challenging zoning and environmental studies. Crying about confused turtles or some nonsense. There were two of them fighting this. An old woman and her granddaughter. The old woman is gone now."

"Died?"

"Or given up, I have no idea, but she's left the property to this one. All in all, they delayed the schedule for nearly *a year* with all their antics."

"Wow." I've gotta give this woman credit not only for her ambition but for having the guts to go up against the Wolf family. Too bad it might bite her in the ass. Henry doesn't easily forget.

"Yes. Well, now that she's lost her battle, this is what she has resorted to." She flings a manicured hand at the signs. "Digging up old newspaper headlines in some sad attempt at a smear campaign."

"What does Henry say about the signs?"

"He expects them down before the media open. Otherwise, everyone will be writing about this nuisance instead of what they should be focused on."

"Right, that circus." I remember when the Alaska location launched, they flew in a bunch of high rollers and journalists. It was a whole dog-and-pony *make sure you shine your boots and straighten your bow tie* show. "So, give her money."

"You don't think Henry already tried? She keeps tearing up the checks the lawyers bring."

"Sue her."

"For freedom of speech and the right to peaceful protest? On her own property?"

"How about for slander."

"She's pulled directly from the headlines of major print companies. Even a hack lawyer could put up a good fight, and it would be a long, drawn-out mess. They've already threatened her, and she's dug in her heels. Besides, a lawsuit would attract more media attention that Henry doesn't want around the opening."

I shrug. "Have someone hop the fence at night and rip them down."

Belinda's laugh is wicked. "It's been thrown out there, trust me. But knowing this lunatic, she has a gun trained on us right now. She's probably sitting in a tree, waiting."

My gaze drifts to the branches. "That's a little unsettling."

"Henry wants to keep everything above board. He has plans for that lot."

"He thinks she'll sell?"

"Not in a hundred years." Belinda shakes her head. "Henry's tried. The last check the lawyer handed her was for *two times* what the property is worth. She tore that one up too."

I whistle.

"See? Crazy."

"Have you met her?"

"God no. If I ever find myself face-to-face with this troll, I will destroy her," Belinda growls.

I love this scorned neighbor's dedication, I'll give her that. And I don't think I ever want to be on Belinda's bad side.

She sighs heavily, as if the move will expel the anger. "I suggested building a wall, but that is a lengthy property line. It would be astronomically expensive and visually unappealing. And we're already over budget. Trees would work in the long-term but they need time to grow, and I've been told too many trees will stunt the growth of quality turf. I don't know what to do, but we need to come up with something to screen that PR mess."

It's a true David and Goliath situation. In this case, it appears David is winning. Or should I say Davida. "What do you know about these people?"

"Only what Henry told me when he tasked me with opening *another* hotel for him. Frankly, I have more important things to do than focus on this pest. This is *your* problem."

"Great ... Tell me what you know." So I can offer no help whatsoever because I don't even understand why I'm here.

"The old lady had one of those old lady names. The grand-daughter ... I can't remember." Belinda groans as if it's an effort to talk about her even now. "She runs a local tourist business. You'd think she'd be happy that a Wolf is here to draw in more people."

"Unmarried?"

"No idea." Belinda pauses. "Why?"

I shrug. "Just curious."

Her glare narrows. "Henry warned you to keep your dick in your pants with that one."

I chuckle. "Hands and dick inside the bus at all times. Already got the memo."

"I'm serious. That one is bitter and unhinged. Enough that I wouldn't put it past her to make up stories to create ammo, if you catch my drift. Henry doesn't need another scandal like that last one." That lecturing pointer finger goes up in the air. "If I find out you're sniffing around her, the first call I will make is to Henry, and he will fire your ass in his next breath. I will make sure of it—"

"Okay!" I've never seen Belinda so passionate. I don't doubt her. "I've got it. Look, I may not have been a Boy Scout in Alaska—"

"You ran a fuck club," she deadpans.

"Not one of my prouder moments." I'm still not sure how that all transpired, but I blame Connor. "Things have changed. *I've* changed. And batshit crazy doesn't appeal to me."

She purses her lips. "Come on, we have a lot of ground to cover today."

Movement on the porch catches my eye, but all I can see are tan female legs. Attached to a disgruntled woman who has nothing better to do than plaster her property with lame signs, apparently.

Leaving my spy post, I climb into the cart and drive us back toward the path.

A horrendous rooster caw cuts through the peaceful silence then, sending a flock of warblers perched on a nearby pine tree flapping into the air.

"See?" Belinda's expression is triumphant.

"Okay, you may have a point," I admit with a cringe.

36. Sloane

"Good job, Ralph." I toss a chunk of carrot over the rail as I tuck my phone back in my pocket.

The fourteen-pound Jersey Giant rooster struts over to collect his treat—a reward for singing to our Wolf Hotel scouts. Who says you can't train birds ...

I was hauling trash to the can when I spotted the golf cart coasting over the grass toward my property line and the male figure climb out. I couldn't make him out from here, but I assumed he was coming to hop the fence and rip down my signs. My first move was going to be to dash over and record the fool. The second was to call the police to report trespassing and vandalism.

They haven't sent any sleazy lawyers with fat bribery checks lately. Have they given up on that angle?

A horn honks and a moment later, the familiar white Volkswagen Beetle eases up my lengthy driveway. All thoughts of Wolf vanish from my mind.

I squeal as I scurry down the stairs and rush to the yellow single-wide trailer in anticipation. Even though we text regularly, I haven't seen Rebel and Skye since they left for school in August. I've missed them terribly.

"We're here!" Rebel launches herself at me the second she gets out of the driver's seat, roping her toned arms around my neck in a tight grip.

I inhale the familiar citrusy scent of her black hair, now cut short in a pixie style. "What are you doing here so early?" I wasn't expecting them until dinnertime.

"We were all packed, so we said 'Fuck it' and left last night to avoid the traffic."

Skye climbs out of the passenger seat and stretches her arms over her head, showing off her toned stomach. "If I never eat at another Burger King, it'll be too soon."

"I see that." I nod toward the empty food wrappers that spilled out with her, the last remaining fries scattering over the dirt, drawing the hens and Ralph in.

She rounds the car for an equally affectionate hug.

"How were your exams?" I ask, clinging a beat too long.

"Ugh, *awful*." She groans dramatically. "But they're done, and I passed and that's all that matters."

"Your hair has gotten long." I emphasize my point with a tug of her corn-silk blond braid.

"And it's about to blow up like a puffball in this humidity."

"An adorable puffball." My heart swells as I listen to Skye's Southern twang. She comes by it honestly, having grown up in rural Georgia.

Of all the seasonal staffers who have lived here throughout the years, I've always felt a special connection to Skye. I think it's because, like me, she lost her mother to ovarian cancer at an early age and never knew her father. Whatever the reason, she's always felt like a little sister.

"Whatever. I don't care because this feels like coming home." Her blue eyes are alight with thrill as they skim over "Rainbow Alley," as Gigi affectionately named the row of mobile homes nestled between two lines of big, gnarly trees. Each is painted and meticulously decorated —a passion of Gigi's in the quiet winter months. The yellow one that the girls occupy is the nicest by far, with turquoise shutters and a pineapple theme interior. Hence the name: Pineapple Express. There's also the purple Palmy Daze trailer, the green and pink Monstera Hut, and a teal blue Dolphin Around trailer. The only one not painted is Frank's silver Airstream, but he has surrounded it with surfboards and tiki torches to give it some flair.

"Frank just put a brand-new air-conditioning unit in there last week. It cools down fast now."

"Oh, great. No more sweating at night." She shudders for effect. "Anyone else here yet?"

I falter. "You're the first!" Dave and Ted were supposed to move into Palmy Daze on Saturday. I'm still not over the shock of that betrayal, but I don't want to ruin this reunion by sharing the news yet.

"Ralph! My big boy!" Rebel exclaims. "Stop playing so hard to get." The rooster runs at surprising speeds in the opposite direction as Rebel chases, earning our laughter.

"Okay, your place is all set. I'll help you unload so you can get some sleep." The back of their car is packed to the roof with their belongings and, knowing Skye, she has Red Bull coursing through her veins.

"Ugh, that'd be great. But first?" She grins with childish mischief.

I smile and toss an arm around her shoulder as we head toward the sandy shore.

37. Ronan

A female screeches, the sound quickly followed by a splash.

I lean over the railing of the rooftop deck to the pool below, where Connor and four local Wolf staffers lounge. Fucking guy. One shift and they're flocking to him.

But I don't know what I'd do without him. I'd be lonely in this giant house, that's for sure.

"You comin' down?" Connor hollers, his deep voice carrying through the peaceful neighborhood. Two-thirds of the houses are empty, waiting for summer visitors.

"Enjoying the view."

"What view? It's dark!"

I chuckle. The sun may be long gone, but the salty sea air is balmy, and the roar of the nearby ocean is palpable.

"Come on. We're playing Marco Polo."

"*Pass.*" Connor's version involves losing articles of clothing, and two of those girls work in administration, which means they inevitably report to me. "Keep the glass away from the pool."

"Aye-aye, boss," he mocks.

My phone vibrates in my pocket. I dig it out to check the screen and smile as I answer. "What took you so long?" I texted Abbi twenty minutes ago to tell her I don't know what the fuck I'm doing here.

"She's busy," a deep male voice retorts, his voice laced with smugness.

I groan. Henry has her phone. "What do you want?" He never calls me. The only time I hear from him is when he's chirping in the background *while* I'm talking to Abbi.

His gulp fills my ear. I can picture the asshole stretched out on his leather couch in their New York high-rise penthouse, sucking back a glass of scotch that only zero-point-one percenters can afford. "How'd your first day go?"

"Belinda didn't stab me, so I call that a win. But I'm sure you've talked to her, so why don't *you* tell *me* how my first day went?"

His dark chuckle tells me Belinda gave him an earful. "She has high hopes for you."

"Yeah, I'll bet." I smirk. "The managers seem equally pleased." Belinda introduced me to Chester, Dorian, and Mike. The reception was polite but decidedly unimpressed.

"Pleasing them is not my concern. How's the house? The car?"

"House is on the small side," I deadpan, stealing a glance at the pool as a brunette peels off her bikini top and tosses it to a nearby chair. I move away before I get myself into trouble. "The car could be nicer." I haven't had a vehicle at my disposal since I was living in Indie and booting around in an old Tacoma. The black BMW waiting for me in the parking lot today dropped my jaw.

"I'll be there for the media open," Henry says, smoothly ignoring my gibes. "I hope you know how to golf."

"Barely." Mention of golf reminds me of the tour. "Saw your neighbor's art display."

Henry's responding sigh is laced with irritation. "Ruby Parker and whoever lives in that commune have already lost."

"And the signs? How are you going to deal with those?"

"Me? I'm not. That's what my director of operations is there to figure out."

Of course. He and Belinda are in lockstep. I mutter dryly, "No problem."

A moment of awkward silence hangs and then Henry says abruptly, "All right, then. Abbi wanted me to check in with you."

"Don't say that!" Abbi hisses in the background.

"Hey, Red," I call out, hoping she'll hear me.

Henry muffles the receiver, his words incoherent but his tone gentler with her.

"Roh-nan!" Connor's deep voice bellows from the pool below.

"Tell him to shut up!" Henry snaps in my ear. "I have neighbors."

Wait. "Is this *your* house?"

"Of course it is. One of many." He hisses. "*Fuck, Abbi, teeth ...*"

It dawns on me then exactly what's going on over in the Wolf household. "You've got to be kidding me."

"I'll touch base next week."

"You motherfu—"

The line goes dead as my hand tightens around my phone, the mental image of Abbi on her knees for him instantly swelling my cock. "Fuck." *Well played, you son of a bitch.* He wants to remind me what I can't have.

And now I'm right back to that night in Alaska.

With that memory fresh in my mind, I head for the shower.

———

I'VE ALWAYS HATED JOGGING.

Hated it when I was a pimple-faced thirteen-year-old at Creekside High. Double my age and I *still* despise it, but the scenery makes it tolerable.

My heart pounds as I jog along the beach, the morning sun hot against my bare chest, the sand packed beneath my runners. Henry was right—it's like white sugar.

The shoreline seems endless. I wonder how far I could run before I was forced to divert. One day, I'll find the answer to that.

But I might collapse before I make it to Wolf because I seriously misjudged the distance and how humid it would be this early in the day. I'm gonna have to call Connor to pick my ass up because there is no way I'll make it to work on time.

"Fuck me," I curse, my breathing ragged as I slow to scan the buildings along the boardwalk ahead, until I spot a little white one that I instantly recognize. It's not anything special from the outside, but the inside has a cozy tropical theme, with teakwood and reed thatching. Best of all though, it smells like freshly brewed coffee.

An OPEN sign glows in the window. A quick glance at my watch tells me it's seven thirty. Would Sloane be there this early? I'll bet King Kong is. That fucking guy makes Connor look like a runt and gives off *stay away from her* vibes that I probably shouldn't ignore. He didn't seem like her boyfriend though. Who is he to her? Brother? Cousin?

I'm *so* curious.

And sweaty. Beads roll down my chest and my back. How will Sloane react to my soaked ass strolling into her shop? Plus, if I consume a coffee now, I'm liable to pass out. No ... what I need is to cool down first.

I kick off my shoes and peel off my socks, dropping them into a pile along with my empty water bottle. There are people here and there, watching the sun climb into the sky and the waves roll in, but no one's in the water yet. With a sigh of satisfaction, I venture out, the refreshing salt water already soothing against my feet.

Fuck, yeah ... I could get used to this life.

38. Sloane

People always ask me what my favorite time of year is, and I can never give them just one answer because there are two spectacular seasons in Mermaid Beach. The first is in the spring, when the day's temperatures are rising but the humidity isn't oppressive yet, and the water is still refreshingly cool. The second is in the fall, when the days are cooling off but stepping into the Gulf is like swimming in a bath.

In both cases, the beach is quieter but not deserted. It's never truly empty here. Even in January when locals bundle up in sweatshirts, people will lounge in the sand, listening to the waves lap while basking in the sun and watching the odd pelican linger. I've spotted swimmers in February when the Gulf is twenty degrees colder than in season. Northerners, usually, venturing down from Michigan or New York, reveling that the white powder beneath their feet is not snow.

It's all relative, I guess, but you won't catch me in the water at that time of year. I don't enjoy the bite of cold. Even the sand is frigid against your bare feet.

I shut my book and finish the last drops of my coffee. The first days when seasonal staff start rolling in are the best. We're on the verge of the boom, but we're not there yet, and we usually have hands to spare. My life feels temporarily lighter in these early days.

Rebel opened the coffee shop this morning with the help of the new girl, Amanda, reacquainting herself with the menu and machines, and letting Frank sleep in for the first time in months.

I wish I could sleep in, but my internal clock is hardwired. Still, I don't feel guilty about taking twenty minutes for myself with this calming view before help Frank with moving equipment.

Except for the bobbing head I spot out in the water. *Way* too far out, especially to be swimming alone. Ten bucks says it's an ignorant tourist who's never heard of a rip current and has no idea how bad they can get around here with the sandbar. That, or they were so enthralled by the lapping waves—like a mermaid's call, impossible to ignore, Gigi always says—that they didn't notice the giant red and purple flags flapping in the breeze. Now they're trying to swim back to shore like an amateur. If they keep it up, they'll exhaust themselves and drown. It happens every year.

With a groan, I abandon my things and march along the beach toward the water, waving my hands. "*This* way!" I yell, gesticulating wildly to my right. "Swim this way!"

My phone sits heavy in my pocket. Do I call for help yet? Do I go in after them? Ugh, it's too early for this shit.

The guy—I think it's a man?—finally clues in because he follows my direction, swimming parallel to the shoreline, getting himself out of the dangerous current.

Relief washes over me as I watch him approach.

By the time he reaches the beach, he's on his hands and knees, crawling, and collapses in a heap on the sand.

"You've gotta pay attention to those currents," I chastise, closing in. "They'll pull even grown-ass men out before you know it." And grown-ass, this pile of sculpted flesh definitely is.

He rolls onto his back, his bare, muscular chest heaving as he tries to catch his breath.

My jaw drops. "It's *you*." The guy who came into the shop two days ago. "Ronan, right?" I'd be lying if I said I hadn't thought of him more than once, hadn't glanced up when the door jangled with a customer, hoping he'd make another appearance.

His mouth opens but he can't seem to manage words, waggling his finger, gesturing for me to come closer.

I drop to my knees beside him. "Do you need me to call for help? I can get someone here—"

"Sea witch. Sloane," he squeezes out through ragged breaths before his arm flops to the side. He closes his eyes.

I bite my bottom lip against the urge to grin. He remembers my name too. That's ... *something*. "I thought you said you were from Miami. Did you not notice the flags?"

"Indianapolis, originally, and I was jogging ... The water looked so inviting."

I wait as his breathing evens out. "You're going to be okay."

His Adam's apple bobs with a hard swallow. "I need mouth-to-mouth, just to be sure."

Now I can't contain my smile. "Barely alive and flirting already."

"I know where my skills lie."

What *are* this guy's skills, besides wielding that deep, grating voice that I feel deep in my core?

A passerby calls out, asking if we need help.

Ronan answers by raising his arm and giving the thumbs-up sign but otherwise makes no move to stand.

"You didn't come in for that coffee."

"I was on my way there today, I swear." He cracks an eyelid but flinches against the morning sun.

I shift to block the blinding rays for him. "But decided to almost drown first?"

"I like to keep things interesting." A crooked smile

stretches across his full lips, reminding me how attractive this man is. Not that I haven't already gotten an eyeful, him in nothing but a pair of shorts that cling to his groin in an obscene way. My effort to keep my focus above his waist leads me to study the sleeve of intricate ink curling up over his shoulder.

And he's watching me ogle his body shamelessly.

"Find another way. I don't need floaters outside my place of business. That's not very *interesting* for my sales."

His stomach clenches as he pulls himself up to a sitting position, showing off a well-honed washboard of muscle and bringing his face to less than a foot from mine. "Probably wouldn't impress my boss either if I didn't show up for my second day on the job."

"Oh?" I can't help the surprise—and delight—in that single word. "You're not just a finance bro here on vacation?" Which means he's going to be here for at least a few months.

He chuckles. "Definitely not. I hate numbers."

"Where are you working?"

He checks his watch before jerking his chin toward the west. "At the new hotel."

"You mean the new *Wolf* Hotel?" I can't help the accusation in my tone.

"Yeah ..." Ronan's brow pinches as he regards my face. "Why do you say it like that?"

My disappointment swells. That stupid place is infiltrating *every* aspect of my life. I can't even flirt with a guy now without being reminded of its existence. "If you're going to run into the water, educate yourself so you don't die." With that stark warning, I leave Ronan sitting on the beach as I march back to the shop, my footfalls heavy with frustration.

The glaring HELP WANTED sign greets me.

"Fuck you, Henry Wolf." I shove the rentals office door open.

My mood turns downright caustic when I spot Cody with

his elbows on the counter, chatting up Skye. I haven't been in the same room as him since he picked up the last of his things to move back in with his mother, though I've seen him around town a few times. He's been smart enough to stay away from the Sea Witch on account of Frank promising to rip off his arms and beat him with them if he came around again. I've never seen Frank hurt so much as a spider—he's the type to brave a thorn-coated bush to rescue an injured bird—but the threat was effective.

Skye gives me a wide-eyed *I didn't know what you wanted me to do* look, and mouths *"I'm sorry"* before scooting to the back office. She's incapable of being rude, even when the person deserves it.

"Rentals aren't open yet. If you want a coffee, you know where it is." I toss my book behind the counter and then crane my neck to check the line on the other side, while deftly avoiding his gaze. "It's quiet. Better move quick before that changes. And you're paying full price."

"Already got one." Cody hoists a paper cup in the air. "Gotta support the Sea Witch, right?" A pause and then, "You look good."

"Bet you say that to all the staffers. Oh, wait, you *do*." That was the icing on the cake, hearing that he put the moves on Skye one night last summer at the bar, about a month after we broke up.

I busy myself with my computer screen, his gaze like a hot iron on my cheek.

"Wow, it's like we're strangers."

"No, we're not strangers. I know you too well." Finally, I meet his eyes. It used to send a thrill through my core to have his attention. Now it swells the ball of anxiety in my stomach. I really did love him then, probably as much as I hate him now. "Seriously, why are you here?"

He shrugs. "I came to see how you're doing."

"No." That's the thing about Cody—he's always angling

for himself. He's an opportunist. "You want something. What is it?"

He purses his lips. "I need a work reference from you."

"You've got to be kidding me." I stare at him with incredulity. After everything, he has the nerve to ask for *that*? "What's wrong, can't get one from Logan?" After he left here, our mutual friend who owns Siren's Call, a popular beach bar for tourists and locals alike, gave Cody a chance at bartending. That lasted all of two weeks until Logan discovered Cody was giving away as much tequila to pretty girls as he was selling.

"Come on ..." Cody's jaw tenses. He's annoyed. Good.

"No? What about the Depot, then?" Frank saw him stocking shelves in the tool aisle over winter.

He grins. "Been keeping tabs on me?"

"Yeah, so I can avoid you."

His glee curdles. "Of course I got a reference. A good one too," he scoffs, and I know he's lying. I can hear it in his voice.

"Then you don't need one from me."

"The Depot is grunt work. But seeing as I helped run things around here—"

"Are you serious? '*Helped run things*'?" A maniacal laugh escapes me. "You want my reference? Okay, here it is: You were the laziest person to ever work for the Sea Witch. How's that?"

"Come on. Just 'cause we didn't work out doesn't mean you have to be so bitter."

I take a deep breath to stop the urge to scream. "I'm not bitter, Cody. I'm relieved that I dodged a giant, lethal bullet. But that doesn't change the fact that you did not help run *anything* around here, and I'm not lying to whomever you are going to fool into hiring you—oh shit." It dawns on me. Right. It's Friday. "The job fair." Frank said he heard Cody was aiming for a position there.

"Yeah. And it would *really* help me if you could tell them how great I was as an employee. Come on, Sloane. How about it?" He's shifted to wounded-animal mode, with pleading eyes and a docile tone.

"You mean lie?"

He sighs with exasperation. "Yeah, sure, fine, if you want to call it that. But what do you care, anyway? It's Wolf. You *hate* that place."

"What'd it ever do to you?" a deep raspy voice calls out.

My head snaps to where Ronan fills the doorway between the two sides, still shirtless but with runners on. How long has he been standing there, listening?

He meets my gaze, long and steady, before sizing up Cody through a sip of his coffee.

"Who's this?" Cody asks.

"Nobody." My life is none of my ex's business, and I want him out of here as quickly as possible.

Ronan scoffs, presses a hand over his bare chest. "After all that we've shared?"

Cody's chuckle is dark. "You couldn't have shared too much if you didn't know what a hate-on she has for that place."

"To be fair, we didn't spend a lot of time talking." Ronan winks at me.

"You're not helping." Seriously, why is he here?

The back door creaks open. "Am I mistaken or is that Dead Man Walking's truck in our lot?" Frank appears behind us, his presence eating up space in my tiny shop like a grizzly bear entering a small cabin. "Oh, look. Hey, Dead Man Walking. What, you don't need your arms anymore?" His voice booms.

I could kiss Frank right now.

"Whatever." Cody backs away, shaking his head. "Sloane, I thought you'd have the decency to get over yourself by now, but if not, fine. They'll hire me without your help. I mean ..." He holds out his arms as if presenting himself. If there's one thing he doesn't lack, it's self-confidence.

"Good luck with that."

His responding smile is smug. "I'd say the same to you and the Sea Witch this year. Not sure how you're gonna run things without staff."

"Fuck you. We have staff."

"You sure about that?"

"I already know about Dave and Teddy leaving."

His eyebrows arch. "Dave and Teddy *too*?"

A swell of panic hits me. "Why? What do you know?"

He shrugs. "Nothin' about nothin'." With one last wary glance at Frank, he yanks the door open. The bell jangles noisily with his departure.

I'm relieved that he's gone, but my mind spins as I run through names. I employ sixteen seasonal staffers here, and I'm already down seven. Who else might be bailing on me?

"Ex-boyfriend?" Ronan asks casually.

"Ex fiancé," Frank answers for me, earning my glare as he passes by, on a mission for a cup of coffee.

Ronan lets out a low whistle as he shifts out of the doorway, closer to me. His shorts are damp from his swim and, while not clinging to his groin anymore, hang low enough to highlight the V of muscle cutting downward into his pelvis. It's not helping my concentration.

"Come on." I gesture at the No shoes, no shirt, medi-ocre service sign on the wall while inhaling the scent of clean sweat and salt water that follows him.

He sets his coffee cup on my counter and pulls his shirt on, allowing me one last admiring gaze at a torso that should never be covered. "The hotel hasn't even opened yet. Seriously, what's the hate for?"

"That hotel has haunted me for the past five years, and it won't stop. First, it came after my peace, and now it's trying to ruin my business."

A strange flicker of recognition passes across Ronan's eyes. "*Fuck* ... You're the crazy rooster commune lady."

"*Crazy rooster commune lady?*"

Through the open door, Frank barks with laughter.

"You own the property next door to the hotel," he amends, and it's followed by a muttered curse.

"Employees have heard about me?" That's surprising. Despite all my efforts, I assumed I was nothing more than a gnat on a horse's ass to them.

"Well, yeah, the hotel manager ..." His words trail.

"The hotel manager *what*?" I've never met this manager. I have no idea who they are. What are they telling their staff to do—stay away from me? Harass me until I'll sell?

"So, that's what that reaction back there was about?" Ronan jams a thumb in the air toward the beach, not answering my question. "You ditched me because I work for Wolf?" His tone is mocking.

When he says it like that, it does sound petty, but it's not even 8:00 a.m., I'm already tired, and now I have to worry about how many more staff members plan on deserting me. "Don't you have a job to get to?"

He checks his watch and collects his coffee cup. "Actually, yeah, I do. Thanks for the help in the water. See you around. Maybe." That last word is a mumble. He may as well have said *not likely*.

I bite my bottom lip with a mixture of reluctance and regret as I watch him and his deliciously powerful back stroll out.

Frank sticks his head in. "Making friends everywhere these days, hey, Parker? Or should I say crazy rooster commune—"

"Shut up," I snap. "You live in that commune, remember?"

"I'm getting T-shirts made." His deep chuckle trails him back into the coffee shop.

Rebel appears then, holding out a warmed macadamia scone and wearing a sympathetic smile. "Hungry?"

"You're a godsend." I clamber for the treat—my favorite.

"It's so nice having you guys back." I add loud enough to carry, "Frank *never* does nice things for me."

A responding grunt is all I get.

"So?" Her dimples flash as I moan through a mouthful. "Who was that guy?"

"A customer from the other day."

"Who's got a thing for Sloane," Frank hollers.

"Stop gossiping!" I scowl at the wall between us.

"Could be a customer with benefits." She waggles her eyebrows.

"Not my style, you know that. Plus, I think those benefits just walked out the door, never to be seen again." Ronan is not my concern right now, though. "Have you talked to Jeremy lately?" He and Rebel occasionally wake up in each other's beds together—naked.

"Yeah, briefly. Why?"

"Because he booked today off and ..." I collect the newspaper from my desk and hold up the Wolf job fair ad. "Do you know about this?"

Her gaze darts to the floor but not before I catch the grimace of guilt.

My shoulders sag. "So, it's true. He's applying to Wolf?"

"I don't want to get in the middle of this!"

"Come on. I know I'm putting you in a tough position, but I need to know." I already have nine reservations for next week.

She hesitates, glancing behind me, no doubt to search for help from Skye, who is conveniently still hiding. "Jeremy mentioned something about applying there."

My arm flops to my side with the article. "Great. I knew it. He's as good as gone."

"Not necessarily—"

I glare at her, and she presses her lips together. We both know Jeremy's a shoo-in.

"So, I'm going to be down to one captain for high season."
We normally run three boats a day.

She winces. "I think AJ might be applying there too."

"Are you kidding me?" I shriek. "Why are you just telling
me this now?" My anger flares.

The coffee shop door jangles and Rebel uses that as her
excuse to scurry back to the other side.

Frank swaps places with her, his expression grim.

"What do I do?" I look at him helplessly.

"They got a right to leave if they want to."

"Yeah, fine, but don't commit to me for the season, then!
And when are they going to give me notice?" I press a hand
against my chest as panic sets in. "I have to stop taking bookings today. Now. At least until I know what's happening." But
if I close Sea Witch's calendar, people won't wait, they won't
call in. They'll just move on to our competitors. I'll lose business either way.

Frank holds up a brown paper bag with another scone
inside. In his giant hand, it looks miniature. "Why don't you
take this to Gigi?"

So she can talk me off the ledge, he doesn't have to say.
"She's at the pool all morning. And I don't want to stress her
out about this." She wasn't any happier about the hotel
opening than I was. Frankly, I blame Henry Wolf for her
waning health.

"Okay. I'm gonna head down to the docks to do maintenance on the boats and then I'll be movin' equipment, if you
need me." He sets the paper bag on the desk and wanders
away, leaving me to stew.

Skye is sitting cross-legged on the floor in the office,
surrounded by file folders.

"What do you know about this?" No doubt she heard
every word.

She smiles uneasily. "Jer's tired of juggling jobs through

the year. He wants somewhere full time, with benefits and all that."

"Yeah, I know." I can't blame him. And he did come to me, asking for more hours. "What about the others? Who else besides AJ?"

She hesitates. "Ron texted me a few weeks ago—"

"*No.* Are you kidding me? Ron too!" I paid for that guy to get his USCG Captain's license for pulling riders on that stupid giant inflatable banana boat that Frank convinced me to buy. "He's supposed to be staying in Surf's Up this summer!" What does he think, I'm going to let him pay next to nothing in rent while working for someone else?

"I don't know for sure!" Skye says, her voice high-pitched. "He didn't say anything specific, but I got the feeling he's curious."

How many others are "curious" about the new hotel in town? Is there going to be anyone left? My eyes burn with the threat of tears. "What is Wolf paying people, anyway?" Could I match it?

She shrugs. "I don't know. I always knew I was coming here."

"Because you are a perfect angel who would never betray me.".

"Exactly." She presses the backs of her hands under her chin and bats her eyelashes playfully.

But the weight of my dilemma is too much to shed with laughter. "I can't just sit around here. If I'm going to lose half my staff, I need to know, like, *now*."

Skye gasps and declares, "I have a *crazy* idea."

39. Ronan

That's amazing. Congratulations.

OMG, Carrie is getting married and I just had a brilliant idea for her bachelorette! We should do it at your new hotel! When does it open? I need to organize something soon. Hook a girl up?

Carrie would love you forever (she's still pissed we're not together anymore).

Why didn't you warn me how muggy Miami is?

I reread the string of texts that started last night, the last one coming in while I was using the staff locker room shower. Tasha is clearly trying to open a line of communication after two years of radio silence. Does she remember how we broke up? Because I sure as hell do and it wasn't pretty.

But it's been so long. I don't even think about her anymore until she shows up on my phone screen. This is stupid. Why am I toiling over how to respond and what things might mean? It doesn't matter because we've been done for years. I couldn't say how many women I've slept with since. If Tasha and I can come out at the end as friends? Fan-fucking-tastic.

> I can definitely hook a girl up.

I feel Belinda's dissecting eyes on me, so I dump my phone into my pocket and return to scanning the hordes of people filling the hotel ballroom, in various stages of the screening and interview process. It's a complete shitshow. "What ever happened to emailing résumés and calling people in?"

"Is that how you were hired?" Belinda retorts.

"No," I admit. "It was a college job fair." Wolf Hotels had a table, and people could apply and interview on the spot for everything from administration to collecting trash, working all over the world. I'll admit, Henry's company has a stellar reputation. The line of candidates was long.

Her heels click as she leads me through the crowd at a leisurely pace. "This may be painful, but it allows us an opportunity to evaluate applicants up front and quickly, especially when we're hiring seasonally for a hotel that opens in less than three weeks. For example"—she lowers her voice to a murmur only I can hear—"that one over there is applying to serve in our fine dining establishment."

I follow her focus. "The mullet?"

"Precisely. He wants to serve our clientele thousand-dollar bottles of wine and premium oysters. Do you think his name will reach the hire list?"

"You'd kill someone's future over their hair? You know they're back in style," I add, half jokingly.

"Mullets were *never* in style. The hair is a questionable choice, but he's applying for a high-end customer service job in *flip-flops and torn jean shorts*." She sneers. "He won't get past the first round of scrutiny and if he does, Lena's managers will end that quickly because they know what is required of our employees."

I met my counterpart yesterday and the disapproving once-over she gave me told me everything I needed to know about her. We aren't going to get along. "What if he's qualified to do the job?"

"If he were qualified to work in high-end service, he would not have arrived for an interview dressed like *that*."

"Fair enough." I smirk. "Though, I didn't show up too much better yesterday."

"Precisely. You're not qualified for your job either. But it's amazing what the right clothes can do." Belinda's sharp, assessing gaze drags over the white button-down and tailored palm-green dress pants I changed into. While I'm not thrilled by this location's color scheme, I have to admit, the clothes Belinda chose make me feel like a baller. The double takes I've caught are tenfold the average. This is how Wolf must feel.

But I'm still not wearing that fucking tie.

I assess the vast group of hopefuls. Some of these people will know me as their *boss* beginning next week—a reality I'm still adjusting to. There are a lot of them. "Are these all Mermaid Beach locals?"

"Here and the towns over the bridge. Or seasonals who have come down with jobs already lined up but are hoping to upgrade."

Like Sloane's staffers, based on the tail end of that conversation I overheard. How many of her people are ready to ditch her? No wonder she has no love for Wolf. Still, it's unhinged to react the way she did when she found out I'm working here.

But I already knew she was unhinged.

Damn it, though. How is Sloane, that beautiful creature who knelt beside me in the sand today, *also* the check-ripping, hateful sign-crafting, deranged neighbor who has picked a war with Henry Wolf?

"I imagine some are aiming for permanent year-round positions." Belinda shakes her head. "Honestly, they think they can show up to an establishment like *this* in stained tank tops?

And look, that one just came from the pool." She juts her chin toward a young woman whose bikini has soaked through her T-shirt, leaving two round wet marks across her chest. "She wants me to trust her with cleaning a guest's room? I could cull half these people in the next five minutes." She pauses in her rant. "At least he looks like a serious applicant."

I find her new target, and familiarity hits me right away. It's Sloane's ex, the arrogant fuck I met this morning at the Sea Witch. Well, "met" is a stretch. I witnessed him try to bully her into a favorable reference. I have no idea why they ended their engagement, but it was clearly not on good terms.

"What position is that for?" He's dressed in a cheap suit and tie. It's funny, I didn't know the difference between a suit you buy at a big-box store and one made by a man named Lorenzo who shifts your ball sack to ensure the perfect fit until I met Henry.

"Bartending. Good fit. Pretty faces sell drinks. To be honest, I'm amazed you chose yard work over that. You could have raked in the tips."

I smirk. "Are you calling me pretty?"

"You know you are." She juts her chin at Sloane's ex. "So does he. And barring a criminal record, Lena will take him."

"That would be a mistake," I say before I can stop myself. Why do I care if Sloane's ex gets a job here? She all but told me to go fuck myself. I shouldn't care at all, and yet the idea of him coming out on top burns, especially after watching him taunt her and how her face paled. It sounds like he's not the only one who might want a reference from the Sea Witch—a notion that stressed her out greatly.

"Why? Do you know him?" Belinda asks.

"Not exactly." How much do I want to share? Belinda already wants Sloane's head on a pike. She'd hunt down and hire every Sea Witch employee out of spite. "I know his ex—"

Belinda holds up a manicured hand. "You know what? Never mind. I don't want the sordid details of what you and that fuckboy friend of yours have already gotten up to in your short time here. Speaking of fuckboys, did I hear from Henry correctly that you are giving Connor a supervisory position?"

"That's right." I grin. "I know him and I trust him." For example, I know the idiot will drink too many margaritas tonight and will be nursing a brutal hangover tomorrow, but he'll make sure to escort out the woman he brings home from the bar and lock the door behind her.

She shakes her head. "I give you three shifts until we have an HR complaint and then have fun firing your ..."

Belinda's scathing prediction fades as a swirl of familiar ash-blond hair catches my attention.

What the hell is Sloane doing *here*?

40. Sloane

The Wolf Hotel's grand ballroom is jam-packed with prospective seasonal workers. Still, it took us under five minutes to find Cody.

"This is crazy. I can't believe you talked me into this!" I hiss. And not just talked me into it. We went home and changed first. "We should go."

"I've never seen him in anything but a T-shirt," Skye whispers, ignoring me.

"His mother dressed him." We went to a handful of events —weddings, funerals, family dinners—while we were together, and she chose Cody's outfits every time.

"How old is he again?"

"Thirty."

"Talk about failure to launch."

"Still, I'm sure he'll charm the right people." I scan faces. Where did all these people come from? And did they do any research about Wolf Hotels before they arrived? Half of them look like they rolled out of bed to get here. I'm just a spy and even I threw on my favorite power outfit—white dress pants and a pale blue blazer over a floral print tank top.

Despite my bitterness for this chain, I struggled to keep

my jaw from gaping as we parked and followed the signs in. I've never been in something so fancy in my life. It oozes money, from the gold cornice details to the ornate fixtures in the restrooms. I couldn't afford to stay here even if I wanted to.

Fuck Henry Wolf.

My stomach sinks as Jeremy appears.

He's easy enough to spot, his lanky form towering over nearly everyone else. He's gripping a copy of his résumé in front of him and biting his bottom lip. Sable brown hair that normally settles in every direction is combed and styled with gel. Someone has ironed his white dress shirt. If I know Jeremy at all, he's nervous and desperate to make a memorable impression.

"I guess that settles it." I was right, even before Rebel confirmed it. And there's nothing I can do about it.

While waiting, Jeremy idly scans the crowd.

"Shit!" I duck behind a pillar. Did I move fast enough?

My face burns with indignation. I knew this was a stupid plan the second Skye suggested it and yet I went along with it like a fool—

"Hey, you're back!" Jeremy's familiar jovial tone is suddenly within earshot, on the other side of the pillar.

I hold my breath.

"Oh, *hey*, Jer!" Skye's nervous laugh carries over the buzz of voices. "Yup, I'm back."

"I didn't think you were comin' today."

"Yeah ... I didn't think so either but ..." She fumbles over her words as she struggles for a response.

"Does Sloane know you're here?"

"Nope." She emphasizes the *p* in the sentence. "No idea. None whatsoever."

I breathe a sigh of relief even as I roll my eyes. Skye's always been a terrible liar. But at least Jeremy didn't see me. Yet. Between him and Cody, my chances of escape are slim.

"I feel so guilty applying *here* of all places, given how she feels about it, but I need something stable, ya know?"

"Yeah, I get ya."

"Dave told me he got full time. Him and Teddy both. They moved into an apartment down the street, and they're starting Monday. I should have applied during the first round. I shouldn't have waited. I heard Wolf's benefits for full-time are good."

Unease slides down my spine as I eavesdrop and Jeremy rambles. I can't blame him for wanting more. I wish I could be the one to give that to him.

But I need to leave now, before I'm caught.

I make a break for the door.

And freeze.

Ron stands a mere twenty feet ahead and directly in my path, flipping through a pamphlet.

"You son of a ..." I grit my teeth as a flurry of anger and disappointment flares. I should have made him pay for his own training.

He leans in to say something to a guy beside him, and my jaw drops. That's Mick! And Will is beside him! They're leaving me too? I want to scream.

Shifting from palm to pillar to palm—I swear, Gigi and I watched an *I Love Lucy* episode just like this once—I rush for another exit at the back of the room, veering to the left.

And run smack-first into AJ.

His eyes widen. "Sloane. Uh ... What are you doing here?"

"What am *I* doing here?" There's not much left to do but confront him.

"I ... uh ..." He stalls as he searches for a suitable lie.

"There you are," a familiar raspy voice purrs.

I spin on my heels. "Ronan?" My attention snags on the way his white dress shirt sits unbuttoned at the collar, showing off a hint of that chiseled collarbone I saw earlier. It's a far cry from the half-naked jogger who crawled out of the water this morning.

His gaze rakes over my shocked face. "Let's have that meeting."

"Meeting?" I echo dumbly.

"The one we scheduled. In my office. *Now*."

It finally clicks. He's offering me a way out of this awkward hole I've dug for myself. "Your office. Right."

The corner of his mouth twitches as if with a private joke. "Follow me." Gesturing in the opposite direction of AJ and the ballroom of applicants, he takes a few steps and then stalls, waiting.

"Uh ... see you next week, Sloane?" AJ calls out.

Apparently not if he's applying here. I toss a weak wave in his direction as I trail Ronan away. "You are literally *every-where* today, aren't you," I hiss the moment we're out of earshot.

"I could say the same about you." He skims the faces of people around us, as if looking for one in particular. "And you're welcome."

"For what?"

"For saving your ass before you got caught spying on your ex."

My jaw drops. "I wasn't here to spy on him!"

"Good, because that would have been humiliating." Ronan swipes a key card that allows us through a set of glass doors and into a large office full of Wolf employees. We quickly veer down a hall.

"Where are we going?"

"To my office, like I said."

I follow, secretly admiring his sleek stride, the graceful, confident way he moves. And here I thought he was appealing while half naked and sprawled on the sand but, no, no, no ... business attire Ronan is like a luxurious present waiting to be unwrapped, especially when his clothes look tailor-made for his body and I know what's hiding beneath. Well, not *everything.*

I clear my throat to shake out the intrusive—and blush-inducing—thoughts. "What do you do here?"

"I'm the director of operations for facilities, grounds and, admin. As for what I do ..." He pushes through a glass door, holding it open for me. The door shutters behind him. "I have no fucking clue."

I snort at the unexpected candor. "How old are you?"

Ronan perches himself on the edge of his desk and crosses his arms. The material of his dress shirt stretches across his biceps, distracting me. "Is that polite to ask?"

"I think we've moved past polite." Why does he seem *so* familiar? I've seen his face before, I'm sure of it.

"You're probably right." He studies me with amusement as he seems to consider his answer. "I'll be twenty-seven in the fall."

Five years younger than me. How does a person that young get promoted to a position this high? "Someone up top must have faith in you."

"Yeah, well ..." His green eyes drift over a framed photo of the Emerald Coast waters on the wall. There isn't much to the office—a desk, a computer, a rack holding men's dress clothes. Certainly no personality, and nothing that tells me who Ronan is. "I've questioned Henry's sanity more than once, believe me."

My eyebrows arch. "*The* Henry Wolf gave you this job?"

"The one whose reputation you're intent on smearing with your little art project? Yeah, him."

"I have a right to protest."

"If that's what that is." Ronan's tone is dry. He's hard to read. Is he mocking or teasing me?

"So, you guys are friends?"

"I wouldn't call us that, no." The sly smile curving Ronan's lips is secretive. "Enough about me. Honestly, what were you thinking, coming here to hunt down your employees?"

"I was not ..." My denial fades with a heavy sigh. "It was a stupid idea. And not that it matters, but it wasn't mine. It was my twenty-one-year-old barista—oh, shit! Give me a sec." Skye is likely freaking out, wondering where I've disappeared. I feel Ronan's gaze on me as I quickly type out a text to her, telling her to meet me at her car.

With that done, I turn my focus back to him. "So, why'd the director of operations rescue the crazy rooster commune lady? You could have left me out there to disgrace myself."

"Well, for one, I know why you came here. It must be a kick to your stomach to see the people you rely on abandoning you, especially at the start of your season."

I swallow the flare of emotion, his words hitting deep. *Abandoning.* That's the perfect word. "I guess I have you to thank for that."

"I only started here yesterday, so I can't take credit for the hires up until now."

"Yeah, well ... It's hard to find reliable workers. Impossible when you have no idea they're all quitting on you at once."

"I imagine it is." He studies me intently. There's a different, less playful air around him now than on the beach and at the Sea Witch. Then again, he didn't know who he was flirting with.

Silence hangs in the room.

"And the other reason?" I finally ask.

"Huh?" Wherever he just went, I seem to have interrupted his thoughts.

"The other reason you helped me. You said 'for one,' which usually means there's more than one reason."

"Right." He smirks. "Given your reputation, I was worried you'd cause a scene, which would attract Belinda's attention, and then we'd have an even *bigger scene* once she figured out who you are."

"Who's Belinda?"

"The general manager. I report to her, and she takes her job very seriously. She wouldn't be above having you dragged out in handcuffs, if she didn't claw out your eyes first."

"Belinda sounds like fun."

"She has her moments." That tiny smile appears again but disappears just as quickly, as if he's catching himself. "But it wouldn't reflect well on anyone."

"Especially for Wolf."

"For *anyone*," he reiterates. "So, you're welcome." He lets those words hang.

What's going through his head, now that he knows who I am? Probably that I'm certifiable. "Thanks," I offer after a delayed moment. "I should go. I have to figure out how to keep my business from running into the ground." If I sound dejected, it's because I am. The day keeps getting worse. If Mick and Will are here too, who else is?

I should have stayed in bed.

"You assume we'll hire them all," Ronan says.

"Oh, you will. My tiki captain, Jeremy, is the best employee we've ever had. Ron is eager and hardworking. They're *all* decent people," I admit begrudgingly. "Except for Cody. But he doesn't work for me anymore."

"Your ex?"

"Yeah. Be careful if he's anywhere near the bar."

"Heavy drinker?"

"More like a heavy dicker. Loves to ply women with free shots so he can get into their pants."

"That's a new one." Ronan chuckles. "Is that how he got you?"

"I don't fall for that." I don't even touch hard alcohol. "But I'm sure it's how he got all his side action while we were together."

Ronan nods, as if he's not surprised to hear that Cody

cheated on me. He could be the type to cheat on women too, though.

"He got fired from Siren's Call for giving away bottles' worth of tequila, though he's probably not stupid enough to use them as a reference. But don't expect a solid employee there. Or even a mediocre one. God, why am I giving you advice while you steal people away from me!" I roll my eyes at myself. "If you could show me how to get out of here without walking through that ballroom again, I will be gone, and I promise, I will *never* step foot on Wolf Hotel soil again."

Ronan hums but doesn't move, seemingly in thought. "Jeremy … what's his last name?"

"Smith. Why?" I ask warily.

He reaches for a pad and pen on his desk, the fine material of his shirt stretching across his chiseled torso. "We have a lot of people to choose from. I don't see why we have to hire your staff. Any more of it, anyway. So, we can help each other out. Who are the other ones?"

Shit. My guilt flares. "You're asking me to make a hit list?"

He smirks. "I assumed you already had one."

"I do, but it's for Cody." And Henry Wolf, but admitting that would not be smart.

Ronan opens his mouth but falters. "Why'd you end things with him? The cheating?"

"No, I didn't know about that until after. Let's just say he was more interested in having my money than in having me as a wife."

"Your property. Yeah, that's got to be worth a bit."

"Enough that your not-friend boss tried buying it from me five different times." And that's only my house. I also own the Sea Witch lot and the storage lot. There were two other properties that Gigi acquired over the years—she's also been a shrewd woman with her money—but we sold those to pay for her place at Palm Oaks.

"Five times." Ronan whistles. "He is nothing if not persistent." He shifts back to his pad. "Who are the other employees?"

I bite my thumbnail as I think. Is this right? It's bad enough that I came here but now I'm sabotaging their chances of a job. Frank is right—if they don't want to work for the Sea Witch, who am I to stop them from leaving?

"How much is the high season worth to you?" he asks.

"It's seventy to eighty percent of my annual sales," I admit.

"Exactly." Ronan peers up at me from beneath thick dark lashes, studying me while I continue to waffle over my reluctance. "Okay, how about this—I don't want to hire people who would royally screw over their current employer. We're making offers as soon as possible and training starts next week. You're not getting two weeks' notice from these guys. So, give me some names. I get final say for my departments. I'll see what I can do."

Is his guy saying he'll pass on good employees for me, a.k.a. the crazy rooster commune lady? My hackles rise. "Why are you helping me?"

His brow quirks. "I don't understand."

"I crashed your job fair and now you're helping me." There must be a catch. There always is. "What do you want from me in return?"

"Man, you are cynical." A soft, deep chuckle slips out. "Can't I just be a good guy?"

"No." Beautiful men can't also be good guys. They don't exist, it's that simple. "What is this going to cost me?"

"Who says I expect anything?"

"*You* did. 'We could help each other out'?" I air-quote those words.

"Right, I said that." He nods slowly. "What are you offering?"

"What do you want?" I ask hesitantly.

Steely eyes trace my nose, my cheeks, my lips, and then a devilish, small smile breaks free, one that makes my pulse spike. He knows he has me over a proverbial barrel. Or his desk. I inhale sharply with the mental image that stirs, even as I acknowledge that it would be utterly vile of Ronan to use sex as a bargaining chip. It would also prove my beautiful-man theory.

Would he at least keep it semi-classy and buy me dinner first, or would he just unbutton his pants right here? The office doors are frosted. Do they lock—

"Sloane?"

"Huh?" Oh my God, I've been gaping at him.

"The signs have to come down."

"The signs?" *That,* I hadn't expected, but I should have. "Was this your plan all along when you brought me in here?"

"No. I actually was trying to avoid a disaster out there."

For some inexplicable reason, I believe him.

"You take down all the signs and then I'll steer the managers toward different hires."

The Sea Witch's survival or my petty art project, as Ronan called it. "Frank would be ecstatic to see them gone." He keeps suggesting I find a new way to channel my rage. That, and therapy.

"Frank sounds like a reasonable man."

"As long as you're not on his bad side." But the signs down mean Henry Wolf wins. I may as well have cashed that last fat check he offered. Frank wasn't happy with me about that one either. Outright called me an idiot.

"So? What do you say?"

"I say ..." I weigh my options. I have none. I'm not about to let Gigi's legacy to Mermaid Beach fall apart. "You stop poaching my staff *and then* I'll take down my signs." Getting those up was work. I earned dozens of slivers and scrapes, climbing up into branches.

"Deal."

I still can't believe Ronan is being so kind to me. I wasn't kind to him today. I definitely am not his boss's favorite person. Is there more to this that I haven't picked up on yet? "That's it? That's *all* I need to do?"

Now his gaze slides down, stalling on the fitted tank top that hugs my curves beneath my blazer. "Why? Was there something else you had in mind?"

"I just meant ..." My heartbeat quickens. He oozes confidence and masculinity, but with it a calm assuredness that I find so incredibly attractive. Unlike Cody, who flaunts his appeal to get what he wants, Ronan sits back and lets others gravitate toward him, like he doesn't have a care in the world, one way or another.

What would Ronan be like in bed?

Hell, Frank was right and this guy *is* dangerous. I've been alone in this office with him for five minutes and I've thought of stripping off those expensive clothes at least half of that time. I'm not usually this thirsty. Scratch that, I'm *never* like this and especially not since my heartbreak.

"The rooster."

"Huh?" I blurt, his voice jarring my perverted thoughts.

"It has to go."

My jaw drops, all previous thoughts of sex gone. "*No deal.*" The audacity!

"Okay." Ronan holds up his hands in surrender. "It was just a thought. I didn't realize you were so attached to a bird."

"Ralph is not a *bird*. He's a part of the family."

"Got it. Ralph. Forget I mentioned it." More to himself, he adds, "How long can those things live, anyway, right?"

Eight years for Ralph's breed, and he's only two.

"So ... Jeremy Smith, and who else ...?" Ronan waits with his pen poised.

"Not Jeremy."

He frowns. "Didn't you just say he's your best employee?"

"Yeah." I sigh. "He asked me for full-time hours. I can't give those to him, but that's not his fault. Don't blacklist him on my account. He's doing what he has to do. I'll manage." I hope.

"What about that guy you were talking to when I found you?"

"AJ? You might as well take him, seeing how awkward things will be now that he knows that I know he's applying here."

Something unreadable flickers in Ronan's gaze. "The others?"

My stomach curls. Am I doing this? Yeah, I guess I am. "Mick Wallen, Will Moore, and Ron Sholtz. Those are the ones I know about."

Ronan scribbles on his paper and then sets the pad and pen on his desk, freeing his hands to settle on splayed thighs, the rich green fabric stretched over muscle. "Consider it taken care of."

"And how will I know you've kept your end of the deal?" I ask.

"You'll still have employees next week."

"Right." I hesitate. "Thank you."

"You're welcome. What are neighbors for?"

"It's my neighbor who caused *all* of my problems."

"Fine. But aim that anger at Henry Wolf. Not the hotel employees. Definitely not at me." Humor glints across his handsome face. "I'm far more useful to you as a friend."

How did he make that one platonic word sound sexual? "I'll try to remember that."

The air within the office grows potent with tension as the silence lingers and we stare unabashedly at each other. This can't all be one-sided. He *must* be able to feel it too.

Ronan clears his throat as he stands and reaches for a business card from a holder. I admire his body as he leans over to scribble something on the back of it. His steps are measured as

241

he closes the distance toward me, holding the card out between two long fingers. "You can find me here."

He's standing well within my personal space. That can't be unintentional. And he smells divine—a blend of mint and woody citrus, and musky soap from the shower he must have had after he dragged himself out of the ocean. Why is his scent so intoxicating? It's drawing me in, in a way I can't describe. I inhale deeply.

"Who says I'll want to find you?" My voice cracks on that lie as I tilt my head back to meet his gaze with a challenging one. *Something tells me I'll be hoping it's you every time the door swings open at the Sea Witch.*

A muscle in his jaw ticks. It's the first hint that Ronan might be anything but lackadaisical.

If I thought the tension was thick before, now I'm about to choke on it. He might have been handpicked by the devil himself to help run this hotel, but right now, I've never felt such a strong urge to kiss a man.

His hand with the card hangs in the air, waiting.

Finally, I collect it, our fingertips grazing in the process, my skin acutely aware of his touch and how it lingers a few beats before pulling away.

"If that's *all* I can help you with today ..."

It's a taunt, but he's not going to make the first move.

A rare burst of impulsiveness hits me.

Before I can talk myself out of it, I lift onto my toes to meet that perfect mouth head-on.

For one ... two ... three beats, we're pressed together in a slow, tentative connection.

And then he pulls away abruptly. "I didn't mean ... Let's keep this professional."

"Of course it's professional." I snap as my cheeks burn with embarrassment.

The glass door behind me cracks open with his push. "Go left out here and make another right at the end of the hall.

Halfway down there's an exit that will put you on a path to the parking lot. You'll avoid any more uncomfortable run-ins."

More uncomfortable than this? Spinning on my heels, I speed down the hall, mortified over my temporary lapse in judgment.

41. Ronan

Sloane storms away without a glance back, as if she can't get away from me fast enough.

I bite my tongue against the urge to recall her to explain myself while I watch her tight ass in those sexy white pants until she disappears around the corner.

What a bold woman, showing up to Wolf the way she did.

I duck back into my office and shut my door, my body vibrating with a raw need I haven't felt in forever.

"Fuck me." My second day as a director and I was *this close* to testing the desk's weight capacity. I hadn't meant it to go that way, but then she asked if there was something else I wanted from her, and all blood flow left my brain, heading south.

Yeah, I wanted something, all right. I quickly assessed how frosted that glass is, if the lock on the handle works, how long it would take us to get our clothes off, how the sound of her coming might carry down the hall.

And she certainly wasn't helping matters, what with those gorgeous eyes raking over me countless times.

But she came to Wolf in the first place because she's

desperate. I would have to be a grade A prick to take advantage of that.

Did I send mixed signals? Yeah, probably. But I didn't expect her to kiss me. She's hard to read, but I can tell she isn't the kind of girl to kiss random men. She's also not the kind who will slide her number into a guy's pocket and hike up her dress for him later that night. She's older than me—I'm not sure by how much but definitely a few years. And she was engaged, which means she's the settle-down type.

She's also the one woman who will one hundred percent cost me this job if Belinda makes good on her threats, and I believe she will. As reluctant as I may have been to accept it, now that it's mine, the idea of failing bothers me. So, the last thing I need to do is start something up with Sloane.

Or any woman, for that matter.

I need *fewer* women in my life, not more.

On a positive note, I haven't been this hard for a woman since ... well, Abbi. I also haven't kissed a woman on the mouth since Abbi. I run my tongue along my lips now, still tasting the coconut oil of Sloane's lip balm. She smelled incredible too, a tropical scent that made my pulse spike. She has no idea how difficult it was for me to hit the brakes.

But I'm not helping her so I can fuck her. I'm not even helping her because it solves the problem of what to do about those signs.

Why am I so intent on helping the crazy rooster commune lady?

I guess because it's the right thing to do; I know that in my gut. Plus, she's aggravating Henry, and that doesn't bode well for her.

A knock sounds on the door.

"What?" My annoyance bleeds through my voice.

"Sir ... um ... Ronan?" Archie calls out. "Belinda's asking about you. Should I tell her you're in your office—"

"*No.*" The single word comes out too harsh. I also don't

need *that* woman coming in here while I have a raging hard-on. I temper my tone. "Tell her I'll find her in ten minutes. I need to make an important call."

"Got it." The sound of his hurried footfalls fade.

I briefly consider dealing with my issue the old-fashioned way, but there aren't any blinds on the windows, so I do the only thing I can think of to kill all lewd thoughts.

I call my mother.

———

THE SEA WITCH parking lot is busy when I pull in, on my way to the hotel. I'm already annoyed that I'm working on a Saturday, especially when I was in my office until ten last night, playing a game of "read all these reports and pretend we know what the fuck they mean." Then I came home to a house full of strangers and music blaring. Connor is already living his best life.

I briefly consider skipping this stop, but leaving things with Sloane the way we did has pricked my conscience all night. I embarrassed her, maybe even hurt her. I need to make it right so I can stop dwelling on it.

"Fuck me." I take in the customer line that snakes around the shelves of merchandise and bags of coffee. At six to seven bucks a pour, Sloane's got quite the racket going on here. I'm impressed. I'm also going to be late for the morning managers' meeting if I wait.

The same girl with short, black hair from yesterday is behind the till, her black Sea Witch T-shirt stretched across her chest. She smiles wide as she chats up the customers, as if she landed her dream job and this is it.

In complete contrast, a brunette scrambles behind her to make orders, spilling milk and dropping a spoon with a clatter. Her deer-caught-in-headlights eyes say she's new here and struggling to keep up.

There's no sign of Sloane, but the door between the two halves of the building is open, so I slip through it and into the rentals side.

Rustling sounds in the back office.

"Hello?" I call out and cross my fingers that King Kong doesn't appear. I'm in no mood to deal with his crusty ass this early.

"We're not open yet," a woman with a southern twang answers. "If you come back"—a blond rounds the corner and stops dead when she sees me—"at eleven, we can help you then." Her lips part in a wide grin as she smooths her hand through a lion's mane of golden hair.

I recognize her. She was at the job fair with Sloane. "Is your boss around?"

"Sloane? No. She's visiting Gigi." She says this as if I personally know this Gigi woman.

"Do you know when she'll be in?"

"Not sure. Can *I* help you with something?" she asks, adjusting her stance so her Sea Witch T-shirt stretches tight across tits that are almost too big for her little body. This one is a wet-dream sorority girl, through and through. Connor would be salivating. "No, I really needed to talk to Sloane." To say what, exactly, I'm not sure yet.

I'm sorry I didn't fuck you on my desk yesterday.
I'm not allowed to touch you, boss's orders.
I can't get hung up on another woman right now.
I'm still sort of in love with Henry Wolf's wife.

The truth is, I doubt I'd have the guts to say any of those things, just like I never had the guts to say half the things swimming through my head where Abbi was concerned. I always kept it cool and superficial. It was an act, but it protected me where she was concerned.

"How long do you think that coffee line will take?"

"With Amanda making the orders? *At least* thirty minutes."

"Damn." I mutter more to myself, "All right. Shit coffee from the pit it is." For all the money Wolf spent on construction, you'd think they could invest in decent coffee machines for the staff.

"Hold, please." Blondie holds up a manicured finger. "I'll be right back." She ducks through the doorway before I can say a word, leaving me alone. I wander over to the far wall to the pictures I didn't notice the first day, too enthralled by the beauty behind the counter. It's a timeline of Sea Witch's long history in Mermaid Beach, reminiscent of a family portrait wall—dozens of group photos of staff huddled around the same woman pictured in the original Sea Witch plaque, her long, blond braids adorned with a tropical flower.

In the earliest ones, a teenage girl stands in front of her, Gigi's hands resting possessively on her shoulders. Gigi's daughter, I presume. With each year, the girl grows older, until suddenly she's cradling a baby. She can't be more than twenty.

And I'll bet that's Sloane.

From that point, Gigi and her daughter take turns holding Sloane, then standing with her, the little ash-blond girl wearing a bathing suit and a goofy expression.

There are a dozen pictures of the three generations together through the years as Sloane grows from an impish child to a gangly prepubescent, and then the younger woman is suddenly gone. The smiles are more forced across the group that year. Sloane's is nonexistent.

As I move down the line, I note that her mother never reappears.

A creak of a door opening in the back sounds, and a moment later, King Kong strolls through. He grimaces when he sees me. "This side's closed."

"Yeah, I know. I came in to see Sloane."

"She's not here."

"Thanks. I got that. I'm gonna head—"

"Morning, big guy! Missed you at the fire last night." The

blond swoops past him, patting his trunk of an arm, before she crosses the room to hand me a large coffee. "If you need cream or sugar, you can grab it at the side bar."

"Black is perfect. How much do I owe you?"

"This one's on the house." She winks. "I'm sure Sloane would agree."

I chuckle as I dig out a ten-dollar bill and set it on the counter. "I think she'd charge me double. But thank you ..."

"Skye." Her eyes shift from the cash to me, batting long, salon-made lashes. "Have a great day." She skips back to the coffee shop, stealing a glance over her shoulder to flash me a playful grin.

Frank glowers at me. "She's not interested in you either."

I would beg to differ, but I don't want to die today. Does he know what happened between me and Sloane yesterday? "I'm just gonna ..." I toss a thumb toward the door.

"Yeah, you do that." Frank's distrusting gaze sears into my back.

———

"Late, and you arrive like *this*." Belinda falls into step beside me as she glares at my open collar and rolled-up sleeves. "You love to test boundaries, don't you?"

At least I'm wearing a fucking dress shirt and pants. I despise golf shirts and was *this close* to throwing on my usual jeans and T-shirt. "Since when does senior management work weekends?"

Belinda flips her blond hair over her shoulder, and I'm hit with a waft of perfume. "Henry owns the entire company, and I've yet to see him take a weekend off. He was answering calls on his honeymoon."

"I'm not Henry." I sure as hell would love his bank accounts, though.

"Believe me, *I know*. He personally watched every interview video for Wolf Cove because he was that invested in its success. If you were Henry, you'd be doing the same. But you're not." In a slightly more conciliatory tone, she goes on. "Besides, we're running on a super-condensed timeline. Our people have already done all the heavy lifting. Just approve the final staffing lists that our managers spent *all night* vetting and then run off to do whomever you want for the rest of the weekend."

I smirk. "You mean *what*ever."

"I don't," Belinda snipes, admiring her hot pink fingernails that I once recall digging into my shoulders.

There's no point trying to sway her opinion of me. "So why am I here if all the work is done?"

"So you can take full responsibility if your department hires give me problems." She frowns at the paper cup in my hand. "The Sea Witch?"

"Local shop." I hold my breath a beat, waiting to see if a link between the name and Sloane will form, but Belinda doesn't seem to connect the dots. "The coffee in the pit is shit."

"Oh God, why would you drink that?" She grimaces. "Minnie gets mine from Opal Reef. The Brevilles arrived two weeks ago."

"We can do that?" I didn't even consider sending my assistant to fetch me coffee from one of the hotel's restaurants.

She answers with a snort.

I was actually hoping to run into Belinda before this meeting, but it wasn't to discuss caffeine sources. "Listen, there might be a few names I need to veto today."

"*Veto*?" She adjusts her thick-rimmed glasses to scowl at me. "Explain."

The list is tucked in my back pocket. To say Sloane was reluctant with my idea would be an understatement. I practically had to pull the names from her pretty lips, and she squirmed uncomfortably the entire time. "Our neighbor is willing to take down her signs if I help her out."

Belinda's pencil-drawn eyebrows arch with a mixture of interest and suspicion. "Help her *how*?"

I considered how to approach this long and hard last night, while admiring the stars from our rooftop. I've figured out Sloane's weakness—her family business, her grandmother's legacy to Mermaid Beach. If I give Belinda this information, I don't trust that she won't use it as ammo to punish our menace of a neighbor rather than as a negotiating tool. "It's a long story, and I'd rather not bore you with the details. Plus, plausible deniability has its benefits."

She freezes mid step. "Does this involve my director of operations sticking his dick somewhere it doesn't belong?" she hisses.

"Inside the bus at all times. I swear."

She stares me down as if searching for the lie.

"I did not lay a hand on her, Belinda." My lips are another story, and I didn't instigate that. I sure as hell enjoyed it, enough that it was the first thing that came to mind when I cracked my blurry eyes open this morning. "But I need you to back me up. You do that, and those signs on her property will be long gone by the media open."

That gives her pause. "*All* of them?"

"Every last one."

Her lips twist as she considers this. "I want the rooster gone too."

"That's a no-go." There's not a chance in hell *Ralph* is going anywhere. I saw Sloane's face. I may as well have demanded she drown a puppy. "So? Will you back me up if I need it?" Something tells me I will need it. Sloane wouldn't tolerate idiots. Aside from her ex, that is. All these guys will be Wolf Hotel employees by the end of the weekend if I don't run interference.

I hold my breath as I wait for her answer.

"Fine." Belinda sighs reluctantly. "But don't make me look stupid."

"That's impossible." I cap it off with a wink.

She rolls her eyes. "Be prepared for pushback, though. These are all career Wolf managers who aren't pleased about reporting into a grounds crew worker who weaseled his way into Henry's good graces."

"Got that vibe." But weaseled? I smirk. "Is that what I did?"

"I have no idea what precisely you did, and I'm sure I do not want to know. But Dorian was expecting your job. Frankly, he deserves it."

"And maybe one day, he'll have it. But today, it's mine and I can squash our public relations issue with your help."

A thoughtful expression lingers on her face as she slows her steps. The meeting room is up ahead. "If you want to earn your position, you need to start acting like you care that you have it."

"I *do* care." As much as I might not have wanted this job, now that I'm here, I'm not letting anything or anyone get in the way of it. "But I have a fuck ton to learn."

"And no time to learn it," she agrees. "So, you better learn how to fake it."

"Is that what you did?"

"I've never had to fake a single thing in my life," she scoffs.

I can't help the sly smirk that curls my lips. "That's good to know." Because she screamed like a woman possessed that day in the old Wolf cabin.

Her warning glare has my apology slipping out. I did promise her we wouldn't mention our past again. "Don't you remember what it's like to start a new job and not know what you're doing?"

"No."

"Come on, Belinda ..." I give her an imploring look.

She purses her lips. "Ask yourself what Henry Wolf would do in a particular situation, and do that."

"So ... be an arrogant prick?"

"Exactly. It hasn't failed me yet."

An unexpected bark of laughter escapes me, and she joins in. I don't think I've ever heard Belinda laugh before. At least, not in a way that isn't mocking.

Her steady gaze is on my profile as we close the distance to the meeting room. "What?"

"When did you meet the neighbor?"

"Yesterday. Went by to have a talk," I lie. If Belinda knew Sloane was on hotel property, she'd lose her mind.

That answer seems to satisfy her. "I'm impressed that you managed to negotiate with that menace. Maybe Henry wasn't *completely* wrong about bringing you here."

I bite my tongue against the urge to defend Sloane. Hell, I'd be pissed too, if I owned a property like that and this place moved in next door. And now all she's trying to do is keep her decades-old family business running while we pillage her best workers.

But Belinda isn't the empathetic type, especially when finding empathy requires going against her boss. "I guess we'll see soon enough."

———

"I HAVE a firm list of candidates for HR." Dorian's weathered hands rest on the stack of printouts, but he makes no effort to pass any across the table. The middle-aged grounds staffing supervisor has heavy bags under his eyes. Then again, all the managers tasked with combing through yesterday's applicants look like they haven't slept much. But Chester has handed over his seasonal hire lists for the facilities without question, as if happy to be rid of it.

"Do you have a list for me?" I ask calmly.

"I can cc you on the email when I send it to Mike." A smarmy, counterfeit smile curves his lips. "Listen, Ronan, I've gone through this process a dozen times. I know what makes a good employee."

And you have no fucking clue. He doesn't have to say the quiet part out loud. Everyone in this room can hear it, and they're exchanging furtive, knowing glances.

I steal a peek at Belinda to read her expression, but her attention is on me, her eyebrows arched in a bemused *Now what are you going to do?* way.

"I personally reviewed each applicant forwarded up the chain. Everyone has adequate experience and can start immediately. I'm confident my people have built a solid team."

No shit he's confident. And patronizing and bitter. The guy who wants my job has been eyeballing me since I stepped inside this meeting room, and now he's throwing around words like "my people" and holding on to that list like fucking Gollum with his precious ring.

A soft cough is the only sound in the room.

Dorian's waiting for the twenty-six-year-old out of his league to bob his head and agree. I might have done that, too, if I didn't have an ulterior motive, because the truth is, it's just a bunch of names to me. That would have been a colossal mistake. Belinda's advice has settled in the forefront of my mind, and I can't shake it.

What would Henry do if one of his managers pulled his dick out in a meeting to compare sizes? Because that's what this feels like, and I don't like it.

Would Henry point out the chunk of muffin caught in this fuckhead's bushy mustache? No, he has too much class for that.

I clear my throat—mostly to compose myself—and keep my gaze locked on him as I ask, "Belinda, has there been a change in the management structure overnight?"

"There has not, and I believe I would be the first to know."

"And, as the director, I still make the final decision on all opening hires under *my* departments?"

"That is correct." I could be wrong, but I detect the slightest hint of humor in her voice.

"Perfect. Dorian, I'll have that list now."

With pursed lips, he digs it out from a folder and shoves it across the table. The asshole had a hard copy all along. There was no need for that pissing contest.

I ignore everyone and scan it quietly, searching for the names I memorized.

There they are, near the top. Mick Wallen and Will Moore, placed in outdoor crew positions. Flipping the page, I quickly find Ron Schultz as well. Surprise, fucking surprise.

Grabbing a pen, I draw lines through their names. "These three aren't good options for Wolf."

Dorian glares at my markups before shifting an incredulous expression to me. "Can I ask why not?"

"No." Henry wouldn't explain himself.

"But those are three solid hires," he argues.

"I know for a fact they're not, so do I need to question every name on here, seeing as you were so sure you've built a solid team?"

"No," he mutters.

Silence hangs in the room.

"Do we have what we need, then?" Belinda asks after a beat.

"I do," Lena confirms, nodding to her various managers. "Thank you."

I shrug, my gaze never leaving the disgruntled Dorian. "We'll see. Also, Dorian, Archie will book a meeting with you first thing Monday morning to discuss what we're going to do about the drainage issue on the ninth hole."

He frowns. "What drainage—"

"The fucking swamp you seem to have missed." I took a quick drive out yesterday afternoon to check if it was still there. It was.

His arrogant mask slips. No doubt he'll jump in a golf cart

the second he leaves here to prove me wrong. And when he sees that I'm not? Hopefully he'll arrive on Monday morning with a solution already worked out.

"Okay, then. Thank you, everyone, for your hard work," Belinda announces. "Now go and enjoy what's left of your weekend." Her clawed hand settles on my shoulder, a silent message to stay seated.

I note Lena isn't getting up either. The department managers hurry to get away, as if lingering might get them assigned more work.

"Minnie has sent both of you links to the database that includes all recommended hires. The interview recordings are there, but given timing, I would trust your managers—"

"I don't," I blurt. Dorian has rubbed me the wrong way. My petty side rarely makes an appearance, but when it does, it's highly motivated. I will check every single name on this list just to say I did.

"We don't have a lot of wiggle room, Ronan," Belinda says with forced patience, her hips swinging as she parades around the table. "The sooner HR can verify references and—"

"Is this my department to run?" I respond with a measured tone.

"It is, but—"

"Then I'm going to review these hires until I feel confident in Dorian's choices."

She inhales sharply, her eyes flaring.

I brace myself for a tongue-lashing to put me in my place.

"As long as next week's training sessions aren't delayed."

I falter, not expecting her to roll over so easily. "I'll keep that in mind."

Belinda pauses to size me up, her gaze trailing over the open collar of my shirt, down to my splayed thighs. Either she wants to climb onto my lap or stab me in the groin with her pen. "If there's nothing else ..."

"There is." I'm feeling ballsy today. I turn to Lena. "Do you have a Jeremy Smith in your pile?"

Lena checks her spreadsheet. "I do. He's at the very top. In bar service." She pushes her auburn hair off her forehead and then settles wary golden brown eyes on me. "Why?"

Sloane wanted to leave him off the hit list, but I can't ignore how these guys are willing to royally fuck her over. "I need you to hire him part time. Two nights a week, max." Just enough that he can't afford to quit his day job.

"Are you for real?" She glances up at Belinda before staring at me like I've failed at singing the alphabet. "Why would I do that?"

"Because I'm asking you to."

With a doubtful frown, she rescans the page. "Debbie put him at the top of the list for Seraphina's, which means he impressed her."

The upscale open-air bar on the water, which, from what Belinda said, is expected to be crammed every night with both hotel guests but also visitors hoping to snag a cocktail reservation. "I'm not surprised." Everyone seems to love this Jeremy, including Sloane. "Tell him you'll give him full-time permanent at the end of the season. But, for this summer, I need you to limit his hours."

Her fingers drum with annoyance over the desk surface, the diamonds on her wedding band sparkling under the fluorescent light. "That might have worked on Dorian, but like you get final say, so do I."

"This request comes directly from Henry Wolf," I lie.

Belinda's eyes bore into my face from across the table, but I ignore her.

The name drop had the intended effect. Lena's back stiffens. As far as she knows, Henry is at the top of my Favorites list on my phone. He's not, but his wife is, below my parents and my sister. "Part-time hours, even though we have a strict requirement that seasonal employees must be available full-time. Got it." She scribbles next to Jeremy's name while shooting me an unhappy frown.

Mention of bartending reminded me of something else. "What about a guy named Cody? Is he there too?"

Her eyes skim the list and then she sighs heavily. "*Seriously*? Are you going to tell me I can't hire him either?"

I smirk. "Do what you want with that one, but you should know he was fired from a local bar for giving out shots to get dates with pretty women. I doubt he admitted to that in his interview, and I can tell you for a fact Wolf takes that shit seriously. Considers it theft." My friend Rachel got fired for it at Wolf Cove in Alaska until Abbi stepped in and managed to sweet-talk Henry into rehiring her.

With a groan, Lena strikes out Cody's name with her red marker and then collects her things and marches off.

Leaving me alone with Belinda.

"I think I may have created a monster," she muses, though there is no humor in her voice.

"How so?"

"When I said to be like Henry, I didn't expect such a remarkable impression."

"Too arrogant for your liking?"

Her lips part, but she stalls. "I didn't realize how well you knew him."

"I don't know him well." I rise with a leisurely stretch. "I know his wife *really* well, though."

Something unreadable dances in Belinda's gaze. She's worked with Henry for decades and I don't doubt they fucked around in the past. She must know there's some truth to those scandalous headlines. "Careful how you wield Henry's name. It might burn you in the end."

"Just watching out for his best interests." Will she tell him? Will he care?

"I would focus on your own interests. The next few weeks are going to be overwhelming, and if you don't want to look stupid in front of Dorian and Lena and, well, *everyone*, I would spend every minute of that time learning how to do your job."

Her reminder settles over my shoulders like a cinder block. "On that note, if you don't mind, I have things to do."

"Those signs better be down by Monday morning."

"They will be." I sound far more confident than I feel. Will Sloane hold up her end of the deal after how we left things?

"And I want that final list in to HR by 1:00 p.m.!" she hollers at my retreating back as I march toward my office.

———

"... I want to work at the Wolf Hotel because I know it's a great company with strong values and—"

I click the mouse to end the monotonous drone. I've heard the same bland script in all ten interviews. Hell, I probably said the same bland crap when I applied to Wolf. This is stupid. It's not humanely possible for me to get through this entire list by one. It's already almost 11:00 a.m. I have no choice; I have to trust my managers' work.

I scan the pages again, wondering if any more of them are Sloane's. I really shouldn't care—if they want to leave the Sea Witch and work here, that's their business. I know this, and yet I can't help the urge to ferret them out for culling.

Hit with an impulsive idea, I leave my office and head down to the pit.

The place is buzzing, with more than half the staff here. When Belinda said it's all hands on deck this weekend, she wasn't kidding.

Archie's crop of red hair peeks out from his cubicle.

I lean over the wall and mock hiss, "Dude, what the fuck are you doing here on a Saturday?"

He jumps, throwing his phone in the air as he spins

around in his chair, his eyes wide with shock. "I was just ... uh ..."

"Playing Candy Crush. I don't give a shit, man. Honestly." I made Connor a supervisor, and he takes three breaks a day to jerk off in the restroom stall.

Archie's sheepish smile emerges. "As soon as you approve those hires, I'll be helping them call references and—"

"Okay, got it. Get my ass in gear, is what you're saying." The sooner Archie understands I'm not like regular stuffy managers, the better.

His smile widens. "Sort of."

Enough with the small talk. "Where is Lena's assistant?"

"Mandy? She's three cubes over."

"Perfect. Thanks. Also, people still play that fucking game?" I take off before he has a chance to answer, counting the spaces until I find one with a young, pretty brunette. "Mandy?"

She peers up at me. "Yes, sir?"

Fuck me. People need to stop calling me sir, and especially twenty-something-year-olds who look like Mandy. "Can you email me the link to the hiring list for Lena's departments? I need to run it by someone."

"Uh ... Yeah, I guess?" Her brow pinches with confusion. She's probably thinking it's an odd request, but she's not going to question it.

"It's Ronan Lyle. My email should pop up as soon as you start typing."

"Yeah, I know who you are." Her cheeks pink up as her long nails clack over her keyboard. "Okay. Sent. Anything else?" She bats her eyelashes at me.

Old Ronan would get into a lot of trouble in this role.

This version? He'll likely still fuck everything up, but when he does, it'll be for one specific woman.

I head back to my office and fish out the Sea Witch business card from my wallet.

42. Sloane

"Tournament starts in half an hour! Be there or be square!" Miriam hollers as she ambles past the open door, her four-pronged cane thumping with each step.

"Save me a seat!" Gigi hollers back.

The eighty-eight-year-old catches my eye. "Oh, hey, girl. Good to see you! Can't stop. Gotta get the good table."

I chuckle as Miriam vanishes down the hall. She's been Gigi's best friend for as long as I can remember and has lived in Palm Oaks for almost three years. We should have known Gigi would follow her here. "Tournament for what?"

"One of the fellas taught us how to play euchre and, boy, is it ever fun. You should come and join us. I think you'd like it. Just not today. The competition is mighty fierce. No room for beginners." Gigi leans over to pat my knee before settling back into her rocking chair. Her lengthy white-silver hair is freshly braided and fastened with a fuchsia elastic that matches her painted fingernails and the cardigan over her shoulders. One of the high school girls who volunteers on weekends must have been by already. They always love coming to see her.

Gigi first mentioned moving to Palm Oaks after she fell down the stairs off our front porch and broke her hip. Recovery was long, and she struggled. Frank and I were getting quotes to build a ramp when she announced that she'd put down a deposit on a room.

Of course, Frank and I both argued against it. As far as we're concerned, the only place Gigi belongs is in her little cottage by the water and loitering in the Sea Witch to share stories about Mermaid Beach's history to anyone who might listen. We were so sure she would be miserable here, following scheduled mealtimes and bedtimes and their long list of other rules.

Ever the stubborn one, Gigi was adamant she knew what was best for her.

She was right, as usual. Gigi can fit in anywhere. She's soft-spoken and easygoing. No one expects her to be the type to adore horror movies, a well-timed cuss, and sweet treats—that last one so much so that her doctor warned her about developing diabetes, despite her slight stature. She's only five three and a hundred pounds—and yet to anyone who knows her, she seems larger than life. She's certainly always felt that way to me.

I steal a glance over my shoulder before digging out a paper bag from my purse that holds a macadamia nut scone. "You didn't get this from me."

Gigi snatches it from my grip and digs in. "My lips are sealed." With her mouth full, she asks, "So, what's new?"

Normally, I would spare her worries about the business, but today, I need Gigi's nonjudgmental ear as I unload on her and confess my sins.

"Gosh, Dave too." Gigi picks away at her scone. "But sounds like this director of whatever is helping you out."

"More like helping himself out, so he can win brownie points with the big boss."

"You're splitting hairs, Sloane. He gets what he wants, you get what you want. Just take the win. Lord knows we need it against these big companies comin' in and changin' everything."

"I haven't won yet. We'll see how many people I'm down next week. And, even if Ronan keeps his side of the deal, who says they won't quit on me, anyway?" Are they unhappy at the Sea Witch, or is this a greener-grass situation? The case of the big and shiny distraction.

"It wouldn't be the first time we lost staffers during high season. I remember back in, oh, what was it now?" She frowns at the ceiling. "Had to be '02. Sandy was still around. You were a wee thing." She smiles as she reminisces, the mention of my mother stirring foggy memories. "Anyway, Bill Deckers started a business just like ours. That bastard poached my captains and half my beach workers. Paid them a dollar more an hour." She harrumphs. "All these years later and Sea Witch is still going strong. Where is Bill Decker?"

"Didn't he die?"

"Well, yes, but before that, he was runnin' from creditors. Don't you worry. You'll manage just fine."

"Frank put up a HELP WANTED sign in the window. I don't know how long it'll take to replace all three captains. Until then, I guess it's me and Frank filling the gaps." I still captain the tiki boats every now and again when we're desperate.

"Lord help those poor people." Gigi hoots with laughter. "I love Frank, but keep him on the shore."

"I'll be scheduling myself a lot," I agree. One reviewer counted the times Frank smiled during their trip to Starfish Island—twice, and once it was because a patron fell off his chair.

I already feel better, just talking it out with Gigi, even if there's no solution to be found at the end of the conversation. But Gigi has always had a way to make the biggest disappointments feel minor in the grand scheme of life.

Speaking of big disappointments ...

"Cody came into the shop."

"Oh yeah? What'd that scheming cockroach want?"

Gigi never liked Cody, but she kept her mouth shut until after we broke up. She said she had learned her lesson with my mother, after getting into a row over a man from Texas my mother claimed she loved. Angry, Mom ran off with the guy, only to show up back home two months later, heartbroken and pregnant. He had wanted her to get rid of it.

Of *me*.

To this day, I have no idea who my father is, and no interest in finding out.

"A reference letter for his time running the Sea Witch so he can work for Wolf."

She snorts. "The only thing that boy ever ran was his damn mouth."

"I told him he's not getting anything from me. If he wants to work for Wolf, he'll have to lie his way in."

"If there's one thing he's good at, it's lying."

"Yeah. Well, I warned Ronan about him, so we'll see if Cody can sweet-talk his way into a job."

Gigi studies me as she chews. "This hotel fella ... any interest there?"

I falter on my answer. "I mean, there *was* until I found out who he worked for." Not to mention the fact that he rejected me after I kissed him.

"And now you're suddenly not interested? What should his job matter?" She scoffs. "It's not like he's dealing drugs. It's a perfectly respectable occupation."

"But he's also a liar. Check this out." I dig out my phone and open my photo album to the picture I saved last night.

"Oh dear, this isn't what I think it is." Gigi tsks. "You promised me you'd delete the Henry Wolf file."

"I did, I swear! But something about Ronan seemed familiar, and I couldn't figure out what. Then he told me Henry personally hired him, and it triggered something, so I found the pictures again." I hold up my phone to show her a magazine photo of Henry Wolf alongside his groomsmen. I'd seen wedding pictures before during one of my hate-stalking sessions—they weren't hard to find, splashed all over the internet—but they were nothing more than a group of obscenely attractive people celebrating a man who was destroying our peace. "*This* is Ronan." His dark hair is cropped short—nearly a buzz cut—and he's less muscular, but there's no doubt it's him.

Gigi hums. "That boy's face sure has been blessed."

That's an understatement. "But why was he one of Henry Wolf's groomsmen? He said they aren't friends."

"I'm sure there's an explanation."

"Or he's a liar." And now he and Henry are laughing about the crazy rooster commune lady throwing herself at him. I can't shake the humiliation I've worn since Ronan's rejection. I *never* put myself out there like that.

Gigi's face pinches with worry. "You know, sometimes I think it was a mistake taking up that fight with the hotel. Maybe it would have been better to cash the check. It's just a little house on the water."

I'm already shaking my head. "No, it's our home." It's everything I grew up knowing. "Some billionaire doesn't get to come in and force us out!"

My phone rings, cutting off my rant. Frank's number shows up on my screen.

Gigi's eyes light up. "Oh, let me talk to him!"

I throw the call on speaker.

"You haven't come to see me in two weeks!" Gigi says by way of greeting.

"I know. I'm sorry." Frank's gruff voice carries. "I've been busy getting Rainbow Alley ready. I'll come by tomorrow, if your granddaughter lets me have a day off, I promise."

I roll my eyes, even as Gigi laughs. Frank wouldn't take a day off unless I put a gun to his head. He could be dying and he'd pick up a shovel and dig the hole for his corpse, just so he had something to do.

"Sloane, you got a second?" Frank asks.

He wouldn't bother me while I'm with Gigi unless it's important. "Yeah, for sure. Hold on." I slink away and turn off the speaker. "What's up?"

"Three things. A guy came in askin' for a job. Name's Rolland. Local kid. Not much in the way of experience, and he's scrawny. Not a fucking chance in hell he'll be able to carry four chairs at a time, let alone eight, and a strong wind might blow him over."

"You're not really selling him to me."

"He can start today. And he'll build muscle."

"Okay. Hire him, I guess. We need all the help we can get." My arms and shoulders are screaming at me after loading and unloading umbrellas and beach chairs late into the night.

"You don't want to meet him first?"

"At this point? Just check his references to make sure he's not a criminal."

"Consider it done. Also, AJ called in sick."

I groan. And so it begins. Though I shouldn't be surprised after yesterday's run-in. "Anyone else?" We have two cruise bookings for the afternoon. Will Jeremy bail on me too? And what about Will? He's supposed to be there to ready the boats.

"All good so far. I can play captain, but that means Mick and this new guy are on their own—"

"No, I'll cover AJ today. And every other day," I add, checking my watch. My Saturday has officially been derailed, but this is par for the course when we're in season, even without all the staffing issues. "What else?"

"Just got a call from Lover Boy."

"*Who?*"

"The bro workin' at the hotel."

My heart skips a beat. "Ronan?"

"That one. He said to call him ASAP. Something work-related. Says you have his number but you probably tossed it, so he gave it to me again."

"No, I've still got it." Tucked away in my purse. "I *was* going to throw it out."

"Yeah, sure you were. Anyway, he said you'd want to call him, like, *now*. He was at the coffee shop this morning too."

"Really?" A mixture of curiosity and worry stirs in my stomach. What's this about? Is Ronan going to tell me he can't keep up his end of our deal?

"The guy seems to be working extra hard to *not* get into your pants. You know, because I vetoed him, remember? Give Gigi a kiss for me." The line goes dead before I can tell him to mind his own business.

I fish out Ronan's business card and punch in the number he scrawled on the back.

He answers on the second ring, his voice somehow raspier with a basic, "Hey."

"Frank told me you're looking for me?"

"Sea Witch?"

"How many other people do you call and leave cryptic messages for?" And why are my cheeks burning with embarrassment—again—over the fact that I threw myself at him and he shut me down?

"In general, or just today?" Amusement taints his voice. He sounds more like the flirtatious version sprawled out on the beach.

But my hormones will not sway me today. "What's up?"

"Gotta run something by you, but it needs to be in the next hour. You home?"

"No." I falter, stealing a glance at Gigi. She's cleaning up all evidence of the scone, burying the wrapper and crumbs in the bottom of her wastebasket. "But I can be in about twenty minutes." I need to change, anyway.

"'Kay. I'll meet you at your place."

"Wait, what do you—"

The call disconnects before I finish my question.

"I've got to go. It's something to do with work." I think. Nerves flutter in my stomach at the idea of seeing Ronan again.

"That's okay. You go on and do what you've gotta do. I've gotta prep for my big windfall!" She fishes a folded wad of cash from inside her bra. Gigi has picked up gambling since she moved in here. I'm not sure if I should be worried.

With a kiss on her forehead—and a second one from Frank —I hurry out the door.

———

A SLEEK AND sporty black BMW is parked in front of my house when I pull in. It reminds me of all the times Henry Wolf's lackey would roll up my driveway in his luxury sedan to dangle a fat check in our faces. Only this time it isn't a slimy lawyer waiting for me.

I told myself the entire drive over that I would remain cool —professional—and yet my stomach flips when I spot Ronan lingering over by the vegetable garden we all take turns weeding. Today, he's wearing black dress pants and a pale blue button-down, the collar unfastened to show off his thick, columnar neck, his sleeves rolled up. It's a more casual and yet decidedly sexy look. Or maybe it has nothing to do with the clothes and it's just *him* that continues to appeal.

Inhaling to steel my nerve, I hop out of my Cherokee. Ralph and the hens flock to me.

"I take it you're the one who feeds them," he calls out. Aviators hide those penetrating green eyes, but I can feel them roaming my body. I'm dressed for hauling beach equipment— clingy, black workout shorts, an old cropped tank top made from breezy cotton, my hair scooped up in a clip to keep it off my neck in the growing humidity. There's even a small tear in my shirt. Not clothes I would normally wear in public, but I was planning on heading straight from Gigi's to the compound.

Why didn't I throw on sunglasses too? At least we would be evenly matched, because all I'm thinking about is how much I wish he had kissed me back, and I'm afraid he can read it plain as day.

I clear my throat. These aren't welcome thoughts. "No. Animals love me."

"Snow White, huh?" That gorgeous, crooked smile creeps in. "And here I thought you were Ariel."

"Ariel wasn't the sea witch. That was her aunt, Ursula." I close in, but stop short, keeping a healthy distance. That intoxicating cologne is what dragged me into a fog of stupidity last time—the scent of him. I morphed into a dog in heat.

If he notices my abrupt halt, he doesn't let on. "I seem to remember her having supernatural powers too."

"You sure know an awful lot about Disney movies."

"I have a kid sister. She roped me into a lot of things." The mention of a little sister instantly softens his hard jawline.

"Like what?" I ask.

"You know. Tea parties, makeovers, the usual."

I think of the little kids who visit Palm Oaks. "Did she ever paint your nails?"

His chuckle resonates deep inside me, stirring need. "More than once. They were hot pink for an entire week my senior year."

"And you went along with it."

"Of course. I didn't give a shit. I'm confident with my sexuality."

Such a technical word and it sounds so erotic coming from him.

He's flirting again, and I'm getting drawn in like a bee to honey. What is it with this guy? How does he do it? I came here intent on keeping my guard firmly in place, and yet I abandon it almost immediately when I'm in his vicinity.

I clear my throat, as if that alone can shake this unwanted attraction—a palpable surge of energy coursing through my veins as my body reacts to him, unbidden. "Why are you here?"

Ronan's lips part, drawing my attention to them as he stalls on his words. God, I can still feel them against mine.

I shift my gaze to the ground, keeping my focus on a lurking Ralph as I wait for an answer.

But instead of words, Ronan heads for his car.

I admire his back while he collects a laptop from his back seat. "I'm approving the seasonal staffing lists today and I want you to review them in case there are other employees of yours applying that you're not aware of."

"Seriously?" My voice is laced with shock.

"Inside good?" Shutting his door, he starts moving toward my porch. "I don't have a lot of time. Belinda will have my balls in a vise if I'm late."

Having Ronan in my house was certainly not on my bingo card. "Yeah, I guess." I pick up the pace until I fall into step beside him.

"Rainbow Alley." He reads out the colorful street sign Frank posted to a tree as we pass the trailers, cutting into an awkward bout of silence.

"Gigi's idea. She named all the trailers too. We let staff rent here for cheap during the summer. Basically the cost of utilities and maintenance."

"That's generous."

"Yeah, that's Gigi. She likes having people around, though. Always said it made us more like a family than a business." We pass the Pineapple Express. "That one used to be a lighter yellow. I named it Banana Rama when I was eight. We've gutted and repainted it since, renamed it. Skye and Rebel stay in it every summer." And I am rambling without cause. I only ever do that when I'm nervous. Why does Ronan unsettle me like this?

He must notice—he seems perceptive—and yet he doesn't comment. "So, you grew up here."

"I did. Me and my mom and Gigi. Then, me and Gigi."

He nods slowly, listening but not asking prying questions. His gaze lands on the silver Airstream. "That's different."

"That's Frank's. He bought it new five years ago, I think? He's been here for sixteen years."

"Living in a trailer, outside your house."

"Yeah." I lead Ronan up the stairs, hyperaware of how short and clingy these shorts are, especially with him coming up behind me. "Why?"

"No reason."

I punch in the code to my door and push through, leading Ronan inside. Music carries from the kitchen where I left the radio on this morning. "No, seriously. Why are you asking about Frank?"

Ronan slips off his sunglasses, giving me a full look at his handsome face. "Were you two together?"

I burst out laughing. "Me and *Frank*? No. First of all, he's *a lot* older than me. And, like I said, he's family. A giant, older overprotective brother."

"Is that why he doesn't like me?"

"Frank doesn't like any male who he thinks is sniffing around me, especially after what happened with Cody."

"I'll keep that in mind." Ronan's attention scours the little beach cottage. "Colorful."

"Yeah. Gigi likes character." We've remodeled every square inch over the years. The walls might be crisp white shiplap, but there are punches of the tropics everywhere else—from the teal kitchen cabinets and botanical wallpapered backsplash to the rattan furniture and warm wood plank floors. There's only one bathroom in the entire place and we refinished it in floor-to-ceiling textured cerulean tile.

"How many bedrooms?"

"Two." They talked about adding a third, but then my mom passed away. There was no need after that.

Ronan wanders over to the French doors. The sunlight glancing through casts light over his chiseled jaw. "You have a real piece of paradise here."

"Yeah, I know." I smile. "Gigi bought it years ago, back when you could get acres by the beach. She remembers walking along the shoreline for miles and not running into a soul during the offseason. That was before all the condos and gated communities started flooding the area, ruining the vibe."

He smirks. "We live in one of those gated places on the other end of Mermaid Beach."

"*We?*" Panic flickers inside me. Does Ronan have a girlfriend? Did I throw myself at a taken man?

"Me and Connor. He came in the other day."

"Oh." I sigh with relief. "The mediocre friend."

"And annoying roommate." Ronan regards the view out to the water again. "I can see why you would rip up a giant check for this place."

"How do you know about that?"

"Belinda," he says simply, wandering back to set his laptop on the granite counter. With a few clicks, he has a spreadsheet open. "Here's everyone we're hiring under my department. I also got hold of the other director's list so you can scan that one too. I don't have time to go through everyone's résumés to see if they've listed Sea Witch, so let me know if we're poaching any more of your staff." He slides onto one of the high-back stools and nudges the computer over slightly.

"Isn't this, like, confidential company information?" I muse, edging in, acutely aware of his splayed thighs as he leans back in the seat, resting an elbow on the counter, the tattoos on his corded forearm on display.

I doubt a guy could radiate masculinity more if he tried—and nothing about Ronan says he's trying.

"It is. I could get in a lot of trouble for showing you."

"Then why *are* you showing me?"

His forehead furrows. "Contrary to what you think, we don't want to screw over local businesses. At least, I don't."

"And are you going around to *all* the local businesses, showing them this list?"

"What do you think, Sloane?" He studies me, not his screen, an intent expression taking over his face.

God, I love his gravelly voice, the way he says my name.

"Honestly, I don't know what to think where you're concerned," I admit. Except that he wants to keep this professional. I take a deep breath and, before I embarrass myself—again—force my focus to the spreadsheet, scrolling through the names. I stall on Will and Mick.

"They've been disapproved." Ronan taps the screen on the column labeled Director's Approval heading. *No* is marked beside their names. "They were near the top too. The list is ranked."

And now they're crossed off because Ronan is doing me a favor. The tinge of guilt flares. "Is this wrong?"

"No." He doesn't miss a beat, and I appreciate his certainty. It helps quell some of my anxiety.

I keep going down the list. My attention snags on another familiar name. "Are you kidding me? Brock too?"

Ronan leans forward to read his screen, bringing him closer to me. "Where?"

"There." I tap the name. "He works my rentals with the other guys." A crew that is dwindling quickly. *But we have Rolland now*, I remind myself. A scrawny kid who will have to work twice as hard to keep up and will likely quit by the end of the weekend.

Ronan slips his index fingertip over the mouse pad, guiding the cursor to the approval column and ticks off *no* next to Brock.

"Just like that."

"See this list here?" He flips to another tab. "These are all alternates. We can pull from there. We have options."

"But then you won't have the best people for the job."

"They're outdoor crew. There's leeway with that job. Trust me, I know." He smirks. "Losing these people won't hurt Wolf, but it will hurt you." His eyes drift over my lips before meeting my gaze again. "I'm not going to let that happen."

My pulse races. Does he realize the effect he has on me when he says things like that? When he looks at me like *that*?

Ronan breaks the eye lock first, returning his focus to his computer. He opens his email and clicks on a link to another spreadsheet. "This is Lena's side. She's responsible for all the restaurants, housekeeping, and entertainment."

"That's a lot."

"It is, but she's a pro." He stalls on a tab that reads *Aquarius*. "I'm assuming none of your staff moonlight as mermaids?"

My eyebrows arch. I saw the giant tropical tank featured on the Wolf's website. "That was real? You're actually going to have people swimming around in mermaid costumes?"

"Apparently. But they're not hired through this process. They train."

I frown. "Where do you train for that?"

"The fuck if I know. Mermaid school." He clicks over to a tab marked *Seraphina's*.

My heart sinks when I see Jeremy's name at the top. There's a note in the comments section next to his name. "Part time, two days a week, evenings only?" I read out loud.

"I got Lena to agree to that. The hours shouldn't conflict. That way he can keep doing what he does for you—"

"But I told you to leave him *off* the hit list." I can't help my sharp tone.

"He'll get his foot in the door, make some good cash, and

then he'll get hired full time in the fall. But you still have him for the next few months." He pauses. "It's my choice, Sloane, not yours."

He's only doing it for me, and we both know it. But *his choice* means I only have to hire two new captains, rather than three. As much as I don't like it, I need this right now. I skim the page, noting Cody's name. "He *is* a cockroach," I scoff, but then I note the X in the "not approved" box.

"Told you it's handy having me as a friend."

I can't stifle my smile of satisfaction, even as I counter, "He's a thief. You did that for the hotel, not for me."

"I did it for the hotel *and* for you."

"Why?" I'm close enough that I can pick out the flecks of gold in his irises.

He studies me as acutely. "Because that's what friends do." He taps the counter with his finger. "Anyone else?"

I skim the rest of the list and stall on another name. "Amanda Seymour."

"One of yours?"

"Yeah, she works in the coffee shop. Frank *just* finished training her."

"I'll tell Lena to cut her when I get back." Ronan's hand moves for the laptop cursor.

"No, don't." Without thought, I grab his hand to stall it. For just a split second, I revel in the feel of his calloused, strong fingers, and then I release him.

"You sure?" If he's bothered by the instinctual move, he doesn't let on.

"She's only been there a few weeks and, to be honest, she's struggling."

"If that was her there this morning, then, yeah. She is."

"That's right. You came by the Sea Witch too. You were really trying to get hold of me, huh?"

"Yeah, but not about this. I—" His jaw tenses. "Wanted to

check in, after yesterday. Make sure you weren't sewing a doll in my name to stab with pins."

"I don't sew." My tone is suddenly clipped, but the last thing I want to do is relive yesterday's lapse in judgment. "I can cover Amanda's shifts easily enough," I say, pulling the topic back to safer waters. After a beat, I add, "Thanks, though, for looking out for me."

"You can thank me by taking down every last one of those signs by Monday morning. I guarantee you Belinda will be checking."

"Right." Those. The whole reason Ronan's helping me in the first place. Because this is a professional arrangement, even though he keeps throwing around this *friends* word. "You told her about this?"

"Barely. She doesn't know the details. If she did, she would have hired all of your workers."

"I guess I've earned a few enemies over there." I've never met this Belinda. For all the council meetings I attended and pots I've stirred over the years in the name of Wolf Hotels, I've never met anyone high up in the food chain. Not William Wolf when he was alive or Henry Wolf when he took over. They never bothered to show their faces, always sending representatives instead. Not like the location in Alaska that Henry Wolf personally oversaw, according to the papers.

All that tells me is that Mermaid Beach is nothing more than an acquisition, a cog in the wheel of their empire.

But this place is *everything* to me.

Ronan seems to understand that. It's the only way I can explain his kindness.

He moves to shut his computer.

"Wait. Flip back to that first list for a minute?"

With a curious frown, he pulls it up.

"Him." I tap the line that lists Rick Reynolds. "We call him Rick the Dick. He worked for us a few years ago. He intentionally injured himself and then tried to sue, but he didn't know there were cameras on him. It all got dismissed. But he's a huge scammer. Everyone around here knows about him. He's probably using his brother-in-law as a reference, but whatever they say will be bullshit. The guy hasn't worked an honest day in his life."

A slow smile spreads across Ronan's lips. "You saw his name and were going to let me hire him."

I shrug. "I've changed my mind."

With quick movements, Ronan strikes him off the list and types into the notes, "A.k.a. Rick the Dick. Scammer. Litigious."

"You can't write that."

"I can do whatever the fuck I want. Should I be worried about the others?"

"Let me see." I read through the rest of the names on the various tabs, acutely aware of the heat radiating off Ronan's body and the smell of him, and the way I'm tucked up against my kitchen counter and his thigh has settled in behind me. *Almost* touching me.

So many of these people *aren't* familiar, but that's the nature of Mermaid Beach as it grows. It used to be that if you didn't know them, you could guarantee there was only one degree of separation. "Alvaro and Jose Perez have worked at The Sunken Ship for years." A kitschy tourist-trap restaurant. "Super hard workers. Honest guys." The Sea Witch gives discounts to local industry workers and every year, those two bring their families out for a day cruise around Starfish Island.

I know the owner of The Sunken Ship, and I don't particularly like him. They'd do well to leave.

"So, are you saying we should *keep* them?" Ronan's question cuts into my thoughts.

"Yeah, they're great. Alvaro would make a good supervisor." An impish spark hits me then. "Actually, on second thought, you don't want these guys. I forgot. They don't work weekends and ..." I scramble for another excuse. "They have serious hygiene issues."

Ronan's eyes narrow. "You want to hire them for the Sea Witch, don't you?"

"*Never.*" I fight to school my expression, my laughter threatening. I've offered them jobs before—they'd be a great addition to the beach crew—but they like the kitchen. I'm sure they're angling for permanent full-time at Wolf.

That sexy, crooked smirk curves the corner of Ronan's mouth. "You're trying to poach people from my list. I don't know. That might cost you."

"Oh yeah? How much?" I ask before really thinking that question through.

The mood in the room shifts in an instant as Ronan's gaze skates over my face, along my neck, dipping down to my cropped tank top, his eyes like fingertips trailing over my skin. Can he see the gooseflesh that's erupting?

That same headiness I felt in his office yesterday swirls around us now, taunting me, threatening to pull me under with its spell.

"I need to get back to the office," Ronan says softly, apologetically, even as his square jaw clenches.

I swallow against the flare of nervous excitement as I stare him down, my body vibrating with need. I want this man. Here, now. I want him, and I think he wants me. This *can't* be me misreading the situation a second time. "Are you sure?"

"That I *need* to? Yes."

My adrenaline surges. "Do you *want* to?"

A strangled sound escapes him. "Sloane."

I can't hear myself think as I step in between his splayed thighs. "It's a simple question."

"But it's not a simple answer." He reaches up. My hair clip suddenly loosens, and my hair tumbles down around my shoulders. "No, I don't want to leave." A cool, calloused hand slips around to the back my neck. "But I'm not sure you're up for what I want." His thumb drags back and forth over my skin.

The touch radiates all the way down to my suddenly hardened nipples. Heaviness swells deep inside my belly, my body aching to feel his hands all over me. Everywhere.

It's been so long since I let a man's hands on me, and I'd like the memory of those particular hands—Cody's—erased from memory. I'm tired of being so guarded all the time. Hell, I'm thirty-one and I've never had sex because it was there, in front of me, available.

At this moment, I just want to *feel*.

Emboldened by something I can't understand and throwing caution out the window, I whisper, "Try me."

Heat ignites in his eyes with my invitation, and the seconds seem to hang between us. "Fuck it," he curses, pulling me forward, our lips colliding in a crushing kiss.

I haven't been kissed like this ... ever. I've *never* been kissed like this, with such pent-up energy. Ronan's like a bull released from its cage into the rodeo ring. Somehow, I'm ready for it—I think a part of me has been since the day Ronan walked into the Sea Witch for the first time. My hands settle on his head, my fingers weaving through his silky hair, gripping small fistfuls as our mouths meet each other's intensity, our tongues stroking each other as we both seem desperate to get closer.

I'm vaguely aware of Ronan's free hand sliding up under the hem of my shorts to grip my ass, the tips of his fingers teasing dangerously close to sensitive flesh. I want him closer. I want to feel him *everywhere*.

With ragged breaths, I break free from him long enough to hook my thumbs under my shorts. With a quick tug, they tumble to the floor, along with my panties. I shake them off and then peel off my top and unfasten my bra, letting it fall to the floor with the rest of my clothes.

"Oh, fuck me." A pained expression fills Ronan's face as his eyes rake over my naked body.

"I plan to."

With lightning-quick movement, I'm off my feet, Ronan's powerful hands seizing the backs of my bare thighs as he pins me against the kitchen wall.

Our lips collide once again, the tempo and fervor even more intense as my fingers fumble blindly with the buttons of his shirt, throwing the two sides open so my hands can drag over his beautiful torso, memorizing its hard curves as they make their way down.

He adjusts his stance, giving me access to unfasten his belt buckle, then the zipper, before pinning me to the wall again, this time freeing his hands to wrestle his pants and briefs down over his hips.

"Oh fuck." I echo his earlier words as his erection springs free, hot and heavy and rigid. My fist just barely curls around it when Ronan leans into me, lining our bodies up.

I abandon all thought as I guide his tip into my entrance.

We both curse and moan as Ronan sinks into me, each skillful roll of his hips helping him bury himself deeper.

I cling to his shoulders, momentarily overwhelmed by the size of him, the fullness almost too much. I love this feeling, as my body stretches and primes itself, welcoming him in. I don't want him to stop or even slow.

Ronan begins thrusting with reckless abandon. I'm vaguely aware of the rattling pictures but I ignore it all, my cries growing loud and unabashed as he fucks me against my kitchen wall, our lips a messy tangle of tongues and ragged breaths, my hands groping his straining biceps.

"I'm coming," Ronan hisses suddenly, his fingertips digging into my flesh. Seconds later, his deep, guttural cries fill my house as his cock pulses inside me.

The intoxicating fog that swirled around us seems to lift

instantly, and with it, the sinking realization of what we just did hits me.

Oh my God.

Ronan's body stiffens against me with each new heaved breath. He seems to have realized our mistake, too, as he peers down between us, to where we're still joined. "I don't know what happened. I never skip—"

Gigi's cuckoo clock chooses that moment to pop out of her colorful, refurbished home and noisily announce the noon hour, making us both jolt.

"What is it about this place and loud birds?" he complains.

Shit. "I have to go. I'm late."

"So do I." Ronan pulls out and sets me on the floor. In seconds he has his briefs and dress pants secure.

Suddenly, I'm the only completely naked one standing in my kitchen and I'm nowhere near as brave or confident as I was before. I dive for my shorts and T-shirt, skipping my bra as I hastily redress. "I have to cover AJ's shift. He called in sick. Probably wants to avoid an awkward conversation until he can officially quit."

"You sure you don't want me to ax him?" As fast as my fingers worked to undo those buttons on Ronan's shirt, his seem to be working double time now to refasten them.

"No, we'll manage." Somehow. "But thanks, I appreciate your help." Without Ronan, the Sea Witch would be in deeper trouble than it already is.

And this has turned incredibly awkward.

"I've got to get these names in within the hour or Belinda will kill me." Grabbing his laptop, he moves for my front door.

"Right. The vise ..." On balls that just unloaded inside me. I squeeze my eyes shut, still in shock over how quickly that got out of control. "I'm on the pill," I blurt, though that's only half the problem. "And I'm clean." I got tested as soon as I found out Cody had been cheating on me and haven't been with anyone since.

"So am I," Ronan promises, but the tension hasn't released from his shoulders as he reaches for the doorknob.

"Can you please not tell anyone? About what happened."

A dark chuckle escapes him. "I promise, you don't have to worry about that." With that, he steps out.

And stops dead on the porch.

"Frank!" I smooth a hand through my hair as I spot the looming form standing in the middle of our parking lot. "When did you get home? Ralph didn't make a sound." He gives a signature two-crow salute whenever the black truck pulls in.

"About five minutes ago. And yeah, he did."

That's impossible. I couldn't have missed that terrible racket.

Could I have?

Frank's brooding gaze rolls from Ronan's untucked dress shirt to me.

"What are you doing here?" I ask.

"Needed this." He holds up a wrench. "I thought you were covering AJ's shift."

"I am. I'm heading there right now."

His gaze drops. "Like *that*?"

I cross my arms over my chest, hyperaware of the bra I left by the sink. "Right after I change."

"And I've got to get back to work." Ronan trots down the steps, laptop under his arm, heading for his car.

That is covered in chicken shit.

"Sorry, they do that sometimes." I wince as he pauses to inspect an especially large dropping on his hood. That had to be Ralph.

With a headshake more to himself, he calls out, "Remember the deal."

"Huh?"

Peering over his shoulder at me, he meets my gaze, and a

thousand different things seem to flitter through those eyes, none of which I can read. "The signs."

"Oh, right. Yeah, they'll be down."

He hesitates. "Good doing business with you." With a wink, Ronan slides into the driver's seat. The engine purrs a moment later and then he's gone, his taillights disappearing around the bend of bramble.

Frank's arms haven't uncrossed and now that heavy glare is settled on me. "What kind of business are you doing with the hotel?"

There's no avoiding this. I may as well confess. "I have an arrangement with Ronan. He won't hire more Sea Witch staff, and I'll clean up the property line."

Frank shakes his head. "I regret asking."

"We were going to lose *seven more* people. Seven! We wouldn't be able to operate like that. Now, it's only two." I break the news about Amanda and AJ.

He seems to consider this. "Does Gigi know about this plan you hatched?"

"I told her, yeah."

"And?"

"She said to take the wins when we can." Who knows how many more losses are waiting for us down the path.

His lips twist with displeasure. He's still not convinced.

"Look, Wolf Hotels couldn't care less if they don't get these specific hires. But losing them all at once will break us." I echo Ronan's rationale.

"Yeah, I don't like it, but ..." He pinches the bridge of his nose. "The signs were the *only* condition with that guy, right?"

"Yes."

"Are you sure—"

"*Yes.*" I hold his gaze so he can see the truth in my answer. "Ronan's actually a good guy." And fucking me against the wall was not part of the deal.

"I'd make sure none of them find out about this or there might be blowback. It definitely won't be good for morale."

"They're not going to. I'm not telling anyone except you and Gigi." Not even Rebel and Skye need to know.

With another headshake, he ambles for his truck. "You're gonna be late for your sail."

"I'm leaving in three minutes." I run for the door.

"Hey, Sloane!" Frank calls out.

"Yeah?"

"Your clothes are on inside out."

43. Ronan

"What the fuck, Ronan." I navigate my bird-shit-coated car down the lengthy dirt driveway, veering to avoid the worst of the potholes as I berate myself. "What the fuck!" I've *never* lost control like that when it comes to my dick. I've never kissed a woman like my lips had to be attached to hers for me to get off. Is this what happens to me after months without getting laid? And even longer without truly enjoying it? I turn into a feral humping two-pump fuckboy? Two-pump may be an exaggeration, though, it isn't far off. Twenty might be more accurate.

She whispered *"Try me"* with challenge in her eyes and I snapped.

Then she stripped in record time, and I was a goner.

I couldn't get enough of Sloane's sweet mouth, couldn't get my pants off fast enough, couldn't get deep enough inside her while a condom sat untouched in my wallet. Forgotten.

I haven't raw-dogged it since Tasha and that was intentional.

But—fuck!—did it feel incredible to unload in Sloane's tight pussy, like the dickhead I am. Still, I fucked up. There was no conversation about expectations, about what we are, and, more importantly, what we aren't. What we can't be for several reasons.

I check the clock on my dash and curse. I have fifty-five minutes to get these lists in before Belinda hands me my ass.

With that in mind, I hit the gas pedal.

44. Ronan

My forehead is in my palms as I stare absently at the TCIP report when a knuckle raps on the glass door.

"Yup."

Archie plows through and sets a mug on my desk. "From Opal Reef."

"Oh man, thanks. That stuff from the pit was pure tar. I don't know who brewed it, but they need to be banned."

"I think it was Mandy," he mock whispers.

"*Ban her.*" It doesn't matter how cute she is. I have one vice left, and I'd like to revel in it to the best of my ability.

Actually, what I'd *really* like is my caffeine fix from a certain local coffee shop, but it's been two days since I stepped foot in there and I don't plan on going again until I'm sure my head is screwed on straight.

I think Sloane *is* a real sea witch. Whatever she is, she's been haunting me since Saturday. I can't get her out of my mind.

Just thinking about her hardens my dick. See? It's happening right now.

Archie retrieves a folder from under his armpit. "Updated standards. I know Belinda is pushing for everything online, but here are hard copies. Sometimes it's easier to ... read them this way."

I smirk. "To figure out what they mean?"

Archie looks sheepish. He knows I don't belong here. Everyone knows it.

"Thank you."

"No worries, man."

Despite my foul mood, I smile as he ducks out. The awkward stiffness of the first few days is quickly fading. My assistant will be telling me to fuck off in no time, and I can't wait.

Spreading out the new reports over my desk's surface, I suck back my coffee—it's not half bad—while I review each page.

They're mostly projections—occupancy rates, revenue, budget spend. Yeah, that all makes sense. At least some of the columns do. I grab a pen to circle the acronyms that may as well be in Mandarin, so I can look them up and figure out why I care, and then I open my calendar to see how much time Google and I have together.

My week is already full of meetings—one-on-ones with my managers who think I'm a moron, with Belinda who treats me like an idiot, with finance so I can approve budget spends for equipment I've never heard of, with the golf center media planning committee to talk about a sport I hate, and with the tech department. That last one, I can't even guess why they need to meet with me.

Back-to-back meetings where I bring no value to anyone.

All fucking week long.

Why did I ever say yes to this move? Oh right, because Henry dangled a sheet of paper with a lot of digits and perks on it.

And because Abbi asked me to. *She* has faith in me.

"Ro-nan!" A familiar bellow sounds down the hall from the direction of the pit.

"Not this." I hurry from my chair, spilling my coffee all over the hard copies Archie just gave me as I bolt out the door.

Connor's leaning over a cubicle wall, dressed in a salmon-pink golf shirt and tan pants, flirting with Minnie.

"Hey." My voice is clipped. I jerk my chin in the direction of my office and then march away, expecting him to follow.

He takes his sweet time, sauntering in a whole minute later, a scrap of paper with Minnie's phone number between his fingers.

"*No.*" I snatch it and tear it up.

"Dude!" His face contorts with shock.

"That's Belinda's assistant."

"Damn, even better. We can play a little game of boss and assistant—ouch!" He rubs a palm against his chest where I punched him. "That hurt."

"Good. Stay away from her. I don't need you causing more trouble for me." While Belinda was decent enough yesterday, I don't doubt she'll change direction on me as fast a cobra when I screw up.

"What the fuck is your problem lately, man? You're gone all weekend—"

"Here, Con. I was *here.*" I throw my arms out in my office. "While you were lounging by the pool and picking up random women." Except for that brief window when I was at Sloane's, but he doesn't know about that. "And this isn't Miami. You can't storm into the pit yelling my name. Dorian's a dick. If he gets hold of you—"

"*Dorian* Dorian?" Connor chuckles. "I just left a meeting with him. Me and the other supes."

"And how'd that go?"

"Fine. The guy loves me."

"Why am I not surprised." Because Connor is where he belongs. I, on the other hand, am drowning. But it's not fair that I take it out on him. I inhale a deep, calming breath to try to expel some of this tension. "Did you get your assignment yet?" Dorian was still deciding how to divide the outdoor crew as of Friday.

"Beach," he boasts, puffing out his chest.

I chuckle. "Okay, Ken."

"I got my list of minions already."

I hold out a hand. "Give it here."

He digs his phone from his pocket and pulls up the email.

I scan it. "You've got AJ Brooks." He starts Wednesday. Did he even have the guts to call Sloane to officially quit?

"Yeah. Why, you know him?"

"Not really." But I already don't like him. "Do me a favor and break him in. He needs to earn it." Back in Miami, when a new guy started and he looked like he might not hack it, the supervisor gave him all the shit jobs—scrubbing toilets and dumpsters in the stifling heat.

Connor grins. "With pleasure."

My office door swings open without warning and Belinda strolls in. She stops short when she sees Connor. "Oh. *You.*"

His cheery mood grows exponentially. "'Morning, boss. Love the glasses. Very strong head mistress vibes today."

To anyone else, that might seem innocuous enough, but I know Connor well and he's playing all kinds of dirty scenarios in his mind. At least he's smart enough to keep his big mouth shut this time.

"Ready, Ronan?" Frosty blue eyes dissect me from behind a set of pink frames, ignoring Connor.

"For what?" Rare panic erupts within as I scan my opened calendar. "I don't have anything for another hour." First, my meeting with Dorian to address this drainage issue, and then a meeting with Lena and the head office operations team about the budget. I'm especially dreading that one because there's no way to hide how clueless I am in a Zoom full of people who do this shit for a living.

Her smug smile is downright vicious. "To see how good your negotiating skills really are."

––––––

THE COLLAR of my salmon-pink golf shirt clings to my neck in the heat as I steer us down the path toward the eleventh hole. Last week the course was empty, but today there are signs of life. Truckloads of carts are being unloaded and tested by full-timers while the first group of seasonal workers hired over the weekend get a guided tour of the grounds by a young, athletic guy Dorian tapped for supervisor of the caddies. Hank something, the email that came across my desk said.

"Worried?" Belinda muses, her glasses swapped out for opaque black shades.

That Sloane is so pissed with the way I bolted out of there that she fucks me again, only not in a good way? *Absolutely.* "No." Belinda is too smug this morning. This feels like a setup. "Why?"

"Because you're not your usual self," she muses. She's perched cross-legged in the passenger seat of our cart, the split in her green pencil skirt climbing indecently high up her toned thigh.

"And what is my usual self, Belinda?" I've shared no more than a handful of superficial conversations with this woman over the years. That afternoon at the Wolf family cabin involved very little talking.

"Like you don't give a fuck about anything but having a good time." Her eyes trail over my arms, my shoulders. "You're tense."

She's not wrong there. "I guess stress doesn't become me." I accidently veer off the path around a bend, leaving indents in the freshly watered and manicured grass. Can't wait to hear Dorian bitch about that later.

But my focus is locked on the trees ahead.

The signs are gone.

All of them.

There's no hint of fluorescent poster board, not a single

unwelcome sign, save for the standard Private Property, No Trespassing ones. Nothing but twisted old trees, their branches forming a tangled screen to hide the quaint paradise beyond, with its charming, colorful trailers and garden patch bursting with greens.

My body sinks into my seat. At least one thing has worked out for me.

"Well, would you look at that," Belinda says.

"Hopefully, that's satisfactory for you and Wolf." Enough that Henry will let go of whatever resentment he might still hold for Sloane.

Belinda pivots in her seat to face me, her expression unreadable.

"What?" My voice is wary. Did she figure out that I fucked the one woman she demanded I not?

"Fine."

I frown in confusion.

"I will teach you *everything* you need to know."

"Because you weren't already going to?"

She studies her manicure. "No, I was going to explain things to you with as much reluctance as possible, while making you feel like a tiny, insignificant, stupid man for wasting my time, until you quit." She assesses me like a lioness deciding whether to mate with or kill the male in front of her. "*But I think* I'm beginning to see what Henry sees. So, I will help. If you fail anyway, that's on you."

Her offer is a lifeline—a rope tossed over the edge of a cliff with me clinging to the only jagged rock. "Thank you." And I truly mean it.

"Don't thank me yet. I hope you're ready. These next two weeks are going to be painfully long and especially rough."

Just how you like it, Belinda.

With an almost friendly pat against my shoulder, she goads, "Come on. Let's get started."

45. Sloane

"Who are we scoping out tonight?"

I jump as Rebel swoops in, pressing my phone to my chest to hide the screen. "No one."

"Uh-huh." She sets the filled cooler in the sand and then, fishing out bottles of Sapporo, passes one each to me and Skye before settling into a chair. The ritual of finishing our summer nights out by the oat grass, with a fire crackling and the soothing sounds of crashing waves from the nearby darkness, is a longstanding one. Another tradition from Gigi that's stuck through the years. Any Sea Witch staffer is welcome to pull up a seat and unwind, and many accept the invitation. On any given night, we'll have eight to ten people here, occasionally with someone busting out a guitar. If we're lucky, Frank will bring out his ukulele.

"Okay, spill," Skye pushes.

Right now, it's just the three of us, which is why I'm willing to hold my phone to show them the candid close-up of Ronan from the Wolf wedding. I found it after going down a deep and sordid rabbit hole that led me to the photographer—a French artist famously known for taking close-ups of the female anatomy, mid orgasm. To say I didn't know things like that existed—and that people pay small fortunes for the invasive pleasure of this Joel pervert—is an understatement. Rich people are weird.

She squints. "Ooh, is that the hot guy who came in looking for you last week?"

"Yeah." Exactly one week ago, the same day that we had sex and then he ran out of my house like he couldn't get away from me fast enough. I haven't seen him since. Not a phone call, not an appearance at the coffee shop. Not even a text. Vanished like he never existed.

I guess Ronan got everything he wanted.

And I got what I expected. I'd be lying if I said it didn't bother me, that I hadn't held on to a shade of hope that Ronan would be different from all the others. And then I remember his reaction when I asked him not to say anything, how he chuckled, and swore the last thing he would ever want to admit to is fucking me.

I still can't believe I let him inside me without a condom. After I found out about Cody cheating, I swore I would never allow it again. But with Ronan, there was no thinking involved. I lost all control and sensibility.

"Are you two hooking up?" Skye asks.

"*No.*" It comes out too harsh, so I amend my tone to add, "There's nothing there."

A glance flickers between them.

"I don't want anything to do with him," I declare with conviction. "He's a senior manager at Wolf." He probably has Henry Wolf on speed dial.

"No shit. How'd you find that out?" Rebel asks.

"He mentioned it," I say vaguely, tossing a warning glance at Skye. She's the only one who knows I crashed the job fair, but she doesn't know the devil's deal I made.

"He's hot, Sloane," Rebel says. "Like, *really fucking* hot."

"Yeah. I'm aware." A twinge of jealousy stirs in my stomach as these two fawn over Ronan. How many other women are doing the same, over at that hotel? He'll screw them too, I'm sure. "He's also a giant *dick*." Who happens to possess a giant dick.

"Why? What'd he do?" Skye is pouting like this news personally offends her.

"Look who decided to grace us with his presence."

Frank appears from the darkness to save me from this interrogation, his arms loaded with wood and Rolland trailing behind him.

Frank wasn't kidding when he called the kid scrawny. He's like a newborn giraffe, all knobs and limbs. The obscenely baggy T-shirts he wears hide the protruding ribs I caught a glimpse of one afternoon while he was wiping his sweaty brow. But he's quiet and he tries, and he hasn't quit yet, which is all I care about at this point.

"Welcome, cutie!" Rebel beams up at the lanky kid as she reaches into the cooler and fishes out a beer.

"Uh ..." He looks from it to me to Frank, reminding us that he's only eighteen and, according to the little he's spoken about his family to Frank, was raised in an ultra-strict household.

"I'm not your mother." Frank drops the load of wood with a clatter. "But you better sleep in one of the empty trailers if you have too many."

"Just one." Rolland collects the beer from Rebel with a thanks, his flushed cheeks noticeable even in the fire's glow as he takes an empty seat on the other side of Skye. They turn their interrogation on him, saving me from having to lie about Ronan.

Minutes later, Mick, Ron, and Will show up, and another round of greetings ensues.

I force a smile and pretend I'm none the wiser to their recent plans for a mass exodus. From what Rebel and Skye heard, they received rejection emails from Wolf Hotels the same afternoon Ronan submitted his approvals—and disapprovals.

They showed up ready to work the next day and, according to Frank, no one seems sour or disgruntled, so maybe it really was a matter of chasing the shiny new thing. Still, that prick of guilt lingers every time I see anyone I sabotaged. It's quickly followed by the sting of betrayal.

Amanda never showed up for her Monday shift, making up a story about needing to leave the state to take care of an ill relative. AJ called me on Sunday afternoon to tell me he was taking a job at Wolf and he wouldn't be able to give me two weeks. He thanked me for employing him. There wasn't much else to say.

Jeremy hasn't said a word, but I know through Rebel that he'll be working Friday and Saturday nights at the Wolf beach bar—a ritzy courtyard overlooking the water that serves a menu of martinis and other complex cocktails at twenty-five bucks a piece. Apparently, he's been studying the manual front and back all week. He'll do well there, and I'm happy for him.

Frank wedges his giant body into the chair beside me. "You stopped trying to murder them with your eyes yet?" he murmurs, quiet enough for only me to hear.

"Trying." It's especially hard to fake nice with Ron. He's staying in Surf's Up for the summer. I run into him every morning while feeding the birds.

"Try harder. You gotta let it go."

I know. "Skye made Gigi's chili recipe. Crock-Pot's on the counter inside." There's always something on the stove around here in the summer, with enough to feed a dozen mouths.

"I'll grab a bowl in a bit." He rotates his wrist.

"How's it going over at the compound?"

"Fixed the outdoor shower and a rotten board on the steps. Gonna get Rolland to throw another coat of paint on the trailer. Freshen it up."

"Good idea." Gigi inherited that property two decades ago from a lonely army vet named Bobby who had a soft spot for her. He was highly paranoid and had the place fully fenced and wired against trespassers, making it secure for our needs. Hence, the nickname *compound*. It's only a block away from the beach.

Bobby's trailer was a plain gray single-wide that Gigi insisted on jazzing up with robin egg-blue walls and yellow trim. It serves as an office and resting spot for the staff during the long, hot summer days.

"How you doin' with the tiki boats?" he asks.

"Fine. Tired." I've had to play captain every day this week, taking groups out to Starfish Island where I drop anchor with countless other boats and babysit for four hours while they swim and drink and laugh. I used to love it. Now, I find it exhausting, always needing to be "on" for vacationers, striking conversations, regaling them with fun facts.

And that's all on top of everything else I have on my plate.

"Your banana boat is booking up."

"Told you it'd be a hit." Frank turns his trunk of a neck this way and that to stretch what I'm sure are aching bones. True to his promise, all the Sea-Doos and rental equipment are moved, repaired, cleaned, and ready to be hauled back and forth to the beach daily. Just in time, too, because the first big influx of tourists starts next week, and it only gets busier from there.

So far, it seems the Sea Witch has avoided a crisis. But we're not out of the woods yet. "I hired a new girl to replace Amanda. She starts tomorrow. Her name's Lara."

"Hope she's better than the last one." He chugs his water. "Anyone else come in?"

"A woman named Sage for the tiki captain job."

"And?" Frank's bushy eyebrow arches. "What's wrong with her?"

He can read me so well. "She was high as a kite so ... I'm thinking no."

He chuckles. "How's next week's schedule?"

"Two sails every day. Losing money every day we don't have the third float out there." I've had to block the calendar so we don't book more than we can handle.

"I hear Cody's available."

I snort and beer shoots out my nose. It's a moment of hacking before I can clear it out of my system and then I'm laughing. "Okay, I needed that."

"Why? Is there something else buggin' you?"

I know what he's *really* asking about. He hasn't brought up that day he caught Ronan at the house, and I haven't mentioned it.

"Nope. All good," I lie.

Frank clinks his water bottle against my beer. In sixteen years, I've never seen him touch a drop of alcohol. "One day at a time, Parker."

With a deep breath, I echo, "One day at a time."

46. Ronan

Did Britt tell you I ran into her at a bar?

> She did. That fake ID's gonna get her in trouble.

I can't believe she's twenty!

Getting the hang of things over there yet?

> Yeah, sorry for being MIA. I'm basically living in my office. We're opening next weekend.

I happen to be free. Corporate discount? 😊

I toss my phone onto my desk with a chuckle and rub the tiredness from my eyes. Hell, it's already almost ten. I've been here before the lights come on in the pit and I've been the last to leave every night for the past two weeks.

Heels click in the hallway, warning me of Belinda's approach. True to her word, she has donated hours of her time each day for the past two weeks, pulling up a chair to walk me through systems, explaining reports and even basic details like the company hierarchy lists and operating principles—things that mean nothing for an outdoor crew grunt but are supposed to drive every call I make as a director. She's walked me through decisions I'm pressed for, talking through various scenarios until I can see the best answer at the end of it.

For everything else the woman may be, she's brilliant. She could probably rival Henry himself for running Wolf Hotels. Also, she doesn't seem to think I'm a complete waste of air anymore.

Belinda knocks and a split second later she strolls in, not waiting for my answer. "Update on the course?"

"They finished it this afternoon." Dorian admitted that the pools of water on the ninth hole were an issue, and then I had the displeasure of dealing with the construction company's president. After three days of playing a game of we-followed-the-architect's-plans and we'll-send-you-a-quote-for-the-new-work, I ran out of patience. That's when I learned about the company that lost the original bid. So I contacted them. They were more than happy to send a small army the next morning —engineers, man power, heavy machinery—to tear up the hole and correct the problem.

"Good." She nods with satisfaction.

"I doubt head office will feel that way at our next budget meeting."

"They'll whine for a bit and then they'll release the money from their reserves. We had no choice. It had to be fixed before we opened." She shrugs. "I'm heading out now. You should think about leaving too. It's Saturday night. I'm sure you have better things to do than be here." She carries a soft brown leather computer bag over one shoulder, with her pink blazer draped over it. Even on a quiet weekend, she's dressed to impress, her hourglass figure on display in a pencil skirt and a fitted silk sleeveless shirt. I wonder if she owns sweatpants.

"Soon. I have a few things left to sort out ahead of the

media open." Everyone seems to need my approval before they can sneeze. And with Henry coming in on Monday, people are extra antsy.

"You know you can bring your computer home, right?"

Leaning back in my chair, I stretch. "I live with Connor. I get more done here." And surprisingly, I'm not hating the four walls of my office as much as I expected to, but that could be because I'm too busy figuring things out to notice that I haven't felt the sun in days. "But I'm taking tomorrow off. Gonna rot by the pool and *not* think." Grow a pair and swing by Mermaid Beach to see how Sloane's doing.

"Good." Her gaze drags over my torso. "You deserve it."

I mock frown. "Wait, sorry, what? Did I hear that correctly?"

Belinda rolls her eyes but then her full lips stretch with a rare, genuine smile. "Oh! I almost forgot." She pulls a manila envelope out of her bag and takes the three steps to drop it on my desk.

"What's this?" I dig out a stack of papers. They're letters to "valuable guests," each with the gold Wolf Hotel logo embossed on the top.

"These are what we call golden tickets." Belinda perches her ass on the corner of my desk, the slit in her skirt parting. "In addition to our list of various media, political, and corporate parties, we like to extend invitations to suitable guests for two nights to enjoy all the facilities. They get free spa treatments, meals, drinks within reason. It's a good way to help fill lounge chairs and dining tables, especially for the cameras. Call it a perk for your position."

I leaf through the sheets. There are eight of them in total, each invitation good for two adults. "Can I invite my mom?"

"Does she look hot in a bikini?"

I cringe at the suggestion.

"We can talk about comping a room for dear mom later, but for now, I'd think about any acquaintances you might have, preferably female, who would photograph well in the hotel setting. The cabanas, the pool, the bars. Think influencer type. People who haven't been featured on People of Walmart."

Acquaintances ... a perk ... "So, you want me to find sixteen hot women I've probably fucked at some point to help sell Wolf's image."

Her eyes flash. "You're finally catching on."

"Why didn't you say that." I chuckle. "I may know a few."

"I figured as much. These are good for Thursday and Friday night. Don't waste them." Her clicking heels move away at a clipped rate.

I groan. In addition to everything else, now I have to play this game? Hell no, I don't have time for this.

A thought strikes me. I grab my phone.

> How's Carrie's bachelorette party planning going?

47. Ronan

A fist pounds on my bedroom door. "Come on. Get out of bed! It's almost noon!"

I groan into my pillow. "Fuck off." It's my first day off since I arrived in Mermaid Beach. All I want to do is sleep.

"You decent?"

"*No.*"

"Alone?" My door creaks open.

"Seriously, Con, leave me the fuck—"

"Just how we like you," a female voice purrs.

I lift my head to find Rachel and Katie standing in the doorway, gawking at my bare ass.

"Hey," I croak, fumbling for my sheet to cover my lower half. "What are you two doing here?"

Rachel hops onto my bed first, draping herself over me to deliver a sloppy kiss on my cheek. "Connor invited us here for a few days. Didn't he tell you?"

"No, he didn't mention it."

"Of course I did!" Connor lies.

Katie drops onto the bed on my other side, and suddenly I'm sandwiched between the two flirtatious blonds. "You don't mind, do you?"

"Of course not."

"Good." She leans in to give me a hug.

I guess this means my day of doing nothing is over. I roll onto my back, holding my sheet in place to cover my morning wood. Considering the kinds of things we've done together, it's almost laughable. But we've been platonic since well before Abbi's wedding and I'd like to keep it that way. I search for energy as I say, "Give me five and I'll meet you guys downstairs."

The girls are giddy as they skip out.

"There are five bedrooms in this place. Take your pick," I holler after them. Except for this one. I make a mental note to lock my door tonight.

"Not the one on the first floor," Connor warns. "Ryan and Kyle are staying there. My sis doesn't want to hear me bone."

"Wait. Ryan's here too?"

Connor throws out his hands. "Do you not listen to a word I say?"

"Honestly, *no*, but you didn't tell me this." I'd remember him mentioning Ryan.

He shrugs. "Well, now you know. They're on their way from the airport. Get dressed. We've got *big* plans."

I groan as he leaves, and then fumble for my phone to check messages.

TASHA

Carrie and the girls are in!

———

"So? How do you like Mermaid Beach?" Ryan asks from the front passenger seat of their rental car. They showed up twenty minutes ago, announced they have an afternoon organized and to put on our bathing suits, and we all loaded into this three-row SUV. I was just happy to not have to drive.

"Good so far, but I haven't done much besides work."

"I guess not. That's a big promotion, Mr. Director." She turns in her seat to face Connor and me, her hazel eyes sparkling with excitement. "I still can't believe you guys moved here. You're always doing crazy stuff. I mean, first Alaska, now this."

"Yeah, it was not expected." And still a highly question-able decision on Henry's part. "How's life back in Miami? Building still good?" Ryan and Kyle moved in together right before Connor and I got back from Alaska. Though Ryan says it wasn't the case, I can't help but wonder if my returning had a lot to do with the move—she told Kyle we had hooked up a few times. Regardless, they seem to be going strong. She texts me every now and then, and it's only with good things.

"Same old. Right, Kyle?" She reaches over to squeeze his shoulder with affection as he drives. She looks so happy.

And I'm so happy for her.

"You guys remember Vera?" Kyle meets my gaze in the rearview mirror. "They had to call the fire department because the guy she was seeing couldn't get out of the chains she bound him in. They had to cut him out."

"Yeah, that tracks." Connor shudders at the memory of his scarring night with the older, adventurous neighbor.

I chuckle. "So, not much has changed is what you're telling us."

Turn here." Connor points at a parking lot.

Kyle makes a quick left ahead of oncoming traffic.

"Will you *finally* tell us what we're doing?" Katie whines from the back seat as Rachel smooths sunscreen over her back for her.

"We booked an afternoon tiki bar cruise!" Ryan exclaims, clapping her hands. "Connor gave us the name of a great place."

Oh fuck.

"Remember that coffee shop we went into that one day?" He nudges my arm and points to the familiar mermaid logo on the front of a tiny, festive shed.

"Yeah, I remember." I sigh heavily.

This could get interesting.

Fucking hell.

48. Sloane

The midday sun beats down on me as I cross the pothole-riddled parking lot to our registration booth—a wooden utility shed that Gigi dressed up with turquoise paint and a thatched roof to serve as the Sea Witch's welcome post leading to our three boat slips.

Skye's angelic face is framed within the open window as she sucks back her daily smoothie while waiting for guests to arrive. An oscillating fan flutters strands of her hair but her complexion glows. We call it the Sweat Shack for a reason. A small plug-in air-conditioning unit on the wall above provides some relief, but it's unreliable and, in the height of the season, weak against the humidity.

All in all, this is a tedious job—confirming passenger details and liability waivers—but someone has to do it, and God love Skye for being the willing victim most days.

"Hello, sunshine. Who do I have today?" I only skimmed the schedule.

She pauses mid slurp. "Ryan Tatum. Party of six."

"Ryan Tatum," I echo. "I hope they aren't a bunch of loud, obnoxious bros. I'm in no mood."

"Maybe *you* aren't, but you're gonna put them in the mood

in *that*." Skye eyeballs the red string bikini I threw on under my floral Hawaiian shirt—the official Sea Witch captain's uniform, along with a matching wide-brim hat that Frank refuses to wear.

"Too skimpy?" It's inevitable that I have at least one admirer on a cruise. The outfit inspires some weird fetishes, and the more these people drink, the bolder they get about sharing. Drunk Uncle Phil at Thanksgiving dinner's got nothing on his brother, Drunk Uncle Ned, during a daytime booze cruise.

Normally, I stick to modest two-piece suits, but they're all in the hamper, and I figured my shirt is long enough to hide the thong bottom so my ass isn't hanging out. Besides, it makes me feel good in my skin, and my ego could use a pick-me-up after Ronan's blow-off, which I can't seem to shake weeks later.

This is why I don't do one-night stands. Or one-*day* stands, as it was.

"Just right, I say. But make sure you lube up." She waggles her eyebrows in a cartoonish fashion and then tosses me a full can of sunscreen, drawing my chuckle.

"Oh! Almost forgot. A guy came by today. Where is that ..." She spins on her stool, searching the cramped desk.

"What for?"

"He was asking about the captain's job. Seemed nice. Flirty."

Not surprising that he'd flirt with Skye. "Cute?"

"Yeah! In, like, a beefy black Tom Holland sort of way."

I'm frowning at the unusual mental picture that draws when she declares, "Aha!" and thrusts a paper into my hand.

Excitement flickers at the prospect of a replacement for AJ. "Devon McCloud," I read aloud. "Wait, why does that name sound *so* familiar?"

"I don't know. I've never seen him around," Skye says.

"Devon McCloud." I skim the résumé. When I see the last line, it clicks. "You've got to be kidding me."

"Why? What's wrong with him?"

"Well, for one, he's a friend of Cody's." Not close, but one, nonetheless. Enough that the name means something. "This guy worked at Neptune's one summer." The ice cream shop has served Mermaid Beach for decades. "He got into it with the owner. So he quit and as a parting gift, he flipped the main power breaker off at closing time and opened all the freezer doors. The owner came in the next day to his *entire inventory* melted. On July 4 weekend."

"Ouch." Skye's face pinches. "That's criminal."

"Can you believe he actually included them as a reference?" He probably figured I wouldn't go back five summers to check. "See? *This* is what I'm left with. Potheads and ice cream murderers." I crumple the résumé into a ball and aim for the trash basket in the corner, my hope deflated.

"Have no fear. The next one will be a dream come true. I can feel it in my bones!" Skye hollers after me as I trot down the flight of wooden stairs to the dock. It jiggles beneath my steps as I trudge toward *Tiki One*, already wishing the next four hours over.

Jeremy is backing out of his slip, his group of bikini-clad partygoers chair-bobbing to the music playing over their speaker. Meanwhile, *Tiki Three* sits idle in its space, losing us money every day it's not open for reservations.

"Ahoy, Captain Sloane!" Jeremy hollers from his driver's seat.

I feel his effervescent mood from here. I wave back, but his rapt focus is already on navigating into the steady flow of traffic. Someone once called Mermaid Beach's harbor waterfront the Watery Wild West, and I can't argue with them about that. During high season, the channel is teeming from dawn till dusk, with everything from skilled sailors in their yachts to inexperienced boaters renting pontoons. We've had more than one bump-and-nudge over the years. The fishing charter next to us, Eddie's, lost a boat and half their dock when a group from Louisiana got confused by their throttle and crashed.

My sandaled feet hit the floor of the tiki boat with a soft thud.

A curly blond mop of hair pops up over the ice trough. "Hey, boss."

"Hey, Will." I toss my bag onto the captain's seat and push aside any lingering resentment. "How we lookin'?"

"Uh, let's see ... You're gassed up, engine's purring. You've got Solo cups, lots of ice, bottle opener, straws, trash bags ..." He rhymes off the inventory list, counting down items on his fingers. "Yup, that's it. You're good to go." He caps it off with a grin, his shirtless torso tan and muscular. But all my guys are in shape—minus Rolland. Lugging equipment in ninety-degree humid heat all summer along will do that to you whether you want it or not.

"Perfect."

"Even crammed an extra bag in there." Will slaps the top of the Yeti cooler.

"It's a hot day, so we'll probably need it." I chug a mouthful of water, acutely aware of his bright gaze dancing over my bikini. While I'm used to my staff ogling me when my back is to them, they're not usually so overt about it. Maybe this scant outfit was a bad choice. Oh well, too late now.

"Need anything else? 'Cause Frank wants me back at the compound to do repairs on the umbrellas."

A never-ending task. "You're good to go."

"'Kay, see ya later, boss."

"Actually—" I blurt, then falter. "You like working at Sea Witch, don't you?"

He shrugs. "Yeah, sure. I mean, it's always a good time. Love the guys. You're awesome." He flashes a crooked smile. "Why?"

So innocent, so nonchalant, like he didn't try to stab me in the back.

"No reason." Frank is right. I need to stop taking this whole thing so personally and be thankful I still have a team, though threadbare. "Better get out there before Frank calls."

"Yikes. See you on the other end." He skitters away, grabbing his cast-off T-shirt on the way.

I test the engine to confirm no issues and then spend a few minutes double-checking supplies and setting up the speaker for music until the sound of approaching steps and laughter draws my focus to the incoming group.

It's not a bunch of guys after all, but three couples. That's ideal. They'll be too busy with each other to bother me. A hulking blond in a white tank top is lugging a case of beer in his arms. Hey, wait—he looks like Ronan's mediocre friend—

Oh shit.

It *is* Ronan's mediocre friend. Which probably means ...

My stomach plummets to my sandals as the sleek form bringing up the rear of the line comes into full view, his soft gray T-shirt clinging to that perfect body. Intense green eyes hide behind signature aviators, his stony face half-hidden by a baseball cap.

I haven't seen Ronan since we had sex against my kitchen wall two weeks and one day ago—almost to the hour. I haven't heard a single peep from him. And now he shows up *here,* for a day cruise? Potentially with another *woman?*

I *should* throw my water bottle at his head. A part of me itches to.

And yet my pulse races in his presence.

A short brunette in a fuchsia bathing suit leads the pack. "Hi, I'm Ryan. You must be Sloane?"

"Uh ..." I falter. Do *they* know what happened between Ronan and their captain? Is this why they booked me?

No, Skye gave her my name, I remind myself.

They're all staring at me as I gape like a beached fish. Possibly wondering if they're putting their afternoon and their lives in the hands of an idiot.

K.A. Tucker

I clear my voice, doing my best to draw some semblance of confidence. "Captain Sloane for the next four hours."

"Hottest captain *ever*." Big dumb blond—what was his name again?—declares, peering over his sunglasses at my bikini top, or likely, at my chest. Did Ronan tell him what happened?

"Connor." Ryan elbows him in his rib cage. "My brother thinks he's charming. He doesn't realize he's a pig-slut."

"A pig-slut. Hmm." He mock frowns. "Did you learn that at your fancy MBA school?"

"No, I learned it while living with you," she quips without missing a beat.

"You didn't complain when you were paying practically nothing in rent for all those years."

"Dad gave you your down payment." She smiles sweetly up at him. "And, believe me, I did."

"Is Ronan a pig-slut too?" His responding grin is broad and smug.

Even under the harsh sun, her cheeks redden.

"All right, children," the tall preppy man in the button-down swordfish-print shirt on her left scolds playfully. He's giving off major boyfriend vibes.

But what was that sly dig about Ronan?

Everyone's standing around. Might as well get this awkward show on the road. Or water. I gesture toward the tiki. "Come aboard and get settled in. We'll go over a few safety rules and then we can get this party started. There's ice and supplies for your drinks." Which it appears they've brought a lot of.

"And food?" The preppy guy holds platters in each hand—one of veggies and dip, the other fruit. The two striking blonds behind him carry grocery bags stuffed with chips and soda against their ample bikini-clad chests. *White* bikinis, at that. Brave girls. Who are they in this mix? A jealous twinge in my gut says they're not also Connor's sisters.

Has Ronan fucked either of them?

Is he fucking one right now? Am I about to shuttle Ronan and his girlfriend around for the afternoon?

This is going from bad to worse, very quickly.

"Plenty of ice in the cooler." I force a wide smile and step back, allowing them space to pass. The dock rocks with their shifting weight.

Finally, Ronan reaches the tiki boat, his ripped arms laden with boxes of margarita cans.

I hold my breath as he stalls, his looming body so close taking me back to those shared moments in an instant. My traitorous pulse races once again.

"Hey, sea witch." His voice is as raspy as ever.

I can't ignore him, as much as I'd like to. "Hi."

Simple.

Cordial.

Civilized.

Nothing like our last encounter, which ended with me naked and letting him come inside me.

Chaos erupts as everyone tosses cans into the drink trough, their laughter and giddiness carrying across the slips. It's a suitable distraction.

"I had no idea Ryan booked this until ten minutes ago," Ronan continues.

Steeling my nerve, I meet his hidden gaze head-on. "Will that be a problem for you and your *friends*?"

His lips part but he stalls, studying me for a lengthy moment that weighs me down, even as I do my best to appear unbothered. "No problem at all."

"Good." My tone, by comparison, is clipped.

"And they are all *just* friends."

"I didn't ask."

The corner of his mouth kicks up. With amusement? Is this a game to him? "I wanted to call but—"

"The sooner you take your seat, the sooner we can leave," I blurt loudly, cutting off his lame excuse for ghosting me.

"Yeah, come on, you heard the captain! Stop dragging your lazy ass. These ladies flew here to have some fun." Connor ropes his giant arms around the two bleached blonds, pulling them snug against his chest. For their part, they don't fight it, smashing their curvy bodies into him with giggles, their palms resting on his ample pecs.

I stifle the urge to roll my eyes.

Ronan sighs heavily. "I hope you're ready for a long afternoon."

"You don't say." Every nerve ending in my body seems on edge as he moves away, leaving the delicious scent of mint for me to trail.

"Hey, you got a sound system on here? Sweet. I'm gonna jump on that," Connor declares, pulling out his phone.

"No!" Ryan and Ronan exclaim in unison.

———

"So, everyone just hangs out here all day?" Rachel, the blond with the high ponytail, stares in awe at the cluster of anchored watercraft ahead, a medley of pontoons, speedboats, and modified barges like this tiki bar, plus the odd—and in my view, annoying—Jet Ski. The fact that Sea Witch invested in several for money-making purposes has no bearing on my personal opinion.

"Hang, swim, float, drink." I navigate us toward the left side of the sandbar as a throaty male singer belts out a twangy country song over the speakers—Connor won the playlist battle simply by being too quick on the draw for anyone to stop him. "Any given day in season, we'll have hundreds of boats out here. Once, last summer, they counted over a thousand."

The other blond, Katie, mouths *"Wow"* while Kyle—Ryan's boyfriend—whistles.

"Sounds like I need to get myself a boat." Connor polishes

off the rest of his beer and, first crushing the can in his massive hand, tosses it freestyle into the trash bin beside me.

"Hot dogs?" Ryan points to the nearby dinghy with the bright yellow flag affixed to the back.

"Yup. We have vendors selling everything from ice cream to Chick-Fil-A to slushies. Even coffee." And they're all employed by Ian Sanders, a bloated councilman who convinced the county to limit the Starfish Island vendor licensing to avoid oversaturation. Guess who got all of them? Sanders Sandbar Merchants—*his* company. He has a full monopoly. It's been a sore spot for the Sea Witch for years.

I toss a wave at the sheriff's patrol boat—Jimmy's behind the wheel today. I know a lot of them. Gigi used to know them all. She'd drop off home-baked banana muffins every now and then and memorized their names while ensuring they knew ours.

As much as I hate baking, I should probably get back to that tradition.

"So, when did you guys come up with this floating tiki bar idea?" Ronan asks. The question catches me off guard. It's the first time he's spoken directly to me since we undocked. He's been quiet, in general—nothing more than a "Sure, thanks" or a "Nah, I'm good" to questions thrown his way. But he has texted *someone* several times.

Is it because he'd rather be anywhere than here? It's impossible to read him.

"Gigi built and captained the first one back in 1991 with the help of some friends, paying them in pitchers of margaritas," I recite the marketing copy from the Sea Witch website as I steer. "People loved it so much, she built another one and hired a retired navy officer named Bob Dewar to captain it." I spare a smile as I remember the kindly man who passed away from a heart attack when I was fourteen. He was as much a fixture around our lives as Frank is now. "Since then, Sea Witch has replaced the original tiki boats and added a third to meet demand. We sail seven days a week during the high season, weather permitting. People from all over America come to Mermaid Beach to enjoy the white sands. Families, college kids, business groups. Everyone has a good time here."

I deftly weave past anchored pontoons and a yellow floating carpet holding four girls in bikinis, sun-tanning under a cloudless sky. Starfish Island at this time of year is generally a who's who of hot bodies.

"And it is *much* appreciated." Connor winks at them as we pass, earning their fawning giggles and double takes. His tank top came off seconds after we pulled away from the dock, and now his glorious body—he may be an ass, but he is attractive—is on display for all to see.

Ryan shakes her head at her brother before dismissing his antics, leaning in to steal a kiss from her boyfriend. They're a cute couple. Of the three females, she seems the most level-headed, mature. I haven't heard much from Katie and Rachel besides them sharing tawdry Wolf Hotel gossip. It sounds like Katie works in the spa and Rachel rakes in tips from sleazy businessmen lingering at the hotel bar. Even Ryan was talking about how happy she is to have moved into Wolf's finance department.

They all bow to the devil himself, save for Kyle—a self-proclaimed economics geek working for a hedge fund.

"We're going to anchor near our Sea Witch sister tiki bar." I point ahead to where Jeremy has made room among the revelers and is waving me in. Families usually stick to the far right of the sandbar, where it's especially shallow and less rowdy.

I reduce my speed, and we coast in. Cutting our engine, I quickly drop anchor alongside his, securing it so we don't drift.

"This looks so fun!" Katie exclaims, her bright eyes scraping over the row of guys doing shots nearby. To our left, another group tosses a football around in thigh-deep water, the emerald-green an idyllic backdrop. Far on the right side, where it's slightly deeper, are clusters of pontoons with slides.

"We've officially stationed, so enjoy! But remember, *no diving*." Every year, some fool inevitably goes headfirst into the water and is carried out on a stretcher. "Pay attention to the current and boats. And if you see marine life, appreciate it from a distance!" It's always an exciting time when dolphins or manatees make an appearance.

"You hear that, girls? Go forth and *get wet*." Connor gestures to the platform.

In seconds, Katie and Rachel leap in with giddy splashes, followed closely by Ryan and Kyle, who lets out a comical squeal.

"It's refreshing!" Jeremy hollers with a grin from *Tiki Two*.

"That's polite for ball-retreating cold." Connor surveys the various groups before his focus snags on a brunette with rich brown skin, lying on her pool float, her ample ass on full display in a beige thong that may as well not exist.

I can only imagine the kind of dirty thoughts going through this guy's head. "Sounds like your balls could do with a little retreat," I mutter under my breath.

Ronan chuckles into his beer. "You have no idea."

After a deep humming sound, Connor breaks his focus and snaps his fingers. "Tequila."

Ronan groans. "It's too early—"

"Fuck that. You owe me."

"For *what?*" The incredulity on Ronan's normally stony face is comical.

"You begged me to leave Miami so you wouldn't be alone and, being the amazing friend that I am, I dropped *everything*, abandoned my entire life back home, to come here. For you."

"Are you kidding me?" Ronan slides off his sunglasses to stare in bewilderment at his friend.

Damn, this boy's face has been blessed, as Gigi says. I could admire it all day long.

"I barely mentioned coming to Mermaid Beach and you had your bag packed. You've been throwing parties every night in that monster house. *And* I got you a promotion!"

"Exactly. More responsibility! Since when do I want that? But I did it for *you*!" Connor jabs Ronan in the chest with his index finger, earning Ronan's chuckle. "And then we get here and you're MIA the whole time. Seriously, dude, *where have you been* for the past two weeks?"

Yeah, good question! I busy myself with the ice trough, pretending not to listen as Ronan's friend berates him. But at least I'm not the only one asking. And if I'm not the only one, then maybe he hasn't been avoiding *me*.

Ronan pinches the bridge of his nose. "You know where I've been. Chained to my fucking desk, trying to figure shit out before Wolf fires my ass for incompetence."

"As if. Red would *never* let him."

Who is Red? Besides someone who has control over his billionaire boss.

His wife.

Of course. It *has* to be. She has striking long red hair.

"You're close with Henry Wolf's wife?" I blurt, interrupting their little domestic spat.

"You could say that." Connor snorts, throwing a thumb Ronan's way. "This one was her bridesmaid."

"Man of honor," Ronan corrects dryly.

"You were in *her* wedding party." It all makes sense now. He's not friends with Henry Wolf. He's friends—good friends, clearly—with *Abbi* Wolf.

Ronan peers at me curiously while Connor slaps Solo cups in a row on the counter like a petulant child mid tantrum. "We're all having one." He cracks the bottle of tequila. "Even you, Cap."

My head shake is firm. "Sorry, I'd lose my charter license, and I can't afford that. I'm already down one boat as it is."

"You haven't found anyone to replace AJ yet?" Ronan asks, his tone suddenly somber.

"Nope. A few prospects, but no good ones."

"Wait a minute." Connor's eyebrows arch. "*AJ* AJ?"

Ronan's nod is almost imperceptible.

Connor's attention swings to me. "He worked *here*?"

"He was one of my captains until he quit on me. Why? How do *you* know him?"

"I'm his supervisor at Wolf. You know, because of that *extra responsibility* I didn't ask for?" A sharp glare is thrown Ronan's way. "He's about to know the toilets and dumpster real well." Connor rests his elbows on the counter and levels Ronan with a steady look. "And how do *you* know him again?"

"I told you. I don't ... directly."

Connor studies his friend for a lengthy moment. "Chained to your desk the *whole* time, huh?" There's accusation in his tone.

Ronan's lips twitch, and I sense an entire conversation hidden within that brief exchange.

"Motherfucker," Connor mutters, pouring a round of shots. He picks up a lemon. "What do you say to me doing a shot off you, Cap?"

"I say ..." I falter, not expecting such a direct request. "It's a little early in the day." And it's been a decade since I've let strangers lick me in the name of tequila.

"Yeah? What about Ronan? Would you let him?" His blue eyes are playful, knowing.

I'd let him do that and more, I silently admit, as I feel my cheeks burn. And I think Connor has somehow figured that out too, which means Ronan never told him about us. Should I be insulted or pleased? "Still much too early."

"Later, then." Connor winks and, collecting five Solo cups, drops his brawny body into the water with a gasp. He cuts through the shallows toward the group with powerful thighs.

"Is he *always* like that?" I watch with a mixture of repulsion and wonder as Connor dips down to draw a line with his tongue across Katie's cleavage before downing his tequila. The rest of the group cheers as they do their round.

"Only while he's conscious." Ronan rubs his face with his palms.

Without his sunglasses on, I can see the dark circles under his eyes. A twinge of sympathy stirs for him. "Sounds like you've been really busy." Still ... too busy to text me? I don't buy it.

"It's my first day off since I got to Mermaid Beach. I wasn't expecting house guests and a party. I was planning on sleeping." He pauses. "And coming to see you."

"Sure, you were." I pretend to survey the surrounding scene.

"Look, I'm in a weird place in my life, and I—"

"You comin' in, Casanova?" Connor hollers as he cuts through the water toward the beige thong-clad beauty.

Ronan groans. "If it means you'll leave me alone for five minutes." Whatever he was about to tell me is lost with the interruption.

"He really can't handle being away from you."

"I could probably count the days we've been apart since I met him two years ago."

"Wow. Not gonna lie, that's kind of weird. Do you two do *anything* separately?" The question is thrown out casually, without thought, but the moment the words are out of my mouth, an answer flutters into my mind.

There is *one* thing they don't do together.

By the smirk on Ronan's face, I'd guess he's thinking the same.

"I better get this over with." Ronan stands, empties his pockets, tossing his wallet and phone on the counter.

My stomach clenches as a text pops up on his screen from someone named Tasha, but I'm quickly distracted from my jealousy as Ronan peels off his shirt. He's as perfect as he was in my kitchen, and I can't help getting caught on the V-cut of his pelvis as I remember what he looked like—and felt like—pressed up against me, thrusting into me.

A desperate, traitorous ache stirs deep within my belly. Yes, I'm angry with Ronan for going radio silent, I'll admit, but my body doesn't seem to care.

"I didn't tell Connor about us." Ronan answers my unspoken question from earlier, yanking my eyes upward to find him watching me.

"You mean, you don't share *everything* with him?" They seem awfully close.

A sly smile curves his lips before he schools his expression. "It would appear not. Anyway, I didn't tell him, but he's figured it out and he's gonna be exceptionally annoying for the rest of the day. I'm sorry in advance."

"Can't wait."

"Feel free to tell him to fuck off. I'll write a good review if you do."

"You weren't going to, anyway?" I quip.

"For *you*? I've already written it in my head. I doubt you want me sharing it online."

"And why is that?" We're quickly sliding back into that dangerous flirtatious zone again, the one that led to me peeling off my clothes like they were infested with bugs.

He was ready to join his friends a second ago, and yet he edges around the platform to step through the swing gate, into my space. "Might get flagged for indecency." He reaches up to turn his baseball cap around.

My pulse races through my veins. I didn't think he could get any sexier, but he has a thin layer of stubble across his jaw, and that, coupled with the hat, is ejecting all common sense from my brain. *Again.* "What would it say?" I taunt, backing up into the nautical ship wheel to make room.

"That it was a quick ride but a wet one that I thoroughly

enjoyed. I wish I'd lived up to expectations, though." His voice turns so low and gravelly.

I clear my throat. "You were fine." More than fine. He may not have made me come that day, but he has every night since, as I've replayed those stolen moments in my head with the help of my hand.

The responding chuckle is dark, bitter. "I'm never just *fine*. But with you, I wasn't ..." A muscle in his square jaw ticks. "I don't know what I was. Not myself." He grasps the hem of my floral shirt between his thumb and index finger, holding it open. "I like this."

"Yeah?" I'm suddenly *very* thankful that I wore it today.

Sharp green eyes flash to mine. "I'd like it better *off*."

He may as well have peeled off my clothes with his words because I suddenly feel naked, my skin acutely aware of his. I struggle to play it cool as my breasts grow heavy, my nipples tightening with anticipation. "Not included in the cruise rate."

"We can renegotiate later." His focus swings to *Tiki Two*, anchored twenty feet away. "Is that your golden boy over there?"

I follow his gaze, relieved for the reprieve from innuendo so I can catch a breath. "The one and only." Jeremy is chatting up a cute girl with French braids in her lengthy strawberry-blond hair. Thankfully he's not paying attention to us.

"Has he admitted to taking the job at Wolf yet?"

"Not a word to me."

"Chickenshit."

"But at least we can both avoid an uncomfortable conversation." The last thing I'd ever want to do is make Jeremy feel bad. "How's he doing over there?"

"Still in training."

French Braids tips her head back and belts out a laugh that seems far too big for her petite body. "I'm sure he'll do well." And, as much as I want to, I can't begrudge him for succeeding. At least I've got him for the summer.

"The real test will be next weekend when we open to the public."

"*Next* weekend?" I groan. "Already?" I've been so busy juggling things and worrying, I've lost track of entire days.

Ronan chuckles. "There'll be a lot of activity this week ahead of it. Media and stuff. It's a real circus." A pause. "Your favorite guy's coming in tomorrow."

There's only one person he could be talking about. "I'll be sure to make a welcome sign for him. I'm kidding," I quickly add when Ronan's expression falls. "A deal's a deal." Ronan did me a huge favor before he—literally—fucked me.

"It is." Rough hands slip under my shirt to seize my hips, spinning me around.

My breath catches on a sharp inhale, and no doubt Ronan hears it. "What are you doing?"

"I also made a deal with Henry and Belinda." He steps in closer to me until his body brushes against my backside. "Actually, no, that's not accurate. It wasn't a deal. More like a demand. They told me to stay away from you."

"Me?" My voice is breathless as hot palms smooth over my skin, rubbing back and forth. I've never met either of them, but it doesn't take a genius to figure out *why* Henry Wolf and the hotel manager might insist on that. "Why? Do you have a reputation for *not* staying away?"

"Some may say that. Belinda promised me she'd fire my ass if I laid a finger on you." He confesses this as he lays *many* fingers on me, toying with the strings that keep my bottoms from tumbling to the floor.

It dawns on me. "Is *that* why I haven't heard from you?" Because he broke Henry Wolf's strict rules about fucking the crazy rooster commune lady?

"Partly, yes."

I bite my bottom lip, struggling against the urge to ask what other parts there might be to that answer—he did say he's in a "weird place," whatever that means. "And what happens if he finds out?"

Ronan steps closer until his erection is pressed against the small of my back. "I'll likely lose my job."

"Your big fancy director's position?" I manage a whistle, even as I'm about to choke on my pounding heart. "You'd risk that for *this*?"

"For *you*?" His breath skates. A heavy sigh sails into my ear. "Apparently, yes, seeing as I can't keep my hands to myself whenever I'm around you."

Something sparks in my chest—an odd, warm feeling that hasn't existed there in a long time, not since Cody killed it.

"I need to know something," Ronan murmurs.

"What's that?"

I'm expecting a question, so I gasp with shock when instead of words, Ronan's hand slips under the seam of my bikini and between my thighs, his fingers tracing my slit with a gentle stroke.

"Thought so."

All other thoughts vanish as Ronan's middle finger slides deep into me, to discover a truth I can't hide there—that I'm insanely attracted to him.

His capable hand moves at a languid, teasing rhythm, his thumb drawing lazy circles over my clit.

It takes every effort for me to pretend I'm simply standing here, observing the merry band of revelers as they splash and drink and toss the football while Ronan finger-fucks me. I *cannot believe* I'm allowing this to happen out here in public, with people *all* around us. And within ten minutes of being left alone with him.

"Relax. No one can see anything," he purrs.

"You think I'd let you do this if they could?" I've offered no resistance to his invasion because he's right. The tiki bar walls surrounding us are high enough to hide what Ronan is doing. There's a swinging section to fully close off the bar—not like

Tiki Two, which has a wide-open passageway between the two sides. The thatched roof hangs low, providing ample protection from the helicopter flying above. Out there, everyone and everything is on display, but in here, it's a shady, protected refuge.

As long as his friends don't climb back up for a drink, or they'll get a show they didn't pay for.

All these thoughts are flying through my mind and yet, I can't find the words to tell him to stop.

Because I *don't want* him to.

"I wish I could fuck you right here," he whispers, voicing the words that were just flittering through my overloaded brain.

A rush of warmth floods me. "Yes, you're so disappointing."

His deep chuckle somehow travels down to where his fingers touch me. "At least let me make you come."

"Okay." I sound helpless, shaky.

Wedging his foot between mine, he shimmies my legs farther apart, giving him better access that he takes full advantage of, sliding a second finger in. Each stroke is fluid and easy and deep, my body responding like it's been starved for a man.

Not just any man.

Him.

"You're soaked."

"Uh-huh."

"And swollen."

"So are you."

He presses himself against the crack of my ass in answer, and I whimper. Swollen isn't the right word for what Ronan is. Ramrod, fire-poker hard. I roll my hips in response.

Ronan hisses and shifts behind me.

Material rustles.

The back of my floral captain's shirt lifts.

And suddenly, his hot, velvety-smooth length is pressed against my bare skin.

"Ronan—"

"No one can tell. I promise." He adjusts his stance to lower himself and, with his free hand, he angles himself. His tip prods, then slides between my thighs from behind while his thumb keeps stroking my clit.

A casual glance over my shoulder confirms that he's so discreet about it, he may as well be standing still. All the work is happening at his hips, as he pretends to watch the horizon while he slowly guides his cock, the slickness making each casual thrust easier. There is nothing clumsy or inexperienced about this guy.

All it would take is a shift of my pelvis, a tug on my skimpy suit, and he could be inside me. Just the thought stirs an unbearable ache.

I look around. Still, no one pays us any attention.

My body vibrates with need, and it is *so* tempting.

On his next pass, I rise to my tiptoes and arch my back.

"Careful," he growls, but he tugs my bathing suit material aside and presses his head against my opening.

"Oh fuck," I hiss.

"Not quite. Stay still, or I *will* fuck you right here and I won't care who watches." There's an edge of warning in his tone. "Let me finish you off." His hand regains its rhythm, and my core hums with anticipation.

"What is that perfume you're wearing?"

"I'm not ... It's probably sunscreen." It could be his skill or my desperation, or it could be the insanity of allowing this, but the orgasm he's promised me is already there, drifting along my spine, just out of reach.

"No, you smelled like it before too." He inhales deeply. "Pineapple and coconut."

"My shampoo." I bite back a moan, my hand reaching for his forearm, to feel the corded muscles strain beneath my fingers as he plays me like an elegant instrument. Hell, I've never been touched so thoroughly.

"I *love* it."

This is getting out of control, fast. I scan our surroundings. Katie and Rachel are busy flipping their hair as they chat with a group of guys who look barely legal, Kyle and Ryan have swum off to investigate the floating jungle gym, and Connor is chatting up Beige Thong. Even Jeremy is suitably occupied with his flock of ladies. No one is paying us any heed.

Ronan and I are in our own little world.

And I am desperate to come.

Maybe that's why I adjust my stance more and demand, "Faster."

Ronan slides in a third finger. "You don't need faster, babe. You need *deeper*." He hooks his middle finger to hit a spot inside. "That'd be a lot easier to reach with my cock."

Which is *right there*, its tip anxious to slide in. My left hand fists the steering wheel. "I wish, but you're doing fine."

"There's that word again." He chuckles, but it sounds strained. "How many hours left in this cruise?"

I close my eyes, willing everyone around us to disappear as I do my best to remain calm, unflustered, heading for my climax. "Too many?" I admit on a desperate moan.

"Definitely too many."

He changes his stance and suddenly his tip is no longer nudging but prodding, pushing in, teasing sensitive flesh that is desperate to feel more than his fingers.

"You know what I've thought about since that day?" Ronan's uneven breaths skate across my cheek as he leans in.

I think he might kiss my neck and I tilt my head, welcoming his lips on me. "What's that?"

"What you'll taste like when you come in my mouth."

A stark visual of Ronan's face between my thighs hits me then, and I climax, my legs shaking and my nails digging into his corded flesh as I struggle not to make a sound.

It takes me a moment to come back down and when I do, I feel disoriented.

And sticky.

A quick glance around reassures me that we haven't earned an audience. Ronan just brought me to orgasm in the middle of Mermaid Beach's tourist sandbar, and no one is the wiser.

"That was fucking hot," Ronan whispers.

I can only hum in agreement.

"Look down."

After a deep, steadying breath, I do as asked and regard his coated fingers and palm. "You did that, babe."

That couldn't have been all me. "You came too?" I was so overwhelmed with focus over my own climax, I didn't realize he was having one too.

"As if I could stop it."

"Hey, Ronan!" Connor booms. "Come meet Sasha and Mira!"

My jealousy flares as I spy Beige Thong's equally curvy and beautiful friend hovering around them now. Ronan's hand is literally still halfway inside me, and Connor is trying to set him up with someone else. Something tells me that's a never-ending day's purpose for his friend.

"He's such a toddler today," Ronan mutters. Behind me, I sense him tucking himself into his shorts. Finally, his hand slips free.

I feel the absence instantly, but I play it cool, fixing my bottoms. I'll need to jump in the water to clean up. "Better go give him what he wants, then, before he throws a tantrum."

"It's like you know him." Ronan's slick hand crawls under the hem of my shirt to squeeze my ass cheek.

"Ugh. *Seriously?*"

I jolt at the sharp slap against my bare skin.

Ronan follows it up with a soft stroke before leaning

forward to whisper in my ear, "If you think that's messy, wait until I come all over your face."

My mouth drops with his filthy words, even as my heart rate spikes with excitement over a next time with him. I've never had a guy talk to me the way Ronan does. I never thought I'd like it.

He backs up, adjusting his shorts in the process.

The move draws my gaze down. Even though he came, he's still hard. "You're going to your friends like *that*?"

"They've seen worse."

Where to even begin with a statement like that?

"How many hours left in this cruise?" He asks again.

"Three, give or take."

"Until then." He reaches over the counter to grab the Solo cup. With a knowing smile, he pops his index and middle finger into his mouth and drags them back out, his eyes locked on me the entire time. It's a promise that I feel like an electric current rippling through every intimate spot on my body.

He downs the tequila with one swig and then hops into the water to join the others.

And I finally allow myself a deep exhale.

What is it about this man that compels me to behave so recklessly?

49. Ronan

"Sasha, anchor!" the driver of the pontoon boat shouts. He's a stocky, dark-haired guy who's been shooting daggers at us for the past half hour, since I left Sloane to appease Connor.

A decision I am woefully regretting, though I had no choice. I was seconds away from begging her for a blow job, nowhere near spent. I haven't been able to shed the mental idea of having her lips around my cock since. I can't wait until this cruise is over.

"Let me help you." Connor hauls the cumbersome and hefty weight out of the water with one hand and climbs up the ladder on the back of their pontoon, to settle it in the corner where Sasha and Mira are perched, their backs arched so their barely covered tits are on display. "Dude's an asshole, hey?"

"Ignore him. That's my brother." Sasha casts a dismissive hand toward the stewing chauffeur. "He has a thing for Mira, who *doesn't* have a thing for him."

No, she has a thing for *me*, if the overt flirting is any indication. Would she still be so friendly if she knew that before I came over here, I made our tiki boat captain come with the tip of my dick inside her?

Sasha thrusts a business card at Connor, her heavy, dark lashes fluttering. "Call me. We're here until Thursday."

"I will. Definitely." Connor drops back into the water, holding the card up so it doesn't get ruined.

Her chocolate-brown eyes rake over his sculpted torso. "I'll be waiting."

Connor flashes his signature smile. "You know *I* will be." The propeller suddenly starts, and he jumps back with a booming shout.

Yelling erupts as the pontoon pulls away, clumsily navigating around the anchored boats and people, nearly hitting another vessel in their hasty exit.

"Guy could have chopped me up with that stunt!" Connor growls, glaring after them. "Just for that, I'm going to fuck his sister."

"You're gonna do that, anyway."

"True, but I'll shout his name while I'm in there." He pumps his hips to emphasize his words.

"You've got issues."

"My only issue is how soon before I get to fuck that ass. *Damn*, did you see it?"

"Hard to miss." It was on display like the centerpiece on a buffet table. But to be honest, I barely noticed, too busy searching for every escape route back to Sloane. "I need another drink."

"Yeah, same. I'll come with. Hey, guys! Bevvies?" He makes a drinking gesture and they all nod and begin moving back toward our bar.

I stifle my groan. I was hoping for alone time with her again. This is for the best, though. I can't be trusted to keep my hands to myself.

"So, tell me." Connor slaps his big mitt over the back of my neck, squeezing tightly as he slows our stride, letting the others get ahead of us. "How long has *that* been goin' on?" He jerks a chin toward the tiki boat.

"It's not."

"Fuck off, man." Annoyance laces his tone. "I've tried to be supportive through this whole monk-life thing you've got going on, but I am seriously starting to worry about you."

"We hooked up once, weeks ago, and I haven't seen her since," I admit reluctantly. "It's complicated."

"Complicated how? Like, she's married? Has a baseball team of brats at home? Or she has an army of creepy dolls that she talks to."

I burst out laughing. "No, you jackass. None of those things. It's just ..." There's no point keeping Connor in the dark. It'll only make things more painful for me as he needles to get answers. "You heard about the neighbor at the hotel, right? The one with all the 'Fuck you, Henry Wolf' signs aimed at our green?"

"Oh, yeah. Heard they're a real whack-job."

"She's not."

"*She.*" Connor's eyes widen. "Oh, wait. *That's her?*" He jams a finger in the tiki boat's direction. "The crazy neighbor?"

I knock his hand down so it's not so obvious that we're talking about Sloane. "Yeah. And she's not crazy. She's just not happy about having a massive hotel next to her. I don't blame her. I'd be pissed too." Wolf Hotel has invaded her home and her livelihood.

Connor studies Sloane like he's seeing her again for the first time and she's suddenly grown a horn on her forehead. "Well, the signs are all down now from what I've heard, so what's the problem?"

"She and Wolf have beef. It's been goin' on for years. And Belinda wants to mount her head on a pike at the front gate. They both warned me to keep my distance before I even met her."

Realization dawns on Connor. "So, you fucked the one woman Wolf told you explicitly not to fuck."

"Basically." He said she's off-limits. It *could* leave room for interpretation. For an idiot.

"Not basically. *Exactly*. Because he knows you."

"Yeah, well ... fuck him. He doesn't get to cock-block me." Besides, he already has Abbi.

Connor seems to ponder this. "And what happens if he finds out?"

"He'll fire my ass. Belinda will make sure of it." I'll lose the job I've been killing myself to learn. I know this, and yet I'm incapable of staying away whenever Sloane's around. The second everyone hopped into the water, I was moving for her like a kid slinking toward a cookie jar, desperate to get a taste of what was inside.

So, fuck Henry Wolf. What he doesn't know can't hurt me.

Connor hoots with laughter. "You're right, man. That is *way* more complicated than creepy dolls."

———

TASHA

Flights are booked! Oh my God, we're so excited. Party of ten heading your way. Thank you! Thank you! Thank you! I can't wait to see you! XOXO

Glad I could help. I'll send you the codes tonight so you can register.

"So, how long have you lived in Mermaid Beach?" Ryan leans against the bar, gazing dreamily at Sloane.

I chuckle. She's four margaritas and a tequila shot in and slurring her words. I've never seen her drunk before. It's cute.

"My whole life." Sloane tosses a used straw in the trash behind her. "It's all I know."

"That's so nice." Ryan studies Sloane's tan, svelte body

unabashedly. There's nothing but wistfulness in her expression. She's always been like that since I've known her—acutely aware of other female bodies. At first, I wondered if she was secretly into pussy, but then I realized it was more about her obsession with anyone with a form that doesn't match her compact, curvy one. Either way, Ryan seems more confident in her own skin since meeting Kyle, which I'm happy to see. She has a lot going for her—in beauty, brains, *and* personality.

But I guess it's hard not to admire a figure like Sloane's. I know because I've been ogling her long torso and perky breasts since I parked my ass on this stool, counting down the minutes until I can touch her again. This afternoon cruise feels like an eternity, and she's been keeping her distance. Probably smart. Just the thought of her coming on my hand makes my dick hard. I'm going to have to go chill my erection in the Gulf again.

"Here, you should drink this." Sloane cracks open a bottle of water and sets it in front of Ryan. "The sun's extra hot today."

"Oh, good idea. I don't want to get drunk." Ryan chugs from the bottle, missing Sloane's smirk. "Where did Kyle go, anyway?"

"Up there." I point to the top of the giant red inflatable jungle gym. "That's him and Katie, about to come down the slide."

"They're so high up." Her face is scrunched. "Is that safe?"

"Relatively. The water's deeper there. Still, I've seen a few injuries." Sloane stoops to join us in watching them teeter at the top.

Ryan squints. "Is it me or is Katie naked?"

Sloane chuckles. "A white string bikini. Imagine that."

"Did you notice, Ronan?" Ryan asks.

"Nope." *Yes*, but I've seen Katie and Rachel naked so many times, it doesn't faze me anymore.

"Wait. Of course *you*'ve noticed." Ryan waves off my answer. "I forgot about you guys."

"Forgot what?" Sloane reaches for her own bottled water.

Oh fuck. "Nothing—"

"Every time those girls come to town, they end up in Ronan's bed. Or my brother's bed. Or all of them end up *together*." Ryan's hands splay overhead, her fingers clumsily intertwining, I assume to mimic a tangle of limbs.

Sloane chose the wrong moment to take a sip. Water sprays from her mouth, and then she's choking on remnants that went down the wrong tube.

I take it back. Ryan is *not* cute when she's drunk. I climb over the bar to slap Sloane's back, sparing a glare at my friend.

"What?" She shrugs. "I thought you guys were open about that stuff."

Ryan knows damn well I don't talk about my business, unlike Connor who broadcasts to anyone who will listen.

Sloane's coughing fit finally subsides, allowing her to swing heated, accusatory eyes on me. "So, have you already fucked them this weekend or is that tonight's plan after you're finished with me?"

I stifle my groan.

"*Oh.*" Ryan presses a palm over her mouth. "Oh my God. I'm sorry. I didn't know that you two"—she draws her fingers horizontally between us in a sloppy line—"were a thing."

"We're not *anything*," Sloane snaps, before taking a deep breath. "We're not anything," she repeats calmly.

Her words prick me unexpectedly. I don't know if I'd go *that far.*

Ryan offers me a pained expression as she mouths "*I'm sorry.*"

It's not totally her fault, but I move her half-finished can of margarita out of reach, anyway. "I haven't been with Katie or Rachel in over a year, and nothing will be happening with them tonight, regardless of who else I'm with." Which is

335

supposed to be *nobody* because I'm staying away from women, and especially not Sloane, who I have—*had*—plans on fucking in that little registration hut the second my feet touch gravel.

Sorry, Belinda, the bus is racing forward and all *my extremities are hanging out the window, waiting for you to cut them off.*

Sloane's expression hasn't softened with my assurances.

Ryan squirms in her seat, visibly uncomfortable with her gaffe. "For what it's worth, Ronan doesn't mess around when he's with someone. *Believe* me, *I* know." She reaches out to squeeze my hand in hers. "When we were together, he didn't bring anyone home from the bar. Not once."

I groan. *Not helping.*

Sloane's jaw drops. "You slept with *her* too? With Connor's sister?"

"Half sister," Ryan corrects. "And it was only for, like, a week two summers ago, when we were all living together. My ex had just broken up with me and I was feeling so sorry for myself."

A mixture of shock and horror twists Sloane's features.

Can I put my hand over Ryan's mouth to muzzle her? Would that be wrong?

"Before they took off to Alaska. Oh, ice cream!" Ryan suddenly blurts as a dinghy with a tall pink flag weaves through the boats, heading our way. "They take cash, right?" She digs into her beach bag for her wallet with one hand while the other waves wildly in the air, trying to grab the vendor's eye.

Sloane leans over the counter. "So, tell me, is there *any* female in your life who you *haven't* screwed?"

"A few." But the list is woefully short, and her icy tone says she'll find no humor in it.

"Can I get a vanilla, please!" Ryan hollers, sliding off her seat.

I hop down after her and grip her shoulder to make sure the drunken fool doesn't tumble off the platform.

"Vanilla, you said?" The vendor roots around in his cooler, shirtless and tanned. Next to the pink flag is a yellow one for boiled peanuts. Quite the combo.

Golden Boy, a.k.a. Jeremy, at the next boat over, shouts, "Hey! How's it goin'?"

The vendor sees him, and waves. "Oh, hey, Jer. It's all right." Retrieving an ice cream bar, he turns and faces us.

Recognition hits me a beat before a glower settles across his face.

"Cody?" Sloane's voice is filled with incredulity. "What are *you* doing here?"

He nods at Ryan, swapping cash for her treat, finishing the transaction, before turning his displeasure back to Sloane. "What does it look like I'm doin'?"

Sloane exits through the swinging door and comes around to stand on the edge. "You work for Sanders now?"

"Well, yeah. It's all I could get after you torpedoed my job at Wolf." Cody's gaze drags over her body, even as he spews accusations.

You could have had that for life. You royally fucked up, buddy, I want to say.

"What are you talking about?" Sloane's eyes dart to me. "I didn't get a call from them for a reference for you."

"I didn't put the Sea Witch on my résumé. I'm not stupid."

"We'll agree to disagree there." She folds her arms across her chest. "So then why are you accusing *me*?"

"Because I have contacts at Wolf."

"No, you don't," she scoffs.

"Yeah, I *do*. In HR. And they told me that my name was on the hiring list until it was crossed off by a director."

Fuck. Who has this weasel been talking to inside Wolf?

Ryan's knowing eyes land on me. Her mouth opens—

"Better eat that before it melts." I shove the ice cream bar into her waiting lips and flash her a warning glare to shut the hell up. Seriously, drunk unfiltered Ryan is worse than Connor. Clearly a hazardous gene their shared father passed along.

"So? How does that relate back to me?" Sloane wears an incredulous mask, but I can sense the panic swelling underneath. On the tiki float beside us, Jeremy listens quietly.

Cody's smug smile tells me he's not finished yet. "Because I asked if there were other names that made it to the list and were also crossed off, and you know who was on there? Will, Mick, Ron, Brock ..." He counts down on his fingers. "*All* Sea Witch employees. *Weird*, huh?"

Sloane's throat bobs with a hard swallow. "I didn't get reference calls for any of them. If I had, I would have said they're great workers."

"She said they didn't even make it to reference checks."

She. That narrows it down for me tomorrow. My anger boils. "You're a regular fucking detective."

Cody spares me a dirty look before he turns to Jeremy. "You were on the list too, with a note saying you can only work two days a week."

"What?" Jeremy's face screws up.

"Yeah, the only one on there with a note like that. Ja—my contact"—he catches himself before he divulges her name—"said seasonal hires have to be available for full-time hours. It's a hiring requirement. And hey, what do you know! Jeremy works for the Sea Witch!" Cody laughs, a fake, maniacal sound, as he reaches for the motor throttle.

Sloane's face has paled. She's run out of deflections to throw at him.

I grip the back of the bar stool to keep myself from reaching out and clocking the asshole. "Get the fuck out of here before I call your new boss and let him know you're harassing tourists." Sanders. I make a mental note of that name.

"It's fine. Sloane's not a tourist." Cody smirks, easing his dinghy away. "She's just a raging bitch."

My pulse explodes in my veins. I hoist Ryan onto the nearest chair—for both her safety and to get her out of my path —and then drop into the water, my fists balled as I charge toward him.

"Ronan! Help!" Connor's voice booms from my right, his distressed words distracting me. He's limping toward us in the water, a tear-streaked Katie cradled in his arms.

My rage evaporates in an instant.

———

"HERE, I'VE GOT HER." Kyle stoops, and Rachel helps Katie loop her arms around his neck so he can carry her piggyback style. "You've got *her*, right?" He nods to Ryan, who's slouched against the rail.

"Yeah, I got my drunk-ass sister." Connor winces as he puts weight on his left leg. "Come on, drunkie. I'm behind you, but don't fall or you'll take us all out."

Carefully, they all move up the steep set of wooden stairs from the dock, leaving me alone with Sloane.

"You weren't kidding about those slides being dangerous." I watch as she ties an impressive sailor's knot with ease.

"You probably should have let the paramedics do their thing." She hops up on the dock. "I'd get Katie's ankle checked out right away. It could be broken."

"Yeah, we're gonna get her back to the house so she can change and then head in. Connor, too." He doesn't know what happened, except he landed weird and now his knee is swollen. "So much for a leisurely cruise." It went sideways, fast.

"Yeah, I guess that wild orgy tonight might not work out for you guys," she deadpans, her arms again folded across her chest. Closed off.

With all the commotion, she hasn't forgotten that part. *I owe you one, Ryan.* "Look, I meant what I said earlier. That isn't happening."

"But it *did* happen."

"It did." And I won't be ashamed. I definitely won't apologize.

She bites her bottom lip, and I can almost hear the litany of questions screaming for answers inside her brain.

How many women has he fucked?

Has he fucked men?

How many other people is he fucking right now while he's with me?

She won't believe any answer I give her except the one that paints me as shady as her ex.

Sloane takes a step back and then another, away from me. "I've gotta close up here before Jeremy comes back in an hour, so I can deal with *that* mess."

"I'm going to find out who Cody's been talking to," I promise. And fire her ass.

She shrugs. "Does it matter? They're all going to quit on me when they hear about this, anyway."

"Maybe not."

"I would, if I were them." She nods toward the stairs. "You should go. They're waiting for you." That's a dismissal if I've ever heard one.

I stall for another long beat. "We'll talk soon."

"Yeah, sure, in another couple of weeks?" She shakes her head. "There's a lot of drama here. Too much. You could lose your job, and you're in that weird place, remember? And I'm very vanilla, compared to you. I can't even believe I let today happen." A nervous laugh escapes her.

"You didn't enjoy it?" I hold my breath and wait for her to lie. I *know* she did.

"It's not about enjoying it." She falters. "I just ... I don't think we want the same things."

We could. I wasn't looking for anything, but now that I've met Sloane, she's the one I keep gravitating back to, everything else be damned.

"Ronan! Come on!" Connor hollers.

Shit. "Coming."

"Take care of yourself." Sloane hops back onto the floating tiki, the weight of whatever fallout is to come squarely on her shoulders.

50. Sloane

"One more!" I force a smile as I aim the phone camera at Jeremy and his cruise girls. "There, got it. Make sure you tag us when you post. And thanks again for coming. Leave us a review!" All my standard parting lines.

"Oh, we will. Definitely." French Braid waves at Jeremy before trotting away to join her friends.

"You've got a fan."

"Yeah, Charlotte's sweet." He counts the fold of cash they must have tipped him, then tucks it in his pocket.

It reminds me that I didn't get a tip. Then again, the cruise was cut short due to injury.

And I did get an orgasm.

I shake my head at myself and brush those dirty thoughts aside. "So, good shift?" I prod, bracing myself for the inevitable confrontation.

"Better than yours." Jeremy crouches and sets to tying another rope to secure the float. "Have they gone to the hospital?"

"Probably, by now." They left an hour ago. The right thing to do would be to text Ronan and ask. I know this, and yet I can't bring myself to do it. Ronan is dangerous, like Frank said, but probably not in the way he meant. He's dangerous *for me* because I'm not myself when he's around. I'm reckless. I allow crazy things to happen that I never dreamed of when I was eighteen and brash, let alone thirty-one.

It's best that we cut ties completely. Best for both of us, from the sounds of it.

"You should probably follow up, seeing as they got hurt while on our tour."

"Yeah, I have Ryan's number in the booking. I'll call her tomorrow and check in when she's sober."

"Sounds like a plan." Jeremy stands, scratches the back of his head. "Hey, so what was all that back there, with Cody? What was he talking about?" He asks this, and yet by the displeasure etched across his face, he already has a pretty good idea.

So, I spill my guts. I tell Jeremy *everything*, from the day Dave and Ted quit to the day I let Skye talk me into crashing the job fair. By the time I'm done, I feel both a hundred pounds lighter and like someone tied a cinder block to my ankle and is waiting to toss it into the deepest part of the Gulf.

Jeremy scratches his chin absently. "Why didn't you come talk to me?"

"And say what? 'You're my best employee. *Please, please, please,* don't abandon me?'"

"Well ... yeah, that would have been a start."

"I don't know. Maybe I should have. I didn't think I had the right to do that, though. Especially not after you asked for more hours."

"Wait, so you didn't have the right to ask me not to quit, but sabotaging my chances for a job at a great company—"

"I know!" The urge to bury my face in my hands is overwhelming. "What I did was awful. I'm evil. I'm sorry."

Jeremy studies me, as if weighing my sincerity. "Does Frank know about this?"

"After the fact, yeah, and don't worry, he made me feel plenty guilty about it."

Jeremy's gaze flitters to the top of the stairs. "Will's here to close up."

"Please don't tell him. Or the others. At least not until the season's over. They can all quit on me then. I deserve it."

He purses his lips. "I won't, but I can't control what Cody does."

"Yeah, he's a problem," I agree. For another day.

"What up!" Will says by way of greeting, slapping Jeremy's hand in a friendly fashion. "How'd the day go?"

"Oh, you know." Jeremy's eyes shoot to me. "The usual."

Will frowns at the empty drink trough in my boat. "Where's all the ice?"

"My cruise got cut short, so I had time to clean up."

"You could have called me to come early. Oh well, I've got it from here." He hops onto *Tiki Two* and gets to work. "See you later, boss."

"See you at the bonfire." If he hasn't learned of my crimes by then.

My back's to him when he calls out, "Hey, meant to say earlier, that suit looks good on you."

"Thank you," Jeremy calls back, his easy nature sliding back in.

"No, not *you* ..." Will shakes his head, his face flushed with embarrassment.

I wink at him, a silent thanks. "Have a good night." Jeremy and I head for the stairs, and the momentary levity vanishes.

"Are you mad?" I ask.

"Yeah, Sloane. I am, actually."

His admission feels like a slap across my cheek. Jeremy is one of the happiest and most conscientious guys I've ever met. It's like disappointing Gigi. Worse. "I get why you did it. It's just ... I was never trying to screw you or the Sea Witch over."

"I know that. That's why I wouldn't let Ronan ax you. I

told him to leave you there. He's the one who came up with the two-days-a-week thing, figuring you could do both. And he said he'd push for you to get hired on full time at the end of the season. But he wouldn't have done any of that without me interfering." I can rope Skye and Ronan into my scheme all I want, but at the end of the day, this is all on me.

"So, that guy on the cruise today is a director at Wolf Hotels?"

"Yup."

"He was seconds away from bashing in Cody's face."

I recall that moment, right after Cody called me a bitch, and Ronan calmly lifted Ryan into a chair like she was a small child. There was pure murder on his face as he jumped into the water. But then Connor called, and in an instant, his priority shifted to his injured friends. It's commendable. Sexy, actually.

Still, I would have enjoyed seeing Cody knocked unconscious.

"So, what's going on with you two?" Jeremy asks as we reach the stairs.

"Nothing."

"You sure about that?" He smiles, like he knows more than he's letting on.

A wave of mortification washes over me as I start climbing. "I'm sure."

Absolutely nothing anymore.

———

RONAN:

> Doc says Katie's ankle isn't broken. Bad sprain, though. She's on crutches. Getting her home will be a treat.

MY THUMB FLOATS over my keyboard, stalling on a suitable

answer. And I feel that familiar pull. It's like gravity, forcing me to move in one direction: toward Ronan.

Guys like him, though?

They take what they want while shattering hearts.

I tuck my phone into my pocket and stick to my plan.

I'll call Ryan tomorrow.

51. Ronan

I knock on Belinda's office door.

Her soft sigh of irritation is followed by, "Come in."

She's hunched over her laptop, her hot pink suit jacket draped over her chair, her matching stilettos kicked off. A half-finished smoothie sits next to her mouse. She was here before me this morning. For all else that Belinda may be, no one can claim she doesn't work hard for Wolf. That seems to be all she does.

"Henry didn't get in early, did he?" She checks her watch. "His plane should be landing right now."

"No, I have an issue I have to deal with in the boardroom, and I'd like you present."

Her perfectly drawn eyebrows arch, waiting for me to elaborate.

"I need to fire someone, and I've never done it before. I need you."

"This should be interesting." Tossing her pen onto her leather blotter, she slips on her heels and jacket and rounds her desk. "Walk and talk."

I hold her door for her, and she strolls through, head held high, hips swinging. "One of our employees in HR shared information about hires from our job fair. Names of people who made the final cut but were crossed off when they reached the director's approval." It wasn't hard to figure out who the culprit was. A female HR employee whose name starts with the letters *Ja* and who accessed the documents? It took Archie less than five minutes to track down Jasmine Guilly for me.

Belinda smirks. "The cuts for that little negotiation of yours."

"The deal that got all those signs down ahead of media open," I remind her.

Her lips purse. "Shared with whom?"

"One of the people who we cut." Technically, Lena cut him.

"Which we're fully in our right to do at any time in the process," Belinda retorts.

"True, but she's sharing sensitive company information." We'll ignore the fact that I did the exact same thing. Nobody but Sloane knows and, besides, I'm the fucking director.

"Why would she do this?" Belinda asks.

"That's what we're about to find out." But I have my suspicions when it comes to a guy like Cody.

Don't worry. Sloane's not a tourist. She's just a raging bitch.

My fist clenches. I can't wait until the next time I run into him. It's been a while since I've punched anyone.

"Mike is the HR manager," Belinda cuts into my vengeful thoughts. "He needs to sit in for this—"

"Already there."

Her eyes bore into the side of my face. "I don't think I've seen you so zealous about a cause before."

Not a cause. A person. One who never responded to my text last night. It was an innocuous one at that, about Katie, and yet Sloane didn't respond.

Maybe she didn't get it.

I know that's not true, and it's bugging me more than it should.

Belinda checks her watch again. "So you're aware, we have fifteen minutes before we need to be in the lobby to greet Henry."

"To *greet* him? What, are we rolling out a fucking red carpet?"

"No, a green one," she retorts without missing a beat.

I grunt. "Fine, I'll make it quick." I plow through the meeting room door, holding it open for Belinda before pushing the frosted glass shut.

At the far end of the table, Mike sits wearing a *What the fuck is this about, now? I've got shit to do* expression. Beside him is a young woman with long, cinnamon-brown hair and bold blue eyes that brim with apprehension.

Mike gestures at us. "This is Ronan Lyle, the director of operations, and Belinda Cartwright, the hotel's general manager."

"And you are Jasmine Guilly," I say.

"Yes, sir." She croaks and attempts a smile. She's probably around my age.

I pull out a chair for Belinda.

Her brow flickers a beat—surprised that a Neanderthal can have manners—before she takes it with a murmured "Thanks."

I round the table and sit down, willing myself to relax. "Hi."

"Hi." Jasmine clears her throat. "I don't know what this is about."

"Let's get right to it, then. Did you share potential Wolf Hotel employee names and hiring decisions from the recent job fair with a man by the name of Cody Wilson?"

"I ..." Her jaw drops in shock. "Yes, but ..."

"But what?" I press.

Her bottom lip quivers, and then the floodgate of tears opens.

————

"You've FIRED your first employee. How does it feel?" Belinda's heels click as we head for the lobby.

"As shitty as I expected." According to Jasmine, she and Cody were "dating" for a couple of weeks. She met him at Siren's Call before the job fair, and they "really hit it off," which, in my books, means he found out she worked in Wolf's HR and saw an opportunity to give her dick in exchange for a job with us. Good plan. Jasmine was part of the team vetting people at the job fair. She admitted to making sure his résumé got pushed through. She was shocked when he got the rejection email.

Cody was angry and insisted she find out why. That's when she started fishing around in the main drive for files. He ended things with her the day after she confirmed those names for him. His reasoning? He can't handle a serious relationship so soon after ending his engagement.

What a motherfucker.

And now the girl—a four-year Wolf Hotel employee and a transfer from Chicago—is packing her things, a prosperous career with the company ended over an opportunistic asshole. "Is there any way we can *not* fire her?" I ask.

"It wouldn't be a good look for you, but stranger things have happened at Wolf. Still, we can't have someone like that working for us in HR. The guy manipulated her into getting him a job in exchange for sex." Belinda adds under her breath. "Must be one hell of a cock."

I snort. Her thought process works a lot like mine.

"But for a bartending job? Who does that?"

"A thirtyish-year-old guy who is now selling boiled peanuts and ice cream from a dinghy."

She cringes. "Seriously, who is this guy again?"

"Why? You want his number?" Belinda would eat Cody alive. I'd enjoy that.

She huffs. "Maybe. I could use a good dicking."

I falter a step, not expecting that answer.

"What?" She shrugs. "It's been too long since I had a good lay." There's humor in her tone.

"Just under two years, if my memory serves me accurately," I tease. "You really need to get away from this place once in a while."

"Not this week. Neither will you."

"Yeah, Archie walked me through my calendar." It's rammed to the teeth with meetings and golf sessions—with journalists I need to smooth-talk, politicians I need to ass-kiss, and corporate big dogs I need to make feel special. I may as well book a room here if I want any sleep. "Where do you live, anyway?"

"Why? You want to come over later?"

I chuckle. And then I meet Belinda's gaze, see the heat in it. *Fuck me.* I've seen that look before. She's not joking.

"Need to talk to you!" Dorian charges in to join us, uninvited, but I'm thankful for the interruption. I wouldn't know how to turn down Belinda without earning her wrath—I doubt she's rejected often.

"It's about the sprinklers." A bead of sweat trickles down Dorian's cheek and into his bushy mustache.

I briefly wonder if I can use the clean-cut employee policy to make him shave that broom brush off. "What about them?"

"They're not working."

"What do you mean, they're not working?"

"I mean exactly what it sounds like I mean." The attitude is thick with this one today. "They're programmed to work during the night and the entire system in the front didn't go off last night."

"*That's* a problem." We've spent millions on landscaping,

it's supposed to be eighty-five degrees all week, and we're hosting guests in three days. We can't greet them with wilted palms and brown grass.

Beside me, Belinda remains quiet. No help whatsoever.

"What are the engineers saying?"

"They're on it. The sprinkler company is here too, but so far they're stumped."

"Okay. So, what do you want me to do?"

"You? Nothing. I'm letting you know, in case we have to get outside specialists in."

Which I'll have to sign for, and then I'll get reamed out by head office. I already have a meeting request from them to discuss the golf course rework invoice our finance department approved. "I'm already over budget, thanks to that fucking moat on the green, so how about we see if these guys we're paying salaries to can earn their keep before we bring in outside help? Give them the day. If they haven't found the problem by tonight, then we move to plan B. And get the crew guys out there with hoses." And I'll replace these engineers with people who know how to fix fucking sprinklers.

Look at me, on a firing tear today.

"Already got the hoses out," Dorian confirms. "Hey, what's with your guy, Connor, callin' in sick? Is that legit?"

"Yeah, he fucked up his knee yesterday. Doc said to stay off it for a day or two, plenty of ice, that sort of thing. We're hoping it's not something serious."

"Oh, bummer." Dorian frowns, appearing genuinely distressed. "He brings a good energy to the group. Hope he's not suffering too much."

I smirk. "I think he'll be okay." When I left the house this morning, Rachel was with him and, by the sounds coming through the door, doing a great job taking his mind off his discomfort.

"I'll give you an update as soon as I have one." Dorian storms off.

"That was less painful than usual," I declare as we pass the mermaid fountain.

"You have good people working for you. Sometimes they just need to check in and you need to give them confidence that they're making the right calls."

"Or so they can pass the buck on making the wrong call." Should I be scrambling to get outside people in to fix this? What if this ends up being an open-heart surgery nightmare on the front lawn of the hotel as reporters roll in?

"Have more faith in yourself, Ronan," Belinda scolds. "You have a lot to learn but ... you're learning." She adds after a beat, "Who knew you could?" As if paying me a compliment and leaving it at that is too much to handle for her.

I snort. "Love you too."

"What's happening with those golden tickets?"

"Twelve are committed. Ten to my ex and some friends from back home, and two to my sister. Who looks too good in a bikini for my liking, before you ask," I add quickly. Britt was thrilled to accept the plane tickets I paid for her and her best friend, Dani. They're making a long weekend of it, crashing at my house for a few nights.

That means I have four left. I had an idea—crazy as it is—to offer a ticket to Sloane. She'd probably tear it up. Still, it'd be worth it to try. It's the least Wolf Hotels can do.

"You invited your *ex*?" Belinda notes. "Is she a good friend?"

"No, actually. We broke up a few years ago and it was ugly. Just got back in touch."

"This should be interesting." A look passes over Belinda's face that I can't quite interpret, but it's gone in the next second as Henry Wolf appears. "Right on time."

"Ten minutes early, actually. Hello, Belinda." He offers her a rare, wide smile and a hearty handshake.

I scan the lobby, but there's no sign of the pregnant redheaded woman of my dreams.

353

"Ronan." Henry extends his hand.

It feels foreign to accept, but I do anyway, and the contact is ... civil.

"My wife is up in our room, resting," he confirms with a smirk, reading right through me. "I'll tell her you said hi."

I smash a grin. *I'll tell her myself when I text her in about five minutes, you prick.*

"Lena had a meeting with her staff, but she said she would be here to greet you—oh, there she is."

We turn as one to watch my counterpart stroll across the lobby floor, cheerful in head-to-toe salmon pink. I'll admit, the tropical colors are growing on me.

But I still won't wear that fucking tie.

Even Henry is dressed down—if that's possible—in a plain black golf shirt and beige dress pants.

Fifteen minutes of polite chatter about reservation numbers later, Henry suddenly holds out his hands. "Okay, who wants to start with the tour?"

"Tour of what?" He's seen the hotel before. The bastard is such a control freak, he probably dictated every screw and board of wood to the architects and engineers.

"You first, then, Ronan." He smiles and moves toward the front doors.

I trail after him. "And what am I showing you?"

"All of it."

———

"They've guaranteed their work?" Henry asks as I coast along the path past the ninth hole, his hand gripping the roof of the golf cart for purchase.

"With a pretty little seal on their paperwork and every-thing," I mock. "I've got the guy's personal number. Just waiting for the first big rainfall to see if I believe him. I think we should break whatever agreement we have with those other assholes and use these guys going forward."

"We'll see what our legal team can do. According to ParMasters, we've in breach of contract by going to Legacy Greens—"

"Fuck them. They shouldn't get paid to do work they did wrong in the first place, and they weren't going to have it done in time anyway."

"I agree, and I would have made the exact same call. Good job."

His words boost my confidence more than I'd like to admit. I don't need Henry's approval, damn it.

But it does feel good.

"And how are things with Belinda?" he asks.

"Surprisingly good. I don't think she hates me anymore." Based on the thinly veiled proposition earlier, she may want to fuck me again. That is a situation I do not need right now.

We round the corner to the infamous eleventh hole.

"Hold up a minute," Henry commands.

I bring us to a stop.

He leans back in the seat. "Would you look at that."

"What?"

"Nothing." He waves a hand. "Not one slanderous sign. Just trees. You did what my lawyer and my fat checkbook couldn't convince Sloane Parker to do."

Hearing him speak her name sets unease along my spine. "Have you ever met her?"

"Nope. I've seen pictures, though." A small, knowing smile curves his lips. "Which is why I told you to stay away from her."

I school my expression on the trees ahead. So, he knows she's a smoke show. I'm amazed he didn't try to fuck a property sale out of her back before Abbi came into his life.

"How'd you pull that off again?"

I sense a tone behind that question—that it's not entirely

innocent, like he's fishing to see how honest I'll be with him. But I learned to always assume Henry knows far more than he lets on. He's got investigators on permanent payroll.

"It wasn't that hard, actually," I begin. How much do I want to tell him? About the negotiation, that is. Definitely not the fucking. If his PI caught me, let him throw down the damning photos. I'd like copies to jerk off to. "I found a weakness, and I exploited it." It sounds shitty when I say it like that, but I really did help her with all the best intentions. "She had staff she didn't want to lose to Wolf, and we had more than enough people applying, so I made sure we didn't clean her out."

"The Sea Witch. Coffee shop and"—he frowns in thought—"tiki boats?"

And there Henry is, proving my damn point about always knowing far more than you'd expect a busy billionaire to waste his time learning.

"Smart. No fight, the signs are down. Now my wife doesn't have to come out here and see all her dirty laundry hanging in broad daylight for these fucking reporters to make a meal of." His jaw clenches.

"Is that why you had an issue with them? For Abbi?" That's commendable, but I've never doubted his love for her.

"Definitely a sore spot, but no. We need as little attention on that property as possible now, with the eminent domain claim coming soon."

"I'm sorry, *what*?" Did I hear him correctly?

"Eminent domain. It's where state officials can claim private property—"

"Yeah, I know what it is." Alarm bells go off in my head. "For *that*?" I point at Sloane's little piece of paradise, with its kitschy trailers and colorful beach house, its noisy-ass rooster. "But I thought *you* wanted that land?"

"That land. Other land. I tried to play nice." Henry's smile is downright wicked. "I have *big* plans for Mermaid Beach, and a lot of connections to help make it happen."

52. Sloane

Frank marches into the rental shop and stops in front of the counter to loom over me like a storm about to erupt. "Just had an interesting conversation."

This can't be good. "With?"

"Jeremy, about your run-in with Cody yesterday."

I groan. "How much did he mention?"

"He told me about *that*." He checks over his shoulder, spots Rebel at the coffee, and leaves it unspoken. "But what did Cody call you?"

"Let me see." I mock ponder, a pen pressed under my chin. "I believe it was 'a raging bitch.'"

Murder shines in Frank's eyes. "If he steps foot in here again—"

"I'll punch him myself. You know, because I'm a *raging bitch*. That's what we do."

He shakes his head. "Why didn't you tell me?"

I toss the pen on the counter and throw my hands in the air. "What good would it do? Yesterday was a long day, and I was worried. I'm still worried." How long before Cody drives the knife fully between my shoulder blades? I deserve that, though. I *did* cost him his job at Wolf. "Plus, I don't know. I've been so tired the last couple of days." I rub my face to emphasize my point. "I had to drag my butt out of bed this morning. I don't even know what day it is."

"It's Monday. And it feels like a Monday." He tests my empty coffee cup. "Let me get you a refill."

"Wow. This is a first."

He lifts his middle finger in the air in answer. "I'll take the cruise this afternoon."

"Damn, you must *really* feel sorry for me." I chuckle.

It's Monday.

Henry Wolf is flying in today. He's going to be here all week. And the Wolf Hotel is opening this weekend. After five long years, the day has finally come.

I pull out my phone and open my texts. Ronan's is still sitting there, at the top. Unanswered.

I really should reply. It's rude not to. It's not his fault he's a pig-slut. An orgy boy. It's just more proof that Ronan and I are not meant for each other. Even if I like him, and I *really* do. I could have gotten over the fact that he's not-friends with Henry Wolf and that he works for the hotel. But starting a relationship with a guy like Ronan won't end well for me. I can't possibly keep him interested. All those body parts jumbled up? That's not for me. I'm a one man kind of woman. And definitely a man.

Oh my God, have he and Connor ...?

I mean, they *are* oddly close.

I should get tested, especially seeing as we—so stupidly— did not use a condom *twice*.

Maybe I can get to the clinic today. Shifting to the computer, I scan the calendar and my list of to-dos: payroll, schedule, bookkeeping. I've got to put in an inventory order ...

It's the twenty-first already? Why does that date bother me?

Wait a minute.

But it *can't* be the twenty-first. That would mean ...

Oh my God.

"No, no, no ..." My stomach is in my throat as I frantically dig through my purse, pulling out the dial that holds my birth control pills. I recheck the calendar to see when I took the last one.

I should have gotten my period on Saturday.

I'm two days late.

And I am *never* late.

Just when it started to get good... the next book turns up the heat. Don't miss what Ronan does next.

This story continues with
SAVE ME
(The Wolf Hotel Mermaid Beach, #2)

Preorder Now

Have you met Henry Wolf?

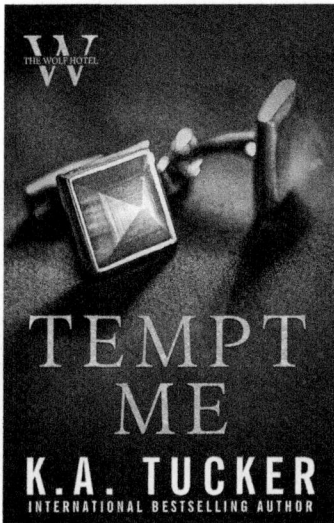

Also by K.A. Tucker

Want news about upcoming books, sales, and other exciting things?
Sign up for K.A.Tucker's newsletter.

For K.A. Tucker's entire backlist, visit katuckerbooks.com

About the Author

K.A. Tucker writes captivating stories with an edge.

She is the internationally bestselling author of the Ten Tiny Breaths and Burying Water series, He Will Be My Ruin, Until It Fades, Keep Her Safe, The Simple Wild, Be the Girl, and Say You Still Love Me. Her books have been featured in national publications including USA Today, Globe & Mail, Suspense Magazine, Publisher's Weekly, Oprah Mag, and First for Women.

K.A. Tucker resides outside of Toronto. When she's not writing, you can find her reading recipes she'll never make or chasing rabbits away from her hostas.

Want news about upcoming books, sales, and other exciting things? Sign up for K.A.Tucker's newsletter. Visit her website at katuckerbooks.com

Spotify Playlist

1. Slower: Tate McRae
2. Open Up: Gallant
3. Sail: AWOLNATION
4. Would That I: Hozier
5. West Coast: Lana Del Rey
6. Go Fuck Yourself: Two Feet
7. We're No Good Together: Tesla
8. Watermelon Moonshine: Lainey Wilson
9. Doin' Time: Lana Del Rey
10. Paradise Circus (Gui Boratto Remix): Massive Attack
11. Nobody Knows: Shawn Mendes

Printed in Dunstable, United Kingdom